falling
softly

ALSO BY MARIA DUFFY

falling
softly

a novel

Maria Duffy

Skyhorse Publishing

For Lorraine Hamm and Angie Pierce
Two of the best

Chapter 1

Summer 1990

'Promise me we'll be best friends forever,' said Holly, swinging her legs as she balanced on the silver-coloured railings outside her house. 'Say it.' She looked pleadingly at the seven-year-old boy who'd been her friend since preschool. 'You have to say "best friends forever" and we link our little fingers and then it will come true.'

He sighed and rolled his eyes but Holly knew. He pretended to be tough but she knew he secretly loved her. And she loved him. One day they'd get married in a big castle on a hill. It would be Christmas time and it would be snowing. Her dress would be white and she'd have red roses for her bouquet. It would be like a fairy tale and they'd live happily ever after. One day.

Holly Russo felt like the luckiest girl in the world. The previous week, her dream had come true when her boyfriend, David, proposed. She wasn't afraid to admit that she'd dreamed of her wedding since she'd been a little girl and there were times she'd thought it would never happen, but now she could start planning to live her dream. The proposal wasn't exactly the wonderful, romantic moment

1

she'd always dreamed of. It was more like a suggestion. A casual mention that perhaps they should take things to the next level. They'd been sitting having dinner in their kitchen when he'd popped the question – or rather made his statement. 'I suppose it's time we made this official and got married,' he'd said, as he shovelled baked ham into his mouth. But still. David was fabulous. He was handsome, hard-working and he adored the ground she walked on. Only for him, she'd be festering in a spinsterly depression, with a high risk of becoming a bingo-addicted, matronly cat-woman, baking cakes for the church fund-raiser and sitting between her parents watching a string of soaps every night. In truth, David had saved her.

'Are you almost ready, Holly? She's on her way.' David's voice boomed up the stairs with urgency, filling her with the dread of a schoolgirl sitting outside the principal's office. She was Mammy Wood, although David hated when she called her that. 'It sounds derogatory,' he'd say. She'd argue that it was a term of endearment but the former was closer to the truth. David was an only child and, due to his father's leaving when he was just six, had been brought up by his mother alone. Holly wasn't completely indifferent to the woman's hardship – in fact she admired her for rearing her son alone. But he was thirty-five years old now and didn't need his nose wiped. He owned his own house, had a great career in the bank and was about to get married. And yet his mother still felt it necessary to involve herself in every aspect of his life. And to make matters worse, he encouraged it.

She looked down at her lilac velour tracksuit and, for a moment, considered changing into something less comfortable. No doubt Mammy Wood would click her tongue and furrow her brow when she saw Holly hadn't stood on ceremony and worn her Sunday best, but Holly didn't care. That woman always had something to say about everything. She didn't really approve of Holly's job as a receptionist in a veterinary practice and had once made a joke about her wearing 'Eau de Dog'. Both she and David had thought it was hilarious but it had freaked Holly out and caused her to have multiple showers every day for weeks. Well, Holly was in her own house today so she was going to dress the way she wanted.

She glanced at her face in the mirror and sighed. Her once-chiselled cheekbones had filled out a lot of late and she was beginning to see the sprouting of a double chin. She elongated her neck, as she'd seen the girls do on *America's Next Top Model*, and the extra chin disappeared. She dusted a bit of bronzing powder over her pale face and pulled her mousy hair back into a ponytail.

'Holly, she's here,' came an excited voice from downstairs, just as Holly heard the front door swing open. She stuck on a smack of lipstick for good measure and hurried out of the bedroom. But at the sound of her soon-to-be mother-in-law click-clacking on the cobbled driveway, her bravado escaped her. She rushed back into the bedroom and grabbed a pair of black trousers and a peach blouse from her wardrobe. She discarded the tracksuit on the bed and quickly changed before running down the stairs. Maybe when she and David were married she'd find the courage to defy the great Mammy Wood.

'Lovely to see you, dear,' Mammy Wood said, air-kissing Holly somewhere in the region of her face. 'And don't you look lovely.'

Holly's inner child beamed at the compliment, which most certainly wouldn't have come had the lilac tracksuit remained. 'And you too, Doreen. Come on into the sitting room and I'll bring in some tea.'

She took the woman's Italian wool coat and ushered her and David into the warmth of the front room while she went into the kitchen. She was happy to play host while David schmoozed with his mother because, in reality, it was the lesser of two evils. She rolled out the hostess trolley from the utility room, a monstrosity of a yoke which David had insisted they buy for occasions such as this, and proceeded to set it with their best Ikea china, bought for the very same reason. She made tea in the large white teapot and took the tinfoil off the sandwiches she'd prepared earlier. A selection of biscuits from an early Christmas tin of Afternoon Tea spotted in Tesco the previous day, and she was ready to wheel the lot in.

Doreen was perched on the edge of the sofa when Holly entered the room, pen and paper in hand, glasses fixed halfway down her nose. 'I was just saying to David,' she said, tapping the paper. 'We'll need to start booking things now because all the good venues get snapped up ages in advance. I was thinking, if we decide a date tonight and make a list of churches and hotels, at least it would be a start.'

Holly's heart sank. 'I'm not sure we've decided what sort of wedding we want, Doreen. I mean, there's all sorts these days. It doesn't have to be traditional.'

'Don't be silly, dear. Of course you want the big white wedding. Don't all girls dream of their fairy-tale wedding?'

She couldn't argue with that. 'Maybe so, but it doesn't have to be in a church or –'

'Not in a church?' Doreen laughed manically. 'Well, that's not up for negotiation.'

Not up for negotiation? Bloody cheek, thought Holly. She glanced over at David, expecting him to jump to her defence.

'Maybe Mum is right,' he said, pouring tea into the three china cups. 'If we decide on the main things, i.e. the church and the hotel, at least we'll have the venues sorted.'

Holly's mouth opened but no sound came out. Firstly, had he not heard her say she wasn't sure about a church? She hadn't stepped inside one for years and he knew damn well about her views on the Catholic Church. And secondly, if there was one thing that drove Holly mad it was David's use of *i.e.* when he spoke. He must have noticed her annoyance because he reached over and placed his hand over hers.

'Sorry, Holly. Are we bombarding you with too much stuff?'

'It's not that. It's just … there's just a lot to think about.' She badly wanted to say something but there'd be plenty of time for that when Mammy Dearest went home.

Doreen shoved the hostess trolley aside and pulled the coffee table closer to her. 'Right,' she said, poising her pen above her notes. 'Let's talk dates. I was thinking maybe June or July. It's the best chance we have of a bit of sunshine.'

'But that's only eight months away,' said Holly, trying to regain some sort of control. 'And besides, David and I have discussed a winter wedding. Maybe around Christmastime.' It wasn't exactly true. After the proposal, she'd told David how she'd always pictured herself getting married in the snow. He'd teased her about being a kid at heart and that had been the end of the conversation.

'I don't mean *next* summer,' said Doreen, looking at her with a tight smile. 'We'd never have everything organised by then. I was thinking maybe summer 2017. That would give us a good year and a half to get organised.'

Holly took a sip from the cup in her hand, not trusting herself to speak.

'And you wouldn't want a winter wedding,' Doreen continued. 'You'd get your death of cold in your lovely dress and so would your bridesmaids.'

Holly let her rattle on about dates and venues for the next hour, nodding her head and telling her they'd have a think about it all. Then at last, she breathed a huge sigh of relief when Doreen finally stood up and smoothed down her over-the-knee shift dress, announcing that she must go home. Holly walked behind her to the hall, where her coat was hanging, and she couldn't help admiring the woman's figure. For a sixty-two-year-old woman, she looked really well. Her legs were shapely and her tiny waist must have been the same size as one of Holly's thighs. She never allowed a speckle of grey to appear in her blonde hair, which she wore in a youthful bob. Holly was suddenly conscious of her frame as she reached forward to accept the air kisses thrown in her direction.

'Thanks for that, love,' said David, putting his arm around her after they waved Doreen off and closed the front door. 'I owe you one.'

'For what?' She looked at him questioningly.

'You know what.' He grinned. 'I know she's hard work and I know she gets on your nerves but I really appreciate you playing along with her.'

'So is that what we were doing? Just playing along with her? And we're not going to let her take over the wedding?'

'Of course not. It's *our* wedding and it should be our decision.'

Her heart leapt for joy. She'd thought she was in for a battle – her against the two of them – and she hadn't fancied her chances.

'So why don't we continue this discussion in bed?' he said, taking her hand and pulling her towards the stairs. His eyes told her what was on his mind and she knew she was in for a rare treat.

David didn't do spontaneous. At least not very often. Everything in their house was planned with military precision, from the time they sat to eat dinner every evening to the nights they made love. But every now and again, the mischievous David appeared. He'd fly in the face of his own rules and bring a bit of excitement into their lives. Holly loved that David. Not that she didn't love the other one but *that* one reminded her of why she'd fallen in love with him in the first place.

Half an hour later she was in bed looking at the ceiling and listening to David's contented snores. She went over the evening's events in her mind and realised a number of things. One, she should have had more trust in her fiancé. Although he adored his mother and sometimes acted as though she was the second coming, his loyalties lay with Holly and he would never let his mother take over their lives. Two, she was a very lucky girl to have a man who loved her so much. Her friend Milly would often say that David was boring but Holly liked to think of him as steadfast and reliable. She'd kissed a lot of frogs and had her heart broken more times than she cared to imagine so a bit of stability in her life had to be a good thing.

'I was just thinking,' David said, startling her.

'I thought you were fast asleep.'

'I was just resting my eyes. We should go and buy a ring this weekend.'

A bolt of excitement shot through her. That was the first time he'd mentioned a ring and she had begun to think he wasn't going to bother. She'd thought of bringing up the subject when he'd proposed but it hadn't seemed like the right time.

'Holly?'

'Sorry. I was just thinking. Yes, a ring would be nice.'

'How about tomorrow then? Maybe we could even …'

'We could what?'

'No, it doesn't matter. It was a stupid thought.'

Holly wasn't going to let him fob her off. 'Let me be the judge of that.'

'Look, I meant what I said earlier about not letting Mum take over, but I still want to keep her included in things. She's asked me to bring her into town tomorrow for a few things so maybe she can come and look at rings with us.'

Holly's heart sank but what could she do? Still, she was marrying the man she loved and nothing or no one was going to get in the way of that. Mammy Wood could stick her nose in all she wanted but, at the end of the day, Holly would be David's wife and his loyalties would have to be to her. She closed her eyes and tried to sleep but something was whirring around in her head and keeping her awake. A little tiny voice pecking at her brain and, much as she hated to admit it, she knew it was the voice of doubt.

Chapter 2

'Come on, Josh. We're just going to have to make a start somewhere. If you weren't such a hoarder, this job would be easier.'

He nodded and sighed. He found it was the best thing to do these days. Ever since Stephanie had become pregnant, her moods had been all over the place and he, her loving, supportive boyfriend, was the one who suffered her wrath if things didn't go her way.

'I'll make up the boxes while you load up the books,' she said, walking into the study. He followed her without argument. There were hundreds of books there, not just on shelves but in piles on the floor. Josh's job as a primary-school teacher required him to possess a lot of literature but, as Stephanie said, he was a hoarder too. Some of those books he'd had since the early nineties, when he'd discovered the Goosebumps series and it was as though he'd uncovered a hidden treasure. His love of books had grown from there and he'd spent every free moment reading. Stephanie told him all the time that he should have a proper clear-out of his collection but he couldn't bear to part with any of it.

'I don't mind making a start on things, Steph. But are we sure about this? The move, I mean. I know the van is booked and the deposit is paid, but it's not too late, you know.'

Her head shot up and he prepared himself for the onslaught. 'How many times do we have to go over this? I told you I want to be settled in the new place before the baby is born. It will be twice as difficult to move afterwards. Why are you so against the move? Why are you always fighting against me?'

'You know that's not true. I'm just thinking of you. Moving is very stressful and with you being four months pregnant, I don't want to risk anything happening to you or the baby. I'm not talking about putting it off forever – just until after the baby is born.'

'You worry too much, Josh. I'm absolutely fine. And so is this little one.' She patted her expanding belly and smiled. Her face lit up and he was putty in her hands. Stephanie was the most beautiful woman he'd ever known. Three years his junior, she had the face of an angel and his breath would catch in his throat every day when he'd wake up beside her. He looked at her long blonde hair falling over her face as she concentrated on assembling the boxes and his heart swelled with love for her and their unborn child.

Three hours later, they were exhausted and they hadn't even finished packing up one room yet. 'How about we stop now and order a Chinese,' he said, watching as Stephanie rubbed her back. 'There's no point in overdoing it. We have the whole weekend ahead.'

To his relief, she relented and he ushered her into the sitting room while he went to get the menu from the kitchen drawer. He smiled sadly to himself as the drawer stuck and he had to expertly twist it slightly to the left and pull quickly to get it open. It had been like that since he and some of his college friends had hosted a house-warming party when they'd moved in ten years ago. He definitely had some great memories of the place. He'd loved living there and would be sad to leave.

An hour later they were tucking into their mixed vegetables with black bean sauce while watching Graham Norton, and he knew he'd be still hungry when he was finished. He wasn't a vegetarian but

10

Stephanie was, and lately he'd been avoiding meat when he was with her because she said it grossed her out. Under normal circumstances, he'd have ordered a meat dish anyway, but with her being pregnant, he cut her a bit of slack. She threw her head back and guffawed at something Graham had said and he was reminded of why he loved her.

The last few months had been difficult for him. Stephanie's pregnancy hadn't been planned and when they'd found out, she'd been inconsolable. As a model and actress trying to make a name for herself, the last thing she'd wanted was a baby. Josh, on the other hand, had been delighted. Of course he hated to see her in so much turmoil but he believed in fate. Fate was giving him a second chance at the life he wanted and it just felt right. It had taken a number of weeks to convince her that everything was going to be okay but, eventually, she'd accepted the pregnancy and had even begun to get excited. Now her biggest fear was getting fat or developing stretchmarks, but looking at her stunning figure with just the beginnings of a tiny bump, Josh couldn't see that happening.

She muted the telly when the ad breaks came on and turned to him, placing her half-eaten food on the coffee table. 'Are you getting excited about the move?'

He couldn't lie. 'I'm excited about the baby. But you know how I feel about moving.'

'It will be a fresh start for us,' she pleaded. 'A new life for you, me and the little one.'

'But we don't need a fresh start or a new life. What's wrong with this one?'

'I told you, Josh, this place just doesn't feel right. The house, the area, everything. It's your college digs. Your first bachelor pad. It wouldn't feel right to bring our child up here.'

'But you've been happy here, haven't you? Seven happy years we've lived here together and you never once said you wanted to move.'

'It's different now.' She patted her barely swollen stomach. 'And besides, the rent on the new place is only slightly more and it's far more suitable for a child.'

He relented. Again. It was an argument he wasn't going to win. It felt as though he'd been battling with her about everything from the moment she'd discovered she was pregnant, and once she'd gotten it into her head to move, there'd been no changing her mind. She'd been like a bulldozer, steaming ahead with plans – finding a house, negotiating rent, giving notice to the landlord and even picking out some new furniture which they could scarcely afford. The new place was just twenty minutes' drive away so it wasn't going to affect his job. He worked in a school just off the Navan Road so, if anything, he'd get to work a little quicker in the mornings. But no matter what he said, the move was happening so he knew he'd just have to get used to it. Besides, they'd be together and soon there'd be three of them. His mother had always said that a house was just bricks and mortar – they'd make a home wherever they lived.

He glanced at Stephanie again and realised she'd dropped off to sleep. She could sleep on the point of a needle these days and nothing could wake her up. It made him nervous for when the baby came along. He didn't mind mucking in with night feeds but he certainly didn't want to be the designated night-time parent. She'd already said that she didn't want to breastfeed, so he had a sneaky suspicion she was grooming him for the night shift.

'Come on, Steph. It's bedtime for you, I think.'

She didn't budge, so he gathered up their plates and glasses and brought them into the kitchen. He discarded the uneaten food and loaded the dishwasher. He wouldn't claim to be a domestic god, but he was pretty well house-trained. He wiped down the counters and stuck the heating on for an hour. Their room was at the front of the house and it always seemed to be freezing. Back in the sitting room, Stephanie was still fast asleep so he shook her gently until she woke.

'God, Josh. What's wrong with you? Can't you see I'm sleeping?'

'Yes, but you need to get yourself up to bed. You'll get a crick in your neck sleeping here. Come on, we'll go up together.'

She turned to face the back of the sofa and curled her knees up to her stomach and he knew it would take more than words to move her.

'What are you doing?' she said, as he secured one arm behind her knees and another around her upper back.

'Carrying you up to bed.'

She opened her mouth to protest but changed her mind and wrapped her two arms around his neck. He stumbled beneath the weight as he carried her up the stairs and placed her as gently as he could on the bed. He pulled back the duvet to roll her in and she curled up on her side and continued to sleep. He watched for a moment, envying that wonderful dreamy state of oblivion.

Josh knew he wouldn't be able to sleep for a while yet so he headed back downstairs and filled the kettle with water to make some tea. While he was waiting for it to boil, he was gripped with a pain in his stomach. He leaned against the kitchen counter as the pain took his breath away and he prayed for it to pass quickly. When it began to ease, he grabbed a packet of paracetamol from the cupboard and downed two quickly with a glass of water. It had started about four months ago – roughly the same time they'd discovered Stephanie was pregnant. He'd joked about it with his friend Shane, who'd suggested that maybe he was having a sympathetic pregnancy. He'd googled it and apparently it was an actual thing.

He made his tea and took it into the sitting room, where he flicked on the telly and found a channel where they were rerunning episodes of *Fawlty Towers*. He knew he should get the pain checked out. Especially given his family history. And he would. Just as soon as Stephanie had the baby and things settled down. Or maybe Shane was right and his pain would disappear when she had the baby. Either way, he had enough to think about at the moment, and once the tablets did their job, he wasn't going to worry. Stephanie and the baby were his priorities now and he was going to put all his energies into them.

Chapter 3

'Do you think maybe you should wear something a little more casual?' said Holly, eyeing up David's very smart navy-blue suit, complete with shirt and tie. Although she had to admit, he did look very handsome. 'I mean, we're just going into town for a bit of shopping.'

'But not any old shopping.' He smiled, straightening his tie. 'I think we'll get better attention from the jewellers if we're well presented. Take your time. I'll just go and give Mum a ring and tell her we'll be on our way shortly.'

He headed downstairs and Holly stuffed her blue ripped-knee jeans and over-sized T-shirt back into the wardrobe. Shit! When she was twenty pounds lighter, she had an array of clothes to choose from, but since her waistline had exploded, she hadn't bothered to buy anything new. She always had a plan to lose weight. *I'll join Slimming World on Monday*, she regularly promised herself. *I'll start back at Weight Watchers next week. I'll just reduce my portion size.* But none of those things ever happened, except in her head. It wasn't that she was fat. Well, not *really* fat. But her previous size-ten frame had gone up to a fourteen and most of those extra inches hung over the top of her knickers.

She eventually settled on a loose-fitting grey wool dress, which covered a multitude, and pulled on a pair of thick black tights to go with it. She wished she could say she was looking forward to the day ahead but she was actually dreading it a little bit. She'd always imagined that a marriage proposal would come complete with a sparkling diamond ring and a man down on one knee declaring his life and his love for her. But that just wasn't David's style, so it was never going to happen. Even a romantic day together would have been nice, choosing the ring and celebrating over an intimate lunch where she'd run her stockinged feet up his leg under the table and they'd talk dirty with their eyes. They'd giggle as the waiter poured the wine, oblivious to the foot sex going on beneath the table, and they'd rush home afterwards to bed. Instead, what she had was a trip to town with David and his mother where they'd all pick the engagement ring together and then take Doreen to Tesco to do her shopping on the way home. Romantic, eh?

As they headed outside to the car, old Mr Fogarty from two doors down was walking past with his dog. 'Well, don't you two look lovely,' he said, stopping while Simon, his golden Labrador, peed against the wall. 'Going somewhere nice?'

'Just into town for a bit of shopping,' said David, scowling at the dog. 'And we're already running late so we'd better get going.'

Holly's eyes twinkled as she bent down to let Simon lick her face. 'But not just any old shopping. Engagement ring shopping.'

Mr Fogarty beamed. 'Is that right? Well, isn't that wonderful. I won't delay you so. Be sure to make the most of your day. It's a special time, so it is. Congratulations to you both.'

'Thanks,' said Holly, opening the car door. 'Enjoy your walk.'

'Bloody dog peeing on our wall,' said David, zooming out of the driveway at breakneck speed. 'I've a good mind to say something to him about it.'

Holly laughed. 'To the dog? I'm not sure he'd take you seriously.'

David shook his head but Holly could tell he was amused. He was so serious at times and Holly loved nothing more than to disarm him and make him smile. David expertly navigated the traffic as they headed to pick up his mother at the other side of the village. Holly knew she'd have something to say about them being late but she wasn't going to let it spoil their day.

'Are you excited about choosing a ring?' he said, glancing at her briefly. 'I can't wait to get it onto your finger and tell the world we're getting married.'

Holly's heart melted a little. 'Yes, I'm excited. And I can't wait either. I love you, you know.'

'I love you too, Holly. You're the best thing that ever happened to me and I'll never let you go.'

Perhaps the day wouldn't be so bad after all. She'd loved seeing that spark in him the previous night. He'd been attentive and loving and had made her feel wanted. Maybe the engagement had made him realise that she was his future and, although his mother would always be there, she wouldn't be the centre of his life any more. She felt buoyed up by David's words and was filled with generosity of spirit as Doreen came out her front door and headed for the car. She was pointedly checking her watch but Holly wasn't going to give her the chance to complain.

'Doreen, why don't you sit in the front?' said Holly, hopping out to get in the back. 'You'll have more room to stretch your legs.'

'Thank you, dear. That's very kind.'

'Your hair is gorgeous pinned up like that, by the way. Very modern.'

They headed off and Holly's generosity continued. 'David and I are delighted you're coming along today to help us choose a ring. I know you have such good taste.'

'Well, as I said to David,' she said, staring straight ahead so that Holly had to look at the back of her neck, 'we don't want you ending up with something gaudy.'

'I was thinking, Mum,' said David, just as Holly's generosity began to wane, 'why don't we park in the Brown Thomas car park and you can have a look around the store while Holly and I do a few things. We can all meet up after an hour or so.'

She looked at him uncertainly. 'Wouldn't it be better if we all just stayed together? And what few things do you and Holly have to do?'

Holly bit her tongue and willed David to be strong. 'Oh, just a few things we have to sort out in the pharmacy. We need to pick up some stuff and I need to talk to the pharmacist about a … a thing.'

Holly almost wet herself in an effort to stop a peal of laughter from escaping her lips. She couldn't see Doreen's face, but judging from the red blotches on the back of her neck, it was safe to assume she'd turned scarlet. Nothing more was said until they parked, and David kissed his mother on the cheek, assuring her they'd see her at the door of Brown Thomas in exactly an hour.

As they headed out onto Grafton Street, Holly noticed that some of the shop windows were already displaying Christmas decorations. Soon the street lights would be turned on and the excitement of the festive season would begin. Holly adored Christmas. And this year would be all the more exciting because she was engaged to be married. Married! She, Holly Russo. About to become somebody's wife. There were times when she'd thought she'd never see the day.

'So, come on then. What's this *thing* you have to talk to the pharmacist about?'

'Shh, will you?' David looked cagily over his shoulder. 'She has supersonic hearing, don't you know? And I wouldn't put it past her to be following us.'

'So what are we *really* going to do then? We have a whole hour to ourselves.'

'We're going to go and look at rings. Just you and me.'

'But what about your mum?'

'Well, I think we'd be saving her the job of traipsing around the place with us. If you pick one out that you like, then we can bring Mum to see it.'

Holly's heart leapt with excitement for a second until the reality of the situation sank in. 'She won't like it. I guarantee you, whatever we pick out, she'll have something to say about it because she wasn't involved.'

They arrived at the door of Weir and Sons on Grafton Street and David took Holly's hand and pulled her to him. 'And I guarantee you, if you choose a ring you love, I won't let her change your mind. This is *our* engagement, *your* ring, and we should be the ones to choose it.'

'But I thought –'

'I know you think I pander to Mum too much but I just want to keep the peace. I know the right thing to do and, although I'll make her feel as though she had some input into this, it will be solely our decision.'

As soon as they walked into the shop, Holly knew her decision to wear a dress rather than torn jeans was the right one. The shop assistant, on realising they were in the market to actually buy a ring, took a keen interest in them and couldn't have been more helpful. It didn't take Holly long to fix her eyes on the one she wanted. A small solitaire on a band of white gold. The assistant tried to get her to look at others – larger stones and clusters – but her mind was made up.

'It's perfect,' she said, holding her hand out and marvelling at how the diamond twinkled under the light. 'I think anything bigger would just look silly on my hand.'

David nodded his approval. 'You have such lovely, slender fingers. It's beautiful on you. And it won't break the bank.'

Holly cringed slightly at the mention of money but he was right. David was always the sensible one, keeping track of their spending and making sure they didn't get into debt. Well, he was a banker after all, so she wouldn't expect anything else. But there was no doubt he was right on this occasion. It would be foolish to spend thousands on a ring when they had a wedding to pay for and Holly also knew that she'd be terrified to wear a massively expensive ring on her finger.

'So is that the decision made then?' The shop assistant smiled and looked from one to the other. 'And it looks as though you won't need a size adjustment.'

He was right. The ring fitted Holly perfectly. It was meant to be. But they'd definitely have to bring Doreen in to see it before they finalised anything. And Holly was surprisingly okay about that, especially now she knew David was just humouring his mother. So they told the bemused assistant they'd be back shortly and then headed out to meet Mammy Wood.

She was waiting impatiently at the door when they arrived, checking her watch again, her lips pursed. 'I was just thinking,' she said, proffering her Brown Thomas bags for David to carry, 'I know it's a bit of a walk but we should probably go to McDowell's on O'Connell Street for the ring. It's a bit of a tradition in Dublin. It's where mine is from.'

And look where that ended, thought Holly, but of course she kept her lips sealed. Doreen began to walk in the direction of O'Connell Street and David looked panic-stricken. Holly prayed for him to say something to stop her.

'Listen, Mum. Why don't we have a look in Weir's first? They have a great reputation and it would save us going over to the other side of the city.'

'Don't be silly, dear. It's not as if it's miles away. You can look in Weir's if we don't find anything in McDowell's.'

Holly wanted to butt in. To say something. But she also wanted David to stand up to his mother and, thankfully, after a moment, he did.

'Actually, Mum, we had a little look in Weir's while you were in Brown Thomas and I think we might have found the perfect ring.'

She stopped dead and glared at him. 'But we were supposed to do it together.'

'I know, but we just had a bit of time and couldn't resist looking.'

'But I wanted to look with you. I wanted to have input. You said I could.'

Holly felt like she was in some parallel universe. It was absurd. David and his mum were arguing about her engagement ring. *Her* engagement ring. It was as though she was a bystander in her own life. They were both staring at each other and Holly knew she'd have to take charge.

'Doreen, of course we want you involved. We just peeped in to see what they had and we just happened to see a lovely one. We could have bought it there and then but we wanted to wait until you were with us. Now, will you come with us and have a look?'

'But McDowell's. It's the Happy Ring House. It's where dreams are made.'

Oh, for God's sake. Now she was quoting the ad campaign. Holly tried again. 'This ring isn't unlike yours, actually. It's a little bit smaller but they're quite similar. Come on. I bet you'll love it.'

Doreen relented and David's shoulders relaxed. He mouthed a thank you to Holly and she smiled in response. But her eyes warned him that she wasn't happy. They couldn't go on like this. They couldn't have Doreen ruling their lives. They may have won today, but it was exhausting having to pander to her like that. And what about Holly's own parents? It wasn't fair to them that Mammy Wood got all the attention. Her mum and dad were elderly too and were the loveliest, most easy-going people in the world. They'd been delighted to hear the news about the engagement. All they wanted was for their daughter to be happy. They kept their noses out of her business but she also knew that they'd always be there if she needed them.

The shop assistant looked confused as they ushered Doreen in and asked to see the ring again. Holly couldn't blame him. He was probably used to couples coming in together to choose the ring, holding hands and kissing over the perfect fit. Or men coming in alone, clueless but determined to find something to surprise their girlfriends. Holly wondered how many mammies had come in to give their seal of approval.

'So what do you think?' David asked, watching as his mother examined the ring. 'Let Holly put it on and you'll see how perfect it looks on her.'

Doreen sniffed and they waited. Like two children in a sweet-shop. Eventually, having inspected the ring thoroughly, and inspected it some more with her glasses on, she handed it over to Holly to be modelled. Holly put it on and again she was struck by how comfortable she felt with it. How perfect it was.

'Couldn't you have picked a gold one?' Doreen said, an accusatory look on her face. 'Silver doesn't seem right.'

'Oh, I can assure you, Madam,' the assistant couldn't help himself, 'this ring *is* gold. It's white gold rather than the red gold you're probably familiar with.'

'White gold? I've never heard such rubbish. It's as silver as the knife and fork I eat my dinner with.'

The assistant balked at that and opened his mouth to speak but David took charge. 'Mum, it's gold all right. As the man said, it's just a different type to what you're used to. Now, I hope you like it because, to be honest, we both do and I think we should buy it.'

'Well, then you don't need my opinion.'

'Mum, please. Don't be like this.'

'It's not me who has to wear it so do whatever you like. I'm popping back to Brown Thomas to treat myself to some Jo Malone so come in to me when you're done.'

All three of them stared as she turned and exited the shop without a backward glance. Holly was mortified. The shop assistant must have thought they were the weirdest family ever, and Holly sort of agreed with him. What had they been thinking bringing her with them in the first place? What had David been thinking?

'So …' ventured the bemused assistant, looking nervously at Holly's hand. He probably thought they were going to do a runner with the ring still on. 'The ring?'

Holly looked at David and half-expected him to say they'd have to think about it, but to her surprise and delight, he pulled out his wallet and slapped it down on the counter. 'We'll take it.'

'Will we?' said Holly, surprised at his decisiveness.

'Unless you've changed your mind?'

'No, no. I mean, yes. I want it. I haven't changed my mind. I love it, David. It's perfect.'

'Well, then it's yours.'

A few minutes later they were walking back towards Brown Thomas and Holly linked her arm through David's. 'Thanks, love.'

Although he usually spurned public displays of affection, he pulled her closer to him as they walked. 'For what?'

'For putting me before your mother. For knowing what I want. And just for being all-round lovely.'

'Well, you're going to be my wife soon. The woman I'm going to spend the rest of my life with. Mum will get over it.'

Holly felt happy as she glanced down at the ring on her finger. She hadn't really wanted to wear it home. She'd hoped David would take it away and give it to her in a romantic gesture over dinner or something. But he'd felt it would be safer on her finger. He had a point. Safe and secure. Sensible. It was good to have a partner who was all of those things.

Chapter 4

'Remind me to never, ever move again,' said Josh, as his back almost broke beneath the weight of some of the boxes. 'Or at the very least, remind me never to move while my girlfriend is pregnant.'

'Don't be cheeky,' Stephanie chided, as she sat on the wall outside the house, watching him lift box after box into the van. 'I'm just taking a break. I've been doing my fair share.'

'I know you have, Steph. I'm just teasing. Right, I think we're almost ready for our first trip.' He shoved one last box into the back of the van they'd rented for the weekend. 'I don't think there's room for any more.'

'Great. Let me just grab my bag and I'll come with you.'

'Why don't you stay here? I'll unload and be back as soon as I can.'

'No, I'll come with you. I want to –' Her phone vibrated in her pocket and she pulled it out to answer it. Josh watched as she checked the screen, rejected the call and stuck it back into her pocket.

'Who was that?'

'Nobody.'

'Well, it was definitely somebody.' Her face had changed. She looked awkward. Upset. The phone rang again but she completely ignored it this time and walked into the house. Josh followed her.

He couldn't help being suspicious. It wasn't the first time something like this had happened. He'd been in Africa last summer on a charity building project and when he'd come home, she'd been acting a little strangely. There'd been a lot of phone calls which seemed to upset her. She'd dismissed them as work-related issues but he hadn't entirely believed her. But then she'd got pregnant and he'd been so happy that he'd forgotten all about the phone calls. Until now.

'So who keeps ringing you?' he persisted. 'And why aren't you answering their calls?'

'It's just a girl I did an acting job with last year. She keeps ringing to ask me to go to some stupid audition with her next month.'

'Why is it stupid?'

'What?'

'You said the audition was stupid. You usually tell me that all auditions are opportunities and even if you don't get the job, they give you valuable experience.'

She glared at him. 'What is this, Josh? The Spanish Inquisition? I just don't like the girl and I don't want to go to any audition with her. Is that okay by you?'

She stormed upstairs before he could reply and he felt slightly guilty for upsetting her. He should have known by now that her hormones were all over the place and questioning her integrity was probably the worst thing he could have done. He went up after her and she was in the bathroom with the door locked. He knocked gently.

'Steph, I'm sorry. I didn't mean to upset you. You seemed a bit distressed when you got the call so I just wondered why.'

The door swung open and she stood there, her long blonde hair pushed behind her ears, her make-up-free face red and blotchy from her tears. Josh felt like such an idiot.

'Come here,' he said, folding her into his arms. 'Don't cry. I'm sorry.'

She stayed nestled into the crook of his neck and neither of them spoke. He stroked her hair and breathed in the musky scent of her perfume. He wasn't sure how much time had passed but eventually she pulled back and looked at him.

'I feel guilty,' she said.

'Guilty about what?' A chill ran down Josh's spine.

'I feel guilty because I've had a lot of opportunities for jobs these last few months and I've turned a number of them down. I'm exhausted all the time and sometimes the thought of getting up at five in the morning to do full make-up and hair and traipse over to the other side of the city in the freezing cold to do an audition that I probably won't even get fills me with dread.'

'Oh, Steph,' he said, relieved. 'Is that what you've been thinking? That you should be doing more?'

She nodded. 'Yes. I see how hard you work and everything you do for me and I know I should be bringing more money into the house. And I promise I will. After the baby is born, I'll work something out. I'll get my mojo back and find some well-paid jobs.'

'Steph, Steph, Steph. We're a team. It doesn't matter who brings what money into the house. Once we have enough to pay the bills and keep a roof over our heads, that's all that matters. And I certainly don't want you pushing yourself too hard while you're pregnant. You're carrying this baby for both of us. Remember that.'

She looked relieved and Josh was glad to have reassured her. But the truth was he *was* worried about their finances. Despite telling Stephanie everything was okay, he knew that his money alone wasn't enough. But he'd work something out – he always did. The last thing he wanted was for Stephanie to get stressed while she was pregnant.

'Right, I'll tell you what we're going to do,' he continued. 'We're both going to head over to our new place. We'll stop for a few supplies on the way and we can have our first cup of tea there. What do you think? And then you can watch while I unload the boxes. I'll need somebody to tell me where to put everything.'

She nodded and smiled, and his heart skipped a beat. Sometimes when he looked at her, she seemed so young with her innocent blue eyes and luminous skin. She looked exactly like she had when he'd clapped eyes on her seven years earlier. He'd just graduated from college and their eyes had met across a crowded pub. She'd been like a vision and his world had stood still. With the help of a few beers and a slug of whiskey, he'd found the courage to go and talk to her and that's where it had all begun.

They sat in companionable silence in the van as they headed off with their first load. But Josh couldn't stop thinking back to those phone calls and wondering why he found it difficult to quell his suspicious mind. It was stupid, really. He should have learned to trust her by now but a little part of him still felt wary. Stephanie had a great social life and loved to flirt and, despite her assurances that she loved him and didn't want anyone else, sometimes he wondered. From the bits she'd told him, her past was quite colourful. But then again, didn't everyone have pieces of their past they'd rather forget?

They took a slip road off the Navan Road and wound their way through the housing estates towards their new home. Josh felt a little bubble of excitement, which took him by surprise. It was a lovely area and maybe Steph was right. It would be good to have a fresh start. Their first proper home together – all three of them. He glanced at Stephanie to see if she was excited too but she'd fallen asleep. The pregnancy was really taking its toll on her. She'd spent the first couple of months vomiting almost every day and, although that had stopped, there were still certain foods she couldn't face and her energy levels were low most of the time. He stopped at a petrol station to grab a few essentials and she was still sleeping when he came back to the van, her head drooped to the side, her lips parted and relaxed. They arrived at their new house a few minutes later and he reversed the van into the driveway.

'God, I can't believe I slept all the way,' said Stephanie, waking up and stretching her arms above her head. 'You should have kept me awake.'

'You need your sleep,' he said, hopping out of the van and going around to her side to help her down. 'Come on. Let's go in and switch the heating on. It's going to be freezing in there.'

They stood for a minute and looked up at their new home. It was a mid-terrace three-bedroom house with a small garden and drive-way in front and a reasonably sized garden out back. The front of the house was covered with a rustic red brick and the window frames were dark brown PVC. The windows in their last house were wood-en-framed and there was no keeping the wind out. It seemed to be a quiet street with a green area at the top and Josh could already pic-ture himself running around with their little one, playing football or chasing or whatever made him or her happy.

'A penny for them,' said Stephanie, jolting him out of his reverie. 'You were miles away.'

'Sorry, I was just thinking …'

'About?'

'I was just thinking about the fact that you were right. This place is perfect. I can see us being very happy together – you, me and the little one.' He felt strangely emotional. He was finally getting every-thing he'd ever wanted.

'Well, are you going to let us in or what?'

'Of course,' he said, fishing the keys out of his pocket and open-ing the door. 'But first I have to do this.'

He suddenly swept her up into his arms and shoved the door wide with his foot. She squealed as he carried her inside before letting her down in the hallway.

'What was that all about?' she giggled, straightening her long white T-shirt over her little bump. 'You'll break your back if you keep doing that. I'm like a baby elephant at the moment.'

'You are not,' he said, kissing her on the top of her head. 'You're beautiful. And it's traditional. A man should carry his partner over the threshold in a new house.'

Stephanie frowned. 'I think you have that wrong. It usually applies to weddings, when a husband carries his new *wife* over the threshold.'

'Maybe you're right. But there's no reason I can't do it too.' He opened the door to the little kitchen and shivered with the cold. He flicked on the switch for the heating and hoped it wouldn't take too long to warm up. He looked behind and Stephanie was still standing in the hall, a slight pout on her lips. He knew what was wrong with her but he wasn't getting into it again.

'Come on,' he said, changing the subject. 'I'll bring in the bag of shopping and maybe you can make tea while I carry in some of the boxes.'

She sighed heavily. 'Fine. And bring in the box of cups too. I don't want to use the ones that are here.'

Stephanie had brought up the subject of marriage a number of times over the last few years and even more frequently since she'd become pregnant. It wasn't that Josh didn't want to marry her. He did. Eventually. But something was holding him back. Telling him to wait. To be sure. Which didn't make sense because he couldn't be any surer than he was about Stephanie. But he just didn't feel ready to enter into a marriage and it had been a bone of contention between them for a long time.

Ten minutes later, they were sitting on some of the more sturdy boxes in the sitting room, their hands wrapped around steaming cups of tea. It was only late morning but they had a lot more journeys back and forth to do before it got dark so Josh didn't want to delay too long.

'So can we stay here tonight?' Stephanie asked, like a child anxious to try out a new Christmas present. 'It's warming up nicely now. I think it would be really cosy.'

'Definitely not,' said Josh, horrified at the thought of his pregnant girlfriend sleeping in those conditions. 'It'll take a few days to get things in order so we should wait until then.'

'But –'

'Seriously, Stephanie. I'm not going to have time to assemble the bed and unless you want to camp down on the floor – and I wouldn't recommend it in your condition – then we'll just have to wait.'

The sound of Taylor Swift's 'Shake It Off' came from the kitchen where Stephanie must have left her phone. 'Why don't I get it?' Josh said, jumping up from his box. 'If it's that girl again, I can just say you're not well or something.'

'No!' She pushed past him in an effort to get to the kitchen first and, again, he found himself feeling suspicious.

But it was just her mother. She turned the phone towards Josh so he could clearly see the word *Mum* on the screen. He knew that once she got talking to her mum she'd be there for ages so he headed back outside to continue unloading the van.

The early November sun was surprisingly bright and he was glad he'd thought of bringing his sunglasses. He grabbed them from the dashboard and walked out to the front of the garden to look around at what was now their new street. A woman passed by wheeling a buggy with a sleeping child and she nodded a hello. Another woman, elderly, with two supermarket bags and an old man with a Labrador on a lead went by too while he stood there. They were all friendly and Josh felt suddenly at home on the little street.

He scanned his eyes along the houses and was pleasantly surprised at how neat and tidy everything looked. All the gardens were well kept with nice greenery and leaves neatly swept to the side. The cars in the driveways were all pretty decent and one in particular caught his eye. It was a brand new black Audi A3 and he could feel himself salivate as he stared at it. He couldn't help but wonder why somebody with a car like that would live in a three-bedroom terraced house. He'd expect to see a beauty like that parked in the leafy driveway of a detached house in Ballsbridge. But then again, who knew what went on in people's lives. Maybe they'd spent so much money on the car, they couldn't afford a bigger place. Josh's little Nissan Micra was going to look pretty miserable in comparison but his dream was to one day trade up to something a little fancier.

The blinds twitched in the house with the Audi and Josh felt suddenly conscious he'd been standing staring across for the last few minutes. He must have looked like a right weirdo. He turned back to the van and began unloading the boxes, hoping that his new neighbours didn't think he was some lecherous man trying to see beyond their windows.

'Moving in, are you?' came a voice from the end of the driveway.

Josh looked around the side of the van and saw it was the old man with the dog who'd passed a few minutes before. 'Yes, we are. Well, at least we're moving some of our things. Josh O'Toole.' He walked over and held out his hand for the man to shake.

'John Fogarty.' He nodded his head towards the houses across the road. 'Number forty-four. And this is Simon.'

'Hello, old boy,' said Josh, bending to give the dog a scratch. 'Aren't you a beauty?'

The old man nodded. 'He's a good one, all right. Thirteen years old, he is, but he can still run like the best of them.'

'They're a great breed. Maybe when we get settled here we'll get one ourselves.'

'You should. There are plenty of green spaces around for dogs to run and Simon would be delighted to have a doggie neighbour.'

Josh smiled and nodded. 'Right, I'd better get on with unpacking these boxes. It was lovely to meet you, John. I'm sure we'll be seeing you around.'

'Bye, son. And the best of luck to you in your new home.'

The sound of Stephanie's laugh reverberated through the house as Josh watched the old man shuffle down the street. He had a good feeling about this place, and as he began stacking box after box into the hall, he smiled contentedly. Who knew what the future was going to bring but Josh had a feeling that they were in for an exciting ride.

Chapter 5

September 1995

'So how was it?' Holly said, flopping down on his bed. 'Did you miss me?'

'It was okay. The sports facilities are good but it's weird not having any girls around.'

'Weird good or weird bad?'

'Good, of course.' He grinned and she pretended to slap him across the face.

It was their first day in secondary school. They'd been in the same class all their lives and now at twelve years old, they were finally going their separate ways, him to an all-boys school and her to a community college.

'By the way, your mum said to tell you she was going to the shop to get something for dinner and you're to empty the dishwasher while she's gone.'

He nodded and looked at her strangely.

'What's up?' she said, unnerved by his stare.

'This,' he said, and moved forward and planted his lips on hers. It was the most wonderful feeling. Holly's insides did a flip as she felt the moist, sweet lips meet hers. She entered some other universe and wanted to remain there forever. It was their first kiss. They'd been best friends all their lives but never like this. Holly closed her eyes and imagined that snow-covered castle and felt this was just another step towards her dream.

Holly dropped the blind quickly and stepped back from the window. Shit! She thought he'd seen her looking. She and David had been dying to know who was going to move into the vacant house across the road and it looked like the new neighbours were in. From what Holly had seen, it was a young couple, with no sign of children. It would be nice to have people their own age on the street. Some of the other neighbours were more settled and middle-aged and they didn't really have anything in common with them.

She peeped out again cagily and noted that the guy was working hard emptying the van of its contents. He had sunglasses on so Holly couldn't see his face properly, but there was something about him, something about how he'd stood, hands on hips, surveying the street. His aura felt familiar and yet she couldn't place him. But the way he'd petted Simon, so gently and enthusiastically, told Holly that he must be a decent guy. Working with animals every day, Holly tended to judge people on how they treated their four-legged friends.

'I'm off, love,' said David, appearing at the sitting-room door, wearing a pair of loose red golf trousers and a top with the first few buttons open and the collar up around his neck. A sun visor completed the outfit and Holly couldn't help staring. It never ceased to amaze her how even the most fashion-savvy men could lose all sense of style when they entered the golf course. Why were all the clothes so unflattering? There seemed to be some sort of unspoken golfing law that trendiness or sexiness was a complete and utter no-no.

'Our new neighbours have arrived,' she said, turning her attention away from his attire. 'They have a vanload of stuff and they're bringing it in at the moment.'

David came in to have a look. 'It will be good to have somebody living in that house again. Did you see them? What are they like?'

'A young couple, I think. I just saw her briefly as she went into the house but he's been in and out to the van for the last while.'

It didn't take David long to lose interest. 'So what time are you meeting Carina at?'

'Two o'clock on Grafton Street. I'll be home around tea time.'

'Same here. Do you want a lift to the bus stop?'

'No thanks,' she said, keeping an eye on the activity across the road. 'I don't need to leave for another hour.'

'Okay, love,' he said, coming to kiss her on the cheek. 'Have a good time and tell Carina I said hello.'

Holly watched him load his golf clubs into the boot before hopping into the driver's seat and heading off. Her eyes were drawn back to the house across the road but there was nothing to see. The guy must have gone back inside – all was quiet. She went upstairs to get ready for her lunch date and it wasn't long before she was heading out into the bitter cold. Just then her mobile rang and she juggled to pull it out of her handbag while locking the front door. It was one of the customers from the veterinary clinic. She needed a favour. A bit of help with her little Maltese dog. Holly glanced at her watch before turning around and heading the opposite way down the street. Carina wouldn't mind waiting for a bit. Holly always welcomed the chance to spend some time with her furry friends. They were loyal and uncomplicated and all they needed to make them happy was a bit of love.

'Hi, Holly,' said Carina, warmly folding her into a hug. She smelled of their childhood, due to her unflinching loyalty to one particular perfume from the age of fifteen. Her hair had got longer since Holly had seen her and somehow seemed even shinier. She looked beautiful in a light-grey trouser suit that moulded to her size-ten figure. Working as a stylist, Carina knew how to dress and Holly envied her effortless chic.

'Let me see it then.'

Holly knew immediately that she was talking about the ring so she proffered her left hand for her sister to have a look. She *ooh*ed and *aah*ed for a few seconds before hugging Holly once more. Carina had to be the warmest human being on the planet. Holly was ten years younger and she'd grown up envying her for just about everything. It wasn't a jealous type of envy. She adored her sister. It was more an 'I want to be like her' envy. Carina was taking Holly to lunch to celebrate her engagement and Holly couldn't wait to sit down with her and catch up on all the news.

They settled on a little Italian restaurant just off Grafton Street and managed to nab a lovely table right at the window. They ordered a glass of wine for Holly, a coke for Carina and a pizza to share before settling down to the gossip.

'So,' began Carina. 'Have you started to make wedding plans yet? I'm so excited for you.'

'We haven't decided on anything for definite, but if Mammy Wood has her way, she'll organise the whole thing singlehandedly.'

Carina laughed, even though Holly wasn't trying to be funny. 'The poor woman. She must be excited that her only son is getting married. I'm sure she doesn't mean any harm.'

'But, Carina, you should have heard her when she came over. It was unbelievable. My opinion counted for nothing.'

'I'm sure you're exaggerating, Holly.' The waiter stepped in just as Holly felt like strangling her sister and placed the drinks in front of them.

'Carina, I know you like to see the good in people but, honestly, she's a right battle-axe. I wish she'd just let us get on with things ourselves instead of wanting to be involved in every aspect of our lives.'

'Jason's mum is very involved in our lives too. And do you know what? I probably felt much the same as you some years back. But now that we have children, her input is invaluable. We'd never be able to get away by ourselves for weekends or go out as often as we do if it wasn't for Rosie. We only have to say the word and she'll come over to babysit the girls. Wait until you and David have children. You might think differently then.'

Holly bowed her head. 'David and I have a long way to go before we think about that.'

Carina's almost-black eyes looked worried. 'But you must have discussed children – you and David. You're a brilliant auntie and you'll make an even better mum.'

Holly felt a lump in her throat and didn't trust herself to speak.

Carina persisted. 'Now that you're getting married, you must have some idea whether you're going to try straight away or wait a little while.'

'We've talked about it, but not at length. David has always said he'd like two children – a girl and a boy.'

'Babies don't come to order,' Carina said, her face turning dark. 'You of all people should know that.'

Holly looked at her and her eyes filled with tears.

'Oh God, Holly, I'm sorry. That came out all wrong.'

'It's okay. But you're right. David is very organised in every aspect of his life. He expects things will fall neatly into place but, as you say, life doesn't always happen like that.'

Carina looked at her quizzically. 'Holly, is there something wrong?' She reached across the table and put a hand over Holly's. 'I expected you to be glowing today. Revelling in your status of bride-to-be.'

That caught Holly off-guard and she willed the tears not to fall. She didn't want to cry. Not there. Not now. Carina knew she'd touched a nerve, so she continued.

'Because if there *is* something wrong, if you're not happy, if it's something to do with David, you need to speak up now. What is it, Holly?'

Oh God, she was giving her that look. She only ever looked at her like that when things got really serious and Holly knew she meant business. She was like a ninja when it came to extracting information from her and Holly knew she'd have to tell her.

'Holly?'

'It's just … it's just that –'

The pizza arrived and the waiter hovered, offering them black pepper, mozzarella, another drink – and Holly was given a lifeline.

'Go on,' said Carina, waiting intently for Holly to finish her sentence.

'It's just that I'm a little disappointed David doesn't want a party, that's all.'

Relief flooded Carina's face as she sat back and let out a long sigh. 'Is that all? Thank God for that. I thought you were going to tell me something awful.'

'Don't be silly,' Holly said, a nervous laugh escaping her lips as she tried to compose herself. 'I'm getting married. How could anything be awful?'

'And do *you* want a party?' Carina asked, expertly cutting the pizza and dishing it up onto both plates with the skill of a well-practised mother. 'Did you ask him about it?'

'Well, no, not exactly. You know what David is like. All practical and no romance.'

'Ah, Holly, don't say that. He's so good to you. Romance isn't all flowers and chocolates, you know.'

'I know, and I'm probably being unfair. Don't get me wrong, I'm delighted about the engagement and I want to marry David. Of course I do. But it's just all happened so … I don't know … so matter-of-factly. No big proposal, no romance around the buying of the ring and no talk of a party to celebrate.'

'I see where you're coming from. I really do. But surely what matters is that you're marrying a good man. He's kind and reliable and he loves you to bits. And unless I'm wrong, you love him too.'

Holly nodded. She remembered back to the day she told her parents about David. 'A banker!' her mother had said. 'Well, now that's a man you want to keep.' Holly had felt vaguely annoyed at the time, since they hadn't even met him and he could be an absolute idiot for all they knew. But she also knew how her parents had struggled when she and Carina were kids. They'd barely had enough money to survive and Holly remembered well the hunger pangs when she'd lain awake at night. It was no wonder her parents wanted so much more for their daughters.

'I just had a thought,' said Carina, jolting Holly out of her reverie. 'Why don't Jason and I do a meal for you two and we'll ask Mum and Dad over as well. We can make it an engagement celebration.'

'That's very kind of you, Carina. But I know how busy you are. I wouldn't want to intrude.'

'Nonsense! It's ages since you visited. I won't take no for an answer.'

Holly was delighted. 'Okay, thanks. Just tell me when and we'll be there. Now come on and fill me in on all your news.'

Carina leaned forward and lowered her voice. 'Well, you have to promise me you won't breathe a word of this to anyone …'

Carina always had loads of juicy gossip from her job and Holly loved to hear her stories. They chatted amicably for the next hour until it was time to go. They paid the bill and headed out into the bitter cold.

'So we'll organise that meal for next week then?' Carina said, as they came to the end of Grafton Street where they'd part ways. 'Just check with David and let me know what night suits.'

Holly nodded, then hugged her tightly. 'I will, and thanks again.'

She watched as Carina strode purposefully down the street and she envied her completeness. Because that's what Carina was – complete. She had a lovely husband whom she adored, two gorgeous children, a job to die for and the looks of a goddess. That's why Holly couldn't tell her. She couldn't tell her about her doubts. She had the opportunity to be as happy as Carina was. She had a good man who loved her and wanted to marry her. She loved David. And she really wanted to marry him too. But sometimes, just sometimes, she remembered what it was like to have passion. To love somebody with such ferocity that your insides exploded into fireworks when you were with them. That passion had broken her heart in the past so she shouldn't have craved it, but sometimes she did.

She gave herself a mental shake as she headed towards the bus stop. David would never break her heart. That's what was important. She smiled as she passed a shop window filled with blinking Santas and was reminded of how close they were to Christmas. Only eight weeks away. She increased her pace as a cold wind cut into her face and she felt suddenly brighter. She needed to start planning. Maybe she and David could have their first Christmas together in their own house. Their first one as an engaged couple. They'd usually each go to their own families for Christmas dinner and meet up again in the evening, but maybe they'd do it differently this year. Holly would have a chat with David about it later. Maybe they could even buy some new Christmas decorations too and decorate the outside of the house with lights. Holly felt all her earlier doubts dissipate and she smiled to herself. She and David were going to be married and she couldn't wait to see what their future held.

Chapter 6

Josh breathed a sigh of relief as he drove out of the school gates. He adored his job but sometimes teaching thirty feisty twelve-year-old boys took its toll. The sixth class at St John's primary school were at that stage where they were ready to move on to the next level and got bored very easily. Josh had to constantly come up with new, innovative ideas to hold their attention. But thankfully he held the trump card of being a football coach as well as a teacher. And for most twelve-year-old boys, football was everything. The school principal always said that they shouldn't use bribery to get the children to do what they wanted, but Josh liked to think of it as incentivising them. If they knuckled down to their work during the week, he'd give them two hours of sports on Fridays, and if he wanted a little extra from them, he'd promise a kick-around during lunch on another day.

He was out on the Navan Road in minutes and heading in the direction of home. He felt like he was playing truant because it was only half past one, but thanks to a burst pipe and some necessary maintenance work, they'd had to finish up early. Stephanie was at home waiting for him. They'd decided that they were going to make the final move to their new house that day. Josh still felt a little sad to be moving, but as they'd emptied the old house over the last week, it had begun to feel less and less like home. His mother always said 'Home is where the heart is' and he was beginning to realise what that really meant.

He turned his silver Micra onto their street and pulled into the driveway for what would probably be the last time. He was surprised to feel a lump in his throat as he stepped out of the car. He'd had some fantastic times in that house. If the walls could have spoken, he was sure they'd have had plenty to say. It seemed like no time since he'd walked up to that very door, a shiny new key in his hand, about to step into adulthood for the first time. The front door swung open and Stephanie stood there, looking gorgeous with her hair pinned on top of her head, her sleeves rolled up and her make-up-free face flushed and glowing.

'Come on,' she said, like an excited schoolgirl. 'I have everything cleaned so I'm just waiting for you to sort out the rest of your stuff.'

'I hope you haven't been pushing yourself too hard,' said Josh, kissing her gently on the lips. 'I told you I'd do whatever needed to be done when I got home.'

'I know, I know. But I'm just excited. I hate being between houses like this. I just want to move into the new place for good.'

Her excitement was contagious and Josh worked like a Trojan for the next hour, sorting out all his bits and pieces and loading the car one last time. Then it was time to leave. Stephanie headed out to the car while Josh double-checked each room, making sure they hadn't left anything behind. It was funny, just as this house had welcomed him to his first real taste of adulthood, the new house was going to introduce him to a whole new level of responsibility. It would be the first house he'd be a dad in. He'd no longer be a reckless student or a party-loving free spirit. He'd be a proper grown-up, a responsible adult with a family to support. The horn tooted impatiently and his moment of reflection was lost. He finally closed the front door behind him and joined Stephanie in the car to head to their new life.

*　　*　　*

'Why don't you head up for a bath and I'll order us a takeaway,' said Josh some hours later when they'd finally settled themselves in. 'You'll be aching from all that work today so a good soak will ease your muscles.'

'I might have a shower, actually. A few of the gang are meeting up in town and I thought I'd go in and see them.'

'Tonight? Our first night in the house?'

'I'm sorry, babe. We can sit in tomorrow night but I haven't seen Brigitte or Coco in ages and they're going to be there.'

Josh tried not to be judgemental but it was the fourth night she'd been out in the last couple of weeks and he worried about her. 'I'm glad you're seeing your friends, Steph, but you'll be exhausted tonight after the day we've had. And I've had a beer so I can't drop you into town. You'd have to get the bus.'

'I might just get a taxi, actually.'

Josh opened his mouth to say something but changed his mind. Stephanie's social life wasn't cheap, but he knew that if he made any reference to money, she'd have one of her meltdowns and accuse him of being miserly.

'You could always come too,' she continued. 'We could celebrate the new house.'

He paused before answering and he thought he noticed a flicker of panic cross her face. 'No,' he said eventually. 'You head on in. I'll sort out a few things here and see you later.'

'Thanks, babe,' she said, jumping up from the sofa and kissing him on the top of his head. 'And I'll cook for us tomorrow night. I'll do some shopping while you're at work and get everything in.'

Josh felt old. Stephanie loved to go out to clubs and gigs whereas he was more a pub and cinema guy. She hated to be home before daybreak and he'd usually start to wane after midnight. He could tell she really hadn't wanted him tagging along on her night out but he was actually quite relieved. He didn't have much time for those pretentious friends of hers. None of her old school friends lived in Dublin so the friends she had now were an arty bunch she'd met over the last few years. Brigitte and Coco! Apparently their real names were Ann and Martha but, according to them, 'The name really matters in this business, dahling!' Josh liked real people so the less time he had to spend in their company, the better.

He settled down to watch some football on the telly and poured himself another beer. He wasn't planning on a party for one but, as he sprawled out on the sofa, he was beginning to think it mightn't be such a bad thing after all. He almost forgot Stephanie was still upstairs and she frightened the life out of him an hour later when she appeared in the sitting room.

'Wow!' he said, looking her up and down. She looked spectacular. Her long blonde hair was curled and falling over to one side and her face was breathtaking. She was wearing a silver shift dress that fell way above her knee and did a good job of hiding her pregnant stomach. Her favourite Kurt Geiger black heels made her legs look endless and Josh couldn't stop staring at her.

'I take it I look okay then?' she asked, her dark-red lips forming a smile. 'Aren't you going to say something?'

'Gorgeous!' was all he could manage.

'I have my key so you don't have to wait up. I won't be too late, though.'

'Just be careful, won't you, Steph? You look amazing. You're bound to get lots of attention.'

'You know me. I can look after myself.' She kissed him and disappeared out the front door. Josh knew she was tougher than she looked but he couldn't help worrying.

An hour later, Josh was already beginning to feel bored. It felt weird to be in a new house alone. He stood up and went to the window to see if there was anything happening on the street but all was quiet. He looked forward to getting to know a few people and finding out more about the neighbours. It would be nice if there was a crowd of people their own age whom they could socialise with. They hadn't had anything like that at their old place.

He was about to go back to the sofa when he noticed the gorgeous Audi from across the road pulling into the driveway. Without taking time to think it through, he dashed out the door and went over to introduce himself. He probably wouldn't have bothered if it was a Fiat Punto or a Toyota Yaris, but he'd always been drawn to fancy cars and he just couldn't resist. The driver, a man of about forty, well dressed, serious face, stepped out of the car.

'Hi,' said Josh, feeling slightly awkward. 'I'm Josh. I just wanted to introduce myself. Me and my girlfriend have just moved into number three across the road.'

The other man smiled and extended his right hand for a hand-shake. 'David Wood. It's nice to meet you.'

'You too. This seems like a lovely street.'

'It's fine,' David said, looking around him. 'Mostly people keep themselves to themselves. There are a few elderly people on this side, and over beside you there's a young couple with a baby and a single mum with a few kids. It'll be nice to have someone our own age here.'

Josh recoiled slightly. He wondered if they really looked the same age. The guy seemed nice enough but Josh would have put him at maybe eight or nine years older.

David continued. 'So is it just you and your girlfriend? Any children?'

'Not yet, but one on the way.'

'Well, congratulations. When is the little one due?'

'End of April, all going well. How about yourselves?'

'It's just the two of us for now. We're planning a wedding at the moment so who knows. Maybe sometime after that.'

'So I've been admiring this beauty,' said Josh, changing the subject. 'It's pretty special.'

'It is, isn't it?' David said, stroking the bonnet in a gesture only car geeks would understand. 'I'll take you for a spin in it someday, if you like.'

'That would be amazing, thank you. I love cars, although you wouldn't know it by looking at that clapped-out thing in my driveway.'

David looked over at Josh's Micra and laughed. 'I've had one or two of those in my time. Not a bad car, really.'

'It'll do me for now. But *this* is what I strive for. Some day.' Josh dared to stroke the precious car too until he suddenly felt awkward and realised he'd already taken up too much of this man's time. 'Anyway, I'll let you go on in. It was nice to meet you.'

'You too,' David said, turning to open his front door. 'You and your girlfriend should drop over to us some night. I'll speak to my fiancée and we'll arrange it.'

'That would be lovely. Thanks again.'

Josh headed back in and felt suddenly contented. They had a lovely house on a lovely street and it seemed they might have made some new friends too. Stephanie had done well choosing this place. It ticked all the boxes and Josh felt that they were going to be very, very happy here.

Chapter 7

Holly had decided two things while she'd lain awake listening to David's snores the previous night. Firstly, she needed to start appreciating what she had. She was engaged to a wonderful man who adored her and it was about time she realised how lucky she was. Secondly, she needed to do something about her appearance. She'd caught a glimpse of her reflection in a shop window the previous day and she couldn't believe it was her. She used to wear her five-foot-eleven height with pride, choosing skinny jeans or leggings to accentuate her long legs and fitted tops to show off her tiny waist. What she'd seen yesterday was a woman who'd lost all pride in her appearance. She looked frumpy and overweight and was even walking with a stoop. There were seven weeks left until Christmas and she was determined to get some of the old her back before then. She was going to buy herself a size-twelve figure-hugging dress as an incentive and she was going to make sure she fitted into it for the festive season.

She checked the clock on the cooker display and saw it was almost eight. David would be home soon and she wanted everything timed to perfection. She'd finished work at four and had picked up a few bits in the local supermarket on the way home. She was making them a proper home-cooked meal, something she'd probably only done a handful of times over the last few years. She wasn't much of a cook and it was easier to just throw something frozen into the oven or order takeaway. She'd never be one of those domesticated wives but she reckoned she could brush up on her kitchen skills at the very least. And besides, if she was going to get lose weight, the best way to start was with a bit of decent home cooking.

The smell coming from the oven was making her mouth water and she hoped David didn't get delayed any longer in work. She wasn't good when she was hungry. Hangry, they called it. If she didn't get food when she needed it, she lost all sense of reason and had been known to cry. A lot. But, thankfully, the sound of a car in the driveway alerted her to David's arrival so she could rest easy that they'd be eating soon. She opened the oven to check on the tuna pasta bake, a recipe she'd taken from the Jamie Oliver website, and she felt a sense of pride at the sight of the cheese bubbling on the top and the pasta crisping at the edges. Just like Jamie had said it would.

'Hiya, love,' said David, arriving into the kitchen. 'Something smells delicious.'

'I cooked for us,' she said proudly. 'Something proper and healthy. It's almost ready. Do you want to go for a shower while I dish up?'

He came over and kissed her on the cheek. 'To what do I owe this pleasure?'

'Nothing in particular. I just thought it would be nice to have a bit of home cooking. Go on, this will be on the table shortly.'

A few minutes later, David arrived back into the kitchen, slipping his arms around her waist as she dished up the dinner. 'You smell nice,' he said.

She turned to see if he was mocking her. 'I smell like tuna and broccoli.'

He took her by surprise then by kissing her full on the lips. 'And you taste even better. I love you, Holly.'

'I love you too, David.' If this was the reaction she got from simply cooking a meal, she was definitely going to do it more often. He was a great kisser and she suddenly realised that they just didn't take enough time to be intimate together. And that was another thing she was determined to change.

They tucked into their food and, to Holly's relief, it tasted okay. She'd even made a green salad to go with it and had cut a wholemeal baguette into fancy little slices. She wouldn't say she'd uncovered her inner culinary goddess yet, but it was a start.

'I was just speaking to our new neighbour,' said David, stuffing a large forkful of the tuna bake into his mouth. 'Seems like a nice chap.'

'Really? How did you get talking to him?'

'He came over when I parked. Wanted to introduce himself.'

'Go on then. What's he like?'

'It's just him and his partner,' David continued. 'But they have a baby on the way.'

'How old are they? I couldn't tell from seeing the guy the other day because he had sunglasses on.'

'Mid-thirties, I reckon. I've invited them over.'

'You what?' She stopped the fork just before it got to her mouth. 'When?'

'I said I'd chat to you and we'd let them know. It might be nice to have a couple our own age on the street. What do you think?'

'I think it's a great idea,' she said, delighted that David had taken the initiative to ask him. 'Maybe this weekend?'

David looked pleased. 'Grand. I can drop over tomorrow after work and suggest it, if you like.'

Holly shook her head. 'No, let me do it. It will give me a chance to introduce myself.'

'Fine by me.' He had already finished his plate of food and sat back, stretching his arms behind his head. 'That was delicious, thanks. You're turning out to be a pretty good cook.'

He was in great spirits so it seemed like as good a time as any to talk to him about the festive season. 'David, you know how it's only seven weeks to Christmas?'

'Is that all it is? Where does the time go?'

'Well, anyway, have you given any thought to what we'll do this year?'

'You mean on Christmas Day? I'd just assumed we'd do the same as always.'

'How about we change things this year?' she ventured. 'Now that we're engaged to be married, why don't we start as we mean to go on and have Christmas dinner here?'

'Here?'

She continued while the going was good. 'I know I'm no Nigella but I reckon we could rustle up a nice dinner between us and it might be nice to celebrate it in our own house for a change.'

Holly could see his mind ticking and wasn't sure how he'd react. After what seemed like minutes, he finally spoke. 'You could be right, Holly. Maybe we should start our own traditions. Out with the old, in with the new, and all that.'

That was easier than she'd thought. 'Exactly,' she said, delighted he agreed. 'I was thinking we could take an early trip to Kildare to see my parents on Christmas morning and then call to your mum on the way back. What do you think?'

She knew by the way he was looking at her that she'd said something wrong. 'David?'

'If we stay here for dinner, Mum will have to come to us. I can't believe you thought she wouldn't.'

'But –'

'Holly, there's no way I'd leave her alone on Christmas Day. Of course she'd have to come to us for dinner.'

Holly's heart sank. He was probably right but what about *her* parents? When would *they* be considered? He must have read her mind because he continued.

'Your parents have each other so it's not as though they'll be lonely. Mum only has me.'

She wanted to point out that Doreen had her two sisters and three brothers, along with a heap of nieces and nephews, all of whom were constantly inviting her to their homes. But she knew she'd be fighting a losing battle.

'I suppose,' she relented. 'I just wasn't thinking.'

'So that's settled then,' he said, taking a cloth hanky out of his pocket and blowing his nose loudly. 'We're going to have dinner here. I'll tell Mum later.'

She could have cut her tongue out. Her worst nightmare. Not only did she have to cook Christmas dinner, which wouldn't have been so bad if it had just been her and David eating it, but now she'd have to have it scrutinised by Doreen. You'd think from how the woman behaved that nobody else in the world could cook Christmas dinner like she could. Apparently, she had a recipe for the ham that had been handed down through generations and had a secret ingredient to make sprouts really tasty. Sprouts, in Holly's opinion, were the food of the devil and nothing on earth could make them edible. Oh God, what had she let herself in for? She'd have to retrieve the situation.

'Actually, maybe hold off on asking her for a while. It's still early so we've plenty of time to make decisions.'

David looked at her quizzically and she couldn't blame him. 'But I thought you just said –'

'I know, but the more I think about it, the more I realise that we should probably stick to our usual plan, at least until we're married.'

'No,' he said, with uncharacteristic decisiveness. 'You were right first time. I think it's time we set down some proper roots here. We shouldn't be parting ways on Christmas Day at this stage. Not when we're engaged to be married.'

'Well, I suppose we could …'

'Great. Now have we anything for dessert?'

That was it. Conversation dismissed. But there was no point in dwelling on it any further. She sighed and took a tub of Ben & Jerry's Cookie Dough from the freezer. As her culinary skills were still in development, she hadn't ventured into the sweet zone yet.

'Have you seen the house around the corner?' she said, in an effort to banish the dark cloud she felt threatening to engulf her. 'The one with the lights.'

David nodded. 'Ridiculous, isn't it?'

'I think it's lovely, actually. Do you think we could put up some outdoor lights this year?'

'It's a monstrosity. And I think outside lights are just tacky.'

'It doesn't have to be like that house. Just a few twinkly ones to brighten up the place. I think it would look fabulous.'

He seemed to be mulling it over so she kept talking. 'It's just that if we're having your mother over and trying to set down roots here, it would be nice to make the house more Christmassy. Come on, David. I know you're not a fan of lights but can't you just get into the spirit this year? Just for me?'

'I suppose a *few* lights wouldn't do any harm,' he said. 'Once they're subtle.'

'Done,' she said, her hopes of recreating Lapland in the garden slipping away.

'And definitely not those blue lights. I don't know how anyone could think they're even remotely Christmassy. They look more like the lights of a brothel.'

She was tempted to ask how he'd know but stayed quiet, lest he decided they couldn't have lights after all.

'Oh, and no twinkly ones,' he continued. 'Those flashing lights give me a headache. I certainly don't want to be sitting here watching the news with lights going on and off outside the window.'

Scrooge had nothing on her husband-to-be. Christmas was stressful on so many levels but Holly loved it. She loved everything about it, which was why she wanted to get married at that time of year. And she wasn't letting go of her dream. Mammy Wood thought she'd had the final word on the wedding but Holly wasn't giving up on her snowy castle on a hill.

Chapter 8

Josh rubbed his eyes in an effort to stay awake. He was in the staffroom at work and had never felt more exhausted in his life. He'd taken a book so that he could sit in the corner and keep himself to himself. He wasn't actually reading the book but by holding it up somewhere close to his face, people tended to leave him alone. It wasn't that he didn't like his colleagues – in fact they were great and he enjoyed their company – but today he needed peace. He glanced at his watch and was glad to see he still had twenty minutes left of break-time. The watch was old and battered and Stephanie was always telling him he should get a new one – something trendy like Michael Kors or Emporio Armani – but he wasn't ready to part with this one just yet.

He'd eventually gone to bed the previous night at 3 a.m. and there still hadn't been any sign of Stephanie coming home. Josh had planned to stay up until he knew she was back safely but two things had eventually changed his mind. One – he had a seven o'clock start the following morning. Trying to teach a group of highly charged twelve-year-olds when he'd had no sleep was something he hadn't wanted to face. And two – he wasn't her father and she wasn't a teenager. So instead of sitting on the sofa watching senseless telly until she came home, he'd lain in bed wide awake until she'd crash-banged her way into the room at 5.37 a.m. precisely.

His first thought when he'd heard sounds akin to a herd of ele-phants coming from downstairs was that she must have been drunk. He'd quickly ruled that out, but when she'd come into the bedroom, turning the light on and flinging bits of her clothing on the floor before falling into bed, he'd begun to wonder again. A wave of panic had overcome him and he'd turned to look at her on the bed. She'd already fallen asleep, sprawled over the outside of the duvet with just her knickers on. She'd left the bedroom light on, which had forced him out of the bed to switch it off. He'd been torn between annoy-ance and concern. They'd agreed right from the start of the preg-nancy that she wouldn't drink any alcohol for the duration and he'd hoped she'd kept her promise. By her own admission, she'd been a bit of a wild teen – drinking to excess and dabbling in some recre-ational drugs. There was a part of him that had been scared she'd slip back into her old ways – now that she was pregnant, he was even more worried.

He'd crept back into bed, pulling the duvet gently from under her and placing it over her exposed body. She'd been lying on her back, her lips slightly parted, so Josh had taken the opportunity to smell her breath. He'd quietly brought his face close to hers, half expect-ing to smell alcohol, but all he'd gotten was a whiff of garlic. It hadn't completely put his mind at ease, but he needed some sleep so he'd turned on his side and closed his eyes for the short amount of time that was left before the alarm went off.

Now he was exhausted and, on top of that, the stomach pain had come back earlier and it had been pretty bad. He'd popped a couple of pills before he'd left the house and thankfully that had kept it to a dull ache. At least he'd already gotten through the worst of the day – just another two hours to go before home time. He'd promised the lads football in the afternoon but he was going to have to cancel. They'd moan and look at him as though he'd committed a cardinal sin, but he'd just have to suck it up. He glanced at his watch again – ten minutes of break left – so he sank a little lower into his chair and allowed his eyes to close.

'Josh. *Josh!*'

He opened his eyes a slit and for a moment couldn't think where he was.

'Josh, wake up. Are you okay?'

He squinted as the sunlight trickling through the window blinded him and he tried to focus. It took him a few moments but when he realised where he was, he jumped up in panic. 'Donal! Jesus, I must have dropped off.'

'Ms Heffernan heard chaos coming from your class,' said the school principal, a stern look on his face. 'She went to investigate and found the boys running wild with no supervision.'

'I'm so sorry. I'll head in there straight away.'

'Are you up to it?' Donal asked, looking at Josh with concern. 'You're not sick, are you?'

'No, no, I'm fine. I just didn't get much sleep last night, that's all.'

Donal chuckled as they walked out of the staff room. 'Pregnant girlfriend not getting sleep and making sure she doesn't suffer alone, eh?'

He wasn't entirely wrong. 'Something like that.'

'I remember when my Sally was pregnant with our Jack. Up all night with heartburn, she was. And she had me running up and down those stairs through the night to get her Gaviscon, cups of tea, dry crackers. By the end of the pregnancy I felt like I'd carried the child myself.'

'I know what you mean,' said Josh, following him out the door. 'I'd better go and sort these boys out. Sorry again.'

Almost half past one. The boys had had a half hour to cause chaos in the classroom. They must have been delighted with themselves. At least now Josh wouldn't have to make an excuse for not giving them football. He could tell them it was a punishment and if they behaved and read quietly for the rest of the day, they'd be rewarded tomorrow. He just couldn't wait to get home. He was angry at Steph, but he was also worried and he needed to talk to her. Calmly. He didn't want to argue with her but he wanted to make her understand why he was so concerned.

He could hear them from down the corridor. Much as he loved teaching the boys, he'd rather have been anywhere else at that moment. But he knew what he had to do so he took a deep breath and swung the door open. They knew immediately by his face that they were in a whole lot of trouble. At least they respected him enough to go quiet and return to their seats. He stood at the top of the class and it dawned on him that this was where he had control. It was easier to manage thirty twelve-year-olds than one pregnant girlfriend. It would be funny if it wasn't so worrying.

When he finally walked in the front door of his house, he exhaled a sigh of relief. He'd honestly thought he was going to drop off to sleep again on that drive home. He could hear the telly on so Stephanie was obviously up and about. That was something at least. He closed the door behind him and walked into the sitting room, where she was sprawled on the sofa watching *Mad Men*. She looked a stark contrast to the previous night. She was wearing a pair of his tracksuit bottoms with one of his sloppy jumpers. Her hair was dishevelled and clipped up haphazardly on top of her head and the remains of last night's make-up streaked down her face. She looked up as he came in and her eyes were bloodshot. A cold chill ran through his veins.

'You look awful,' he said, too tired to bother with niceties. 'Good night?'

She pulled her feet towards her to make room for him to sit down but he stayed where he was. 'It was the best. All the gang were there and we haven't all been together in an age.'

'You were very late.' He searched her face for something. Guilt maybe.

'I know. I'm sorry. Coco and I were sharing a taxi and I couldn't drag her away. She's been after Jeremy for months now and was finally getting somewhere last night.'

'Hmm.' He knew he sounded like a disapproving dad. Again. But he couldn't help it.

'Aw, don't be like that, Josh. You know what it's like when you're having a great night and lose all track of time.'

Josh wished he could remember. He relented and sat down on the end of the sofa. 'As I said last night, Steph, I want you to have a good time, but shouldn't you be taking it a little easier with the pregnancy and everything?'

'Pregnancy isn't an illness,' she said, sitting up straighter. 'I'm still young and my body is fit and well. I should be able to live my life normally.'

Josh idly wondered how she figured pregnancy wasn't an illness when it came to her social life and yet it was a completely different story when it came to working. 'You look terrible, though, Steph. If I didn't know better, I'd say you were hungover.' He let the words hang there and waited for the onslaught.

She began to laugh and then, just as quickly, her expression turned serious. 'Oh my God. You actually think I was drinking? Is that what all this is about? I can't believe you think I'd go out and get drunk in my condition. I don't have to be drunk to have a good time.'

He felt slightly guilty but not convinced. 'But have you looked in the mirror today? Your eyes. Have you seen how bloodshot they are?'

'Yes, I have. And I'm bloody exhausted. That's why they're bloodshot.' She got up from the sofa, sending a cup smashing onto the wooden floor, and stormed out of the room.

Josh knew he needed to sort this or he'd be in the doghouse for days. 'Steph, come back. I'm sorry. I'm just tired. I was waiting for you last night and only got an hour or two of sleep before I had to get up again. Steph, please.'

She was already upstairs and he was left in no doubt about how she felt by the ferocity with which the bedroom door was slammed. He sighed and followed her up and into the room. He dearly wished he was better at dealing with these types of situations. At dealing with *her*. But she was like a bull in a china shop when she was in a strop and Josh would usually end up regretting he'd even opened his mouth.

'I don't want to talk to you,' she said, shoving him away as he went to put his arms around her. 'Honestly, Josh. Stay away from me, if that's what you think of me.'

'Steph! Don't be like this. I don't think anything of you, except that you're my girlfriend, you're carrying our baby and I just want to keep you both safe.'

'And I don't?' She got into bed with her clothes on and turned on her side, pulling the duvet over her head.

He sat on the edge of the bed and tried to pull the duvet back, but she was clinging tightly to it. 'Come on, love. You know me. I just say stupid things sometimes.'

She wasn't budging and had fallen silent. He knew the best thing to do was to leave her to simmer for a while, so he reluctantly stood up and headed back downstairs. What a palaver. He hadn't even taken off his coat yet and, the way he felt, he could just head back out the door again. But he wasn't going to do that. In a way, he didn't blame her for being so defensive. Especially if he'd been completely wrong in his accusation. But he still had his doubts. To quote his old friend Shakespeare, 'The lady doth protest too much'.

Chapter 9

September 1997

Holly sang to herself as she wrapped the present. It wasn't expensive – just a cheap watch from the jeweller's in the village. She wished she'd had more than twenty pounds to spend but even at that she'd been saving for weeks. Still, she was making it look nice with the gold wrapping paper and the red ribbon. And she was sure he'd appreciate it. He was like that. Appreciative of everything. Kind, loving and adorable. Today was their two-year anniversary. They'd been going steady for two whole years and she was the happiest girl in the world. Most of their friends had sniggered when they'd announced their togetherness at just thirteen. She wasn't stupid – she'd heard all the comments behind her back: 'That will never last.' 'It's just puppy love.' 'I'll give it two months, max.' But they'd proven the doubters wrong. They had lasted and would continue lasting. Holly knew that they'd be together for the rest of their lives.

'So go on then, tell me.'

'What?' Holly looked at Milly questioningly. 'Tell you what?'

'Why you're looking so gloomy. You should be singing "I'm getting married in the morning" and beaming from ear to ear.'

Holly laughed at that. 'Firstly, you've heard me sing – mostly when I'm drunk. So you know that it's not something I should inflict on our poor customers. And secondly …'

'Yes?' Milly was waiting for her to finish but Holly didn't know if she wanted to say too much.

'It's just, you know, stuff.'

'Oh, well, that tells me everything. Not! Come on, Holly. I know there's something wrong. Talk to me.'

Just then Mrs Jackson arrived in with her stuck-up shih-tzu, Kylie. Kylie was wearing a pink tutu and had an oversized bow on the top of her head. Her face, as usual, was grumpy and, although it was the natural appearance of the breed, Holly was sure Kylie was extra miserable because she was forced to wear such ridiculous attire.

'What can I do for you, Mrs Jackson?' Holly said, as the woman approached the desk. 'You don't have an appointment for Kylie, do you?'

'No, no, I didn't have time to ring. She's not well and I don't know what's wrong with her.'

'Okay,' said Milly, taking over immediately. 'I'll take a look at her. What are her symptoms?'

'She's been a bit listless these last few days but this morning she wouldn't even eat her tuna.'

'Oh, well, we can't have that, can we, Kylie?' Milly rubbed the little dog's head, causing her to growl viciously.

'See,' said Mrs Jackson, looking as though she was about to cry. 'She can't even bear somebody touching her.'

Holly didn't like to point out that Kylie was a vicious bully who would bite the hand off anyone who dared invade her space. Instead, she smiled sweetly and marked her down in the book before Milly led them both into the treatment room.

Milly had arrived at the veterinary surgery as a trainee vet a few years before, and she and Holly had clicked straight away. Only five foot three, with fiery red hair and the brightest blue eyes Holly had ever seen, Milly had immediately brought spirit to the old veterinary practice. Fintan, the owner and head vet, was lovely but he was getting on in years and he didn't exactly fill the place with energy. The customers loved him. He was brilliant at what he did and was kind and generous with his time, but his soft voice and slow manner sometimes made Holly want to go to sleep. Milly, on the other hand, was like a little pocket rocket. She'd fly about the place, getting through customer after customer, either whistling or singing and generally lightening the mood.

The practice was very quiet while Milly was seeing Mrs Jackson and Kylie and, except for a cat with an itch and a post-op Labrador, the appointment book was empty for the rest of the day. Business had been very slow generally these last few weeks and it made the day drag on. Holly had already done a stocktake and sent in an order for supplies, but, never one to be idle, she then began to rearrange the items for sale in the reception area. Holly adored her job and her only regret was that she hadn't gone to college when she left school. If she'd worked harder and got decent points, she would have studied to be a veterinary nurse. Her life had taken a different path and she'd ended up with no real qualifications. But she'd always known she wanted to work with animals so fronting reception at the clinic was the next best thing.

Just then the door opened to her right and a low growl told her that Kylie wasn't happy. Holly adored dogs, all shapes and sizes, but Kylie just wasn't one she could warm to. It wasn't the dog's fault that she was the way she was.

'So, all sorted then?' Holly looked at Mrs Jackson and was shocked to see she was crying. 'Mrs Jackson? Are you okay?'

'She's pregnant,' said Milly, following the woman out of the room.

'Mrs Jackson is pregnant?' Holly gasped, looking at the old lady in horror. She must have been almost seventy.

'Kylie! *Kylie* is pregnant.' Milly tried to stifle a giggle and all of a sudden Holly couldn't stop the tears of laughter from pouring down her face.

Thankfully Mrs Jackson mistook them for tears of sadness and nodded vigorously. 'Terrible, isn't it? I can't believe it. It's that horrible mongrel from down the road. I know it is. They let him out to wander the streets on his own and I've caught him a few times in my back yard. My poor little Kylie. He's about five times her size. I hope he didn't hurt her.'

Holly had to excuse herself and go out the back for a moment for fear a guffaw would escape her lips. She leaned against a supply shelf and gulped in some deep breaths. She shouldn't have laughed really but there was just something funny about the whole thing. Once Kylie was healthy, that was all that mattered. And at the end of the day, she'd have some gorgeous new puppies. Motherhood might even make her a nicer dog. Holly began to laugh again at the very idea.

When she went back out to reception, Milly was talking to Mrs Jackson. 'I reckon she still has a few weeks to go so come straight back to us if there are any problems. But I think she'll be fine.'

'How can she be?' sniffed the distraught woman. 'She's been defiled by a monster.'

Holly let a guffaw escape from her mouth but covered it well by launching into a fit of coughing.

'And furthermore,' continued Mrs Jackson, 'I don't think she'll be able for delivering pups. She's very delicate, you know.'

'Listen, don't worry about anything for now,' said Milly, gently leading her to the door. 'Dogs are resilient and she might surprise you. Give me a ring tomorrow and let me know how she's getting on.'

Finally Milly closed the door and leaned her back against it with relief. She and Holly looked at each other and burst out laughing. It was exactly what Holly needed. Something to distract her. Something to take her mind off other things. And it felt like a long time since she'd properly laughed.

'Fancy a drink after work?' said Milly, checking the diary for appointments. 'Just a quick one, though, because Greg and I are heading into town later.

'Actually, I'd love a drink. And maybe I'll finish what I started to tell you earlier. I could do with a bit of your honesty to set me straight.'

Milly arrived back at the table with two pints of cider and Holly knew she meant business. They usually had a glass of red wine when they'd drop in to O'Malley's for a quick one – the cider would only appear when they had something serious to discuss.

'So,' Milly said, taking a large slug of her drink. 'You've never made a secret of the fact you'd like to get married, your lovely boyfriend has just proposed and you're walking around with a face like a slapped arse. What am I missing?'

Holly wasn't even sure she could answer that honestly. All the ingredients were there. Everything in her life was good and, on paper, she should be dancing around with joy, but she wasn't. And she wasn't entirely sure why. She took a sip of the cold cider before answering.

'I *am* happy, Milly. I really am.'

'Well, I'm certainly not buying that!'

Holly tried again. 'What I mean is that I'm happy generally. Life is good. But I just feel like something is missing.'

Milly looked at her intently. 'Is this to do with David, or something else?'

Holly thought for a moment. 'It's just the whole wedding thing. I know it's what I've always wanted but it doesn't feel … it doesn't feel …'

'It doesn't feel what, Holly? It doesn't feel right?'

She shook her head. 'No, it's not that. It's more that it doesn't feel like I'm in control of it. Mammy Wood is sort of taking over the whole thing, and before we know it we'll be marched up the aisle of a church I don't want to be in, hosting a hotel full of people I don't want there and, God knows, maybe wearing a creation I don't even want to wear!'

'Ah,' said Milly, as if Holly had offered the solution, rather than the problem. 'Is that all?'

'What do you mean, is that all?'

Milly pushed her glasses up her nose and sat forward, ready to impart her wisdom. 'I mean, it's the wedding you have a problem with, not the marriage.'

Holly was confused. 'Aren't they one and the same thing?'

'Completely different,' said Milly knowingly. 'Your problem doesn't lie with the fact you're getting married but how it's going to happen.'

Holly thought about it for a moment. 'Well, yes, I suppose.'

'Isn't that what you just told me?'

'Yes, but I …' Milly had made it all sound so simple, so reasonable. Holly almost felt done out of a drama. 'I'm not sure that's all.'

'Oh, right. Well, then that's a different story. I think we might be needing a couple more drinks for this one.'

Holly didn't argue and headed straight to the bar. She was back moments later with two more drinks, anxious to bear her soul to her friend.

'So you and David,' said Milly, sitting back and sticking one leg up under her bum. She obviously wasn't going anywhere for a while. 'You're having problems?'

'Not at all.' Holly was quick to answer. 'But getting married is scary. I mean, how do you know? How do you know that the person you're with is the right one?'

Milly thought for a moment. 'Do you love him, Holly?'

'Of course I do. You know I do.'

'And how's the sex?'

Holly blushed furiously. 'Milly!'

'What? It's an important part of a relationship.'

'Well, there's no worries on that count. Our sex life is just fine. Perfect, actually.'

'Are you sure about that, Holly? I mean, I can't see Mr Boring providing a lot of excitement in the bedroom.'

Holly glared at her. 'Behave yourself, Milly. And don't call him that.'

'Sorry,' said Milly, looking sheepish. 'I'm just trying to get you to think about why you're having doubts.'

'I … I'm not having doubts. It's just … it's just …' Holly suddenly felt teary and wished she hadn't downed almost two pints in quick succession.

'Holly?'

'I love David, Milly. I really do.'

'But?'

'He's handsome and charming and honest and kind. And most of all he's good to me.'

'But?'

She took a moment before saying it. 'But I remember when his love made my insides explode and my head swim with happiness. I remember the feeling that nothing else mattered when we were together. When butterflies flew around my stomach when he kissed me. When I melted when he made love to me. And having his arms around me made me feel like the luckiest, richest, most blessed girl on the planet.'

'Wow! That sounds like heaven. So what's happened to change things?'

Holly felt a lump in her throat but knew she had to tell Milly. Even to her own ears, her voice sounded strangled as she barely whispered the words: 'I'm not talking about David.'

Chapter 10

It was Saturday morning and Stephanie was still in a strop with Josh. His head was wrecked. *She* was the one who'd gone out partying until the early hours. *She* was the one who'd come crashing into the house keeping him awake. And yet *he* was the one trying to make amends. And to top it all, he wasn't feeling too good today himself. He'd had a flare-up of stomach pain during the night and even painkillers hadn't really helped. So he hadn't had a proper sleep in two nights.

'Do you fancy some eggs?' he asked, as she came into the kitchen to fill the kettle.

'I've eaten.'

He tried again. 'But you've only had porridge, and it'll be a while before it's ready anyway. Will I stick on enough for us both?'

'No, I'm fine.'

She breezed out of the kitchen and Josh sighed. That was how it had been since the previous evening. Him trying to make conversation and her giving short, sharp answers. He was fed up with it. He took the pan and threw it loudly back into the drawer. He couldn't be bothered with breakfast either. What he needed was a long, hot shower to clear his head and put him in better form. He took a look at the mess he'd planned to clean up but decided against that too.

Let her bloody-well take some responsibility for a change. See how she liked it when he didn't pander to her every need.

He felt a lot better half an hour later as he stepped out of the shower. He shook the water from his hair and wrapped a towel around his waist before walking back into the bedroom. Stephanie was sprawled on the bed reading a magazine but she didn't acknowledge his presence.

'Steph, can we stop this fighting? It's not good for us and the stress is not good for you and the baby.'

'Fine.' She didn't even look up.

Josh sat down on the edge of the bed. 'Maybe we should go back to bed for a while. Cuddle up and have a lazy Saturday morning, like we used to.'

She looked at him then and he could see he'd said the wrong thing again. 'Do you ever think about anything except sex?' she said, almost spitting the words out.

'That's not fair,' he said, hurt at the vicious tone of her voice. 'You know I'm not like that.'

She closed her magazine and threw it on the floor. 'I'm going to ring Mum. You can get back into bed if you like but don't expect me to be joining you.'

He stared after her and sighed as she left the room. Bloody hormones. It was a good job he understood her because the way she was behaving would test the patience of a saint! He went to the dressing table and squeezed out a handful of serum and expertly applied it to his hair before smoothing it down with the hairdryer. As he looked in the mirror, he noticed a slight paunch that he hadn't had before and made a mental note to get back to the gym. Another thing he'd been neglecting lately with the moving and everything else going on.

When he switched off the hairdryer, he heard animated chatter coming from downstairs and assumed Stephanie was talking to her mum. But he soon realised that she wasn't on the phone at all and was talking to somebody at the front door. He secured the towel around his waist and made his way over to the window to have a look. There was a click as the front door closed and he saw a girl walk across the road and disappear into a house. Curious to find out more, he dressed quickly and headed downstairs.

'Was that our new neighbour you were talking to?'

She looked at him and sighed. 'Yes. She came over to ask us over to theirs tonight for a drink.'

'Oh, that's nice of them.' David had said they'd have them over but Josh had thought maybe he'd said it without thinking and hadn't really meant it. 'So what time?'

'She said eightish. But I'm not going.'

Josh looked at her but her gaze was still on the telly. 'Why not? I thought you'd be dying to see what they're like.'

'They asked us for a drink. I can't drink, remember?'

Another dig. 'Oh, for God's sake, Stephanie, it doesn't have to be alcoholic. You can still have a mineral – or a cup of tea even.'

'I think I'll pass.'

He tried another tactic. 'Come on. Let's see what sort of people can afford an amazing car like that. I could do the subtle questioning and you could check out their bathroom cabinet.'

A glimmer of a smile. 'I don't know.'

He almost had her so he continued. 'You know you want to, Steph. Come on, let's not fight any more. Let's go over there and we can have a good old gossip about them later.'

'Maybe,' she said, getting up off the sofa. 'But I need some fresh air so I'm going to go out for a walk first. I'll see how I feel later.'

'I'll come with you,' said Josh, jumping up to get his shoes. 'It'll be nice to suss out the area together.'

'No! I just want to put on my headphones and listen to music.'

He was a bit taken aback at the rebuff but she turned to him and kissed him on the cheek. 'It's just a walk, Josh. You know how music relaxes me and, to be honest, I feel so uptight at the moment. An hour out in the fresh air with good music in my ears will do me the world of good.'

He sat back down and sighed. 'Okay. But be careful of icy patches out there. It's freezing.'

He flicked around the channels when she was gone and settled on *Football Focus*. Weekends used to be fun-filled and exciting. Now he couldn't help wishing it was Monday and he was back in work. But maybe Stephanie would come back in a better mood and they could go to the neighbours' later. She and this girl might even hit it off and become friends. He thought how nice it would be for her to have a friend close by, and he would also love a mate on the road to go for a pint with. Most of his friends lived on the south side so it wasn't easy to go for a spontaneous drink. The telly became a dull buzz in the background as he felt his eyes starting to close. He relaxed down further into the sofa and began to drift off into a lovely, hazy sleep.

The sound of the hall door banging jolted him awake and it took him a few moments to realise where he was. Cold air drifted into the room and he looked up to see Stephanie standing in the doorway, her cheeks red, a smile on her lips.

'Having a sneaky sleep?' she said, grinning. 'I guessed you would.'

At least she seemed to be in better form. 'I was just having a little snooze. What time is it?'

'Quarter past two. I had a gorgeous long walk. You barely feel the cold when you keep going but when you stop it's absolutely freezing.'

Josh sat up and motioned for her to sit down beside him, which she did. 'Gosh, I can feel the cold air coming from you. Stay here and I'll make you a cup of hot chocolate.'

'Nope,' she said, jumping up. 'You stay where you are and *I'll* make us some hot chocolates.'

It was a miracle. She'd gone out for a walk and come back as the old Stephanie – the funny, caring, considerate one. He wasn't complaining, though. Her behaviour lately had been stressing him out and he'd begun to wonder if pregnancy had changed her forever. A few minutes later she was back in the sitting room, coat and shoes off, two mugs of creamy hot chocolate in her hands.

'Thanks, love. This is gorgeous.' He took a sip and it really was. She'd added mini marshmallows and a dash of squirty cream, and they sat side by side with their hands cupped around the drinks. Neither of them said anything for a few minutes and Josh was happy just to have no arguments. Eventually she broke the silence.

'I don't want to fight with you any more, Josh.'

He nodded vigorously. 'That's exactly what I've been saying. I don't want to fight either.'

'Good.' She laid her head on his shoulder and he kissed the soft, wispy blonde hairs straying from her ponytail. 'Let's have a nice evening together. Just like we were going to do the other night.'

'Definitely,' he said, glad the drama was over. 'If we just go across the road for an hour, we can watch a movie and get takeaway when we come back.'

She sat up and looked at him. 'I don't want to go over there tonight, Josh. I thought we'd have a night together, just the two of us.'

'And we can. But surely we should go over and say hello at least.'

'Please, Josh. I'm exhausted. I just want to have a bath and get back into my pyjamas. We can go another time.'

He sighed and nodded. 'Okay. I'd better go and let them know.'

'Thanks. Tell them I said sorry but I'm just not feeling up to it tonight.'

'Right,' he said, standing up and looking out the window. 'David's car is there so there's somebody home. I'll head over now.'

He didn't bother putting on a jacket just to cross the road but the nip in the air bit at his bare arms. A light dusting of snow had begun to fall and his inner child whooped. Josh loved snow and he hoped that it would become heavier and stick to the ground. It had been a pretty mild winter so far but this weather reminded him that Christmas was just around the corner. He couldn't wait. It was his favourite time of year and it excited him more than anything to think that from next year Santa would be coming to their little boy or girl.

He was just about to ring the bell when the door swung open and David was standing there. 'Come in, come in,' he said, gesturing for Josh to go inside. 'We were just talking about you two.'

'I won't, but thanks. It's just a quick call to say we won't be able to make it tonight after all. I'm really sorry.'

David looked genuinely disappointed. 'That's a pity. We were looking forward to it.'

'We were too,' said Josh. 'But I think I told you Stephanie is pregnant and she's not feeling too good today.'

'Sorry to hear that. Are you sure you wouldn't like to come in and have a cup of tea? You haven't met Holly yet, have you?'

'Not yet, no. And thanks for the offer but I'd better get back. Maybe some time next week?'

'Hang on a sec. Holly, come and meet – sorry, what did you say your name was?'

'Josh!' The word came out as a gasp from behind David and he stepped aside in confusion. Josh's eyes almost popped out of his head and his mouth fell open. He couldn't get any words out but instead just stared at her.

'I thought you two hadn't met,' said David, looking from one to the other. 'Holly?'

'Hello, Hols,' Josh said finally. 'It's been a long time.'

*   *   *

July 2000

Josh took Holly's hand as they walked on the warm sand. He couldn't believe they were finally free. School was finished forever and the Leaving Cert was over. The world was their oyster and he couldn't be happier. They'd come to Majorca with a group of friends for a week after the exams and the two of them were taking some time out alone. Neither of them had been abroad before and he was completely in awe of his surroundings. The calm, blue sea rose to meet a cloudless sky and the golden sand was like feathers beneath his feet. He looked at Holly and saw she too was lost in thought.

'How are you feeling, Hols?'

'About what?'

'Everything. It's crazy to think we're here, isn't it? So far away from home, never to return to school again.'

Her eyes squinted with the sun and she squeezed his hand. 'Crazy, yes, but also a little bit scary.'

He stopped and looked at her. 'How is it scary? I'd have said exciting, not scary.'

'It's exciting all right,' she said. 'But I worry that things will change.'

'Well, of course things will be different, but you and me will still be together.'

'I hope so,' said Holly, a look of sadness crossing her face. 'But with you going to college in Dublin, I worry we'll drift apart.'

Josh smiled and enveloped her in a hug. 'That would never happen, Hols. You and me are destined to be together. I'll never let you go.'

Chapter 11

Holly felt as though she'd just stepped back in time. She couldn't believe that Josh O'Toole was standing right there. At her front door. Staring at her. She did her best fish impression by opening her mouth and closing it several times without any sound coming out.

'Don't tell me you two know each other?' said David, breaking the silence. 'What a small world.'

'When we were kids,' said Josh, keeping his eyes fixed on Holly. 'We grew up together.'

Time stood still for Holly. His words spun around and around in her head. They were kids in the beginning, yes. But they were so much more than that by the end. She searched his eyes but she couldn't read them. He had a smile on his face and his expression seemed to say that it was the most normal thing in the world to come face to face with the person you thought you'd spend the rest of your life with, the person you hadn't seen for over thirteen years.

'Holly, are you okay?' David looked at her with concern and she knew she'd have to pull herself together.

'I'm fine. I'm just surprised to see a … an old friend. Hi, Josh.' She took a few steps forward and held out her hand to shake his. Never, ever had she imagined she'd be in a situation like this, shaking Josh's hand politely after thirteen years apart.

'Holly.' He nodded politely and took her hand. He held it a moment too long and Holly noticed a flicker of something in his eyes. 'Good to see you again.'

David clapped his hands together and laughed. 'Typical Ireland, what? Imagine you two growing up together and ending up on the same street. Well, you'll have to come in now, Josh. You two can catch up over a cuppa.'

Josh must have noticed the panic in Holly's eyes and he quickly shook his head. 'I'd love to catch up but I'd better head back over. I don't want to leave Stephanie on her own when she's not feeling well.'

Of course, thought Holly. The pregnant girlfriend. She still couldn't find any words.

'Well, we'll all have to meet up soon,' said David, totally oblivious to Holly's discomfort. 'I hope Stephanie feels better. Tell her we're looking forward to meeting her.'

'Will do,' said Josh, beginning to back away from the door. He looked directly at Holly and her heart leapt. 'Nice to see you again, Hols.'

If David noticed a strange vibe between the two of them, he didn't mention it. He waved to Josh as he headed back across the road and closed the door.

'Crazy that, isn't it?' he said, as they headed into the kitchen. 'Were you two good friends?'

Holly's mouth was dry and all she wanted to do was go some-where quiet to think. She certainly didn't want to discuss Josh with David. She shook her head and poured a large glass of water from the tap, gulping it down, to buy herself some time. He was still looking at her when she finished, waiting for an answer.

'No,' she said eventually. 'Well, yes. But as he said, we were kids.'

For a split second, David's face darkened but then he smiled, and Holly wondered if she'd imagined it. 'And the Hols thing?'

Nobody had ever called her that except Josh and her heart had done a flip when she'd heard the word after all those years. She managed an awkward giggle. 'We were just three years old when we met. That's what he called me then and I suppose it stuck.'

'Well, we'll have to put him straight. I know you hate when people try to shorten your name.'

She nodded in agreement but would never be able to tell him that the reason she didn't like people to shorten her name was because it reminded her too much of Josh.

He picked up the kettle and filled it with water. 'Right, let's have a cup of tea and decide what we'll do tonight, since our neighbours won't be joining us.'

She perked up a little. Maybe what she needed was a good night out with David to remind her how happy they were together and try to banish thoughts of Josh from her mind.

'What are you thinking? We could always go into town for something to eat.'

'I can't think of anything worse than the city centre on a Saturday night, actually. All those youngsters falling around the place drunk. Not my scene at all.'

She tried again. 'Well then, maybe just down to O'Malley's for a few drinks and some bar food. I heard they have a new chef and the food is supposedly delicious.'

'Actually, now that I think of it, I have a couple of hours' work I need to do so maybe tonight would be a good time to get it done.'

'Can't you do it during the day?' she pleaded. 'It's still early and then we can have tonight to ourselves.'

'I won't have time today I'm afraid. I've promised Mum I'll bring her shopping so I'll be heading over there shortly.'

'But your mum isn't an invalid. She can go shopping herself.' She immediately cursed her loose tongue that tended to spit out words before her brain filtered them. Not surprisingly, David looked at her angrily.

'Holly, that's not fair. Even if I wasn't bringing her shopping, I'd be visiting her. She's my mother and she's alone.'

'I know and I'm sorry. I didn't mean it to come out like that but it's just … it's just I was looking forward to a nice evening.'

'I'll tell you what,' he said, making a pot of tea, 'let's have a bite to eat here together before I go to Mum's. We can have a chat about wedding stuff and I can tell Mum all about it.'

'And when you come back?'

'I'll pop into the shop on the way home, get you a few snacks, rent you a DVD and you can have a nice relaxing evening while I get my work done. And if I'm finished early, I can even join you. How does that sound?'

Exhilarating. 'Fine.'

She didn't want to think about Josh. She didn't want to think about the fact that he'd moved into the house across the road. She didn't want to imagine him snuggled up on the sofa with his pregnant girlfriend. She didn't want to picture Josh as a dad. It was way too painful. She didn't want to see him happy and fulfilled and complete. Without her. But David was forcing the memories upon her by giving her so much alone time. If only he knew.

Holly was on her way to meet Milly. After sitting in all day and driving herself mad peeping out the front window, hoping to catch a glimpse of Josh, she'd had enough. When David had arrived home with *Love Actually*, it had been the final straw. That movie would make her cry at the best of times but today she'd be a complete and utter blubbering mess if she watched it.

'I thought you loved that movie,' he'd said, his face full of disappointment. 'I thought you'd be thrilled I picked it.'

'I *do* love it but it's just that Milly rang. She and Greg have had a row and he's gone out. She didn't want to be on her own so I said I'd meet her in O'Malley's for an hour or two.' The lie just tripped off her lips.

'Trouble in paradise, eh? I thought they were the perfect couple.'

Holly nodded. 'They are. Well, most of the time. It's nothing serious. And you don't mind, do you?'

He looked at her for a moment and she was afraid he could tell she was lying. Then he smiled. 'Of course not. Tell Milly I said hello.'

He headed upstairs to where he kept his laptop and Holly grabbed her mobile to make her arrangements. O'Malley's was pretty packed when she arrived there an hour later, so she was glad to see Milly already sitting on a stool at a high table at the back. There were two pints of cider already on the table and, before saying a word, Holly downed almost half of hers.

'Oh God, Holly. It's something bad, isn't it?'

'I'm not sure what it is, to be honest,' Holly said, unwrapping herself from the layers of clothing she wore to fend off the freezing November air. 'But it's sent my head into a spin.'

Milly leaned forward on her elbows and urged her to go on. Holly didn't need much encouragement and the whole saga began to spill out. She told her how Josh had just appeared at her front door and she'd felt as though she'd walked straight into her past. How he'd looked at her. How she'd felt. How time had stood still. Milly's eyes were almost popping out of her head by the time Holly was finished her story, and she sat back and let out a long, low breath.

'So what do you think?' Holly asked, vainly hoping her friend had a magic wand she could wave to make sense of everything.

But Milly shook her head. 'I don't know what to say. Talk about coincidence. I can't believe we were just talking about him yesterday and he comes back into your life today.'

'I know. It's like I've made him appear with the power of my mind. Stupid, I know. But that's the first thing I thought when I saw him. That I'd wished him here.'

'Well, they do say to be careful what you wish for,' she said, a glint in her eye. 'You must be excited to see him again. Especially after what you told me yesterday.'

Holly took another mouthful of her drink. 'I'm not sure how to feel, Milly. It's confusing.'

'And he's actually living across the street from you now? Right across the road where you can see him coming and going every day?'

The enormity of the situation hit her and she felt her eyes well up. 'We're going to have to move, aren't we? Me and David. We can't go on living there. Oh God, what am I going to say to David? It's not as though we're even renting. He'll have to sell up and we'll have to find somewhere else and I don't even know if –'

'Holly, stop! You're getting way ahead of yourself.' Milly placed a calming hand over her friend's and Holly stopped talking to allow her breath to return to normal.

'You're not thinking rationally,' Milly continued. 'Let's deal with the facts.'

The facts were clear. At least according to Holly they were. There was no way she could live across the road from the man she'd spent so much of her youth loving, seeing him every day and thinking about what could have been. There'd be just no way. The tears she'd been holding in began to fall and she rooted in her jacket pocket for tissues. Milly waited patiently while Holly cried quietly. A few minutes and a lot of tissues later, Holly was ready to speak again.

'I loved him, Milly. I was so in love with him for so long.'

'But it's a long time ago, Holly. Surely you can't *still* be in love with him.'

'Of course not! But it's just dredged up a lot of stuff from the past.'

Milly's eyes lit up then and she opened her mouth to speak. Holly waited expectantly for her words of wisdom but she fell silent.

'Milly?'

'I was just going to say … no, never mind …'

'What? You can't say that and not tell me.'

'It was just a thought, but a stupid one.' Milly brushed the air with her hand as if to dismiss her words.

'Tell me.'

Milly smiled sheepishly. 'What if it's fate?'

'Go on.'

'I don't know. It just seems like a mad coincidence that you should be telling me about Josh yesterday and today he appears like magic.'

'It's strange, all right,' Holly concurred. 'What are the chances?'

'Very small, I should think,' Milly said, her eyes dancing with mischief. 'What if this Josh really is *the one*? What if fate is trying to intervene and tell you that you shouldn't marry David?'

'But I love David. I couldn't do that to him. To us.'

'I know, and I feel bad even saying it. But sometimes we have to follow our destiny. What do you think Josh thought when he saw you?'

'I think he was just as shocked as I was. But I couldn't read his face.'

Milly swallowed the last of her pint and sat back. 'I suppose you'll just have to let the whole thing play out. See what happens over the next few weeks. But you said he had a girlfriend, didn't you?'

'Yes, and he seems very happy.'

'But she's his *girlfriend*, not his wife?'

She knew what Milly was hinting at but Holly hadn't told her everything. 'Yes, they're not married. But there's more.'

'Go on.'

'His girlfriend is pregnant. Josh is going to be a dad.'

The words hung in the air for a few moments and, annoyingly, Holly felt tears spring to her eyes again. But this time she kept them under control.

'Wow!' said Milly, letting out a low whistle. 'That certainly puts a different spin on things. It's his first, I presume?'

Holly shifted awkwardly on her chair but Milly didn't wait for an answer. 'Did you speak to David about any of it?'

'I didn't say much, really. We never talk about past relationships, and when he saw that Josh and I recognised each other, we just said we grew up together. He seemed happy enough with that. Said it was a small world and typical Ireland. The usual clichés.'

The lounge girl arrived with two fresh pints they'd ordered and they both took lingering sips before Milly spoke again. 'I think you need to speak to Josh alone when you get a chance. Find out about his relationship. Just catch up and see how it feels to be with him again. You might find there isn't a connection there any more and that David is the one for you.'

Holly shook her head. 'I won't be speaking to him, Milly. At least not alone and not about the past.'

Milly looked confused. 'But why not? If seeing him again has unsettled you, if you're unsure about your feelings, you need to talk to him.'

Holly had never spoken about how she and Josh had broken up. Milly had asked her but she just hadn't wanted to talk about it. Even now, after all these years, it was way too painful.

'Holly?'

'I won't be talking to him, Milly. Josh broke my heart. He broke it so badly that I vowed I'd never, ever give him a chance to do it again.'

Chapter 12

Stephanie and Josh were sitting on the sofa watching *Miss Congeniality*. Josh hated that movie but it was Stephanie's favourite and she always seemed to get her own way when it came to movie night. She laughed out loud as she watched, and Josh smiled, but his mind was far from the movie. It was full of Holly Russo. He couldn't have been more surprised to see her standing in front of him earlier. She'd looked at him in shock with those gorgeous eyes. Those deep pools of darkness that seemed to look right into his soul.

It had taken Josh a long time to get over Holly. His life had felt empty for a number of years after they'd split and he'd thought he'd never find love again. He'd dated, of course, and even had a few steady girlfriends, but he'd compared everyone to Holly and they'd all paled into insignificance. That was until he'd met Stephanie. She had been his saviour. She'd made him fall properly in love with her and had helped him to forget. Until today. In just that moment, a moment that had felt like an eternity, all the old feelings of love and hurt had flooded back and threatened to explode inside him. How he'd managed to keep his composure, he'd never know.

The movie credits appeared on screen and he glanced over at Stephanie. She was fast asleep and he stared at her for a few minutes. She looked beautiful when she slept, her features relaxed and her blonde hair falling in wisps over her face. But the most beautiful thing about her then was her baby bump. He reached his hand over and touched it gently and marvelled at the fact that there was a little life in there. His son or daughter. It filled him with excitement but it also made him a little anxious. What sort of a dad would he be? Would he be good enough? Patient enough? Loving enough? Would Stephanie and he manage to muddle through those baby years and keep their relationship intact? He really hoped so because this baby meant everything to him and he would do all he could to welcome him or her into a safe, secure and loving family.

He and Holly used to talk all the time about their future. They would imagine living in a little house with a big garden and having maybe three or four children running around. Youth was a strange thing. It made you believe in your dreams. They used to speak about those things with no doubts at all in their minds. They believed they'd always be together and their future had felt secure. But they'd been forced to grow up way too quickly and had learned never to take anything for granted. They'd learned the hard way that dreams could be taken away in the blink of an eye.

'Oh, is it over?' said Stephanie, waking suddenly and stretching her arms over her head with a yawn. 'You should have woken me.'

Josh smiled and continued to stroke her stomach. 'You looked too peaceful. And besides, I love watching you sleep.'

'I thought you said I snored.'

He laughed at that. 'But it's a pretty snore.'

'So do you think you and that girl – What did you say her name was?'

'Holly.' He really didn't want to get into a conversation about her.

'Right, Holly. Do you think you and this Holly will meet up to chat about old times?'

He wasn't sure how to answer that. Stephanie knew some of the details about his past with Holly but not everything. There was no point dredging stuff up that could cause hurt. Maybe some day he'd tell her more about his past, but now wasn't the right time.

'Well? *Do* you?' She glared at him.

He tried to think of the right thing to say. 'Not specifically. But I'm sure if we all meet up, we'll touch on old times – old friends, that sort of thing. We lost touch a long time ago.'

'Right,' she said, hauling herself up off the sofa. 'On that note, I think I'll head to bed. That walk earlier wore me out. I can't wait to get rid of this bump so I can get back to proper exercise again.'

Josh winced at her harsh words but she didn't notice. He was glad she'd changed the subject, though, because he really, really didn't want to talk about Holly. At least not until he had time to think.

He took their empty bowls and glasses and headed towards the kitchen. 'You go on up, Steph. I'll clear away here and be up in a minute.'

He pottered around for a while, cleaning up but mainly buying time. He wanted her to be asleep when he went up so that he could think in peace. For years he imagined what it would be like to reunite with Holly. He'd bump into her somewhere, their eyes would meet and they'd fall instantly in love again. He'd fantasised about that moment for so long. But in time, when he'd realised they weren't going to meet across a smoky room like people did in the movies, he'd begun to detox her out of his mind. And it had worked. Eventually. He switched off all the lights and set the house alarm before heading upstairs. Thankfully Steph was snoring softly so he gently pulled back his side of the duvet and slipped quietly into bed.

'So what happened with you two then?' Steph's voice cut through the darkness and scared him half to death.

'I thought you were fast asleep. You were snoring a minute ago.'

'Maybe I was just breathing heavily,' she said, turning towards him. 'I was just thinking that you never really told me much about your relationship with Holly.'

'I told you, we went out for a few years but we were young. Practically children.'

She snuggled in closer to him. 'And why did you split up?'

'Do you know, I can't even remember. It seems so long ago. I think we just drifted apart. I moved home with my family then and she went off travelling.' It was a lie. Well, partially. He could remember every last detail. Every single heartbreaking moment.

'And did you love her?'

He wanted to be honest so he nodded slowly. 'Yes, I suppose I did. But young love is different. It's nothing like what we have now, you and me.'

'Are you sure? I won't have to worry about you sneaking across the street to see her or anything, will I?'

'Of course not, Steph,' he said, and he was glad she couldn't see him blushing. 'Why would I want to do that?'

She turned to put the bedside lamp on and sat up. 'I don't know, Josh. You tell me.'

'Steph, what's this all about? There's nothing for you to worry about.'

She sighed. 'Is she the reason?'

'The reason for what?' He wasn't sure he liked how this conversation was going.

'The reason you don't want to marry me.'

Oh God. Not this again. 'Steph, I never said I don't want to marry you. I just … I just –'

'You see? There you go again. Making excuses. If I'm not right for you – if I'm not enough – you should just tell me now.'

'Stop, Steph. Don't do this. You're just being ridiculous. I love you. You know that. I don't know what's gotten into you.'

She turned onto her back and stared at the ceiling. 'I'm pregnant, Josh. And scared and unsure about everything. You're supposed to reassure me and make me feel better.'

'Oh, Steph,' he said, rolling in towards her and wrapping his arms around her. 'You are the love of my life and I plan to spend the rest of my days with you. You and bubs here.' He bent down and gently kissed her stomach. 'So stop worrying. You have absolutely nothing to worry about.'

She reached over and switched off the light. 'Okay. I'm going to sleep now.'

And just like that, the conversation was over. He stayed still for the next few minutes until the room was filled with her soft snores. But sleep wasn't so easy for Josh. Thoughts whirred around and around in his mind, driving him crazy. He'd been surprised by Stephanie's questions. She didn't often show her vulnerability and, in a way, it was nice. He'd assured her as best he could but he knew that what she really wanted was a ring on her finger.

He couldn't get comfortable so, careful not to wake Stephanie, he gently pushed back the duvet and stepped out of bed. He went to the window and looked across at number forty. There was just enough light from the street lamp for him to see the curtains of the upstairs bedroom twitch just a fraction. He instinctively knew it was Holly. She was there looking over at his house, just as he was looking at hers. He had the strangest feeling that they were staring at each other, even though they were too far apart to tell. For a moment, he couldn't move. Nor did he want to. He felt as though somebody had cast a spell on him. Eventually, her curtains were dropped and Josh reluctantly moved away from the window. He suddenly felt terrified. But also very, very excited.

Chapter 13

'Bye now, Mr O'Grady,' said Holly, waving at the old man and his beloved cat. 'I hope Tinker feels better soon.'

'Thanks, love. A few days of the medicine and Fintan says she'll be as right as rain.'

Holly smiled as the bell tinkled on the door closing behind him. She was happy when there was an easy resolution to a problem. Worried owners came into the clinic every day with their sick pets and Holly loved to see them leaving with smiles on their faces. She'd often watch the treatment room with trepidation to see the looks on their faces as they'd come out. Sometimes there'd be bad news and she'd have to comfort the customer with tea and sympathy. But more often than not, Fintan or Milly would have been able to work their magic and there'd be smiles all around.

She glanced at her watch and saw it was a quarter to two. Wednesday was her early finish day and usually she loved having the afternoon free. But not today. Today she'd promised to go looking at churches with David and his mother and she was absolutely dreading it. She'd rather poke her own eyes out with a blunt instrument but David had reassured her they wouldn't spend too long looking around and they didn't have to commit to anything. It was just to keep his mother happy. Again.

'Holly, can I have a word please?' Fintan's voice broke into her thoughts and she looked up to see him standing right in front of her.

'Sorry, I was miles away.' There was something in his eyes. Sadness. Worry. 'Is there something wrong?'

'Please,' he said. 'Just step in here. I want to talk to you.'

She suddenly felt worried but followed him into the little room where he indicated for her to sit down. She took a seat and looked around her. It was where they usually brought customers to tell them bad news about their pets or to discuss treatments. She'd cleaned in there a thousand times but it was the first time she'd been asked to sit. Fintan sat down in front of her and she could see he looked distressed.

'Fintan, what is it? You're worrying me now.'

He coughed and cleared his throat. 'Holly, I …' He coughed again.

Holly froze but said nothing – she just waited.

'Holly, I'm really sorry about this but … but I'm going to have to let you go.'

'Go? Go where?'

He sighed and looked at her. 'I can't keep you on here any more, Holly. I'd love to, I really would. It's not a reflection on your work or your dedication. It's just I can't keep on paying a receptionist when business is so slow. I'm really sorry.'

Holly opened her mouth to respond but no words came out. He was firing her. She couldn't believe it. Tears sprang to her eyes and before she knew it they were falling down her face.

'Oh God, Holly, I'm so, so sorry.' He jumped up and grabbed a box of tissues from a shelf behind him and handed them to her. 'You know I wouldn't do this unless I had to. And if – *when* – business picks up, I'll definitely take you back. All the customers love you. You're a huge asset to this place. But you're a luxury I can't afford at the moment.'

She blew her nose and finally found her voice. 'It's okay, Fintan. I understand. It's just a shock, you know?'

He nodded. 'I know. And I wish I could say something to make it better. But you know I'll write a glowing reference for you and I'll keep an eye out for anyone else who's looking for a brilliant receptionist.'

'Thanks,' she said, twisting the tissue around in her hands. 'When … when do you want me to leave?'

'Let's say two weeks. I know it's close to Christmas and I'm sorry for that too. But I think you know how quiet we've been of late.'

She nodded. 'I'm going to miss this place.'

'We'll miss you too,' he said, standing up.

Holly stood up too and they looked at each other awkwardly for a moment. She didn't know whether she should shake his hand or give him a hug but the decision was made for her as he wrapped his arms around her. She was sure she saw tears in Fintan's eyes too as she exited the room and grabbed her coat from behind the reception desk. She couldn't believe her days there were numbered. She'd somehow thought she'd stay for the rest of her working career. She felt desperately sad as she walked the short distance home, and when she saw David's car there, she remembered their plans for the afternoon. But she wasn't in the mood. She'd just tell David what had happened and he'd understand. There was no way she could concentrate on wedding plans today.

Bloody churches. When Holly had told David earlier what had happened, he'd been sympathetic but had insisted they keep to their plans. His mother would be waiting and of course they couldn't let her down. At that moment, they were having a look around the Church of the Holy Ghost. Honestly! It sounded like something from a scary movie and not somewhere Holly could picture being full of love and romance.

Doreen was giving it a thorough once over, including running a finger along the top of the holy-water font to check for dust and even dead-heading some of the flowers on the altar.

'This could be the one,' she said, before lowering her voice, lest God himself might hear. 'A little dirty but it's definitely the best we've seen.'

'It's nice all right,' said David, as they trailed along behind her. 'What do you think, Holly?'

You know what I bloody well think, is what she wanted to say, but instead she smiled sweetly. 'Lovely.'

David shot her a look of gratitude. 'Okay, Mum. I think we've seen enough for today. Why don't we drop you home and you can go through those notes of yours and give us your thoughts later.'

Holly breathed a sigh of relief but she sensed Mammy Wood wasn't ready to go home yet. 'David,' said Doreen, glaring at her son. 'We've only seen three churches and it's still early. No, I think we'll continue for the next hour or so.' She checked her list. 'I want to see St Paul's and The Sacred Cross at the very least today.'

Holly wanted to grab her list and rip it to bits but she managed to restrain herself. 'Maybe we can do those another day, Doreen. Both David and I came straight from work so I wouldn't mind getting home for some dinner.'

'Dinner!' she declared, as though she'd had a revelation. 'That's a great idea. Why don't we all go and get something to eat in that nice deli on the corner? Then we'll be fuelled up for another few hours.'

Holly didn't know what to say. She wasn't in the mood for any of this and just wanted to go home. She looked at David pleadingly, hoping he'd object, but he seemed to think his mother's idea was a great one.

'Holly, what do you think?' They were both staring at her, waiting for her response, and again she cursed David for not manning up and just telling her that they wanted to go home.

'Fine,' she said, and barely had the words left her mouth before Doreen high-tailed it out the church door and towards the deli.

'You should have said no,' she hissed at David. 'What were you thinking?'

He looked at her in confusion. 'Why? We need to eat anyway so why not here?'

'Don't you have any cop-on, David? I've just had my world shattered and I still came out on this silly jaunt. The least you could do is support me.'

He was about to say something when Doreen stuck her head back in and asked them what was keeping them. 'Coming now, Mum,' he said, looking at Holly pleadingly.

Holly sighed but relented. She'd be as civil as she could during the meal and then she'd cry off sick and say she needed to go home. David could do the holy tour of the city with his mother if he liked. It was all irrelevant anyway, since she wouldn't be getting married in a church. She gritted her teeth and followed David and his mother outside.

'David, I've had enough.' Holly spat the words out as soon as they walked in the front door. None of them had spoken in the car on the journey home, Doreen obviously put out that her day had been cut short and David annoyed at Holly because he knew damn well she was faking her headache. After they'd dropped Doreen home, they'd both silently fumed until Holly couldn't take the tension any more.

'*You've* had enough,' he said, taking off his suit jacket and neatly folding it over the bannister. Holly had a sudden urge to throw it on the floor but refrained.

'How do you think *I* feel?' he continued. 'I'm trying to keep two women happy and all I get is grief. From both of you.'

'That's the problem, David. Why do you need to keep us both happy? Surely at this stage of your life you don't need to pander to your mother's every whim. You're thirty-six years old, for God's sake!'

'What am I supposed to do?' he said, gesturing wildly with his arms. 'Tell her to get lost? Cast her aside because there's a new woman in my life? Cop on, would you, Holly. She's my mother and that's not going to change, even when we get married.'

She was slightly taken aback by his fieriness. David was usually the peacemaker and she wasn't used to him standing his ground. But she wasn't backing down. She was sick of going along with things to please Mammy Wood. They were still standing in the hallway, glaring at each other, so Holly stormed into the kitchen and David followed.

'David, I'm happy for your mum to be part of our lives,' she said, leaning against the counter. 'I wouldn't want it any other way. But the way it is now – it's just too much.' She waited for him to object, but instead he came to her and folded his arms around her.

'I'm sorry, Holly. I'm trying to keep Mum happy by getting her involved but maybe you're right. I'm sorry you feel neglected and I'm sorry about your job.'

She nodded, and leaned her head against his shoulder.

'And there's no need for you to worry,' he continued. 'We're doing fine financially. I earn more than enough for both of us.'

She pulled away from him. 'I know you mean well, David, but I want to earn my own money.'

'But we're getting married, Holly. My money is your money.'

'Oh, for God's sake, David. It's not all about the money!'

'Well, what is it about?' he said. 'Is there something else going on with you?'

She bristled. 'Like what?'

'I don't know,' he said, filling the kettle with water. 'You seem on edge since the weekend. Snappy. Not yourself.'

'I don't know what you're talking about,' she said, sitting down at the kitchen table. 'I'm perfectly fine.'

'Is it something to do with *him*? Josh? You've been acting strangely since you saw him at the weekend.'

'No, I have not.' The words came out too quickly. Too defensively.

'I've seen you look across at their house every time we get in or out of the car. Was there more to your friendship than just a childhood thing? Do you two have history I should know about?'

How could she tell him? How could she reveal the depth of her relationship with Josh when they had to live across the road from him? David wasn't really the jealous type but surely it would make things uncomfortable. For her, at the very least.

'So was there?'

He wasn't going to leave it alone so she'd have to give him something. 'We went out for a while, that's all. But as he said, we were kids. It was more friendship really.'

David nodded. 'I hate arguing with you, Holly,' he said, looking at her with sad eyes. 'And I'm sorry again if you think I'm pandering too much to Mum. It's just difficult, you know?'

'I know. And I should be more tolerant. But I want our wedding to be special, David. I want a day that represents *us* – not something fabricated or forced. We haven't even sat down and discussed what *we* want for the day. It's all been about your mother picking dates and churches and hotels – none of which I particularly want.'

He sighed. 'Well, why don't we discuss it now? It's still early and we have the whole night to ourselves. Let's start to make some plans of our own.'

Holly suddenly didn't want to talk weddings any more. 'I'm tired, David. And I honestly do have a headache. I might just go for a shower and maybe we can order some food and watch a DVD later?'

'Fine,' he said, standing up. 'But there's no point in ordering in food. It's only Wednesday and there are some pork chops in the fridge that are almost at their use-by date – it would be a shame to waste them. I'll peel some potatoes while you're in the shower and get dinner going.'

There was nothing left to say so she headed upstairs. That's what drove her crazy about David. His sensible side. Milly would call it boring but Holly liked to think of it as sensible. He'd seldom break out of the norm. She wanted him to go mad and order a curry. On a Wednesday. Dump the chops in the bin. Fly in the face of good sense and throw caution to the wind. But even as she'd suggested it, she'd known he wouldn't. He was David, not Josh.

She gave herself a mental shake as she stood under the warm jets of water. She really needed to put Josh out of her mind and concentrate on David. Her family thought he was the perfect man for her, and they couldn't all be wrong. Her parents weren't the interfering types but they'd made it known that David, with his clean living, his dedication to her and his good, pensionable job, was a wonderful catch and they couldn't wait until she was Mrs Wood. Although taking his name was still under negotiation.

She heard David clattering about in the kitchen as she stepped out of the shower and she could smell the dinner cooking on the stove. Her parents were right. She was lucky and it was about time she started to realise it. She might be losing her job, but she still had her man. And that was more important than anything.

Chapter 14

Josh thanked God for the sunshine because he was determined to make the front of the house look like Santa's grotto. Stephanie had been out late again the previous night so he'd crept out of bed early, leaving her to sleep, and headed for a newly opened Christmas shop just outside the village. Although he was worried about the state of their finances, he reckoned a little splurge to cheer them up would be a good investment. He'd been like a child in a sweetshop, picking out various lights and decorations, and he couldn't wait to get them all up.

He secured the ladder, which he'd borrowed from a guy in number seven when he'd spotted him cleaning his windows earlier, and headed up with his string of lights over his shoulder. He'd gone for single strings of clear, twinkly ones for the sides of the house and icicle ones for over the windows and door. He'd decided to keep to the white theme and had gotten a set of bell lights for the gable and a reindeer made of twisted white lights for outside the front door. He worked like a Trojan for the next couple of hours until he finally had everything set up properly. When he stood back to admire his work, he knew it had been worth the bother. It looked amazing. And now he was excited for it to get dark so he could see the lights in their full glory.

'That's a *lot* of lights,' said Stephanie, arriving out to have a look. She was wrapped up in Josh's leather jacket with a big woolly scarf and gloves. 'You really meant it when you said you wanted to brighten up the house, didn't you?'

He laughed. 'Yep. It's worth it, though, isn't it? Doesn't it make you feel all Christmassy?'

She shrugged. 'A little. But I'd still prefer to be celebrating it somewhere hot and sunny.'

'Christmas and sun do *not* go together.' He laughed. 'The colder the better for me.'

'One day I'll drag you off to a warmer clime for Christmas. But for now I'd better go and get ready.'

Josh followed her inside. 'Are you going somewhere?'

'I told you, Josh. The shampoo ad. They're shooting it today so I'll be gone for a few hours at least.'

'Oh, right.' He couldn't remember her mentioning it before and he tried to stop suspicion creeping into his mind. But if she was genuinely going to a job, he was delighted – she'd barely worked these last few months.

'And tonight?' he said, hoping she wouldn't have plans to go out with her friends again.

She thought for a moment. 'Why don't you ask the new neighbours over since we didn't make it over to theirs last week?'

'I'm not sure.'

'Why?' She glared at him. Testing.

'I just thought we could go out or something. Just the two of us. But if you want to ask them over, that's fine.' He wasn't ready. He wasn't ready to have Holly sit across the table from him in his own house, talking about her wedding to another man.

'Right,' she said, heading upstairs. 'You ask them while I'm gone. I should be back around six so any time after that suits me.'

He stared after her as she disappeared into their bedroom. It was bound to happen sometime. He and Holly were going to have to face each other, no matter how awkward it might be. But the day loomed ahead of him and he needed something to take his mind off things. And he knew just the person to help with that.

'Honestly, Josh,' his mum said, wiping a tear from the corner of her eye. 'Those kids of yours are a scream. I don't know how you keep a straight face in class.'

'Oh, it's not all fun, you know. There's a lot of responsibility in teaching kids of that age.'

She was still laughing at his stories. 'I know that, love. And you're brilliant at it. The kids are lucky to have you. And on that note, I think I'll head off. Erica and Simone are coming over to play bridge later so I've got to go to Tesco for some nibbles.'

Josh walked to the door with his mum. He'd rung and asked her over to lunch earlier and he was very glad that he had. They'd spent a pleasant hour chatting about his job and her slightly eccentric bridge friends and between them they'd laughed almost non-stop.

'It was good to see you,' said Josh, kissing his mother on the cheek. 'Drive home safely.'

'I will, love. And thanks for lunch. It was a lovely surprise.'

Suddenly she was almost knocked off her feet and Josh had to grab her arm to steady her. 'Mum! Are you okay? And Simon! How did you get out?'

'Sorry about that, Josh.' Mr Fogarty rushed over to retrieve the dog. 'I opened the door to put something out in the bin when he must have seen you and made a run for it. Are you okay?' He turned his attention to Josh's mum.

'I'm fine,' she said, bending down to pet an excited Simon. 'He's gorgeous. I've been thinking of getting one myself.'

Josh raised an eyebrow. He'd often tried to talk her into getting a dog. He thought it would be great company for her. But she'd always refused, saying she didn't want the hassle.

'Really?' said Mr Fogarty. 'And where are my manners. John. John Fogarty. Number forty-four.' He stretched out a hand to shake hers.

'Maura,' she said, and Josh noticed how her eyes lit up. 'And, yes, Josh is always trying to persuade me to get one.'

'Well, if you're serious about it, give me a ring and I can put you in touch with some breeders.' He took a pen and a piece of paper out of his jacket pocket and wrote his number down. 'You need to be careful who you buy from and I have a few friends who could help you with that.'

'Thanks very much,' she said, stuffing the paper into her handbag. 'I'll definitely bear that in mind.'

There was an awkward moment when they all stood in silence looking at each other until Mr Fogarty finally spoke. 'Well, it was nice to meet you, Maura. And sorry again about Simon.' He tipped his cap and took the dog by the collar to lead him inside.

'Bye, Mum,' said Josh, kissing her lightly on the cheek. 'I'll give you a buzz over the next few days.'

He waved until she disappeared around the corner then turned his attention back to his precious lights. It would be dark soon enough so he wanted to make sure everything was in place before he switched them on. But minutes later he was distracted by the sound of approaching footsteps. His heart almost leapt out of his chest when he saw it was her. It was Holly. And she'd seen him. Oh God. He was rooted to the spot. She knew he'd seen her so he couldn't rush inside and pretend he hadn't, but how was he going to hold a conversation with her? What would he say? The decision was taken out of his hands as Holly took her earphones out and walked towards him. His only consolation was that she looked just as uncomfortable as he felt.

'Hello again, Josh,' she said, standing about a foot away from him. He was glad she didn't come nearer. Even at that distance, he could sense her body close.

'Hi, Holly. Have you been out?' Of course she'd been out. He was such an idiot.

She nodded. 'In work. I finish up early on Saturdays.'

'So where do you work?' It dawned on him that this was a totally new Holly – one he knew nothing about.

'In the veterinary practice down the road.'

'You're a vet! I always knew you'd end up working with animals. Even when we were really little, you used to say you wanted to live in a house with hundreds of cats, dogs and rabbits.'

She flushed and gave a nervous laugh. 'I remember. But I'm not a vet – just a receptionist. But it's great. I love working there. And you?'

'Primary-school teacher at St John's. Sixth-class boys. My dream!'

'You're saying that sarcastically,' she said, her brown eyes boring into his. 'But I bet you love it. You were loving the teacher training when we … when we …'

They both fell silent. He could tell she didn't want to finish the sentence. *When we were together*, was what she was going to say. Josh really didn't want the conversation to go there. To get into the reasons why they'd parted. It was all in the past and they needed to move on. He tried to lift the heaviness in the air with humour.

'I do love it, actually. I shouldn't say this, but having the summer off is fabulous.'

'I bet it is. What do you do with your time for two whole months?'

'I try to be as productive as possible. I actually went to Cape Town last summer on one of those house-building projects for charity.' He watched her carefully. He and Holly had often talked of doing something like that together.

'Oh.' Her voice dropped. 'I regret never having done that myself. Maybe I still will someday.'

'It was great,' he said. 'Very rewarding. Although Stephanie said she couldn't think of anything worse.'

'Stephanie,' Holly said. 'Is that your girlfriend?'

He nodded and felt awkward all over again. 'She's out at work at the moment. She's a model and an actress.' He wanted to take back the words as soon as they were out.

'She must be very beautiful.'

What could he say to that? *Beauty is only skin deep? It's what's on the inside that counts? She's no more beautiful than you?* He never thought he'd see the day when things between him and Holly were so awkward. They'd spent more than half their lives together, for God's sake. Surely it had to be easier than this. Maybe he was wrong in trying to avoid speaking about the past.

'Holly,' he said, watching as she shifted awkwardly from foot to foot. 'Do you want to talk?'

'What do you mean? We're talking now, aren't we?'

She knew what he meant. 'I mean properly talk. About you and me.'

'There is no you and me, Josh.' He noticed how the words caught slightly in her throat and she wasn't looking him in the eye.

He tried again. 'I mean about back then. If we're going to live across the road from each other, surely we need to find a way to move forward and not have the past hanging over us.'

'Nothing is hanging over *me*, Josh.' She glared at him. 'The past is the past and I'm looking forward to a lovely future now with my fiancé.'

She practically spat the word fiancé out and he knew she was trying to hurt him. But they were past all that. 'I know what you're saying, Holly. And I've moved on too. But we're living across the road from each other so for the sake of our sanity, I don't want things to be awkward between us.'

She leaned against the pillar and sighed. 'So what have you told Stephanie? Does she know our history?'

'Not fully. She never really wanted to know many details from my past so she just knows we were together for a while when we were younger.'

She nodded and smiled. 'Same with David. We both had history when we got together so we agreed that there was no need to drag it all up. I told him you and me were close in the past. But we were just kids.'

'Stephanie wants you both to come over tonight,' said Josh, watching her carefully. 'She left me with orders to go and ask you.'

'Oh.'

'What do you think? We can't keep avoiding each other.'

She stood up straight and it was as though a spell had been broken. 'As you say, we can't keep avoiding it so why don't we drop over for a while? We've talked now so let's just move on.'

She held his gaze for a moment longer than was necessary and he saw everything in those eyes. No matter how much she talked about moving on, she, like him, was still a little stuck in the past.

'Okay,' said Josh reluctantly. 'Let's say seven o'clock?'

'That's fine by me.' She turned to leave. 'I'll see you then.'

Josh watched her walk off but then she stopped halfway across the road. She turned around and looked at him, and his heart began to beat faster. It was like a slow-motion scene in a movie and his mind was trying to guess what was going to happen next. He thought, for just a second, that she was going to run back into his arms. But then he realised that he was being ridiculous.

'Josh,' she said, so softly he could barely hear. 'Congratulations. I hear you're going to be a daddy. I'm very happy for you. I know it's what you've always wanted.'

She disappeared into her house and Josh stood looking across at the closed door. Yes, it was what he'd always wanted. But hearing the words coming from her lips was like a knife to his heart. He felt tears sting the backs of his eyes but he fought the urge to cry. He pictured a scared seventeen-year-old Holly crying her eyes out. *'Don't worry, sweetheart,'* he said. *'Someday we'll have a whole house full of kids and this will be a little less painful.'* She looked at him and laid her head on his shoulder. *'I hope so, Josh. I really do.'*

Chapter 15

January 2001

'What are we going to do, Josh?' Holly said, sticking her hands down further into her pockets to fend off the bitter cold. 'I ... I just can't get my head around it.'

He sat forward on the park bench and put his head into his hands.

'Josh. Say something. What are we going to do?'

He looked at her then, his face pale and worried. 'I honestly don't know, Hols. How could this have happened? We were being so careful.'

'I know,' she said, her voice catching in her throat. 'But we knew the risks. We just need to decide what happens now.'

'What do you want to happen?'

She thought for a moment. 'I'm not sure. But maybe it doesn't have to be such a bad thing. It was always in our plan – it's just happened a little earlier than we would have liked.'

'Holly! We're only just eighteen years old. I'm in college and you're working full time. How will we make it work?'

She snuggled into him. 'I don't have all the answers, Josh. But I know this. I love you more than anything in the world, and if this baby is a product of that love, we're all going to be just fine.'

The sound of the doorbell startled Holly and a little bead of sweat trickled down the back of her neck. When she'd told David earlier about the invitation from Josh and Stephanie, he'd insisted that *they* should be the ones to host the evening, since they'd suggested it first. She would have preferred to go across the road because then she'd be in control of when to go home. But having them in her house meant that, no matter how uncomfortable she felt, she'd have to wait until *they* decided to leave. She opened the bedroom door slightly to listen to the voices downstairs.

'Come in, come in,' David said, in his deep, cheery voice. 'Welcome to number forty.'

'Thanks,' came the voice of a woman, who Holly assumed was Stephanie. Her voice seemed to have a Cork lilt which, for some reason, Holly hadn't been expecting. She didn't hear Josh's voice, but then again, his was soft and understated. There was the sound of laughter before the voices became a dull murmur and Holly assumed David had ushered them into the sitting room. She was dreading the thought of sitting down with Josh and his girlfriend as though it was a normal situation. Speaking to him earlier had been awkward. She'd listened to how happy he was – how he loved his job and how his life was sorted, with a beautiful girlfriend and a baby on the way. Holly hadn't even been able to tell him about losing her own job. She hadn't wanted to seem like a failure.

Suddenly she heard footsteps on the stairs and realised she still wasn't dressed. She'd already changed six times and applied and removed her make-up twice. She knew it was stupid, but she just wanted to look right. Stephanie, she assumed, was a glamorous woman, given the job she did, so Holly wanted to make an effort. But she didn't want to look like she was trying too hard either, so she just couldn't decide what to wear. God, she was such a bloody mess.

'Holly, what's keeping you?' David's face appeared around the door as Holly was flapping around in her knickers and bra, and he

didn't look happy. 'Come on, will you. I don't want to have to entertain them on my own.'

'Sorry,' she said, grabbing a black pencil skirt from a hanger. 'I
stubbed my toe on the leg of the bed and I was trying to get it to stop
bleeding.'

'Give me a look,' he said, walking into the room. 'There should
be plasters in the –'

'No!' She immediately took a step back. Why did she tell such
stupid lies? 'It's stopped now so just give me two minutes and I'll
be down.'

He sighed but relented. 'Okay, but hurry up.'

Now multiple beads of sweat were trickling – not just down the
back of her neck but under her arms too. She felt like screaming. But
if she didn't hurry up, David would be back up the stairs in a moment,
so she rushed into the en suite, gave herself a quick rub down and
applied some more deodorant. It would have to do for now. She
teamed the black pencil skirt with a grey top from Penneys, not too
casual, not too dressy, and stuck her feet into a pair of grey heels.
Even though her make-up was a bit of a disaster, because she'd run
out of one foundation and had to continue with another which was
a different colour, she had no time to fix it again. So she dusted a bit
of powder over it, prayed for the best and headed down to meet their
guests.

'Ah, there she is,' said David, looking relieved. 'I've poured you a
glass of wine, Holly. This is Stephanie. And I think you already
know Josh.'

She nodded at them both. 'Hi, Stephanie, Josh. Glad you could
make it.'

Stephanie stood up to greet her properly and Holly immediately
envied her waif-like figure. She was also annoyingly beautiful. They
kissed each other on the cheek and Stephanie floated back to her
seat. Everything about her was elegant and polished and Holly felt

like a baby elephant beside her. Thankfully Josh didn't stand to kiss her and just waved his greeting from the armchair.

'So how long have you lived here?' said Josh. 'It seems like a decent sort of street.'

David was quick to answer. 'Just over two years for Holly – a little more for me. I bought this place before we even met so she moved in when we started to go steady.'

Holly cringed at his use of 'go steady'. It was like something her mother would say. But Josh didn't seem to notice and continued, 'I hear the pub down the road is decent too. What's it called? O'Mahoney's or something?'

'O'Malley's,' Holly said, finding her voice. 'And, yes, it's a great spot. We should go down some evening.'

Everyone looked at her and she could feel the redness start at her neck and creep up her face. 'I mean all of us. Not just both of us. I mean we should *all* go down to O'Malley's some evening.'

'Sounds good to me,' said Stephanie. 'It's great to have a pub like that so close. In our last place, we had to drive to the nearest one.'

Holly found herself watching Stephanie enviously. She was relaxed and self-assured, everything Holly aspired to be. She also had the face of an angel and Holly couldn't help thinking she looked too young for Josh. But Holly's eyes were especially drawn to her stomach, which was just slightly protruding through her white T-shirt. She was wearing a pair of skinny jeans too and looked like she'd just walked out of the pages of a catalogue for trendy maternity wear.

'So have you met any of the other neighbours yet?' David asked, taking a sip of his drink.

Josh smiled. 'Just one. Some old guy. Said he lived in number forty-four. John, I think his name is.'

David nodded. 'John Fogarty. Nice enough man. His dog is a bit of a nuisance, though.'

'Oh, I met Simon too,' said Josh. 'Beautiful creature.'

Holly smiled enthusiastically. 'He *is* gorgeous, isn't he? He's exactly the sort of dog I'd want if we were getting one.'

'Well, that will *never* happen,' said David. 'I'm not keen on dogs at all, if I'm honest.'

Holly had to bite her tongue. She didn't want to argue in front of their guests but she hated how David was so firm in his opinion about getting a dog. It was a contentious issue in the house and Holly had often been tempted to just rescue a dog from the Dogs Trust and bring it home before David even knew what was happening. Thankfully Stephanie chimed in and changed the subject.

'So when are you two getting hitched? I hear you got engaged recently.'

David sat forward and nodded. 'Yes, only a few weeks ago. And we haven't set a date yet but we're hoping to in the next few days. It will probably be summer 2017.'

'Summer?' The word came in a high-pitched tone from Josh's mouth and he looked like he wanted to disappear. Everyone looked at him and he cleared his throat. 'Sorry, I'm just surprised you said summer because Holly –'

'I mentioned winter to you today, didn't I?' said Holly, quickly interrupting him. 'We really haven't decided for sure yet.' She knew what he was going to say. She and Josh had spoken so often about getting married. In their plans, it would always be winter and there'd always be snow. Nothing else had ever been an option.

David threw her a quizzical look. 'But I thought we'd ruled out winter because of the cold and the possibility of snow and ice?'

Josh raised an eyebrow and Holly felt trapped. 'We didn't rule anything out for sure, David. I know your mother would prefer summer but *she's* not the one getting married.'

The room fell silent again and Holly knew David was fuming with her. But she didn't care. She probably didn't have to let their visitors know it too, but she hadn't known what else to say.

'So what about you two?' Holly said eventually, not able to bear the silence any more. 'Any plans for a wedding?'

A look passed between them and Holly immediately sensed she'd said the wrong thing. Again. So she tried to recover the situation. 'But I suppose you're way too busy planning for this baby without thinking about a wedding too.'

'Josh's not really keen,' said Stephanie, her voice clipped. 'He thinks we're fine just the way we are.'

'Hang on, Steph,' he said, glaring at her. 'That's not exactly true.'

'Come on, Josh. We've been together seven years and you haven't proposed. I doubt you're going to do it at this stage.'

Holly was mortified for her. For them. They were just staring at each other and the tension in the room was palpable. Holly glanced at David, who shrugged, and she suddenly wanted to giggle.

'To be honest,' said Josh, looking from Holly to David. 'The time has just never been right. And as you say, we have a lot on at the moment and we're concentrating on the baby.'

Stephanie gave a little harrumph and Holly's urge to laugh increased.

'Nuts,' said David suddenly. 'I knew I forgot something. Holly, will you pour the wine there and I'll go and get some. Nobody's allergic, I assume?'

Both guests shook their heads and David clapped his hands together as though it was a triumph. Holly noticed a look pass between the couple and wished she knew what it meant. Were they bored by her and David? Making fun of them? Did they have some secret code to indicate it was time to go home? She and Josh used to have secret codes for everything. They'd had this strange ability to read each other's eyes. Holly noticed Josh looking at her and suddenly became self-conscious. What if he could still read her eyes? If he could tell what she was thinking?

'So how's your sister these days, Holly?'

'Carina is great, thanks. And so are Jason and the two girls.'

'Two! She had another baby?'

'Yes. She had Lilly a couple of years after … after …' Holly realised what she was about to say, so she faked a cough to cover it up, '… after Elaina. There's just two and a half years between them.'

He nodded. 'She was born to have children. I remember her with Elaina and she was a great mother. Tell her I was asking for her.'

'So do you think you'll have children?' said Stephanie, sliding in a little closer to Josh.

Holly didn't know what to say but thankfully Josh chimed in. 'That's a very personal question, Steph.'

She glared at him. 'Well, she asked about us getting married. So fair's fair.'

'It's not exactly the same –'

'It's okay, Josh.' Holly didn't want them to have another row. 'We've no plans for children yet, Stephanie. We'll just see how things go over the next couple of years.'

'You shouldn't wait too long,' she said, smugly rubbing her baby bump, 'or you'll be too old to do all the fun stuff with them. I'm glad I'm having this little one while I'm still in my twenties.'

Her twenties. So Holly was right. She was definitely at least three years younger than Josh. And she acted like a precocious teen. At least he looked sufficiently mortified by her behaviour. But Holly decided to rise above her immaturity and just be nice.

'So do you know if you're having a boy or a girl?' Holly smiled sweetly at them.

Josh shook his head. 'I don't want to know but Steph does and she's trying to talk me into finding out.'

'Oh, but wouldn't it be great to know the sex of the baby?' she said, taking his hand and placing it on her stomach. 'We could be so well prepared rather than just having generic clothes and stuff.'

It was just a quick glance, but Holly caught it. Josh was thinking about her too. Holly had often wondered if he did, and that glance had told her everything she needed to know. Holly thought about him all the time, but she knew that men tended to handle things differently. They tended to push stuff out of their minds so they wouldn't have to deal with their emotions. But Holly should have known. Josh had never been like that. He'd always been able to show his emotions and that was one of the things she loved about him. *Used* to love.

'Here we go,' said David, proudly wheeling the hostess trolley into the room.

Holly was mortified but David was oblivious. Josh and Stephanie probably thought they were so old-fashioned. She noticed a smirk form on Josh's lips and she knew he was thinking about making a smart comment.

'Nice trolley,' he said, winking at Holly. 'Isn't it the same as the one Mrs Doyle has on *Father Ted*?'

'You could be right there,' said David, completely missing the sarcasm. 'Handy little yokes, they are.'

Somehow that lightened the mood and Holly felt a sudden rush of love for David. He may have had his flaws, but he had so many good points too. He had an ability to steer an awkward situation back to safe ground and that's exactly what he'd done just now. The conversation began to flow more easily and the four of them continued to chat animatedly about lots of things. Stephanie told them about her shampoo ad and some of the other high-profile jobs she'd done and Josh seemed happy to let her take centre stage. Holly hadn't warmed to her exactly, but there was something fascinating about her. Maybe it was because she was with Josh. Holly was interested to find out more about the woman who'd managed to snare Josh O'Toole. What was it about her that kept him interested, made him want to spend the rest of his life with her? What did she have that Holly had obviously lacked thirteen years ago?

It was fairly late when they finally stood up to leave. They all kissed each other politely on the cheek but when Holly felt Josh's breath against her skin, her legs turned to jelly. What the hell was wrong with her? They walked to the door and David put his arm around Holly, as their new neighbours stepped out into the cold.

'Thanks again for a lovely evening,' said Josh, turning to look at Holly. 'We must do it again sometime.'

Holly was mesmerised by those eyes. Those bright blue, beautiful eyes. Even after all these years, they could still do it. They could still talk to each other with their eyes, and Josh was telling her that they had some unfinished business and they were going to have to deal with it very soon.

Chapter 16

Josh hopped off the treadmill and tried to catch his breath. There was a time when he could have run twice as fast and twice as far but he was out of practice. He used to be a frequent visitor to the little city-centre gym but events of the last few months had kept him away. Today he was hoping it would give his mind a rest from all the things that were driving him crazy, especially the evening spent with Holly and David two days before.

It had been the strangest of situations. He hadn't been able to take his eyes off Holly and he'd felt guilty because of it. His life had moved on. *Their* lives had moved on. They weren't a pair of love-struck teens any more. They were proper adults with proper responsibilities and they were absolutely nothing to each other any more. But seeing her again had stirred up a whole myriad of memories – some wonderful and some he'd rather forget.

He thought about getting back up on the treadmill and continuing his run but he couldn't face it. He sat down on a wooden bench which ran along the side of the gym and wiped the trickles of sweat from his forehead. Sometimes he wished he was a woman. Stephanie always said that any problem could be solved by a chat with her girlie friends, but it wasn't so for Josh. The conversations he had with his mates usually revolved around football and other sport and rarely ventured into anything personal. And that suited him most of the time. But today he wished he had somebody to talk to.

As he headed into the changing rooms to take a shower, he knew his legs would suffer later from the gruelling workout. He could already feel his body begin to stiffen up so he was glad to let the warm water soothe his aching bones. But just as he'd finished lathering himself with shower gel, he was gripped with that awful pain in his stomach again. It was like something crushing his insides, and he doubled over in agony. He stayed that way until it passed and he could finally breathe again. Bloody, bloody pain. He knew he'd have to sort it out sooner rather than later, but he still didn't want to face it.

When he finally stepped outside into the mid-morning sun, he felt emotionally and physically drained. But he didn't want to go home. And then it struck him. There was one person who always listened with a sympathetic ear. She never judged him and always knew the right thing to say. He suddenly wanted to feel her arms about him, telling him everything was going to be okay. Without hesitation he headed off to where he knew he'd be truly welcomed.

He stepped inside and she put her arms around him. 'Josh! What a lovely surprise. What brings you here? Are you okay?'

He felt himself relax in her embrace. 'I'm fine, Mum. I was just passing and thought I'd pop in and say hello.'

'Come in then, love. I've just taken a batch of scones out of the oven so your timing is perfect.'

He followed her into the little kitchen where the smell of baking filled his nostrils and reminded him that he hadn't eaten yet. 'They look delicious, Mum. Just what I fancy.'

She smiled and her eyes disappeared into a bed of wrinkles. 'Sit yourself down then, Josh, love, and I'll make us both a nice cup of tea.'

He did as he was told, and seeing his mother fuss around him reminded him of what it had been like to be a young boy with no cares or worries. Sometimes he wished he was that boy again. But he was an adult now and he needed to learn to deal with the stresses life threw at him instead of sweeping them under the carpet.

'There we go, love,' said his mum, placing two mugs of steaming hot tea on the wooden table and turning to grab a plate of warm scones. A jar of homemade strawberry jam and a bowl of whipped cream arrived to the table too and he greedily tucked in.

'So this is the second time I've seen you this week, Josh. Should I be worried?'

He laughed as he spread a scone liberally with jam and added a dollop of cream. 'Of course not. I know you came for lunch the other day but I haven't been here to visit you in weeks, what with the move and everything.'

'So how's Stephanie doing? Is everything okay with the baby?'

'Everything is fine, Mum. Both she and the baby are doing great. It won't be long now.'

'I know.' She beamed. 'And I just can't wait. I've knitted about ten cardigans already so the little one certainly won't go cold.'

He smiled at her enthusiasm. 'You're great, Mum. He or she will be lucky to have such a fabulous grandmother.'

'Ah, go away with you, Josh. My first grandchild – who wouldn't be excited? The first of many, I hope.'

'Relax now, will you,' he said, pretending to look worried. 'Let's get this one out first before you start wishing more on us.'

She chuckled and her jowls wobbled a little, making Josh smile. They sat in companionable silence for a few minutes until Josh suddenly felt the beginnings of a pain in his stomach again. Thankfully it eased quickly and Josh breathed a sigh of relief. But as he glanced over at the mantelpiece where a picture of his dad stood, a chill ran down his spine. He'd been trying to convince himself that he was not his dad. That lightning wouldn't strike twice. But in reality, these things could be hereditary and he knew he was going to have to face that. A bead of sweat began to trickle down the side of his face and he wiped it quickly with a tissue.

'Josh, are you okay? You don't look so good.'

'I'm fine, Mum. It's just hot in here.'

She stood up and opened the kitchen window. 'Sorry. It gets really steamy when I have the oven on. You should feel a draught now.'

'Thanks,' he said. He knew he had to question her now. To help him remember. But he didn't want to upset her. He began tentatively. 'Mum, you know when Dad first … when he first found out, you know …'

She looked a little startled. 'When he first found out he had cancer?'

He nodded. 'Had he suspected anything beforehand?'

'Where's this coming from, Josh?'

'It's just, I have a friend. He gets a lot of pain. In his stomach. Really low down, you know? And I seem to remember Dad having similar pains.'

She pushed her plate away and sat back in the chair, her face etched with the ache of her memories. 'It started with pain. Down low, as you say. Sometimes the pain would be so unbearable that he'd have to lie down and pull his legs up to his chest to try and get some relief. How bad is your friend's pain?'

She showed no indication she was suspicious so he continued. 'I don't think it's as bad as that, but it can be bad enough sometimes. He says it's like something inside him is contracting. It only lasts for a few minutes but he said it feels like ages.'

'Well, you tell this friend he needs to go to a doctor. Has he not had himself checked out yet?'

'No. At least I don't think so. Had Dad got any other symptoms?'

'He had a few, Josh. Personal ones, you know? Like down there.' She indicated around her backside and he felt the urge to giggle. His parents had always been old-fashioned and prudish and it was part of the reason he'd never really heard the details of his dad's illness.

'Suffice it to say,' she continued, 'that what was coming out there wasn't right. Not by a long shot.'

'So how long did he wait?'

'What do you mean?'

'From the time he felt something was wrong to the time he saw a doctor – how long was it?'

'Too long,' she said, shaking her head. 'By the time he eventually got himself checked out, the cancer had already spread. And, well, you know the rest. So tell your friend he needs to go now, before it's too late.'

The mood had changed in the room and Josh felt bad for bringing up things his mother would rather forget. Their tea had gone cold so he stood up and offered to make some more. They remained silent for the next few minutes and he knew his mother was thinking about his father, wishing he was there.

'Here we go,' said Josh, trying to lighten the tone. 'Milky and sweet, just how you like it.'

'Thanks, love.'

'So how's the hip been these last few weeks? I meant to ask you about it the other day.'

'A lot better now, love,' she said sombrely. 'The doctor put me on a new tablet and it seems to be working well.'

'And the blood pressure?'

She stirred her tea idly. 'Again, it's grand, thank God.'

He could have kicked himself for putting her into such a sad mood and he racked his brain for something to lift her out of it. He'd have to head off home to Stephanie in the next half hour and he didn't want to leave her like that. Sometimes when she'd get down or depressed, it could last for weeks and she'd been doing so well lately.

'One of the kids in school got himself invited over to an English football club after a scout saw him play last week,' said Josh, knowing how she loved stories from school. 'He's a brilliant little player. He could be one to watch for the future.'

'Very nice, love.'

'And another one of the boys got a small part in *Fair City*. Imagine! You might be able to see him on the telly next month.'

'Is that so? You'll have to tell me when he's on.'

He needed something more to bring her out of this mood. And then it occurred to him that maybe he shouldn't be protecting her so much. He'd been afraid that telling her about Holly coming back into his life would upset her, but she was probably the very person to advise him about it. He looked over at her and saw the sadness in her eyes. Her mind had gone to another place – another time – when she was with the love of her life and was happy.

'Mum?'

'Yes, love.'

'I have another bit of news.'

'What's that then?' Her eyes brightened slightly.

He hesitated for a moment before blurting it out. 'Holly Russo is back!'

'What?' Her eyes opened wide and suddenly she was *very* interested in the conversation. 'What do you mean she's back? Where? When? What does she want?'

Josh laughed. 'She hasn't come back to *me*, Mum. But she's living in the house right across the road from me.'

'I don't believe it. Are you serious? Have you spoken to her?'

'Yes. And to her fiancé!'

'She's getting married? My word. How do you feel about that? About everything?'

'I'm all over the place, actually. Just seeing her again … after everything …' He didn't hold back. He spent the next while chatting to his mum about it. And, just as he'd hoped, there was no judgement and no recriminations. She just listened carefully to everything he had to say until he was finished.

'It's a very strange situation,' she said, shaking her head. 'Who'd have thought it? Holly Russo back in your life after all this time.'

'She's not back in my life, Mum. Well, not the way you're implying.'

'I'm not implying anything, love. But clearly you have unresolved issues.'

He sighed. 'I know. What am I going to do, Mum?'

'You're going to figure it out for yourself – that's what you're going to do.'

'But I thought …'

'I'm here, love. I'm always here for you. You can talk to me about anything and I'll help you in any way I can. But this time you need to follow your own heart. Do what you think is right. I know you'll work it out in the end.'

She was right. She was *always* right. He needed to work this one out himself. He stood up and walked around the table to her, placing a kiss on her head.

'What was that for?' she said, patting her silver hair and blushing.

'Because you're fabulous. And I don't know what I'd do without you.'

'Go away out of that. That's what mothers are for.'

He looked at her face and felt a surge of love. She was his rock. She'd always been his rock. And no matter what the future held, he knew there was one woman who he could rely on. Who'd always love him no matter what.

Chapter 17

'Josh? *Your* Josh? I don't believe it?' Carina stared at Holly, her eyes wide.

'Not my Josh any more but, yes, *that* Josh.'

'But, Holly, how could that have happened? How could he have moved onto your street? That's just crazy. It's way too much of a coincidence.'

'You seem even more shocked than I was,' she said, smiling at Carina's extreme reaction. 'Can you imagine how I felt when he was standing right in front of me?'

'Oh my God. This is unbelievable. Forget the tea. We need some wine.' Carina stood up and flipped up a door above the fridge, where she rummaged around and eventually produced a bottle of red wine.

'Not for me, unfortunately,' said Holly. 'I want to get home in one piece.'

Carina grabbed two glasses. 'Just a small one then. Or you could stay. Elaina would be happy to give up her bed and sleep in with Lilly.'

'I wish I could, Carina, but I'm in work at ten in the morning. And I just have one week left so I don't want to be late.'

'Go on,' she persisted. 'You could drive up early. We need a serious chat.'

Holly smiled at her enthusiasm. 'I'll think about it. But for now, I'm happy with my cup of tea.'

Carina nodded and poured herself a large glass of wine. 'So tell me everything.'

Holly spent the next half hour telling her about recent events – from her first sighting of Josh in the hallway of their house and the awkward meeting on the street, to the painfully embarrassing night at theirs. Carina listened carefully, nodding and making all the appropriate noises.

'So what do you think?' Holly said, when she'd finally told her every last detail.

'I don't know what to think, to be honest, Holly. How did you feel seeing him again?'

She thought for a moment. 'Strange. That's how I felt. Really strange.'

Carina nodded. 'I can understand that. And what's this Stephanie like? Are they serious, do you think?'

'She's okay. Young and beautiful. And very much pregnant.'

Carina gasped. 'Pregnant! You didn't tell me that bit. So Josh is going to be a daddy.'

Somehow the words hurt and Holly winced slightly.

'Oh God, I'm sorry, Holly. I wasn't thinking. I'm sure it must have been a shock for you.'

'Yes,' she said, not looking Carina in the eye. Her sister could read her like a book. 'But I can't be stupid about things. It was bound to happen sometime. We've been apart a long time and, for all I knew, he could have had a number of children by now.'

'He hasn't, has he?' Carina looked shocked.

'I don't think so. I think this is his first. *Their* first.'

Carina reached across the table and patted her hand and Holly tried to swallow the lump in her throat. 'At least you have David

122

now, Holly. Imagine what it would have been like if you were still single. It would have been much harder seeing Josh happy.'

Holly knew she was right but somehow it didn't give her much comfort.

'And you have the wedding to concentrate on now too, so that should help distract you.'

'That's true,' said Holly, thinking about the plans she'd made with Josh for a winter wedding. 'But I think I need to talk to him, Carina. I mean properly talk. About what happened back then – how he was able to walk away after all we'd been through. We shouldn't have fallen apart so easily. We just shouldn't have.' Tears sprang to her eyes and this time she didn't try to stop them from falling.

'Oh, Holly, love!' Carina jumped up from her chair to rush to Holly's side. 'Don't be getting yourself so upset. It was so long ago. Don't let it have such an effect on you now.'

'That's just it, Carina.' She sniffled. 'I can't help it. It just shows that I never really dealt properly with the grief of our split.'

Carina handed Holly a clump of tissues from the box on the counter and sat back down. 'Grief? You make it sound like he died.'

'That's what it was like. I felt like somebody had died. We were together for so long, Carina. I loved him so much and he just left. He just walked out of my life and said he didn't want to see me again. How could that have happened?'

Holly looked at her sister and waited for an answer. She didn't understand what had happened then and she still didn't understand it thirteen years later. Josh had been her life and she'd been his. Or so she'd thought. Until one day he'd sat her down and told her he was moving to Dublin with his parents and he wanted to make a clean break from her. Just like that. He'd loved her one minute and the next he was leaving. Gone. Out of her life. And now, all these years later, he was living right across the road from her and she was supposed to just get on with it, as though nothing had happened.

Carina shifted uncomfortably in her chair and Holly could tell she didn't quite know what to say. 'Holly,' she ventured, watching her carefully. 'I know it must be difficult, but you can't let the past spoil your future. If you dredge up everything again with Josh, God knows how it will turn out. Have you even told David about all of this?'

Holly shook her head. 'Just bits. He knows we were together once, when we were kids.'

'You were a lot more than kids, Holly. You both had to grow up very fast …'

She trailed off but Holly knew what she meant. 'I just don't think David needs to know everything. And it's not as though I'm trying to hide things from him. He really doesn't want to know details of my past.'

'And how does he feel having his fiancée's ex-boyfriend living across the road?'

Holly thought for a minute. 'He's okay about it, actually. But things have been a little tense between us since Saturday. He's seen me looking out the window at their house a few times and has asked a few probing questions.'

'Holly!'

'What? It's just curiosity. Obviously I'm going to be curious about Josh's life. It's been a shock seeing him again.'

Carina poured herself another large glass of wine. 'Look, Holly, I sort of agree that David doesn't need to know the details of your past, but I don't think you should discuss it with Josh either. You need to tread very carefully. It could be a dangerous game.'

Holly looked at her quizzically. 'What's dangerous about it? Why are you so against me talking to Josh? I know you don't want me to get hurt, but don't you think it will be easier for me to move on if we have that conversation? If we both stay living on that street, I'll have to see him all the time, and if we haven't cleared the air, I'll always wonder.'

But Carina seemed adamant. 'It's dangerous, Holly, because if you start to dredge up old feelings, either yours or his, it could ruin a lot of lives. Let's say you start to fall for him again. Where does that leave David? And where does it leave *you*, more importantly, if Josh doesn't reciprocate?'

Holly tried to think of a sensible response but she knew Carina was right.

'Or,' Carina continued, 'what if you both fall for each other again? Where does that leave Stephanie? Would you really want him to leave his pregnant girlfriend? Let her bring up his baby alone? Be branded a home-wrecker?'

'Carina! You're getting carried away now. None of that is going to happen. I'm just talking about a civil conversation between me and him. I want to find out once and for all what happened to make him leave so suddenly and maybe then I can move on.'

'I still think you're crazy,' Carina said, gulping down the last of her wine and draining the bottle into the glass. 'It was such a long time ago. It really shouldn't matter any more.'

'What if it's fate?' said Holly, watching her sister carefully.

'What do you mean?' Carina's words were beginning to slur.

'I mean, what if it's meant to be? Don't you think it seems coincidental that Josh should move onto my street just as I'm about to plan my wedding? Maybe it's for a reason.'

'Now you're just being stupid, Holly. So you think that the universe is telling you that you two are meant to be together and you should ditch your respective partners?'

'Don't mock me,' she said, stung by her sister's flippant words. 'I don't mean anything as drastic as that but maybe we just have unresolved issues and the universe is throwing us together so that we can talk. Maybe it's what we need to finally move on properly. Milly said that –'

'Ah! I might have known Milly would have something to do with this. Putting ideas like that into your head.'

'That's not fair. Milly is a good friend to me and, if you want to know, yes, she mentioned fate at first. But once she heard Stephanie was pregnant, she felt that I should leave things be.'

'You see? Even Milly agrees. Honestly, Holly. No good can come from raking up the past. Use all that energy of yours on David now. On your relationship. Throw yourself into the wedding plans and forget about Josh O'Toole.'

Easier said than done. 'I think I'll head off,' said Holly, stretching her arms above her head and yawning. 'I told David I wouldn't be late.'

Carina stood up. She didn't even try to talk Holly into staying again. She'd obviously had her fill of drama for one night.

'And Holly?'

Holly looked at her and saw the worry etched on her face. 'Yes?'

'Just tread carefully. Remember what I said. Don't live in the past. You might just end up sacrificing your future.'

She walked Holly to the door and they said their goodbyes. Carina was a lot older than Holly and a lot wiser. She only ever wanted the best for her little sister and wanted to see her happy. And Holly knew that she should listen to her wise words. But Josh O'Toole was like a drug. Holly had managed to detox from him once before but seeing him again – having him so close – might just be a temptation she wasn't strong enough to resist.

Chapter 18

It was the day of Stephanie's first baby scan and Josh couldn't have been more excited. They'd been due to have one weeks ago but Stephanie had got the dates mixed up and so they'd had to wait. He'd just left work and was heading in to meet her in town. He'd offered to pick her up from home so that they could go in together, but she'd said she was meeting a friend for lunch beforehand. He sighed at the Friday-afternoon bumper-to-bumper traffic, but at least the appointment wasn't until half past four. He smiled to himself at the thought of seeing their little boy or girl moving around inside Stephanie's belly. All their little niggles and arguments would fade into insignificance when they saw the wonderful miracle they'd created. He knew it was going to bring them closer together and he couldn't wait.

In the end, he made it into town in perfect time, and as he rounded the corner towards the hospital, he saw Stephanie was already there. She looked gorgeous in her knee-length cream coat, one she'd got from a designer after she'd modelled some of her clothes the previous year. She was talking to somebody on the phone so didn't notice him approaching her and Josh was slightly alarmed to see that her face looked strained. She was clearly arguing but he couldn't make out what she was saying. Suddenly, she clapped eyes on him and she ended the call abruptly.

'Hi, Steph,' he said, kissing her full on the lips. 'Who was that?'

'Who?'

'On the phone. You looked agitated when you were speaking.'

She shook her head. 'Stupid crank call. It's the third one I've had this week.'

'Really? What sort of crank call? What did they say?'

She waved her hand dismissively. 'Just somebody doing a survey or something. I told him I was sick of getting those calls and not to ring me again.'

Josh wasn't convinced but he let it go for now because he didn't want to spoil the day. 'Right. Are we going in? Are you excited?'

'Actually, Josh, I have a confession to make.'

He looked at her in alarm. 'What? What is it?'

'I'm an idiot,' she said, linking her arm through his. 'I got the times mixed up. Again.'

He breathed a sigh of relief. 'Is that all? You really are a feather-head. So how long do we have to wait? There's probably a coffee shop in there so why don't we go in and get some tea. It's freezing out here.' He moved in the direction of the door but she stopped him.

'No, Josh. It was *three* thirty, not four thirty. I only realised it when I checked the appointment card while I was having lunch.'

He quickly checked his watch and saw it was four twenty. His heart sank but he wasn't ready to give up. 'Come on, then. Let's go in anyway. They might see us if they're not too busy.'

'You don't understand,' she said, rooting in her bag. 'When I realised I'd made a mistake, I got over here straight away. There was no way I was going to miss that scan.'

'Wh– what? You mean you went ahead without me? I can't believe it.'

'I'm sorry, Josh. But I didn't have much choice. It takes ages to get an appointment here and I knew we'd probably be waiting for weeks if I had to make another one.'

'But, Steph, you know how much I wanted to be there. You should have rung. I could have left work early. I would have been here.' He felt gutted.

She shook her head. 'I'm telling you, Josh. There just wasn't time. It all happened so quickly. When I got here I asked if they could change the time to four thirty but before I knew it, they had me on the table and the nurse was scanning me.'

He felt angry and he didn't trust himself to speak.

'Come on,' she said, putting an arm around his waist and pulling him to her. 'Don't be cross. There was nothing I could have done. I'm disappointed too that you weren't there.'

Josh suddenly realised that he'd been so caught up in his own disappointment that he'd forgotten to ask her about the baby. 'So tell me what happened. Is everything okay with the baby?'

'Let's get away from here first,' she said, taking his hand and leading him back down the street.

He felt panic rising again. 'Why? Is there something wrong?'

'No, silly.' She laughed. 'I'm just starving and noticed a lovely-looking vegetarian restaurant just around the corner.'

'But didn't you just have lunch?'

'A while ago. But do you know how much water they make you drink in there before the scan? I must have flushed out my whole system and now I need to fill it up again.'

He laughed at that and again wished he'd been there to see it. 'So everything was okay with the baby then?'

'Perfect,' she said as they arrived at the door of a very veggie-looking place. He would have killed for a big juicy burger but he'd just have to wait until he got home. It was quiet so they took a couple of seats at a window and the waitress immediately arrived to take their order. Stephanie went for a butternut squash curry but Josh was less adventurous with a cheese and tomato panini.

'So, you were saying?' He leaned his elbows on the table, dying to hear all about the scan.

'Everything was fine, Josh.' She smiled but it wasn't quite convincing.

'Are you sure? What did the nurse say?'

'Of course I'm sure. The baby is a good size and everything seems to be in its proper place.'

She looked tired up close. Fed up, even. 'Steph, is there something worrying you? I mean, if you're sure everything is okay with the baby, is there something else?'

She stared at him for a moment and then nodded. 'There *is* something worrying me, actually. And the visit today confirmed it for me.'

'What is it? Tell me.'

'I think I want a C-section. I'm terrified, Josh. I'm scared out of my wits about having something that size coming out of something this size.' She pointed down below and he couldn't help laughing. Mostly out of relief.

The food arrived and Josh waited until the waitress was well out of earshot before continuing. 'Aw, Steph, it's completely normal to feel that way. I wouldn't blame you for being scared. I'm sure every woman is. But you'll be fantastic. I know you will.'

She sniffled and grabbed a serviette to wipe her nose. 'I hope so.'

Josh's heart filled with love for her at that moment. His beautiful girlfriend carrying their beautiful baby. He just wanted to wrap them both up in cotton wool and never let them out of his sight. And then something occurred to him. 'Steph, did you find out?'

'Find out what?' She looked at him blankly.

'The sex of the baby. I know you wanted to. Did you?'

She shook her head. 'No, I didn't ask. I know you don't want to know and it would be difficult keeping it from you. Especially if I was buying all blue or all pink stuff.'

'Thanks,' he said, relieved. 'I definitely don't want to know until the moment the baby comes out. And how did he or she look? Could you make out the hands and feet and everything?'

'See for yourself,' she said, pulling something out from her hand-bag. She slid a piece of paper across the table and Josh's heart jumped with joy.

'Oh my God! Is that him or her? Is that our baby?'

'Yes, Josh. That's our baby.'

He felt tears at the backs of his eyes and he had to pinch the bridge of his nose to stop them falling. It was the most perfect pic-ture he could have ever imagined. It was so clear that he could actu-ally see the fingers and toes and it looked like it was sucking its thumb. It would have been wonderful to see it on the screen, moving around, but holding the picture in his hand, he didn't feel anything other than pure happiness. He reached over the table and kissed Stephanie.

'So am I forgiven for messing up the time?' She looked at him, her eyebrows raised, the beginnings of a smile on her lips.

'There's nothing to forgive,' he said, looking at the picture again. 'These things happen. Now get that curry into you before you fade away from starvation.'

They spent the next half hour chatting about everything. There'd been a lot of tension between them lately, but now that they were talking again, maybe things would get a little easier. They really needed to enjoy this time together because, from what Josh had heard from friends with children, once the baby came along, there wouldn't be a lot of couple time. But it would be worth it.

*　*　*

The weather had turned suddenly and it looked like they could be in for a frosty night. The car showed an outside temperature of minus one and it was still only just after seven. As they pulled into the driveway, Josh was beginning to wish he'd sorted out the timer for the heating because he knew the house was going to be freezing. He glanced across at Stephanie and saw she was still asleep so he nudged her gently to tell her they were home.

'I was having a lovely sleep there,' she said, stretching. 'I can't believe we're home already.'

Josh didn't have the heart to tell her they'd been in traffic for an hour while she snored all the way so he just nodded and smiled. He hopped out of the car and rushed around to her side to help her out. The paths had begun to frost over and he didn't want her slipping on the ice. He noticed a figure walking up the street in their direction as Stephanie stepped out of the car and it took him just a moment to realise it was Holly.

He averted his eyes, pretending he hadn't seen her, but unfortunately Stephanie had spotted her too. 'Oh, there's Holly. Let's go over and show her the scan pictures.'

'No!' The words came out of his mouth a little too quickly, a little too sharply, and Stephanie noticed.

'Why?' she said, staring at him. 'I'd have thought you'd be dying to show everyone.'

'I am, but just not tonight. I don't want them asking us in for a drink to celebrate or anything. I'm exhausted and just want to flake out on the sofa with you.'

Thankfully that seemed to satisfy her and they both waved at Holly as she arrived at her house. 'Hi, Holly,' Josh shouted, a little too loudly. 'Just home from work?'

'Yes,' she said, looking unsure about whether to come over or not. She didn't and Josh was relieved. 'Thank God it's Friday.'

They all nodded and laughed, and Holly disappeared in through her front door. Josh felt his heart racing as he stepped inside the house, and he cursed the effect Holly still had on him. But he was going to have to find a way around it. He couldn't go getting palpitations every time he saw her. They were nothing to each other except neighbours, and Josh would just have to get used to that.

Stephanie headed upstairs to the shower and Josh fell exhausted onto the sofa in the sitting room. He reached into his pocket for the scan and stared at it for a few moments. *That* was his future. *That* was where he belonged. Holly was his past and that was where she'd stay. If he kept telling himself that, maybe sometime soon he'd believe it.

Chapter 19

May 2001

Holly felt empty. It had been the worst few weeks of her life and she wasn't sure she'd ever recover. The physical pain was nothing in comparison to the mental torture. Her mobile beeped again and she rolled over in the bed to see who was messaging her. It was Josh again. She knew he was worried about her but she wasn't in the right frame of mind to be with him just then. She felt bad refusing to see him because she knew he was hurting too, but she was such a mess and she just wanted to be alone. She lay there willing sleep to come but no such luck. It was only 8 p.m. but she hadn't wanted to sit downstairs with her mother fussing around, trying to get her to eat and making inane conversation.

After what seemed like an age of staring at the ceiling, there was a tap on the door. She closed her eyes and pretended to be sleeping, just in case it was her mother with another tray of food.

'Holly, can I come in?'

Her eyes shot open when she heard his voice. It was Josh. He must have gotten fed up sending texts and had come to see her instead. Part of her wanted to curl up and pretend he wasn't there, but the other part of her needed him.

'Holly. Please. I know you're hurting and I want to help. Please let me in.'

She sat up in the bed. 'Come in.' Her voice was barely a whisper but he obviously heard because the door opened and he rushed to her side.

'Holly. Oh, Holly,' he said, holding her tightly. 'Come on. It's going to be all right. We'll get through this together.'

She eventually let herself relax in his arms and they both cried for a long time. She wondered if things would ever feel normal again. If she'd ever get over losing her little girl.

Holly couldn't remember the last time she and Josh had kissed. Since she'd felt his breath on her face ten days ago, memories of the past had been flooding back to her. Lots of memories. Wonderful memories. Memories of everything they'd done together, except for that last kiss. It was like the more she tried to remember, the more she seemed to forget. Josh had been such a huge part of her life that surely she should have been able to remember that last time. But no, it completely evaded her and it was driving her crazy. The only explanation was that she'd blocked it out of her mind sometime in the past to protect herself, to stop herself reliving the memory and making herself too sad. And now, when she wanted to recall it, she couldn't.

She checked her watch as she hurried down the street. She'd spent most of the morning with Mrs Jackson, whose shih-tzu, Kylie, was close to her delivery date. Mrs Jackson had rung the surgery the previous day in a panic. She'd needed to fill Kylie's prescription but she didn't want to leave the dog alone or bring her out when she could go into labour any minute. The pair weren't Holly's favourite customers but she knew Mrs Jackson was genuinely worried so she'd offered to get the medication and bring it to her. The old woman had been very grateful and had been persistent in offering her a cup of tea. She'd reluctantly agreed and had found it difficult to get away afterwards. She realised that the woman was probably lonely. She gave off an air of nonchalance and confidence, but really she was a vulnerable old lady.

Holly breathed a sigh of relief when she finally arrived home. She had a day off and David was finished work at lunchtime, so she was looking forward to spending some time with him. Today was the first day of December and Holly had decided she'd enter the new month with a new attitude and show David how dedicated to him and their forthcoming wedding she was. She owed him that at least. She'd been depressed before he'd come along. She'd realised that all her friends had moved on with their lives while she was still stuck in a rut. And then she'd met David at one of her friends' weddings. He'd been there with his mother and had looked almost as miserable as she'd felt. They'd got talking at the bar and had clicked straight away. By the end of the evening they'd swapped numbers and Holly had felt a glimmer of hope for the future. They'd started dating soon after and she'd finally felt free. Free from the depression of sitting in every night, free from the worry of being alone for the rest of her life and free from living in the past. Her life had been really sorted before Josh had reappeared. Seeing him again had just jolted her out of her comfort zone and forced her to remember things and times she'd rather forget.

She quickly showered and rooted in her wardrobe until she found a pair of skinny jeans that still fit. She teamed them with a tight-fitting navy T-shirt that she'd bought in River Island a couple of years before and for once was pretty happy with how she looked. She wanted to look nice for him. She wanted to make an effort. She brought a nice dusky-pink nail polish into the sitting room and flicked on the telly. Ruth Langsford's face appeared on the screen and she raised the volume. She loved *Loose Women* but she rarely got a chance to watch it. She settled down to paint her nails and listen to the women's words of wisdom.

She and David had chatted for hours the previous night about the wedding and they'd finally settled on a date. Saturday 10 June 2017.

Much as she'd have loved a Christmas wedding, Doreen had probably been right. The weather would be too uncertain, and if there was snow or ice, it could stop people from going altogether. So a summer wedding it was and they had a whole eighteen months to plan it. She'd also given in on the whole church thing. But she hadn't done it for Doreen. She'd done it for David. He was a traditionalist at heart and said he'd feel strange not getting married in a church. So she wasn't getting her castle on a hill with snow drifting down, but the important thing was that they were going to become husband and wife. She'd never be lonely again. Suddenly there was a sound of raised voices from outside and Holly jumped up to look out the window.

A car was parked across the road outside number three and Stephanie was speaking to the driver. She looked agitated. It was difficult to make out what they were saying but Stephanie was clearly not happy. She was gesturing wildly with her hands and shaking her head. Then the driver got out and Holly held her breath. He was a distinguished-looking man, well dressed in a grey suit with shirt and tie, and he was towering over Stephanie. Holly suddenly felt worried for the girl's safety. What if he was going to harm her? Should she go out and say something? Should she check to see if Stephanie was okay? He leaned in close to Stephanie and Holly's heart almost stopped. She should really ring the police. But while she was still faffing around trying to decide what to do, he got back into his car and sped off down the road. Holly breathed a sigh of relief, but it looked like she wasn't the only one. Stephanie leaned against the wall at the front of the house and ran a hand through her dishevelled hair.

Holly suddenly felt foolish for hiding herself inside when clearly Stephanie was distraught. So without a further thought, she rushed out the front door and across the road.

'Stephanie, are you okay? What did that guy want?'

Stephanie looked at her in surprise. 'He … he was just looking for directions.'

'It looked like more than that to me. Do you know him? I thought he was going to hit you or something.'

'Don't be silly.' A nervous laugh. 'And of course I don't know him. He just got out of the car so I could point out the directions to him.'

'Oh. But you look shaken. Are you sure he didn't do something to hurt you? Or threaten you or something?'

Stephanie glared at her, and Holly felt herself shrinking back. 'You're being ridiculous, Holly. And what were you doing spying on me anyway? Don't you have anything better to do?'

'I wasn't spying, Stephanie. I heard raised voices so I just came out to have a look. So you're saying it was just a random man who drove into our estate and asked you for directions?'

'That's exactly what happened. I was out sweeping the driveway when he pulled up.'

'I see.' Holly noticed the absence of a sweeping brush anywhere close by but she refrained from pointing that out. 'Well, in that case, sorry to have bothered you. I just thought you looked upset so I wanted to see if I could help.'

Stephanie's mood seemed to change and she smiled sweetly. 'Thank you so much, Holly. It's nice to know that if anything bad did happen, you'd be there to save the day.'

Holly couldn't figure out if she was being genuine or sarcastic but she chose to believe the former as she bid Stephanie goodbye and headed back to her own house. Thankfully David arrived home at that moment and he looked at her quizzically as he got out of the car.

'Was that Stephanie you were talking to?' he said, following her into the house. 'Are you two friends now or something?'

'Hardly.' Holly filled the kettle and told him about the events of the previous ten minutes. He listened intently before speaking.

'It sounds strange all right, but I wouldn't get involved.'

'Well, I hadn't planned to get involved in anything,' she said, stung by his dismissive words. 'But when I thought somebody was hassling her and she looked upset, of course I was going to check to see if she was okay.'

'But what were you doing spying on her in the first place?'

Not him too. She sighed and told him what she'd just told Stephanie. 'I just think there was more to it than she let on. I'm sure they were arguing. And what man would get out of the car and approach a woman on her own if he was just looking for directions?'

'Leave it, Holly,' he said, folding his arms and fixing her with a stare. 'It's nothing to do with us so whatever happened or didn't happen, it's her business.'

'But what if she's up to something behind Josh's back? Shouldn't we say something?'

He pulled off his tie and sighed. 'Like what? "Oh, hi, Josh. You might want to check Stephanie out. We think she's cheating on you."'

'Well, when you say it like that ...'

'Holly, it doesn't matter which way I say it,' said David, the little vein at the side of his head popping in and out as his voice got louder. 'It's *their* business. We need to keep our noses out. Now let's worry about our own lives and future instead of wasting time on other people.'

Holly stared at his back as he headed out of the kitchen and up the stairs. She didn't think she'd ever heard David being so forceful about an issue. In a strange sort of way, she kind of liked it. And he was right, of course. Whatever Stephanie got up to and whatever went on between her and Josh was none of their business. She poured boiling water into the teapot and rinsed it out before making the tea. The rest of the day was going to be dedicated to her and David and their plans. They were going to look at some hotels for the wedding and Holly was going to put all thoughts of Stephanie and Josh firmly out of her head.

'So what do you think?' David said, as they walked around the gardens at the front of the first hotel on their list. 'Pretty spectacular, isn't it? Couldn't you just see us having photos taken here? Apparently the flower beds are amazing in the summertime.'

Holly had to admit the hotel was fabulous and the gardens were really beautiful. But the thing was, it didn't really excite her. Although everything about it seemed perfect, she didn't feel any connection to it. It felt like it had no soul. She wanted their wedding to be personal to them. To have their stamp on it. Not just another generic wedding done in the traditional way.

'Holly?'

She realised he was still waiting for an answer so she told him what he wanted to hear. 'Yes, it's beautiful. And we'd definitely get some lovely shots out here in the gardens.'

'But?'

She stopped and looked at him. 'But is it really us? It's very posh and almost too perfect.'

'Nothing is too perfect for you, Holly.' He pulled her to him and kissed her gently. 'I want you to have the best. I really love you, you know.'

She was touched by his gesture. 'I love you too, David.'

'And I can't wait to marry you,' he said, placing little feather kisses on her head. 'We're going to have a wonderful future together, you and me. I can't wait to spend the rest of my life with you, Holly Russo.'

She looked into his eyes and saw the man she'd fallen for. The man who'd taken her away from the life she'd hated. Suddenly, the details of the wedding didn't matter, as long as she had David. 'Let's do it!'

'What?' He looked at her, his eyebrows raised.

'The hotel. Let's book it. The date is available so why don't we just decide to go with it?'

'Are you serious? But what about all the other hotels on the list? Shouldn't we go and check them out too?'

She shook her head. 'It's like buying a dress. You love the first one you try on but you feel you should go and try on a hundred more just to be sure. But what happens in the end?'

He laughed. 'You go back to the first shop and buy that dress.'

'Exactly,' she said, taking his hand again and leading him back towards the door of the hotel. 'So why don't we save time and book this place. What do you think?'

'Well, I'm definitely happy about it. But are *you* sure? It's just I know you weren't too keen on the whole traditional thing.'

'It's fine. I've come around to it. Once we're married at the end of it, none of the details matter really.'

They headed inside to find the manager, Geraldine, and to ask her to put them in the diary. Geraldine was delighted they'd decided to book. She promised to ensure they had a wonderful experience and a day to remember. Holly could scarcely believe she was actually getting married. It just didn't seem real. It was so far away and she knew only too well how life could change in the blink of an eye. Geraldine's voice was just a dull drone in the background as a myriad thoughts whirred around Holly's head. Stephanie and the man looking for directions. Something didn't ring true about that. Josh and all of their history. And the beautiful, romantic wedding in a snow-covered castle on a hill that she knew now, with certainty, would never be anything other than a dream.

Chapter 20

Josh sat looking over the household accounts and clicked his tongue. They really weren't looking too good. With the baby coming along soon, he needed to start budgeting properly. He was constantly assuring Stephanie that he earned enough for them both, but it just wasn't true. His salary barely covered the rent and the bills, leaving only a small amount for food and nothing for any extras. He just didn't know how he was going to find the extra cash they'd need for when the baby arrived. He leaned his head into his hands and prayed for inspiration. A few moments later his mobile rang, jolting him out of his reverie. He reached across the table to grab it and smiled when he saw his mum's name flashing on the screen.

'Hi, Mum.'

'Josh. How are you, son? You were just on my mind so I thought I'd give you a call.'

'I'm fine. All good here.' His eyes were drawn to the bills in front of him but she didn't need to know how bad things were.

'Now listen, Josh. I can tell things aren't fine so why don't you tell me what's up.'

He sighed. 'It's nothing for you to worry about, Mum. I just have a lot on, between Stephanie, the baby and other stuff.'

'Other stuff meaning Holly?'

Nothing got past her. 'She's one of the things, yes. But she's not my main worry at the moment.'

'Well, then tell me what is. How can I help?'

He looked at the mess of figures in front of him and was tempted to confide in her. He didn't want Stephanie worried about it and it wasn't a conversation he wanted to have with any of his friends. Sometimes he felt that he'd explode from the worries he was keeping bottled up in his head.

'Josh? There's nothing you can't tell me. I've been your mother since you were born so I've seen the good, the bad and the ugly.'

Josh laughed at that before becoming serious. 'I'm just a bit overwhelmed at the moment, Mum. With the baby and everything. I want to make sure nothing goes wrong.'

'That's understandable. Of course you're going to be worried. But everything is going okay with the pregnancy, isn't it?'

Josh sat back in the chair, gauging how much he wanted to tell her. 'I think so. I mean, medically everything seems to be fine. But Stephanie hasn't been herself lately.'

'How so?'

'She's moody and snappy. And she's going out partying a lot, which couldn't be good for the baby.'

'Is that all?'

That wasn't the response he'd expected. 'But don't you think she should be taking it easy? Looking after herself instead of being out until all hours?'

'Josh, love, I know you're just looking out for her, but there's no harm in her having a bit of fun before the baby is born. Because, mark my words, with a little one in the house, you'll both be more interested in getting a bit of sleep than going out partying.'

'I suppose so,' said Josh, not convinced. 'But the moods, the fieriness – sometimes I feel like she doesn't even like me.'

'It'll be her hormones. They can play havoc with a woman's moods. Honestly, Josh. I think you have yourself worked up about nothing.'

'Maybe.'

'Is there something else?'

He needed to tell someone. 'I'm worried about finances, Mum. I want to provide for my family but with Stephanie not working much at the moment, my salary alone just isn't enough.'

'How bad is it? Are you in debt?'

'No, not at the moment. But with the baby coming there's going to be so much we need. I'm just wondering where the money is going to come from.'

'I can help out a little, Josh. But I'm not sure it will be enough to make much of a difference.'

'Oh God, Mum. I wasn't looking for a handout. I'd never take money from you. But thanks anyway.'

'Well, the offer is there. And would you not think of taking a little part-time job somewhere yourself? You teachers have a lot of free time so maybe something in the evenings or at weekends?'

Josh hated when people suggested that teachers worked less than average but maybe she had a point. 'That's not entirely a bad idea. Maybe I could check out the local pub. I used to love being a barman in my college days.'

'Well, there you go then. They're bound to be looking for help coming up to Christmas. And with the tips barmen get, you could have a nice little extra packet for when the baby arrives.'

Josh felt a little brighter. 'Thanks, Mum. You really are a treasure.'

'Go away out of that, Josh. Now, I'll have to love you and leave you. I'm due over to Molly Sherwood's in an hour and a half. She's making tea for the bridge club and I've promised her an apple pie, which I haven't even started.'

Josh said goodbye and quickly gathered up the papers from the table. He didn't want Stephanie coming home to find them there. When he had them safely put away in a drawer, he decided there was no time like the present. He was buoyed up by the conversation with his mother so he was going to head straight down to O'Malley's and see if they could give him some bar work. He didn't know why he hadn't thought of it before. His mood had lifted as he walked out towards the main road. Christmas was just three weeks from Friday and he couldn't wait. He and Stephanie were going shopping on Saturday and he wasn't going to let their money troubles spoil that. He'd keep an eye on what they were spending but a little extra on the credit card wouldn't hurt. He knew he'd stress about it in January but there was no way he was being too much of a scrooge at Christmas.

Minutes later he stepped inside the door of O'Malley's. The décor was modern but still felt warm and welcoming. The seats were all red leather and the tables had a lovely oak finish. Stephanie wasn't keen on ordinary pubs, preferring the loud disco bar type places she frequented in the city centre, but he'd take her down here some evening and see what she thought. There was just a scattering of people sitting around but no customers at the bar, so he headed straight there.

'Can I speak to the manager?' he said, trying not to feel old.

The barman, who looked about twelve, eyed him suspiciously. 'What for?'

Lovely customer service. 'I just want a word with him, that's all. I won't keep him long.'

He considered Josh's request for a moment before replying. 'He's not here.'

'When will he be back then?'

'Not today.'

'Well, can I speak to whoever is in charge?'

The barman continued wiping a glass with a tea-towel while keeping his eyes fixed on Josh. 'You can talk to me.'

Josh sighed. He really didn't want to ask somebody who looked like one of his sixth-class boys for a job. But on the other hand, he didn't have anything to lose. 'I was just wondering if they're looking for casual staff here. You know, with Christmas and everything.'

'Nah. There's enough of us here.'

'Do you know that for a fact? Maybe if I leave my name and details you could pass them on to the manager when he comes back?'

The barman shrugged. 'Sure.'

He pulled out a scrap of paper from beside the till and handed Josh a pen from behind his ear. Josh wrote down his details, but he felt sure that as soon as he headed out the door, the barman would have the piece of paper ripped up into little pieces and in the bin. He sighed and decided that if he didn't hear from anyone in the next few days, he'd just try again.

He noticed the pub starting to fill up as he was leaving and he suddenly felt envious of the groups coming from work, popping in for a sneaky pint on the way home. They didn't do much of that at school, firstly because they finished at around three, which was pretty early, and secondly because a lot of the staff were much older than Josh and they just weren't interested. He had an urge to stay for a pint himself, but he didn't want to look pathetic on his own – or, worse still, to look like he'd been stood up. So he pulled his coat up tight around his neck and reluctantly headed outside to the bitter cold.

But as he stepped outside, he bumped straight into a girl walking past, and her phone fell from her hands and shattered on the ground.

'Oh God, I'm sorry,' he said, bending down to pick up the broken phone. 'I didn't see you there.'

He picked up the pieces and stood up to hand them to her. But she was glued to the spot, staring at him. Josh was completely taken aback when he saw who it was. He handed her the broken phone wordlessly and there was a moment, a fleeting moment when their hands touched, that he felt that connection. The one they used to have. The one he'd thought they'd have forever. And then, in a flash, the spell was broken by her angry words.

'Nice one, Josh. That was a brand new iPhone, you know.'

'I'm so sorry, Holly. I'll pay for the repairs.' He didn't know what else to say.

Her voice softened a little. 'It's okay. It's insured. David insisted I take out insurance when he bought it for me, just in case.'

Josh nodded. 'Very sensible. Are you just coming from work now?'

'Yep. Finished at six today so I'm looking forward to getting home, getting into my pyjamas and having a massive bowl of crisps while watching *Coronation Street*.'

He laughed. 'You still watch that, do you? And still with the crisps? I remember when –' He stopped himself from saying any more when he saw the look on her face. It was as though she was warning him not to go there. He suddenly felt awkward. As though he was speaking to a stranger. Except she wasn't a stranger. She was Holly Russo. The girl he used to love.

'How's Stephanie?' she said, changing the tone of the conversation. 'Is she keeping well?'

'She's fine.' Another pause. 'And David?'

'Fine.'

This was ridiculous. They needed to get over the awkwardness if they were going to be living across from each other. It was painful trying to think about what to say and what not to say at the same time. They needed to have a proper talk. Clear the air and move on with their lives.

'Holly?'

'Yes?'

'Why don't we go in and have a drink.'

She looked startled. 'I … I'm not sure. I don't know if I want –'

'Just one drink. A half an hour, tops. Let's have a proper chat and maybe then things won't be so difficult when we meet.'

She nodded in agreement and Josh felt a shiver run down his spine. He opened the door and waved her inside. As he followed her in, he felt strange and he wasn't sure if it was a good or a bad thing. He felt nervous, yet excited. Elated to be in her company again, yet sad at the same time. The young barman looked at him questioningly as they approached the bar but, at that moment, Josh couldn't have cared less about the job. He ordered drinks and the barman said he'd bring them over, so they took a seat at the back of the pub. And suddenly Josh realised that he'd just ordered out of habit. He hadn't asked her what she wanted and she hadn't even noticed. Old habits die hard and Josh was beginning to wonder if Holly was a habit that he just wasn't going to be able to kick.

Chapter 21

Holly felt like she was in some sort of time warp. She was actually sitting there in a pub with Josh O'Toole. Just the two of them. Her head was spinning and she wasn't sure how she felt. She'd promised Carina that she was going to leave things and not get into a conversation with him about the past but it was going to be pretty difficult to avoid it. Fancy bumping into him like that. Of all the people. She knew she probably should have just passed a couple of words with him and headed on home but she hadn't been able to get the words out of her mouth and then her legs had refused to move. They busied themselves taking off coats and scarves while waiting for their drinks and Holly couldn't resist a sneaky glance at Josh. He'd barely changed at all except for a few more worry lines around his eyes. And his slight beard and moustache gave him a more distinguished look. Other than that, he looked just like the old Josh. The one she used to love.

'Here we go,' said the barman, placing the drinks in front of them. 'A pint of cider and a pint of Guinness.'

'You remembered,' she said, her voice barely a whisper.

'Sorry, I didn't mean to assume …'

She shook her head. 'No, it's perfect. Some things never change. So tell me. What were you doing in here on your own? Having a sneaky little pint before going home to the pregnant missus?' Shit. Why had she said that? Every time she tried to be funny it came out all wrong. But thankfully he didn't seem to take offence.

'Nothing as exciting as that. I was actually asking about a job.'

'But I thought you were working in a school?'

'I am. But you know how it is. With a baby on the way, there's never enough money. I'm just trying to pull in some extra cash before the big event.'

'What about Stephanie? Is she not doing any work these days?' She couldn't help herself.

He shook his head. 'A bit here and there but nothing concrete. It's a difficult business, especially with her being pregnant. And I want her to rest as much as possible.'

Holly was about to point out that his girlfriend was pregnant, not sick, but she bit her tongue and stopped herself. Instead, she lifted her pint to her lips and took a lingering sip.

'I can't complain, really,' he said, his eyes fixed on Holly. 'Steph has brought in plenty of money in the past with some high-profile jobs and she will again. But the most important thing now is that she stays well during the pregnancy.'

Holly wasn't sure what to say to that so instead she changed the subject. 'David and I have booked our wedding. We just finalised a few things yesterday.'

'Oh, congratulations,' he said, playing with a beermat. 'It must be very exciting for you.'

Holly thought she noticed his face fall – just a very quick expression before he smiled. But why would he care when he was obviously totally in love with Stephanie and they were going to have a baby together?

Suddenly he banged his pint down, sending splashes across the table, and Holly jumped in fright. 'Josh, what was that for?'

'Because we're being silly. Because we're acting like two awkward teenagers who are on a first date and don't know what to say to each other. Because it shouldn't be like this.'

For a moment Holly was stunned, and then she began to giggle. 'You're right. I never thought I'd find speaking to you so difficult.'

'Let's start again then, shall we? We're adults now, Holly. We should be able to put the past aside and get along. Who knows, we might even be friends again someday.'

It all still felt surreal but she nodded. It would certainly make life a lot easier if they could get rid of the awkwardness.

'So how are your parents?' he continued. 'Are they still in the house in Kildare?'

'Yep. And they're doing fine. Dad turned seventy in the summer and Mam will be seventy next year. Thankfully they're in good health and still getting away for holidays in the sun and weekends in Ireland. What about yours?'

'Mam is okay. A bit lonely, though. Dad passed away a few years ago.'

'Oh no, Josh. I'm so sorry. I ... I didn't know.'

'Of course you didn't. How could you?'

She shook her head. 'I always loved your father. He was a real gentleman.' She felt tears prick her eyes but she tried valiantly to stem them. It was Josh's grief, not hers, and she didn't feel entitled to express her feelings.

Josh was watching her. 'And he loved you too, Holly. He was almost as heartbroken as me when ... well, you know ...'

Her grief suddenly turned to anger. Josh heartbroken? How could he say that? *She* was the one left heartbroken. It was *her* heartbreak, not his. *He* was the one who'd caused it. But how could she say that to him when he was telling her about losing his dad. It wasn't the right time.

'So what happened to him? Was it sudden?'

'No, we knew it was coming, but I think you're still never prepared for it. He had bowel cancer.' He dropped his head and her anger dissipated immediately. She badly wanted to reach over and touch his hair. Rub his head like she used to. She knew it would give him comfort, just like it had in the past, but she couldn't do it. He wasn't hers any more. She noticed then that his hand was clutching his stomach and suddenly felt alarmed.

'Are you okay, Josh? What's wrong?'

His head shot up. 'Nothing. Why?'

'You were holding your stomach like you were in pain.'

'No, I wasn't,' he said, a little too quickly. His earlobes turned bright pink and Holly could see a rash start to form on his neck, creeping up towards his face. She couldn't help smiling.

He glared at her. 'What are you smiling at?'

'Just memories,' she said, and suddenly she felt more relaxed with him. 'I remember how you used to get that rash when you told a lie.'

'What rash?' His hand went automatically to his neck.

'That one right there!' She laughed and he seemed to relax a little too. 'So what's really up with you, Josh?'

'Everything is fine,' he said, not looking her in the eye, and she knew then for sure he was lying.

'Josh?' She wasn't sure how much to push it. He was nothing to her any more.

But he looked at her then, his face tired and his shoulders slumped. 'I'm worried that I could have it too, Holly.'

'What? Have what?'

'Cancer. What my dad had. I think I could have bowel cancer.'

It took a moment for the words to sink in, and when they did, they filled her with panic. 'I … I don't know what to say, Josh. And what do you mean, *you think*? Are you waiting for results or something?'

Having ripped one beermat to shreds, he moved on to another and Holly fought the urge to put her hand over his to get him to stop. 'Josh, speak to me. What's going on?'

'I'm such an idiot, Holly. I haven't gone to the doctor about it yet. I know I should, but I just keep putting it off.'

She felt immediately relieved, but confused at the same time. 'Hang on, so you haven't been told you might have cancer? This is just you putting two and two together and making five?'

'It's not as simple as that.'

'Well, explain it to me then. Why are you thinking the worst?'

He looked at her with sad eyes. He'd always had such expressive eyes that he could say a thousand words without opening his mouth. It took him a moment to speak, but when he did, it was like he'd opened a floodgate and couldn't stop.

'I've been getting these pains. On and off for the last few months. Right down here.' He put a hand on the lower part of his stomach. 'I didn't think much of it at first, but they've been coming more frequently lately and, with my dad's history, I can't help worrying.'

'But, Josh, you're wasting time. Cancer, if it is that, isn't always a death sentence, especially if you catch it early.' She felt angry. Why would he put off getting it checked?

'I know you're right, Holly,' he said, running his finger along the rim of his pint glass. 'And that's the advice I'd be giving to anyone else in my position. But it's not anyone else – it's me. And it's hard to think of dealing with something like that alone.'

'But you're not on your own,' Holly protested. 'You have Stephanie. What does she think of all this? Surely she wants you to go and get checked out?'

He raised his glass to his lips and drained the last of his pint. 'Will we have another? One more for the road?'

'I'll get them in a minute,' Holly said, waving a hand dismissively. 'So, Stephanie – what does she say about all this?'

A barman was clearing glasses from a nearby table so Josh indicated for him to come over and take their order. 'A pint of cider and a pint of Guinness, when you're ready,' he said.

Holly noticed he was avoiding meeting her eye and realisation eventually dawned. 'Oh my God, Josh. You haven't told her, have you?'

He lowered his head and she knew she was right. 'Josh! What were you thinking? Stephanie is your partner. She's about to become the mother of your child. Why on earth have you not told her about this?'

He glanced up at her and looked defeated. 'For the same reason I haven't been to the doctor yet. Fear.'

She hated seeing him like that. Broken and upset. So despite a little voice screaming inside her head not to do it, she reached across and put her hand over his. 'Josh, you need to deal with this. I understand your fear, really I do. But it's fear of the unknown. It mightn't be what you think, and even if it is, catching it early could make all the difference.'

He grabbed her hand as though it was a lifeline, and her insides leapt. 'Holly, what if I'm dying? I'm just thirty-two years old. What if I never see my baby grow up? I really don't want to have to deal with it.'

'Listen here, Josh O'Toole,' she said, in her best teacherly voice. 'You need to face up to this, whatever it is. And much as I'd love to, I can't hold your hand through it. That's Stephanie's job.'

He raised an eyebrow. 'Would you really?'

'Really what?'

'Love to hold my hand through it?' He smiled and it was Holly's turn to blush.

'You know what I mean, Josh. But you need to get checked out and tell Stephanie what's going on. It mightn't be as bad as you think.'

'You're right. And I promise I'll do it soon.'

'How soon?'

'You're very demanding,' he said, smiling at her. 'I'll make an appointment tomorrow.'

'Right,' she said, relieved to be finished that particular conversation. 'So tell me what else has been going on in your life. Are you still in touch with Rob and Jeremy?'

The conversation turned to more normal topics and Holly was surprised at how easily they'd slipped back into their old, relaxed ways. All the awkwardness was gone and she was completely comfortable in his company. She still wanted to talk to him about their past, but now didn't seem like the right time. Part of her wanted to forget about the outside world altogether and just enjoy the moment. The moment she'd thought would never happen again. Then all of a sudden, his mobile beeped, breaking the flow of the conversation.

'Shit!' he said, scrolling through the message. 'Stephanie's home already and I promised I'd have dinner ready when she got in.'

Holly drained the last of her pint and reached for her coat. 'You'd better go then. Where will you say you've been?'

He shrugged. 'I'll tell her the truth.'

'Really?'

'Yes.' He slipped on his own coat and wrapped a grey woollen scarf around his neck. 'I'll tell her I was here asking about a job.'

Holly knew he wouldn't mention her to Stephanie. Same as she wouldn't mention him to David. But she suddenly felt guilty. Not that they'd done anything wrong, but just being there with Josh felt like she'd been disloyal to David. Josh had gone quiet and she guessed he was thinking the same thing.

'Do you want to head off first or will I?' he said, nodding his head towards the door.

'You go. David won't be home for a while yet and Stephanie is waiting.'

He nodded and stood up. 'Thanks for listening, Holly. It was good to catch up properly.'

She watched his back disappear out the door and was filled with a sense of disappointment. But she gave herself a mental shake. What had she been expecting? A kiss? A hug? Either of which would have increased her guilt tenfold. She closed her eyes for a moment to remember his face. How he'd looked at her. It had been as though time had frozen for the last thirteen years and they'd looked at each other like they used to. When they'd been in love. But there was still one thing bothering her and she wished she could stop thinking about it. Try as she might, she just couldn't remember that last kiss.

Chapter 22

Josh sat in the doctor's surgery, nervously waiting for his name to be called. He slid over to the next seat to allow a mother and toddler to sit on two chairs at the end of the row, and within seconds he was regretting it. The mother had wedged the boy on the seat between them and Josh was sure the child was on the verge of throwing up. The mother kept whispering to him that it was better out than in and Josh feared the child was going to decorate him with his insides. He didn't want to appear insensitive so he threw her a sympathetic head-tilt, while at the same time edging a little bit further away from the sick child.

He'd been waiting over half an hour and it made him wonder why they gave people appointment times at all. There were so many people coughing and spluttering, blowing their noses and sneezing, that it would be a miracle if he didn't go home sicker than he'd been when he came in. The longer he waited, the more agitated he became and he realised his hands were moist with sweat. He rubbed them on his grey jeans, leaving wet patches on his thighs which he tried to cover with a magazine. He was beginning to think it was a bad idea to have come. Maybe he should just go home and do as he'd planned and wait until after Christmas.

'Josh O'Toole?'

He almost jumped out of his skin when the doctor appeared at the door of the waiting room calling his name. Everybody looked around to see who the lucky one was and he felt the redness creeping from his neck upwards. Much as he'd love to slip out the door, it was too late. There was nothing else for it but to go in.

'Is Josh O'Toole here?' Her voice was loud, commanding, but there was no going back.

Josh stood up and walked towards her and he felt the whole room slump. If one person wasn't there, then they all moved up the list. Josh understood. He'd been thinking the same thing for the last forty minutes. He followed her down a corridor and into a room where she indicated for him to take a seat.

'So, Josh.' She scanned through information on her computer. 'I haven't seen you here since after your African trip last summer. I take it things settled down after a while?'

He nodded. 'Yes, thank God. It took a few weeks but I was fine after.' She was referring to his trip with the Irish charity the previous July. After three weeks of eating unfamiliar food, he'd come home with a dicky stomach and had been off his food for quite a while.

'So what brings you here today, then? Not the same problem, I hope?'

'No. Well, yes, in a way. It's my stomach, but it's not the same.'

'Go on.'

'I've been getting a lot of pain in my lower stomach. It's sporadic, but when it hits, sometimes it's unbearable. I hope I'm wrong, but I think I know what it could be.'

She looked over the rims of her impossibly small glasses. 'And that is?'

It came out as just a whisper. 'I think there's a chance it could be cancer.'

She breathed in sharply. 'That's a very big assumption, Josh. Why would you think you have cancer?'

'My dad. He had it – died from it. Bowel cancer. I have all the symptoms.'

She seemed unsure about what to say and he waited for the sympathy that was sure to ensue. 'So,' she said finally. 'We don't self-diagnose in this surgery so we're going to have to run a few tests.'

'I know. I wasn't saying ...' The words stuck in his throat. That wasn't exactly the reaction he'd expected.

'Look, Josh.' Her voice was softer now. 'I'm sorry about your dad. But that doesn't mean that you have it too. Let's set the wheels in motion and we'll see what we're dealing with.'

He lay down on the bed and she lifted up his top to feel around the stomach area. It was tender in places and she told him he was backed up. He had to ask her what she meant and he blushed when she told him he was constipated. She asked a number of questions while examining him and he could tell she was a woman that would leave no stone unturned.

'Right,' she said, indicating for him to sit up. 'I'll do some bloods and we'll take it from there.'

'Here? Now?'

'Yes, unless that's a problem? The sooner we get things moving the better.'

Before he could object, she had a strap around his arm and was rooting with a needle to find a vein. He'd never been very brave when it came to injections and this was no exception. He bit down hard on his bottom lip as she tried vein after vein to get a good stream of blood, and just as he thought he couldn't take the pain any more, she had success.

'There we go,' she said triumphantly. 'That's a good one. I've got a number of vials here so we'll do a thorough check on everything.

We'll give you a call next week sometime with the results and to arrange for further tests.'

'So is that it?' he said, relieved. 'I can go now?'

'Unless you'd like to stay?' She smiled and her previously stern face lit up. 'I could always take some more blood, just to be sure.'

He felt a weight had lifted because he knew he was in good hands. 'That's okay. I've probably had enough for one day. Thanks, doctor. I'll wait for your call next week.'

As he walked out the door, he thought about his encounter with Holly two days previously and felt grateful that she'd given him the push he'd needed to get himself checked out. He hopped into the car and indicated out of the parking area onto the main road. It was a quarter to five and Stephanie would be home – he needed to have that chat with her. She needed to know what was going on. She was his girlfriend. The soon-to-be mother of his child. Who knew what the future might hold, but if his life was going to be turned upside down in the next while, hers would be too.

Minutes later he parked the car in the driveway and adjusted the rear-view mirror to take a look at number forty. It had become a bit of a habit. Inside their house, Stephanie was lying on the sofa with a bowl of peanuts by her side. She was engrossed in *Les Misérables* and didn't even hear him come in.

'Jesus, you frightened the life out of me,' she said, when she finally noticed him watching her. 'When did you come in?'

He laughed at her expression. 'Just now. You were glued to the screen.'

'Sorry. You know what I'm like with this movie. I love it. Did you bring home dinner?'

'Me? I thought you were cooking.' They'd discussed it the previous night. She'd said she was going to cook them something nice since she was going to be at home all day.

'Did I say that?' she said innocently. 'Baby brain!'

'So no dinner then?' Josh tried not to sound cross.

'No, but even when I do cook, you never really like it much.'

Josh sat down heavily on the end of the sofa. 'But I've been in work all day, Stephanie. Anything would have been better than nothing.'

'Don't come over all male-chauvinist on me, Josh O'Toole. You know I'm not the Stepford Wife type.'

'That's not fair.' He was stung by the comment. 'I cook most of the time and you know it. Any time you're out on a job, I have something ready for you when you get back.'

'But you're *so* much better at it than I am.' She looked at him with her puppy eyes. She knew exactly how to wrap him around her little finger.

He sighed and stood up. 'Right, let's order something in because I'm too exhausted to cook. Pizza or Chinese?'

'Pizza, please,' she said, pressing Play on the remote and returning her attention to the movie.

He silently fumed as he headed into the kitchen, and when he saw the plates and cups piled high beside the dishwasher, he was ready to explode. Stephanie really had become lazy and it was driving him mad. He wasn't the sort of guy who expected the woman to do all the housework, but she was at home most of the time so why not chip in with the chores a bit more? He rang the order through to the pizza restaurant and popped a teabag in a cup. Just then, the sound of Stephanie's laugh reverberated through the house and Josh suddenly didn't want a cup of tea. He reached into the back of the cupboard above the sink and found what he was looking for. A lovely bottle of full-bodied red wine. He'd been mostly supporting Stephanie in her sobriety throughout the pregnancy, but not today. He poured a glass and took a sip before rolling up his sleeves to begin the clean-up of the kitchen.

'You said you had a meeting after work.' Stephanie looked at him accusingly when he told her he'd been to the doctor. 'Why would you lie?'

Josh had no appetite so he threw his half-eaten slice of pizza back into the box. 'This is what I'm trying to tell you, Steph. I haven't been feeling too good and I decided to get checked out. I just didn't want to worry you, that's all.'

She picked at the cheese on her pizza. 'But you're the one who's always going on about honesty, Josh. You're always preaching that we need to be open and honest with each other.'

Josh wondered if she'd heard what he'd said. 'I know and I'm sorry, Steph. But I had good reason, as I said before. And I'm telling you about it now.'

'So what's wrong with you, then?' she said, taking a drink of her fizzy water. 'It's probably that flu that's going around. Don't think I'll be nursing you if you end up in bed with it.'

Charming. 'No, Steph. It's not a flu.'

That seemed to get her attention and she stopped playing with the pizza and looked at him. 'So what is it?'

He wasn't sure what to say. He knew he was jumping several steps ahead by thinking he had cancer but ever since he'd got it into his head, he was convinced that it was true. And he didn't want them to have any secrets.

'Josh?' Her voice was becoming more urgent and he needed to keep her calm.

'Look, Steph. I don't want you to worry because I need to have tests and all that and the doctor couldn't confirm anything.'

'Go on,' she said, leaning forward, her eyes wide.

'Well, you know how Dad had bowel cancer?'

She nodded.

'I'm worried that I might have it too.' There. He'd said it so there was no going back.

She just looked at him for what seemed like an eternity and didn't speak a word.

'Are you okay, Steph? As I said, I won't know anything until at least next week. The doctor took bloods and she's going to send me for some tests too. I could be wrong. But I just have this feeling.'

'God, Josh, I don't know what to say.'

'I don't want you to worry, Steph. I'm young and fit and, no matter what happens, we'll get through it.'

'And will you be able to work?'

The question took him by surprise. 'What do you mean?'

'I mean if you have it. Cancer. You can still work, right? You won't have to retire or anything?'

'Of course not,' he said, puzzled at her line of questioning. Maybe she was in shock. 'If, and only *if*, I have cancer, I assume I'll need some time off for treatment.'

She nodded. 'And will you get paid for that time off?'

Was she serious? He'd just told her he might have cancer and she was worried about money? If it wasn't so sad, it would be funny.

But, thankfully, she obviously realised what she'd said. 'God, that sounded awful, didn't it? I'm sorry, Josh. Money is the last thing we should be worried about. It's just you've sprung all this on me and I don't know what to think.' Tears formed in the corners of her eyes and began to spill down her face.

Josh rushed over to her and bent down on his hunkers beside her, wrapping his arms around her. 'Oh, Steph, don't cry. We'll get through this, both of us. We can be each other's strength. And don't you worry about anything. I'll be paid if I have to take sick leave so all we'll have to worry about is getting me better.'

She nodded and he noticed how her tears had dried up already. Neither of them was really hungry so they threw the remaining pizza in the bin and headed into the sitting room to watch a movie. Josh was glad he didn't have to pretend any more. But the conversation had unsettled him. He couldn't blame Stephanie. Not really. As she said herself, she was probably in shock. But as he looked over and saw her looking relaxed and happy, laughing at some scene of the movie, he wondered if she really loved him at all.

Chapter 23

December 2001

'It's like a wonderland,' said Holly, as she and Josh walked hand and hand along Grafton Street. 'I've never seen so many lights in one place.'

Josh smiled and squeezed her hand. 'It's great, isn't it? And it's wonderful to see you smile again.'

It had been a really rough year but they were finally coming out the other end of it. Not that they'd ever forget. Holly knew she'd remember forever, but they'd found a way to move on. To be happy again. They were in Dublin city centre doing some Christmas shopping and were enjoying having the day to themselves. They both loved Christmas but there was no doubt that it would be a bittersweet one this year. They crossed the road to St Stephen's Green and found a bench where they could sit and relax.

'Let's go travelling, Josh,' said Holly, watching to see his reaction. 'Let's go and see some of the world instead of rotting away in this little country.'

He looked alarmed. 'Where did this come from, Holly? We can't just up and leave.'

'But why not? We could do something worthwhile. Maybe do one of those house-building things in Africa before heading off somewhere ourselves.'

'I've got college, Holly. And you have your job and your voluntary work at the animal shelter. We can't just walk away from all that.'

She knew he was right. 'Well, when you're finished college, can we take some time out before you start working? We're young and we'll be working for the rest of our lives. Let's go and live a little.'

'Right, you're on. As soon as I'm finished my training, we'll head off and explore the world.'

Holly couldn't wait. She needed something to look forward to. Something to wipe the memory of the last year from her mind and make some new happy memories. She just wished she didn't have to wait a few years for it to happen.

'I just want to say,' said Fintan, valiantly trying to stand up but only managing to lift his bum off the seat and lean sideways. 'Holly here is a gem. She's the best worker we've ever had at the clinic.'

'Hey,' said Milly, throwing a beermat at him. 'That's favouritism.'

Fintan plonked back down on the seat and resumed his speech from a sitting position. 'I love you too, Mills, but it's not about you tonight. It's about our Holly here and I think you'll all agree that the place won't be the same without her.'

Everyone nodded enthusiastically and he continued. 'Holly, I hope we'll see you working back behind that desk again, but for now, I want to wish you all the best for your future endeavours. We'll miss you.' He raised his glass. 'To Holly.'

'To Holly.' Everyone clinked glasses and Holly felt teary.

Today had been her last day in work and her colleagues had brought her over to O'Malley's for a few drinks. It hadn't been planned and they'd only intended to stay for one or two but it had turned into a proper session. Most of them were pretty drunk already but Holly was pacing herself because she'd been expecting David to come in. But it was getting late and there was still no sign of him.

'So how are you feeling?' said Fintan's wife, Lizzie, pushing in beside her. 'You must be sad to leave.'

Holly nodded. 'I am. I loved working there. But I won't be idle for long. Something will turn up.'

'That's the attitude.' Lizzie patted her hand. 'Somebody will snap you up – a lovely, positive, hard-working girl like you.'

'Thanks, Lizzie.' Holly beamed at the compliment. 'I hope you're right.'

'So where's this fiancé of yours then?' Lizzie said, raising her eyebrows. 'I thought he'd be here to support you.'

Holly felt her cheeks flush. 'He … he had to work late. He should be here soon, though. Actually, I'll just give him a buzz and see where he is.'

She excused herself and went out to the bathrooms where it was a bit quieter. When she'd checked there was nobody in the cubicles, she dialled David's number. It was true that he'd had to work late but he'd promised to pop in on the way home. But the phone rang and rang with no answer. She hung up and tried again. Still nothing. She sighed and headed back out to the party. It had started with just the few of them from the clinic, but as the night had gone on, they'd been joined by Fintan's wife, Lizzie, and by Greg, Milly's husband. They'd all been asking about David and she felt a little embarrassed that he hadn't turned up. She wanted him – no, she *needed* him there beside her.

'I love you, you know,' said a very drunk Milly, as Holly arrived back at the table. 'You're like a sister to me.'

Holly shoved in beside her. 'Aw, I love you too. *Mills!*'

'Stop!' giggled Milly. 'Did you hear him? Who calls me Mills? He's very drunk.'

'He's not the only one.' Holly laughed. 'Good night, isn't it?'

Milly nodded but the colour suddenly drained from her face. 'I think I'm going to –' She jumped up and pushed past Holly. 'I think

I'm going to be –' She dashed off, hand over her mouth, and Holly quickly followed.

By the time Holly got to the bathroom, Milly had been sick and was leaning her face against the cold tiles. 'I'm an idiot, Holly. I'm sorry. It was that last drink that did it.'

'Don't worry,' said Holly. 'Feeling better now?'

Milly nodded. 'Much. Come on. Let's get back out there. But I think it will be 7Up for me for the rest of the night. So what's the story with lover boy? I thought he was coming in to join us.'

Holly was quick to answer. 'He is. He just got delayed. Actually, you head on out and I'll just give him a quick buzz.'

She waited until Milly disappeared out the door and rang David again. This time he answered. 'David! Where are you? It's already half ten and you said you'd drop in after work.'

'Sorry, love. I was so late getting out and, to be honest, I just want to flake out. I'm exhausted.'

'So you're not coming in?' She was raging.

'You don't mind, do you? I mean, they're all your friends anyway. And it's late.'

She was going to protest but decided she'd leave it. There was no point in making him come in when he clearly didn't want to. She said goodbye and headed back to her friends, stopping at the bar on the way for another pint. If David wasn't coming in, she may as well get drunk like the rest of them. It had been ages since she'd really let her hair down and tonight was just the night to do it.

Holly arrived home and was still in a party mood so she decided it would be a good idea to switch on the bedroom light, wake David up and do a striptease for him, while singing the same line of 'Don't cha' again and again.

'Holly! What the hell are you doing? It's three o'clock in the morning!'

She continued singing as she peeled off her remaining clothes and shimmied right up to David's face.

'Oh, for God's sake, Holly!' said David, a look of disgust on his face. 'Go and put some underwear on at least and come to bed.'

'But don't you want to see my dance?'

'No. I. Do. Not. Look at the state of you. How could you have let yourself get so drunk?'

'You think *I'm* bad? You'd want to see the other guys.' Somehow she found that hilarious and fell onto the bed laughing. It was the last thing she remembered.

Holly felt as though her eyes were glued shut as she tried but failed to open them. She rubbed them and tried again. She could just see a trickle of daylight so she knew at least it was morning. She pushed herself up into a sitting position and winced with the pain in her head. Her stomach felt as though there was a circus happening in there and her tongue was stuck to the roof of her mouth. Basically, she felt like shit.

She lay back down on the pillow and eventually her eyes opened and she glanced at the clock on her bedside locker. Almost 1 p.m.! She couldn't believe it. She was usually an early riser and couldn't remember the last time she'd stayed in bed so late. There was no sign of David and she tried frantically to remember the events of the previous night. And then she realised she was naked and, bit by bit, it all started to come back to her. Oh God. The striptease. The singing and dancing. She cringed at the memory.

She sat up again and pushed the duvet off. Swinging her legs out of the bed, she tentatively placed her feet on the floor to test her ability to stand. But all the blood suddenly rushed from her head and she fell back down onto the bed. God, if David could see her now he'd be even more disgusted. A sudden clatter from the kitchen told her that he was downstairs so she knew she needed to get to the shower before he came up. She'd half hoped he'd gone into work for a while. He sometimes did on a Saturday and she usually moaned about it. But today she would have liked to be free to wallow in her hangover.

She tried to stand again and this time she managed it and made her way into the en suite. Letting the water sluice over her, she began to feel a little more human. A few minutes later she was back sitting on the edge of the bed with a towel wrapped around her. At least David had left a glass of water on her locker. That was something. She gulped it down gladly and, after one terrifying moment when she thought it was all going to come back up again, she began to feel her stomach settle down a little. Her clothes from the previous night were strewn across the floor and she winced again at the memory of her antics.

A smell of cooking crept into the room and made her stomach lurch so she dared not move, just in case. But as the smell filled her nostrils, she realised she was hungry and what she probably needed was a good feed of something greasy. Feeling a little better, she dropped the towel onto the floor and stepped into a fresh pair of knickers. There was a black tracksuit on the back of a chair in the corner which she'd worn once during the week – a quick sniff told her it was fine. Two minutes later she was heading downstairs, slightly worried about what David would have to say.

'Ah, there you are now,' he said, as she peeped her head into the kitchen. 'I was just leaving you to sleep until this was completely ready and then I was going to go up and get you.'

The table was set and it looked as though he was cooking for an army. 'What's all this in aid of?' she said, eyeing up the crispy bacon he was turning on the grill.

He came and put his arms around her. 'It's just an apology. I'm sorry I was so grumpy with you last night, love. You know what I'm like when I get woken up from my sleep.'

'But –' She hadn't expected that.

'I know, I know,' he continued. 'That's no excuse. But for what it's worth, I felt awful this morning for the way I spoke to you. You were entitled to go out and celebrate. Am I forgiven?'

She pulled away to look at his face and she couldn't help smiling at his raised eyebrows and silly pout. 'Of course you are, David. And I'm sorry too. I made such a fool of myself last night. That's why I don't usually drink more than two!'

'Right, well, sit yourself down.' He pulled out a chair and she noticed that he'd placed a glass of water and two paracetamol on the table in front of her. 'Now, get those tablets into you and a nice big breakfast will help soak up all the alcohol.'

She smiled but her stomach lurched again. She wasn't so sure she could handle food at the moment but she was touched he'd gone to so much trouble. Although she was an independent woman, today she was glad to have somebody look after her. The tablets went down easily enough and she prayed they'd start working on her thumping headache soon. She sat and watched for the next few minutes while David juggled pots and pans and eventually placed two enormous plates of food on the table.

'David, I'm really not sure I can eat this. Not yet.'

'Try a slice of toast first,' he said, shoving a plate with a pile of toast in front of her. 'See how that goes down.'

She did as she was told and, thankfully, it seemed to settle well in her stomach. Before long, she was tucking in to the rest of the food on her plate and she was surprised to realise she was ravenous.

'So I take it you had a good night then?' said David, buttering a slice of toast.

'David, I'm sorry. I just –'

'Holly, Holly! I'm not having a go. I'm glad you enjoyed yourself. And I'm sorry I couldn't make it.'

'I really would have liked you to be there, David.' She thought for a moment before continuing. 'It's a big thing, you know. Being made redundant from a job. I think the reality of the situation just hit me yesterday – I'm now unemployed for the first time since I left school.'

He reached a hand across the table and patted hers. 'I'm sure it feels weird but you don't have to worry about anything. Just think of it as an extended holiday.'

'But I don't really want a holiday. I'm going to spend the weekend looking online for jobs and I'm going to register with some agencies. The sooner I find something, the better.'

'What's the rush?' he said, pouring more tea for them both. 'I thought, with planning the wedding and everything, that you'd be glad of some free time.'

'We've been through this before, David. I can't not work. What would I do? Just sit around here all day looking at wedding magazines and staring at the four walls?'

'I'm sure you'd find plenty to do. And it's not as though we need the money. I earn enough for us both.'

Alarm bells began to ring in Holly's head. 'David, I don't want to live on your money. I need to be earning my own money, paying my own share of the bills and everything else.'

'But we're a couple, Holly. What's mine is yours. Surely it doesn't matter who brings in the money. We're a team. And think about it, if we were to have children over the next few years, you'd probably want to give up work anyway.'

Now she was beginning to get angry. 'Give up work? Why would I give up work?'

'Because you'd be having a baby, of course. You can't work while you're giving birth.'

'I know that, David. But I'd have maternity leave like every other woman. I wouldn't be giving up work to be a stay-at-home mother.'

'Oh.'

'Is that all you have to say? *Oh!*'

'Well, it's just that … I just thought –'

'I know what you thought.' She knew her face was getting red and she could feel the food dancing about in her stomach. 'You thought that this was your opportunity to have the perfect little housewife. You thought that now I'd lost my job I'd be happy to stay at home, cook your dinner and make the house pretty. Well, I can tell you now, I will *not* be doing that. I am not, nor will I ever be, anybody's slave.'

He glared at her, his mouth open, and he had no chance to reply before her words came tumbling out again.

'And I'm not trying to be difficult. I don't mind mucking in and doing my share in the house. I'll cook dinner if I'm here and I'll do the laundry at the weekend. But maybe we need to think again about this wedding if you're expecting me to be somebody else.'

'Holly, stop. Where has all this come from? I was just trying to reassure you, that's all. I know how you worry and I don't want you to be concerned about money.'

Holly opened her mouth to speak again but instead began to cry. 'I'm sorry, David. I don't know why I said all that. I'm just scared of not having a job. I've always been independent and I hate the thought of losing that.'

'You won't,' he said, squeezing her hand. 'I'll make sure of that.'

She didn't want to argue any more so she sent David off to read his newspapers while she cleaned up. But she couldn't get their conversation out of her head. How could he think she'd be happy not working? Didn't he know her at all? A picture of Josh came unbidden into her head then. Josh used to know her inside out – every thought she had, every hope, every dream. Until all her dreams had come crashing down around her. And it had all been his fault. He'd broken her. Why then could she not get him out of her head? Maybe a little part of her was still in love with Josh O'Toole. And if that was the case, what the hell was she going to do about it?

Chapter 24

Josh was in great form as he drove home from school. It had only been four days since his blood tests, but the doctor had rung him earlier to say most of them were back and they were fine. He knew he wasn't in the clear yet, but it was a good sign. She was sending him to a specialist who'd run some tests to see exactly what was causing the pain. He felt relieved – as well as a little foolish for making such a huge assumption about what was wrong with him.

It was just after three thirty when he parked his car in the driveway. He was about to adjust his rear-view mirror to take a look at number forty, when he stopped himself. He'd have to break that habit. It was becoming a bit of an obsession – a thing he did every day without fail – and it had to stop. Holly had her life now and he needed to concentrate on his. So for the first time in weeks, he didn't look but instead got straight out of the car, without a backward glance, and headed inside.

'Steph, are you home?' She wasn't in her usual place on the sofa in the sitting room and it was doubtful she was in the kitchen making dinner, so he headed upstairs to see if she was in the bedroom. But there was no sign of her there either. He'd been so excited at sharing his good news that he felt a little irked that she wasn't there. He took his phone out and dialled her number.

'Hi, Josh.' Her voice was animated.

'Where are you?'

'Out to lunch with Coco and Charlie. I thought I told you.'

He remembered now. He'd been tempted to say something to her about yet another lunch when he was worried sick about their finances. But he hadn't wanted to stress her out so, as usual, he'd stayed quiet.

'Josh?'

'Are you coming home soon?'

'In a couple of hours. We're almost done here and we're just heading to Farrell's for a few drinks.'

He bristled when he heard that but she must have read his mind.

'And mine will be non-alcoholic, of course, so you don't need to worry.'

'I wasn't,' he said, turning red, although nobody could see him. 'Maybe we'll go for a drink ourselves when you get home.'

'Lovely,' she said, and he could hear her friends giggling in the background. 'I'll let you know when I'm on my way.'

He hung up and sat down on the bed. He was worried. He felt they were drifting apart and he didn't know what to do about it. He felt a huge burden between his health and his financial worries whereas she was out and about socialising without him more and more often. He wished he could do something to bring back the old spark they used to have – to bring them closer together. Then suddenly it dawned on him. He checked the time and saw it was only a quarter to four. If he hopped back in the car, he could be in there in twenty minutes. He was always refusing to go out with her when she was with those pretentious friends, so now he was going to do something nice for her. He'd go into town, have a drink with them and then he could drive her home. It was perfect. Within minutes he'd freshened himself up and was on his way into the city centre, excited at the prospect of surprising Stephanie.

All the traffic was going in the opposite direction so it didn't take him long to get into town and he was lucky enough to get a parking spot on the quays, close to Caple Street Bridge. Farrell's was nearby so, a few minutes later, he rounded the corner and arrived at the door of the pub. He cupped his hands around his mouth and checked his breath before pushing the door and entering. It was surprisingly busy for an early Tuesday evening, confirming to Josh that the economy was well and truly on the way back up. He walked towards the bar, looking around, but at first he couldn't see them. Then a bellowing laugh came from the smoking area out the back and he knew it was his Steph.

He hated to think of her sitting out there, her friends all smoking and her breathing it all in. But he relaxed when he saw them. They looked like they were having such a good time, laughing their heads off at something or other. He was just about to join the party when something caught his attention and glued him to the spot.

They were passing what looked like a cigarette from one to the other. Each of them was taking a long, hard pull before passing it on to the next person. But Josh was savvy enough to know it wasn't a cigarette. It was a joint. He couldn't move as the joint came to Stephanie next and he willed with all his heart for her to shake her head and pass it on. But she didn't. She took her turn, inhaling deeply and throwing back her head to laugh afterwards. He couldn't believe it. He'd trusted her. She'd promised him she was done with all that.

Without further thought, he turned and rushed out of the pub before they could see him. Part of him had wanted to confront her there and then – but to what end? He'd embarrass her, make a fool of himself and their relationship might never recover from it all. Instead he was going to have a think about what he was going to say. Once outside, he leaned his back against the wall of the pub and tried to get things straight in his head. He remembered back to the other times she'd been out with those friends. When she'd come home acting drunk, even though she'd sworn she hadn't touched a drop of alcohol. Could it be that she was smoking joints on a regular basis? If that was the case, it couldn't be good news for the baby. He was livid.

His stomach was in knots as he headed back to the car. She was a bloody liar. He'd believed her when she'd put on her little-girl-lost voice and assured him that her drug-taking days were well behind her. How easily she'd been able to lie and how gullible he'd been. He was back on the road within minutes, and the more he thought about the situation, the angrier he was becoming. How dare she! If she'd no consideration for herself, she should at least have been thinking of their unborn child. What if the baby was born with an illness or a defect due to Stephanie's substance abuse? It didn't bear thinking about.

He drove all the way home in a bit of a trance and was surprised when he pulled the car into his own driveway sometime later. He didn't bother checking out number forty this time so he almost jumped out of his skin when he got out of the car and Holly was standing behind him.

'Hi, Josh. I saw you driving in and thought I'd come and see how things are.'

'I … yes, everything is fine.' He really didn't feel like idle chit-chat.

'I've been thinking about you since our talk last week. Have you been to the doctor yet? And have you told Stephanie?'

He glared at her. 'Look, Holly, I don't mean to be rude, but whatever is going on between myself and Stephanie is our own business. So if you don't mind, I'm pretty busy right now.'

'Oh, right. I didn't mean … I mean, I'm sorry.'

'It's fine. I'm just in a hurry, that's all.' He couldn't get his keys into the lock fast enough, and when he'd shut the door behind him, he leaned his back against it and placed both hands over his face.

His head was all over the place and it wasn't long before tears sprang to his eyes. He shouldn't have spoken to Holly like that. She was only being nice and she was obviously concerned for him. But he couldn't bear talking to her when she was so loved-up with David and his own life was in such turmoil. He didn't begrudge her happiness, but at that moment, he envied it. Only a few hours ago he'd been feeling on top of the world and now he was devastated. It brought to mind, once again, how life can change in the blink of an eye.

The front door slammed and Stephanie's voice sang from the hall. 'I'm home. Where are you, Josh?'

Josh poured himself another glass of wine and took a huge gulp.

'Ah, there you are,' she said, coming into the kitchen. 'Did you not hear me calling?'

'I did. And I was waiting for you.'

'Josh O'Toole. Are you drunk?' She giggled as she sat down at the table and shrugged off her coat, hanging it neatly on the back of her chair.

'I'm not sure. Are you?'

She looked confused. 'Am I what?'

'Are you drunk?'

'Of course I'm not. What do you think I –?'

'Or high?'

She glared at him for a moment but he could see the fear in her eyes. 'What are you talking about, Josh? I think you've had way too much to drink.'

'And I think you've smoked way too much weed to be able to make a judgement like that.'

She stood up suddenly and walked to the sink to pour a glass of water. 'Not this again, Josh. How many times do I have to tell you?' She took her water and began to storm out of the room.

But Josh wasn't having it. He stood up and shouted after her. 'I saw you, you know.'

She spun around. 'What are you talking about? Where did you see me?'

'In town. In Farrell's. Just a couple of hours ago.' He felt himself swaying and leaned against the door frame.

'How? I don't understand.' She was definitely rattled so he continued.

'I went in there. After we spoke earlier. And I saw you and your friends passing a *joint* around.' He spat the word out. 'And I saw you smoke it, so don't come the innocent with me.'

'No, I didn't!' She stood her ground in the hall and glared at him. 'I admit the others were having one but I didn't touch it.'

Josh couldn't believe she'd be so brazen as to lie to his face. 'Steph, I saw you. With my own two eyes. I watched as you smoked it and threw your head back laughing when you passed it on.'

He could see her resolve begin to falter. 'What were you doing spying on me? Is that any way to treat your girlfriend? The mother of your unborn child?'

'Don't talk to me about being the mother of my unborn child,' he said, taking a couple of steps towards her. 'If you cared about that child, you would *not be smoking dope!*'

She took a few steps back. 'Josh, stop shouting. I don't like it. You're scaring me.'

'Oh, for God's sake, Steph. You know I'd never hurt you. Stop acting like the victim here.'

'I'm not,' she said, looking wounded. 'But it was just one puff. You're acting like I'm some sort of crazed drug addict.'

'So you *did* take a puff then? I thought you said you didn't.'

She rolled her eyes. 'Stop trying to catch me out, Josh. And, yes, I did have a puff. But what harm could it do?'

'And the other times? The nights when you've come home all giggly and loud. Did you have "just one puff" those times?'

'Josh! You're making way too much of this. I've had a puff of a joint. Deal with it!'

'Deal with it? You're carrying our baby, Steph!'

'And don't I know all about it. I'm sick of hearing about the baby and about what our lives will be like when we have this little one. I'm sick of carrying it inside me, sick of getting fat and feeling ill. I'm just sick of the whole thing!'

She burst into tears and stormed up the stairs. Josh was left open-mouthed, still standing at the kitchen door. Maybe he'd been too harsh. Maybe he'd gone too far and pushed her over the edge. His anger turned to worry and he began to climb the stairs to check on her. And then something inside made him stop. This was Stephanie's game. Any time she did or said something wrong, she deflected attention from it by going off to their room crying. Josh would inevitably end up apologising and trying to cajole her out of her mood. But not this time.

He headed back downstairs and into the kitchen. He was about to pour another glass of wine when he had a change of heart. He'd sobered up by then and he needed to get out of there to clear his head. So he poured the rest of the bottle down the sink and went to grab his coat from the bannister in the hall. He'd go for a walk and hopefully the cold night air would calm him down. He looked back at the Christmas lights that he'd so lovingly placed around the house. He couldn't be bothered switching them on at the moment and they looked dark and sad, just like his mood. He zipped his coat up high around his neck to fend off the freezing cold and went outside, slamming the door behind him. A movement in the window of number forty caused him to look over, but he quickly turned away before hurrying down the street. He thought about how he'd felt talking to

Holly the previous week. He'd felt warm and comforted. Safe and happy. He'd felt like he'd come home. But now not only was his relationship with Stephanie in question, he'd probably ruined any chance of Holly ever speaking to him again. What a mess. What a bloody, bloody mess.

Chapter 25

Holly dropped the blinds when she saw Josh look in her direction. She prayed he hadn't seen her. His earlier rebuff had come as a shock to her and she didn't want him thinking she was stalking him. He'd been so horrible to her. That wasn't the Josh she knew – the kind-hearted, funny guy who would have moved heaven and earth to make her happy. In all the time she'd known him, he'd never snapped like that and it had really upset her.

She heard the shower go on upstairs and knew she'd have a few minutes before David came back down so she flopped onto the sofa and tried to make sense of everything. After she'd come back into the house earlier, she hadn't been able to stop crying. She'd felt like a total idiot. And the worst of it was, Josh had probably been right. It was none of her business. Any of it. She'd mistakenly thought that Josh had wanted her input. She'd thought he valued her opinion and he'd even seemed happy to have confided in her. But for some reason, he'd had a change of heart and didn't want her involved any more.

Although it was upsetting, maybe his rebuff was a good thing. A wake-up call for her. After spending some time with him last Wednesday, she'd begun to allow some of those old feelings to creep back in and, really, it was just a recipe for disaster. They both had their own lives now and nothing good could come from trying to recreate the past.

She realised David was finished in the shower because she could hear him pottering around in the bedroom, and all of a sudden she wanted to forget about Josh and his problems and concentrate on her own relationship. Josh had done her a favour, really, by being so mean and speaking to her so dismissively. David never would have spoken to her like that. David was a good guy. And Holly needed stability – not uncertainties.

'I needed that,' David said, walking into the sitting room wearing a fresh pair of slacks and a crisp shirt. 'Work was very stressful today.'

Holly shifted over on the sofa. 'Come and sit down and tell me about it. We don't spend enough time talking about stuff like that.'

He looked at her suspiciously but did as she asked.

'So what happened in work then?' she continued. 'Are people not paying back their loans?'

'It's a bit more complicated than that, Holly. We're dealing mostly with large companies with loans of millions of euros and …'

She nodded her head as he gave her a blow-by-blow account of how the world of banking worked. It was like a different language to her and she couldn't be less interested. But she wanted to show him she cared – that his life was important to her and that he could talk to her about anything. She tuned out as he droned on and on but she managed to keep her eyes focused on him and even threw in the odd 'I see'. She made a mental note to do some googling and find out more about the financial world. Maybe then she'd be able to impress him with her knowledge and maybe, just maybe, his stories would seem more interesting to her.

'Sounds like you've had a bad day all right,' she said, after he'd finished. 'I was just thinking, why don't we head off to the movies or something? There are a few good ones on I wouldn't mind seeing and we'd be at Blanchardstown cinema in less than ten minutes.'

'But it's only Tuesday,' he said, looking at her as though she'd suggested they take a plane to Paris. 'We don't go out on Tuesday nights.'

'Why can't we, though? There's nothing to stop us. I've made a stew so we could have that tomorrow and grab some fast food while we're there.'

'A stew, you say? That's exactly what I fancy after the day I've had: good, wholesome comfort food.'

'Well, how about we have the dinner and then head off? Come on. It would be nice for a change. You can relax once we're in there.'

He looked as if he was going to relent and then he shook his head. 'No, Holly. Sorry, but I'm not in form tonight. Maybe Friday. It's too early in the week to be out gallivanting.'

She sighed. The cinema was exactly the distraction she needed. It was only a few days since she'd finished work but already the four walls were beginning to close around her. She wasn't going to give up so easily.

'A drink then? Just one. In O'Malley's? The walk would be nice. It would help clear your head and I could do with some fresh air myself. We could be home and all in an hour.'

'Why are you so determined to get us out of the house, Holly? I'm just in from work. I know you've been here all day and you're probably bored doing nothing, but I've been run off my feet.'

She'd cleaned the house from top to bottom, done the shopping, made the dinner and he had the cheek to say she'd been doing nothing? 'Okay, okay, I get it. You're not going to budge.'

'We could bring our stew in here and watch something on Netflix?'

She felt irritated for a moment and then she looked at him scrolling through the Netflix menu and her heart softened. That was who David was. The man she'd fallen in love with. He wasn't the most exciting guy on the planet but he would never let her down.

'Why don't we have a chat about the wedding then?' she said. 'I might slip down to the shop and pick up some wedding magazines and we can have a look through them together. What do you think?'

'I think that sounds great. So you're happy with it all then? I mean, with the church and the hotel and having it in summer 2017? Because I was worried that my mother had pushed you too hard. I promised you I wouldn't let her take over and I meant it.'

She snuggled into him. 'Yes, I'm happy with it all, David. The main thing is I'm marrying you and I couldn't really care less where or when that happens.' And she really meant it. She was going to stop finding problems and start looking to the future. After all, she could still have the wedding she'd always dreamed of. Sort of. It would be minus the castle and the snow. But she couldn't have everything.

Holly doubled her scarf around her neck as the cold air bit at her ears. As she passed number three, she wondered where Josh was. She'd seen him heading out half an hour before and wondered if maybe she'd bump into him again. A bolt of excitement shot through her until she remembered how he'd spoken to her earlier, and her excitement quickly dissipated.

'Hello there, Holly, love,' came a voice from behind, making her jump. She turned and was happy to see it was Mr Fogarty with Simon.

'Hi there, Mr Fogarty. And hello there, Simon.' The dog jumped up and licked her on the face and she laughed at his enthusiasm.

'Not bad for an old guy, is he?' said Mr Fogarty. 'I only wish my own bones were as obliging.'

They fell into step together and Holly looked at the old man. 'Why, what's up with your bones? Is there something wrong?'

'My hip. That's what's wrong. Apparently I need a new one.'

'Oh God, that's awful,' said Holly, looking at him and realising for the first time that he was walking with a limp. 'When will you have to go in for the operation?'

'I don't know yet, love. I'm waiting for a call. But I'm to take it easy in the meantime. To be honest, I shouldn't even be out walking but Simon here needs his exercise.'

Holly had an idea. 'I can take Simon out for walks, Mr Fogarty. It would be no problem. I'd love it, actually.'

'Are you serious?' he said, looking at her as though she'd just told him he'd won the Lotto. 'You'd do that for me?'

'Of course I would. I love Simon. You know that. And I'm trying to get myself in shape again so the walk would do us both good.'

'But it's a lot to expect of you,' he said, shaking his head. 'You have your job and everything. I'm sure you just want to relax when you get home in the evenings.'

She noticed him rubbing his leg as he walked so she slowed down. 'You obviously haven't heard the news then?'

'What's that?'

'I've lost my job. I'm not working at the veterinary practice any more.'

'What?' he said, stopping to look at her. 'What happened? I'm due to take Simon in there next week for his kidney check-up. I can't believe you won't be there.'

'They just didn't have a need for me. I'm not qualified so all I can really do is reception work, and the vets can handle that.'

'Ah, Holly, love, that's terrible. What are you going to do now?'

She shrugged. 'I'm not sure. But I'm not going to stay idle. I've applied for loads of jobs but I'd really love to keep working with animals, if I could.'

'Well, that's settled then. If you're free to do one or two walks per day, I'll pay you for it.'

'No way. Thanks, but I'm not taking money from you. I'll walk Simon because I want to. Because we're neighbours and friends.'

'Well, it's no deal then,' he said, a defiant look on his face. 'I was going to look into dog walkers anyway. And when I went into hospital, I'd have to pay to send him to kennels. Maybe now I could leave him in the house and you could pop down to him every day to let him out and feed him. I'd pay you the same as I'd be paying the kennels.'

It sounded perfect to Holly. 'As I said, I'd be glad to walk him, and of course I'll look after him when you're in hospital. It would have to be in your own house, though.'

'Of course. I know your David isn't too keen on our furry friends.'

She was about to argue but he was right. 'So will I pop down to you tomorrow and we can arrange a schedule for walking? And you can let me know if there's anything else I can do for you while I'm at it – shopping or cleaning or anything.'

He chuckled. 'I'm not a complete invalid yet, but thanks. And yes, tomorrow would be great. But as I said, it's no deal unless you'll accept some money for it. Your time is valuable, and with you not working, you'll need every penny you can get.'

'We'll see,' she said.

He stopped to rub his hip. 'I'll let you go ahead, Holly, love. I'm going to turn back. I'll see you tomorrow then. Any time you like. I'll be there all day.'

Holly felt buoyed up as she arrived at the row of shops. Mr Fogarty had offered her exactly what she needed. She already missed the animals at the practice and being at home made her feel useless and unwanted. It was only a couple of walks a day, but being with Simon and getting herself some much-needed exercise at the same time could only be a good thing.

As she passed O'Malley's, her hand went automatically to the phone in her pocket. She remembered how she'd felt when she'd bumped into Josh that day. It was one of the best evenings she'd had in ages. At the time, she'd wondered if it had been fate. If fate had brought Josh to live on her street and if fate had made them bump right into each other. But now she knew that fate was overrated. All of that stuff was just coincidence and she needed to stop living in a fantasy world. What she needed now was to get her head into the real world and that meant organising her wedding and planning to live the rest of her life with David.

Chapter 26

Josh was in the sitting room decorating a Christmas tree he'd picked up on the way home from work. Things had been very strained between himself and Stephanie since the previous day when he'd confronted her about smoking that joint. After her initial outburst, she'd come down from the bedroom looking all sorrowful and remorseful. She'd scraped her hair back off her make-up-less face and was wearing one of his hoodies, which was down to her knees. He'd taken one look at her and his initial instinct had been to fold her into his arms and tell her everything would be all right. Until he'd remembered why they'd been arguing and decided not to give in.

She'd sat down at the table, where he'd been eating a sandwich, and had tried to explain. She'd told him how stressed she was about the baby and how sometimes she just needed something to take the edge off. That's when he'd realised that it hadn't just been a once-off, like she'd previously claimed. She'd admitted to it then. She'd said it had only been a few times and she'd blamed her friends. It was difficult being in their company, she'd said, when they were all smoking weed and she was the only one not. She'd tried to justify it by saying it was better than getting drunk every night. That she'd been trying her best. That it wasn't easy. Josh had listened and tried to be supportive, but he'd still felt angry.

'I was going to make some dinner,' said Stephanie, appearing at the sitting-room door. 'What do you fancy? I could do a chickpea curry?'

'Whatever.' He didn't look up at her.

'Or how about I make the curry but divide it up and throw a chicken breast into yours. There's loads in the freezer.'

'I'm not really hungry, to be honest,' he said, glancing up at her briefly. 'I ate a sandwich when I came home.'

'Well, we can have it later. I'll go and make a start on it.'

Josh sighed as he opened another box of baubles and began hanging them on the branches of the tree. She was definitely making an effort. He couldn't deny that. And he liked *that* Stephanie. The one that wasn't just thinking of herself. The gesture of the chicken breast was a small one but it hadn't gone unnoticed. Maybe she'd realised how selfish she'd been and was trying to make amends. He knew he'd have to get over his anger and they'd have to find a way to move forward. He wanted to be able to trust her again but she was going to have to earn that trust. He didn't want to come across as a nag or a killjoy, but she needed to take responsibility for her own actions and to stay away from any drugs until, at the very least, the baby was born.

He glanced at his watch and saw it was a quarter past five. And it was Wednesday. Exactly a week since the day he'd bumped into Holly. He felt awful for how he'd behaved towards her the previous evening. He'd been so angry that he hadn't been thinking of what he was saying or how he was speaking. When he'd thought about it afterwards and remembered the look of shock on Holly's face, he'd felt ashamed. She'd been a friend to him the previous week when he'd needed somebody to talk to. He'd confided in her and she'd offered him some brilliant advice. And then he'd gone and spoken to her like he didn't care. He really needed to do something to make it up to her.

He wrapped the last string of lights around the tree and plugged them in. It looked fantastic. The room was transformed and the twinkling of the lights made him feel a lot better. He even smiled at the noise of pots and pans clattering in the kitchen, imagining Stephanie doing her best to cook something edible. But despite all the distractions, he couldn't get Holly out of his head. She'd said that she usually finished work at six so if he went out for a walk again now, just like he had last Wednesday, maybe he'd bump into her again and he could apologise. He stepped out into the hall and grabbed his coat from the bannister. Zipping it right up, he added a scarf for extra warmth.

'Stephanie, I'm heading out for a walk. I'll see you later.'

She came to the kitchen door, a wooden spoon in her hand, sweat dripping down the side of her face. 'On your own? Why?'

'I just want to clear my head. Listen, I know we've had a bad couple of days, but maybe we'll sit down to dinner later and have a proper chat.'

Her eyes lit up. 'That would be lovely. I'll set the table for us and we can have the curry when you get home. How long will you be?'

He thought about Holly and about their chat in the pub the previous week. He thought about how he hadn't wanted to leave. He looked at Stephanie and shrugged. 'Dunno. I'll see how I feel when I'm out.'

He plugged in the outdoor lights before leaving and then stood at the garden wall to admire them. He felt his spirits lift as he headed down towards the shops on the main road. But it wasn't long before his mood changed again. Despite lingering around the street for twenty minutes and watching the front of the veterinary clinic, there was still no sign of Holly. The door of the clinic had opened once and he'd held his breath, but Holly hadn't appeared. He hung around for another ten minutes, buying a packet of mints in the newsagent's and standing against the wall at the corner, pretending to be on his phone, but still nothing. It was well after six o'clock when he realised that his mission was futile and he should just go home. He'd just have to find another way to bump into her.

He felt deflated as he rounded the corner back onto his street. But as he approached his house and looked across at number forty, he saw Holly out front on a stepladder, putting Christmas lights up over the front door. He couldn't believe his luck. He crossed the road and stood watching her for a moment. She had a string of fairy lights strung over her shoulder and was trying to get them to stay in place. She was obviously getting frustrated and hammered down a little too hard.

'Shit, shit, shit,' she said, sticking her hand under her armpit, sending the ladder wobbling precariously.

'Hey, hey, watch yourself,' yelled Josh, rushing to her assistance. He held the ladder while she climbed down.

She turned to look at him, her hand still stuck firmly under her armpit. 'What are you doing here, Josh?'

'Saving your life.' He grinned but she just stared at him.

'Thanks,' she said. 'But you can go now.'

'Don't be like that, Holly. I'm sorry, okay?'

'For what? You don't need to apologise to me for anything.'

'I think I do. I'm sorry for how I spoke to you yesterday. I know it's no excuse, but I had a lot going on. I was angry about something and I took it out on you.'

She took her hand out from under her armpit and examined her thumb. 'Apology accepted. Now, I really need to get on with this. David will be back soon and if the lights are up already, he can't object.'

'So he's not a fan of Christmas cheer?'

She glared at him. 'He's just not a fan of too many lights. He loves Christmas. We both do. And we're planning a fabulous one this year, with it being our first one as an engaged couple.'

Josh knew she was trying to hurt him and he couldn't blame her. 'Look, Hols –'

'Don't call me that.'

'But you used to love when I –'

'Josh! Stop talking about what I *used* to love or what we *used* to do. The past is gone. That girl called Hols is gone. I'm Holly. Engaged to David. In love with David. About to be married to David. And you're about to be a daddy to another woman's child!'

She was shaking and he wanted to put his arms around her but something in her eyes warned him not to. He stood uncertainly for a few moments as she breathed deeply to regain her composure. He'd obviously really hurt her the previous day because this girl was far removed from the loving one he'd had a drink with only a week before. He tried again.

'I don't know what to say except I'm sorry, Holly. I even went out to try and meet you coming from work again this evening. I wanted to apologise as soon as possible for my behaviour.'

'Well, you would have been waiting because I don't work there any more.'

'What? Why?'

'I finished last Friday. They were over-staffed.'

'God, I'm sorry. I didn't realise.'

'How would you realise?' she spat. 'You don't know me. We're nothing to each other.'

'Okay. I deserved that.' He was about to ask her more about what she was going to do but realised she wasn't in the mood for a conversation. 'I'll leave you to it, so. Good luck with the lights.'

Her face softened a little. 'Josh,' she said, as he turned to leave. 'Yes?'

'Did you tell her? And did you go and see the doctor?'

He smiled. Despite her steely exterior, she obviously cared. 'Yes,

I told her, and yes, I went to the doctor. I had some blood tests on Friday and they all came back clear.'

Her face lit up. 'That's fantastic, Josh. I'm delighted for you.'

He nodded. 'I'm going to see a specialist next week who'll run a few more tests to see what's causing the pain.'

'I was worried,' she said, her voice barely a whisper.

'I know you were,' he said, holding her gaze. 'And thanks.'

'What for?'

'For being there for me when I needed you.' He turned and headed back across the street. The conversation hadn't gone quite as he'd hoped but at least he knew now. He could see it in her eyes. She still cared about him. Really cared. And despite the fact she was angry with him, and rightly so, they still had that connection and he found himself breathing a deep sigh of relief.

Chapter 27

July 2002

'My parents are moving to Dublin,' Josh said, as they walked hand in hand through St Stephen's Green.

It was a beautiful summer's day and they'd come into Dublin to do some shopping and to meet some of Josh's college friends. This had always been Holly's fear. Ever since he'd started college in Dublin two years before and she'd stayed working at various jobs in Kildare, she feared the day would come when he'd want to move.

'When?' was all she could manage.

'By the end of the summer. Dad got transferred to a new department in Dublin city centre so they're going to rent out the house in Kildare and look at buying here in Dublin.'

'The end of the summer? But it's already July.'

'I'm not going with them, Holly. No way. I'm not leaving you. Not after everything that's happened.'

Holly's heart lifted and she stopped to look at him. 'You're not? But what will you do? Where will you stay?'

He shrugged. 'I don't know yet, but I'll figure something out. I know Dublin is only an hour away but I couldn't bear not to see you every day.'

'But it would be handier for you. To live in Dublin, I mean. With *college and everything.' She felt she had to give him the opportunity. Allow him to spread his wings, if that's what he wanted.*

'Commuting is fine,' he said, 'if it means I get to stay close to you.'

She squeezed his hand as they continued walking in silence. Nothing would ever tear them apart. They'd already been through a lot these last few years and now Josh was choosing her over his family. She lifted her face to the sun and gave thanks for such happiness.

'I think you need to talk to him,' said Milly, as they walked down O'Connell Street towards the shops on Henry Street. 'If you don't have a proper conversation about the past, about what happened, then things will never run smoothly between you.'

Holly sighed. It was the day after Josh had come over to apologise and she was doing some late-night shopping with Milly in Dublin's city centre. She'd relayed the whole conversation to her friend and Milly had listened intently to every word.

'And furthermore,' Milly went on, 'if things continue to be strained between you two, either Stephanie or David is going to notice and begin to ask questions.'

'You're right,' said Holly. 'But sometimes I think if I open my mouth about the past, about how I felt when he left me, it will be like opening the floodgates and I might not be able to stop.'

'But maybe that's what you need, Holly. Have you ever really spoken to anyone about it?'

She thought for a moment. 'Carina was the only one I really spoke to at the time, but she'd just had a baby and was all loved up so I didn't want to bother her too much. I suppose she knew I was upset but I didn't really talk about it a lot.'

They rounded the corner onto Henry Street and began the walk down to the Jervis Centre. 'You know,' said Milly, linking her arm through Holly's, 'I still wonder if fate is trying to tell you something.'

'What do you mean?'

'I mean if maybe Josh is the one you're meant to be with and not David.'

Holly shook her head. 'We both have our own lives now. That will never happen.'

'But would you want it to?'

Holly turned to look at Milly and saw the twinkle in her eye. 'You're such a shit-stirrer, Milly Martin. And I'm not going to answer that.'

'Ah! That's because you *would* like something to happen.'

'No, I wouldn't. And stop trying to put words in my mouth.'

They arrived at the Jervis Centre and were glad to get in out of the cold. 'Look, Holly. Just talk to the guy. Tell him what you told me about how you felt when he left. Tell him what you never got a chance to tell him at the time. I honestly think you're holding on to a lot of angst from the past. Maybe if you talk to him, I mean *really* talk to him – tell him everything and give him a chance to tell his side of the story – then you can put things to rest and move on with David.'

Holly nodded. 'Maybe.'

'Or maybe you two will fall madly and passionately in love again and run off into the sunset!'

'Milly!'

'Sorry, sorry. I'm just a sucker for a fairy tale.'

They spent the next hour happily shopping for Christmas gifts until their legs and their credit cards couldn't take it any more. So they found themselves a nice coffee shop and were glad to take the weight off their feet.

'I should really have ordered a salad,' said Holly, digging into her enormous cream slice. 'I'm not going to get thin by eating these.'

'You don't need to get thin, Holly. You're gorgeous. I just wish I was as tall and elegant as you.'

Nobody had ever called her elegant before and Holly beamed at the compliment. 'What am I going to do about a job, Milly? I hate not earning, especially when David brings so much into the house.'

'You're not even a week out of work,' said Milly, stirring sachet after sachet of sugar into her tea. 'Why don't you just relax until after Christmas and think about looking for something then?'

Holly shook her head. 'That's just not me. I need to be doing something. Even the few days at home this week have driven me mad.' She told her then about Mr Fogarty and his dog and Milly nodded sagely.

'You need to be working with animals, Holly. You were born for it. Why don't you try the other clinics around? There are quite a few between here and the city centre.'

'I've sent enquiries to most of them already. Some have come back to say they're fully staffed and some said they'd keep me on their books. I know the ideal job is with animals but I think I'll have to take what I can get. I'm going to go to Blanchardstown Centre over the next few days and see if there are any jobs going in the shops there. Beggars can't be choosers.'

'I really admire you, Holly. Another woman would be happy to live off her fiancé if he was offering. But not you. You're a very strong person, you know.'

'I don't feel strong at the moment, but thanks.'

'No, really. I think if Greg was earning plenty of money and suggested I stayed at home, I'd be delighted.'

'No, you wouldn't.'

Milly thought for a minute. 'Actually, you're probably right!'

They laughed and continued gossiping for the next half hour until Holly suggested they should probably head home. They'd got the bus in but had agreed to share a taxi home, since they had so many bags.

'You really love Greg, don't you?' said Holly, as they headed towards the taxi rank in O'Connell Street.

'Of course I do. That's a funny thing to say.'

'How do you know?'

Milly turned to look at her. 'How do I know what?'

'I mean,' said Holly, 'how do you know if the person you're with is the right one? How can you be sure?'

Milly smiled. 'When your heart leaps every time he walks into the room. When you can just be together, without words, and feel content. When your first thought in the morning is about him and he's your last thought before you go to sleep at night. When you feel electricity pulse through you when he brushes against you. And when you feel like nothing else in the world matters when you make love to each other.'

Holly nodded wordlessly. Everything Milly had said was exactly how she felt about Josh. How she'd always felt. David was a wonderful man but he wasn't Josh. Josh made her feel all those things so what was she going to do now? Did she continue her relationship with David and hope that, in time, her love would deepen and she'd feel all those things? Or did she let David go in the knowledge that Josh was happy with someone else and he could never, ever be hers again?

'Did you have a nice evening?' said David, as Holly arrived home laden down with bags. 'I see you've bought plenty anyway.'

'Don't worry, David. I have a good bit saved up and I went for all the bargains.'

'Holly, Holly. How many times do I have to tell you? I'm not concerned about money. We're doing okay. And you don't have to use your savings to do a bit of Christmas shopping. As I said, I can help out.'

She dropped the bags in the hall and followed him into the kitchen. She knew he meant well but she was tired of him talking about money. It was like he was secretly glad she'd lost her job so that he could go all caveman on her and be the sole earner. Next he'd be banging on his chest and demanding dinner!

'I'm just in from work myself,' he said, looking in the oven. 'Did you make dinner before you went out?'

She should have been cross but she couldn't help smiling to herself. 'No, David. I didn't make dinner. We can order in or there's plenty of stuff there for sandwiches.'

'I've been out working all day so a sandwich is hardly enough.' He opened the fridge and tutted as he scanned its contents. She pictured him in a loincloth, dragging her by the hair across the floor, and a snigger escaped her lips.

'What's so funny?' he said, turning to look at her. 'I'm starving.'

She was suddenly filled with affection for him. He was a good man. He may not have been the most exciting man in the world but he was loyal and reliable and, most importantly, he loved her very much. She'd been letting her old feelings for Josh mess with her head and make her think David wasn't enough. But God only knows where she'd be now if she hadn't met David. She owed it to him to stay loyal and stop pining after the past. But it wasn't that easy.

'You go on into the sitting room,' she said, putting her arms around him and kissing him on the lips. 'I'll order us some food and I'll bring us in a glass of wine while we're waiting.'

'Thanks, love. That would be great.'

She grabbed the menu for the local Chinese restaurant out of the drawer and ordered straight away. They always had the same things – beef in black bean sauce and chicken with cashew nuts. She'd once suggested to David that they try something new but he balked at the idea. What was the point, he'd said. What if they hated it and ended up with nothing at all to eat? No, it was better they stick to their usual. It was the safest thing to do. Holly worried that maybe she was becoming safe too. Safe in her choices and safe in her decisions. She poured two glasses of wine and brought one in to David.

'Are you not coming in, love?' he said, when she handed him the wine and turned to leave.

She paused at the door. 'I'll be in shortly. I just want to give Carina a ring. The food is ordered and should be here in twenty minutes.'

Carina always gave good advice and Holly felt she needed some of her sister's level-headedness to get her head straight. She dialled the number and prayed that she'd be free to talk.

'Hi, Holly. Great timing. I've just made myself a cup of tea and was going to sit down and watch the news.'

'Carina, I need your advice.'

'Well, hello to you too. And I'm fine. How are you?'

Holly felt bad. 'I'm sorry, Carina. I just don't have much time to talk because we've ordered food and it will be here soon. I need your help with something.'

'Right. Go on.'

She lowered her voice to a whisper. 'It's Josh. I … I don't know what to do about him.'

'What do you mean you don't know what to do?' Carina sounded alarmed.

'We've been dancing around each other since he moved in. We've chatted a bit but not once have we mentioned what happened. Why we split up. It's like the elephant in the room and I think I'll go mad if I don't speak to him about it.'

'I told you before, Holly. No good will come of dredging up the past. I think you should leave it where it belongs.'

'I was out with Milly today and she thinks I should talk to him about it.'

'Of course she does. She loves a drama.'

'Yes, but I'm beginning to think she's right. Maybe if we sit down and talk about that time – about how I felt, how he made me feel – then I can really move on with David and stop thinking about what could have been. I need to put the ghosts of the past to rest.'

There was silence on the other end of the phone.

'Carina, are you there? What do you think?'

She sighed loudly. 'You know what I think, Holly. I think you're playing a dangerous game by bringing all that up again. What is it going to achieve?'

'My peace of mind, perhaps?'

'Holly, you know I love you. And you know I only ever want the best for you. I'm telling you now that speaking to him about some-thing that happened over thirteen years ago will not end well.'

'Maybe you're right,' sighed Holly. 'And of course there's the added complication that I ...'

'That you what?'

Holly wasn't sure she should say anything but, then again, she may as well tell her the whole story. 'I love David, Carina. And I want a future with him. But I think that maybe I'm also still a little bit in love with Josh.'

'Oh, for God's sake,' said Carina, in an untypically angry voice. 'Of course you're not in love with him. Maybe you're in love with what you had in the past. Or maybe you're craving that ideal of young love. But you're not in love with Josh. You're in love with David and you'd better not go spoiling that.'

Is that what it was? Was she just in love with some ideal? With the memories and the plans they'd made when they were younger? Carina was right. They were older now and had their own lives so she needed to be careful not to do anything to jeopardise the good life she had with David.

'And besides,' Carina's voice was softer now, 'don't forget Josh has a girlfriend who, might I remind you, is going to have his baby. He won't thank you if you wade in and damage that for him in any way. Just tread carefully, Holly.'

'I hear you,' Holly said, biting back the tears. 'But I have to go now. The food has just arrived so I want to get it while it's hot. I'll give you a buzz at the weekend.'

It was a lie but she couldn't stay on the phone for one minute longer. Carina and Milly were like her two consciences – one on each shoulder. One was tempting her to do the risky thing. To take a plunge into the unknown, jeopardise her relationship for the chance of reclaiming the past. The other was telling her to play it safe. Stick with the safe bet and not risk losing everything. It was like a game of roulette. Did she go home with her safe amount of money or put it all on red or black for the chance of winning a fortune? Her head was melted.

The sound of the doorbell startled her and she realised she was still standing with the phone in her hand. The food had arrived so she was going to have to put her decision-making aside for another time. But, she wondered to herself, did she really want to have beef in black bean sauce and cashew chicken forever? Or was she going to go for something more exotic the next time and risk going hungry altogether? Only time would tell.

Chapter 28

Josh's day had gone from bad to worse. He'd slept in earlier, after a night tossing and turning and getting little sleep, and then he'd had trouble starting his car. When he'd eventually arrived at the school, he'd rushed inside only to realise his wallet was gone from his pocket. He'd retraced his steps and, luckily, found it just beside where he'd parked, but looking for it had made him even later. The day hadn't improved when his class seemed to have the Friday bug and had been giddy for the whole day. He'd had to send two of them to the principal's office and had given another six extra homework. He was exhausted now and just couldn't wait to get home.

But he had one thing to do first. He was going to stop off at the shopping centre to pick up a frame for the baby scan. The idea had come to him earlier while he'd been thinking about Stephanie and wondering why they were arguing so much lately. He thought that if he put the picture up on the mantelpiece where they could both see it every day it would remind them of what was important.

He pulled into a spot close to the door and headed inside. At the home section of Dunnes Stores, he found what he was looking for and rooted in his wallet for the scan so he could check the size. But to his dismay, there was no sign of it. He couldn't figure out why it wasn't there because he'd looked at it often enough and each time would place it carefully back in the notes part of the wallet. And then it dawned on him. When he'd dropped his wallet earlier, the scan must have fallen out too. It really wasn't his day. He decided to buy the frame anyway. Perhaps the scan would turn up, but if not, he could maybe get a copy of Stephanie's. He was home ten minutes later and happy to smell something cooking in the kitchen.

'You're home,' said Stephanie, coming out to the hall to kiss him. 'I'm making pasta. It'll be ready in about half an hour.'

He kicked off his shoes and threw his jacket on the bannister. 'Great. I'll just head up to the shower. I won't be long.'

He was dying to step under the warm jets and let the water wash away the stresses of the day. But as he began to strip, he noticed Stephanie's handbag in the corner. He knew she kept her scan in there so thought maybe he could borrow it and surprise her with it in a frame. It always fascinated him how a woman could want so much stuff in her handbag. The bag wasn't that big and yet there was a hairbrush, a make-up bag, packets of chewing gum, pens, a notebook, a pair of tights, a packet of crackers and an over-sized wallet all squashed into the little space. Apparently, there were more germs in a woman's handbag than on a toilet seat. He was about to give up when he noticed a zip pocket at the front of the bag and did a silent whoop when he found the scan in there. It was folded neatly so he opened it and smiled at the picture he'd looked at so often in the last two weeks. He quickly closed her bag and replaced it in the corner then breathed a sigh of relief as he heard her footsteps on the stairs. He grabbed his work bag, threw the scan in and took out some documents before she pushed the door open.

'Josh, are you almost ready? I didn't hear the shower go on so I was wondering what you were doing.'

'Sorry. I was just looking at a few things from work. Give me ten minutes and I'll be down.'

She looked at him for a moment and he thought he noticed her glance at the handbag in the corner. 'Right. I'll dish up in ten minutes. Do you want some wine with it?'

He shook his head. 'No, I'll just have whatever you're having.'

'You don't have to abstain because of me,' she said, raising an eyebrow. 'I'm a big girl and I can stay dry all on my own.'

'I know, Steph. But it doesn't bother me, honestly. You head on down. I won't be long.'

When he was sure he heard her back in the kitchen, he took the scan back out along with the little frame he'd just bought. He looked from one thing to the other and realised he'd hugely miscalculated the size. The frame was way too small. He'd been sure the picture wasn't much bigger than the size of his credit card but Stephanie's picture was way larger. He looked at it again, puzzled, and realised hers had writing on the side and across the top. His was just a picture and nothing else. He squinted to try to read the tiny writing, which seemed to be a lot of numbers and letters, most of which he didn't understand. The only thing he could make out was the date and the time of the scan – 27 November at 3.38 p.m. And then he noticed something. Twenty weeks and six days, it said. Almost twenty-one weeks. That couldn't be right. She wasn't even that far gone now. She'd only been eighteen weeks pregnant on the day of the scan so something was wrong there. He stared at it for a moment but he hadn't time to try and work it out because Stephanie's voice came booming up the stairs.

'Josh! Have you not got into the shower yet? Just leave it until later, will you? The dinner is on the table and it's going to get cold.'

He shoved the scan back into his bag and rubbed his face. He'd ask her about it after dinner. There had to be a simple explanation for it because, with him being away for most of July with the charity team, they were pretty sure of their dates. When he'd come home from South Africa with that awful stomach bug, he hadn't been able to make love to Stephanie until after the first week in August. Having abstained for more than six weeks, he'd been fit to burst and it had been the greatest love-making session they'd ever had. Two weeks later she'd found out she was pregnant and he'd joked that it was the build-up of sperm that was responsible for her condition.

'Josh O'Toole!'

He stood up and hurried down the stairs, the smell of cooking filling his nostrils and reminding him how hungry he actually was. 'This looks lovely, thanks,' he said, sitting down and tucking into the plate of pasta. 'You're becoming a pretty good cook.'

She laughed. 'Don't get used to it. I don't mind doing it now and again but I'm hardly Gordon Ramsay. And when the baby comes along, you'll be lucky to get a sandwich.'

'Speaking of the baby,' he said, watching her carefully, 'how are you feeling?'

'I'm fine. The nausea seems to have settled down and I'm finally getting some more energy. Hopefully the last part of the pregnancy will be easier than the first part.'

'And you're twenty weeks gone, right?'

She looked at him quizzically. 'You know I am.'

'And you're sure about the dates. You're due on 29 April, right?'

'Josh, what's this all about?'

He wasn't sure whether or not to say something. Part of him wanted time to think about why she might have lied about the dates but the other part knew the danger in letting something fester when there could be a perfectly good explanation for it. He was sick of secrets. He'd been lecturing her about talking to him rather than going behind his back so he needed to take some of his own advice.

'Josh?'

'I took the baby scan from your handbag.'

'You what?' Her face turned pale as she glared at him. 'You went snooping in my bag? Why?'

'I was trying to do something nice. I bought a frame and I was going to frame the scan. I thought it might remind you, remind us, about what's important.'

'But what about your own scan? Why did you have to go and take mine?'

'I lost mine. But never mind that. I saw the date, Steph. It would mean that you're almost twenty-three weeks pregnant now and not twenty.'

She stood up suddenly and went to the sink to pour herself a glass of water. He watched as she downed a full glass, gripping on to the edge of the counter as she did so. A chill ran down his spine and he wondered what she was going to tell him. Something didn't feel right and he had the sudden feeling that his world was going to be turned upside down. She turned around then but instead of being angry or teary, as he'd expected her to be, she had a smile on her face.

'Sorry, I was parched. And what are you like, questioning the dates like that?' She sat back down. 'They asked me about my dates at the scan and I got myself mixed up. They already had them typed in when I realised I'd said the wrong dates.'

It sounded reasonable enough but Josh was still unsure. 'But wouldn't they check? Wouldn't they have told you that the dates didn't tally with what they were seeing?'

'They did say that but they'd already input the data and had printed the scan. It's no big deal. We know our dates so that's all that matters. It's only a few numbers on a picture. The hospital will have all the proper information on my chart.'

'But what about mine?' Josh said, holding her gaze.

'Your what?'

'My scan. How come the dates were cut off mine?'

'I honestly don't know. I asked them for a second copy of the scan so they must have just printed it that way.'

He was about to question her further but decided against it. She had all the answers but he wasn't sure whether or not he believed her. So he just continued eating his pasta, changing the subject to chat about the tough day he'd had in school. He noticed that she looked relieved, which made him all the more suspicious. Suddenly he didn't want to be there with her. He wanted time with his own thoughts.

'That was lovely, thanks, Steph. I'll clear up later but I want to go and check on some of the lights outside. I noticed earlier that some of the bulbs weren't working.'

'Don't worry. I'll clear up. You go on out and sort it and we can have a cup of tea in the sitting room after.'

Outside, he leaned against the garden wall, looking up at the house. The lights usually lifted his spirits but not tonight. A few minutes later he was jolted out of his reverie by a cold, wet feeling on his left hand.

'Simon! You gave me a fright. Oh, hello, Holly. Why have you got Simon?'

'Sorry, he dragged me over as soon as he saw you. He might be an old boy but he still has some strength. And Mr Fogarty has a bad hip so I'm just doing him a favour.'

'Good on you. He's a nice man. I hope he'll be okay.'

'He should be fine after his operation. Well, I won't keep you. Come on, Simon.'

'Wait!' The word was out of his mouth before he thought about it. She looked at him questioningly.

'I … I just …' He looked at his front window to make sure Stephanie wasn't looking out. 'Can we talk? I mean, like, in the pub. A proper chat. Sometime.'

She looked taken aback. 'Josh, I don't know. Is there something wrong?'

'No! Well, I don't know. Maybe.'

'Not your results? Please tell me you didn't get bad news?'

He shook his head. 'No, nothing like that. I … I'd just like to chat.'

'But why?'

He kicked his heel against the wall and thought carefully before he spoke. When he did, it came out in a whisper. 'Because my life seems to be spinning out of control. Because I think you understand me and you're a good listener.'

She went to say something but he put his hand up to stop her while he continued.

'And because, Holly, I can't stop thinking about you and it's eating me up inside. We need to talk. Properly talk. And not just about my problems. We need to talk about us. Seeing you again has stirred up a lot of old feelings, and if I don't talk to you about them, I'll explode. The truth is you've never been far from my mind and our break-up has haunted me for the last thirteen years.'

Chapter 29

Holly rang Mr Fogarty's doorbell and tried to resist glancing across at Josh's house. She hadn't been able to stop thinking about what he'd said the previous day and she was exhausted from lying awake all night.

'Come in, come in,' said Mr Fogarty, opening the door wide for her. 'We've been expecting you.'

'Thanks. I won't stay long. I'm sure you're busy getting organised. Oh, hello, Simon.' The big old dog launched himself down the hall and jumped up on Holly, his two front paws reaching across her shoulders.

'Simon! Get down.' He didn't listen to a word his owner said but instead continued licking Holly's face.

'He's fine, Mr Fogarty. It's the best welcome I've had in ages.' She gave him a scratch behind his ears and gently lowered him back onto the floor. 'Now, will we go through the instructions for Simon's care?'

'Come on into the kitchen,' he said. 'I've a pot of coffee on and biscuits just out of the oven.'

He'd baked biscuits for her? Holly wasn't sure she liked the sound of that. She'd hate to be rude but she wasn't sure if she could force herself to eat something he'd made. In her experience, old people who lived on their own generally had cupboards full of overflowing, out-of-date food and their kitchens were shabby and musty. She followed him in anyway, ready to make her excuses.

'Right, sit yourself down at the table and I'll bring the refreshments over.'

Holly's eyes almost popped out of her head. The kitchen was ultra-modern with high-sheen cupboards and stainless-steel appliances. There was a cream granite counter top and cream marble tiles on the floor. The back of the house had floor-to-ceiling glass which allowed the sun to fill the room. But the thing that struck her the most was the cleanliness. It was the cleanest kitchen she'd ever seen – far cleaner than hers had ever been.

'Bet you thought I'd have an old man's kitchen.' He chuckled, bringing cups over to the table. 'I always enjoy seeing people's faces when they come into my house. I used to be a chef back in the day and still love to cook. So my kitchen is my pride and joy.'

'I'm sorry … I didn't …' Holly flushed. 'It's gorgeous. And *so* clean.'

'You can blame my OCD for that. I'm a bit of a cleaning freak. Can't stand dirt. Never could. Now don't get me started on labels all facing the right way!'

The cliché of never judging a book by its cover never seemed more appropriate. She gladly tucked in to the delicious cookies and sipped her coffee as Mr Fogarty ran through Simon's routine. He was going into hospital later that morning and she was going to look after the dog while he was away. It would be good for her. A distraction. Because after Josh's revelation the previous day, she hadn't been able to think of anything else.

'So, any luck on the job front?' he said, after they'd discussed Simon's routine.

'Nothing,' she said, nibbling on another biscuit. 'It's probably too close to Christmas to find anything now.'

His eyes twinkled. 'Maybe not.'

'Sorry?'

He stood up and pulled a piece of paper out of a drawer before sitting back down. 'Now, I have a list of people here who need help with their pets. They can pay you for walking their dogs, bathing them and other stuff. It might not be much to start with, but it will keep you busy for the moment.'

Holly stared at the list. 'I … I don't know what to say. I mean, how …?'

'Look at the names, Holly. You know most of them. People you've helped over the years. Most of them go to the club on Fridays and some of us got talking last week. They heard you'd lost your job and they wanted to help.'

'That's unbelievable. Thank you so much.' Holly could feel tears threatening to fall. 'I mean, I won't charge them, of course. It will just keep me –'

'Well, you can stop right there. You *will* charge them and they won't take no for an answer. You were born to work with animals, Holly. You have a gift. And now you have time, so make the calls and work out a schedule. I bet you'll be busier than you've ever been in your life. It could be the start of a whole new business for you.'

'Do you think so?' She could barely contain her excitement. 'I'm not sure I'd have the confidence or the ability to start up a business. But I do love the sound of it.'

'Stop putting yourself down, Holly. You're fantastic. Smart and kind and a great communicator. All the ingredients you need.'

She blushed again. 'I'm good with animals, I know, but maybe not so good with humans.'

'Are you kidding me? What about Mrs Jackson? Didn't you help her out recently?'

'Well, yes, but it was for her dog, Kylie. She needed a prescription and I filled it for her.'

'But didn't you make her tea while you were there and sit with her for an hour reassuring her that Kylie wasn't going to die in childbirth?'

Holly nodded. 'She was in a state worrying about the dog.'

'She told me you were the kindest girl she'd ever met. And what about Mrs Delaney and her dog, Tara?'

'Yes,' said Holly, remembering the beautiful white dog covered in oil. 'I bathed the dog for her. She was in a right state.'

'So I heard. But she also told me that you made dinner for her before you left and just listened to her. She said that nobody ever just listened. You made her feel like she was really someone. Do you know what that makes you?'

She shook her head but he didn't wait for an answer. 'It makes you a really decent young lady who deserves a chance. And that's what they're giving you. Mrs Jackson, Mrs Delaney and all the others. A chance to do what you love and turn it into a career.'

Holly didn't trust herself to speak. She felt overwhelmed. She always enjoyed dropping in on the old folk in the area to help them with their pets but she never thought about the impact her visits had on them. And now she was being given this opportunity. She couldn't wait to start working it all out. Life had thrown a lot of surprises at her over the years but this was one of the better ones.

Holly stood at the window gazing out but she wasn't seeing anything. Her mind was so full of stuff that her head hurt. She was thinking about Mr Fogarty's kind gesture. She still couldn't believe he'd done that for her. But she was also thinking about Josh and what he'd said. He'd practically said he'd thought about her for the last thirteen years. She'd always assumed that he'd moved on easily and hadn't given her a second thought, and that's what had hurt most over the years. But now he was telling her something completely different and it didn't make sense. He was the one to let *her* down. He was the one to finish the relationship. So why then did he want to talk about it? She'd been so shocked when he'd said those words that she'd just nodded and agreed to meet up soon.

'Simon! No!' She looked away from the window just in time to see Simon crouching down on her sitting-room floor and dropping a stinking mess onto the polished floorboards. 'Come on, get outside. Naughty dog!'

She ushered him out to the back garden and closed the door firmly. He looked at her through the glass pane, his head tilted to the side. He seemed to be saying, '*What? What did I do?*' Part of her wanted to laugh but she knew David would be home soon and wouldn't appreciate it if he knew she'd been harbouring a dog there. She'd gone back down to check on Simon soon after Mr Fogarty had left for hospital and hadn't been able to resist taking him home with her. Just for an hour, she'd told herself. Just to keep her company.

She held her breath as she picked up the offending brown mess with a poo bag and sprayed some anti-bacterial spray to try and disguise the smell. She double bagged it and put it into the outside bin. Simon wagged his tail as she did so, thinking it was all a great game. Mr Fogarty had said that he was fully house-trained but Holly had her doubts. Although maybe he was misbehaving because she'd taken him out of his own house. That hadn't been the agreement but when she'd fed him earlier and had been about to leave, he'd looked at her with those big brown eyes and she just hadn't been able to go without him.

She let him back into the house, warning him that there were to be no repeat performances. He wagged his tail and ran around in circles, clueless about what she was actually saying to him. She went back to the window and looked across at number three. Josh's car was there and she pictured them having a lazy morning in bed. She, on the other hand, was usually abandoned by David on Saturdays so that he could go to the office and catch up on paperwork while it was quiet.

When she turned around again, Simon had disappeared out of the room so she went to find out what he was up to. But a sound from upstairs alerted her to the fact that he must be in her bedroom so, with her heart in her mouth, she dashed up to check what damage was being done. She could have cried when she saw him. He was sitting on the bed, her make-up bag in front of him, and he'd already chewed through her best MAC lipstick. It had been a birthday present from Milly and she always kept it for special occasions.

'Simon! Get down. Wait until your daddy hears what you've been up to. There'll be no treats for a month!'

He skulked off the bed and galloped down the stairs. She groaned at the sight of the mess and it made her think that maybe David had been right all along about dogs being more trouble than they were worth. She gathered up the broken bits and put what was left of the make-up back into the bag. There were a few marks on the duvet but it was patterned so David would hardly notice. She'd had enough of Simon by then so she decided to bring him back to his own house. Clearly being in *her* house didn't agree with him. She hurried back down the stairs but almost broke her neck slipping on a pool of water on the floor at the bottom.

'Simon!'

It was a relief to walk out of Mr Fogarty's house ten minutes later, with Simon safely ensconced in his own bed. She was exhausted and was looking forward to a peaceful couple of hours before David got home. Just then she noticed Josh coming out of his house and hopping into his car. He didn't seem to have seen her so she hovered for a moment until he reversed out of the driveway. He spotted her then and pulled the car to the kerb beside her and rolled down the window.

'Hi, Holly. How are you?'

'I'm good, thanks.' The awkwardness had come back now that she knew what he was thinking. And he knew that she knew what he was thinking. Thank God he didn't know what *she* was thinking or the awkwardness would be catastrophic.

'Did you think about what I said about meeting up? Maybe on Monday when I'm home from work? O'Malley's? Just to talk. You know. To clear the air.'

She nodded. 'Okay. What time?'

'Say around five? Is that okay?'

'Yes, that's fine.' They held each other's gaze for a moment and she felt he was looking right into her soul. With those beautiful blue eyes. Those eyes that she'd loved for so long. She looked away then suddenly, as though her thoughts were written all over her face. 'So are you going anywhere nice?'

'To my mother's,' he said, leaning his elbow on the edge of the open window. 'I'm going to spend the day with her. I'm bringing her shopping and then to see her friend in a nursing home.'

'That's good of you. Is Stephanie not going with you?'

He shook his head. 'She said she's not feeling well today so she's staying in bed. I offered to stay with her but she told me to go. She's going to catch up on some sleep.'

'Well, I hope she feels better soon. I'd better head off but I'll see you on Monday.'

He nodded and winked. The dimple on his left cheek jumped in and out and his eyes crinkled up as he smiled. Holly actually took a sharp breath as she remembered Josh as a teenager. She'd always teased him about his dimple. She'd even had a name for it. Charlie, she'd called it. 'Where's Charlie today?' she used to say to him when he was in a bad mood. He'd never been able to resist smiling at that and Charlie would appear. She had tears in her eyes as he drove off and she wondered where it was all going to end.

Back in the house, a gust of wind reminded her she'd left the sitting-room window open so she went to close it. As she did, she noticed the door of number three opening and out came Stephanie. She was immaculately dressed in a purple wool dress that came to just above her knees and showed off her baby bump beautifully. She had on a short black leather jacket and black knee-high boots, and her lovely blonde hair was brushed over to one side, accentuating her model-like face. She certainly didn't look sick, like Josh had suggested, and Holly wondered what was going on.

And that's when Holly's impulsiveness took over. Without a second thought, she grabbed her jacket from the hall and was out on the street in less than a minute. She was just in time to see Stephanie disappearing around the corner. She followed at a distance until Stephanie hopped on a bus and, without thinking it through, Holly joined the queue and hopped on too. She realised that she was acting like a stalker but her curiosity had gotten the better of her. She was thankful for the coins she kept in her pocket so she threw a couple of euros into the slot and moved down the bus. There was no sign of Stephanie so she'd obviously gone upstairs and Holly breathed a sigh of relief. It would be easy now to watch from the back of the bus, and when Stephanie came downstairs, she could get off after her.

She felt both excited and ridiculous. She couldn't believe she was stalking her ex-boyfriend's pregnant girlfriend. Wait until she told Milly about this. She'd be thrilled by the whole thing. Carina, on the other hand, would be disgusted. But she might not tell her about it. The bus was heading into town and it wasn't long before it was sailing up the bus lane on the quays. At the Ha'penny Bridge there seemed to be a mass exodus, and Holly strained her neck to see if Stephanie was among them. Sure enough she came down the stairs and got off the bus. Holly quickly stepped off too and made sure she kept her distance while keeping Stephanie firmly in her sights. She followed her further up the quays towards O'Connell Bridge, until

Stephanie stopped outside a little coffee shop, just before the bridge. Holly held back, pretending to look at something on her phone but keeping an eye on Stephanie, who looked as though she was waiting for somebody.

And then Holly spotted him. The man who Stephanie had claimed was just looking for directions a couple of weeks before. Walking towards her from O'Connell Bridge. His face lit up when he spotted Stephanie. Stephanie, on the other hand, didn't look pleased. He arrived beside her and went to kiss her on the lips but she turned her cheek so he got that instead. Holly couldn't hear what was being said but Stephanie clearly wasn't happy. The man then took her arm and led her inside the coffee shop and Holly stood for a moment wondering what to do. But she'd had enough. What had she been thinking, following Stephanie like that? What Stephanie did with her life was none of Holly's business, and yet she had a morbid fascination with the woman. She turned to cross the road to get her bus back home. She'd need to think about all this. About whether or not to say something to Josh. She sighed as a myriad thoughts went around and around in her head. How on earth had her very simple life become so bloody complicated?

Chapter 30

Josh opened his eyes as a stream of sunlight peeped through the gap in the curtains. He could tell without looking that it was frosty outside because, despite the sun, it was freezing cold. He turned around, expecting to see Stephanie curled up and fast asleep as she usually was, but there was no sign of her. He couldn't remember the last time she'd been up before him in the morning. Picking up his phone from the locker, he saw it was only half past ten. Stephanie would never be up at this time, especially on a Sunday morning, so he wondered what was up.

He felt exhausted but curiosity got the better of him so he swung his legs out of the bed and pulled himself up. Throwing on a pair of tracksuit bottoms and a warm hoodie, he crept downstairs. Halfway down, the smell of cooking hit his nostrils and his stomach danced for joy. It smelled like one of his mother's breakfasts. There was definitely bacon and maybe even sausages. Although, unless Stephanie had been replaced with a meat-eating version of herself, he doubted very much if he could believe his nose.

When he walked into the kitchen, he could barely believe his eyes. Stephanie was rushing around with pots and pans, and it looked as though she was feeding the masses. Her hair was pinned up on top of her head and her sleeves were rolled up. She didn't even notice him standing there and he smiled at the look of determination on her face.

'What's going on here, then?' he said, making her jump.

'Josh! I thought you were still asleep. I was going to call you in ten minutes when this was all ready.'

He walked over beside her to see what she was cooking. 'It looks and smells delicious. But what's it all in aid of?'

She wiped her hands on a tea-towel and turned to face him. 'Us. It's in aid of us. Now just give me ten more minutes and I'll give you a shout when I've finished.'

'Are you sure I can't help?' He looked at the chaos of the many different things she was juggling, between the cooker top, the grill and the oven, and he wondered if she'd ever manage to get it all together.

'I'm fine, thanks.' She ushered him out of the kitchen. 'Just go and read the paper or something.'

'Maybe I'll slip down to the shop and get the papers, so.'

'You don't have to.' She pointed at a stack of newspapers on the hall table. 'I picked them up this morning when I went to the shops for the breakfast stuff. I wasn't sure which ones you'd want so I got a load of them.'

He couldn't believe it. Stephanie had never once made breakfast for them, nor had she ever bought him a newspaper. She was either very sorry for her behaviour of late and was trying to make up for it or she was feeling guilty about something. He'd prefer to think it was the former, but his gut was telling him it was the latter.

However, he brought the papers gladly into the sitting room, plonked himself down on the sofa and took the first one from the pile. He tried to focus on the main story but it was no good. Thoughts of Holly were whirring around and around in his head and he just couldn't concentrate.

'Come on, Josh. Breakfast is ready!'

He sighed and headed back into the kitchen where the table was set with a myriad of dishes. There were sausages, proper pork ones – not those cardboard veggie ones that Stephanie kept trying to push on him. There were thick slices of bacon, black and white pudding, eggs, mushrooms and tomatoes. There was toast and brown bread. Josh shook his head in disbelief as he sat down.

'I can't believe you made all this, Steph. It looks delicious.'

'Well, tuck in. I know how you love your meat.'

He looked at her suspiciously. 'But what's brought this on? You never cook meat.'

She spooned some mushrooms onto her plate and buttered a slice of toast. 'Josh, I just want things to be right between us. I've been a fool. A total idiot. When you were gone yesterday, I had time to think. I realised how selfish I'd been, how inconsiderate, and it stops right here, right now.'

'I don't know what to say, Steph. I mean, a lot has happened these last few weeks. And of course I want us to get back on track again, but you need to be honest with me. And I mean completely honest.'

She nodded. 'I promise, Josh. What we have is too good to throw away over silly stuff.'

'Steph, some of our arguments lately haven't been just silly or trivial. I'd say they were quite serious.'

'I didn't mean that. I just meant that it would be silly to throw everything we have away.'

He reached over then and took her hand. 'I've no intention of throwing it away, Steph. I love you and I love our baby. I want us to be happy, but at the moment, there are trust issues and it can't go on like that.'

She held on to his hand as though her life depended on it. 'Just tell me what to do and I'll do it. I'm telling you here and now, I'll do whatever I need to do to get you to trust me again.'

'Okay. I don't want to keep going on about it, but the smoking dope thing: I want us to go to the doctor and tell her about it. I want to know if it could affect the baby. So you need to be honest about how much you've smoked and how often.'

'Fine. We can go to the doctor and I'll talk to her about it. But I've told you already that it was just a few times. And that's the truth.'

Josh nodded. 'And the scan?'

'What about the scan?'

'Is there anything you're not telling me? Because it just seems strange that the hospital would hand out a scan with the wrong dates.'

'That's exactly what happened, Josh. And I have an idea. Why don't I make an appointment for another scan? Whenever they can fit us in. And this time we can both go in. Would that put your mind at ease?'

'Well, yes, I suppose it would.'

'Great. I'll ring first thing in the morning. Now, tuck in to your breakfast. I don't want it wasted after all my effort.'

Josh felt a wave of affection for his beautiful girlfriend. She was young and made mistakes. It wasn't as though he didn't make any himself. He'd probably been a bit hard on her and she was trying her best to get things back to normal. They'd had a few rocky weeks but maybe that's what would make them stronger. He suddenly felt ravenous and tucked into his plate of food with gusto. Now he just needed to figure out whether or not he should still go ahead with meeting Holly tomorrow.

Josh felt relaxed and happy as he sat on the end of the sofa, Stephanie on the other end, her feet on his lap. He was giving her a foot massage as they watched a movie, and he was finding it almost as relaxing as she was. They used to often have lazy Sunday afternoons like that, but not recently. It felt good to be getting back to normal, getting back to the happy, contented couple they used to be.

The loud shrill of Stephanie's phone startled them both and Josh reached down to the floor, where she'd left it, to hand it to her. But, like a light, she bent down herself and grabbed it, standing up as she answered the call.

'Hello. Yes. I know. Hold on a sec.' She mouthed to Josh that it was her friend Coco, so she headed into the kitchen to take the call.

Josh paused the movie but, if he knew Stephanie, it would be at least an hour before they'd get back to it. He was amazed to hear his stomach rumble, considering the amount of food he'd eaten earlier, but he fancied something sweet so decided he'd make a cup of tea and root around for a biscuit while he was waiting for Stephanie to get off the phone. He stood up and headed towards the kitchen.

Stephanie was talking in a whisper but he could tell she was agitated so he paused at the kitchen door. He couldn't hear what she was saying but he wondered why she was talking in such hushed tones. He pushed the door slightly so that he could listen.

'You need to stop calling.' Her voice was firm. 'I'm serious. It's not fair on me and it's not fair on him. Just stop it!'

'Steph?' he said, stepping into the kitchen. 'Is everything okay?'

She looked up at him and covered the mouthpiece. 'It's fine. I was just finishing up actually.'

He watched as she spoke again into the phone, all traces of her agitated voice gone. 'I'd better go. Something's come up. I'll talk to you soon.'

'Why does she need to stop calling?' said Josh, still looking at her.

'Who?' She looked anxious. Pale.

'Coco. I heard you tell her that she needed to stop calling. Why?'

Stephanie sat down on a kitchen chair and put her head in her hands. He had a feeling she was going to tell him something he wouldn't like. Something bad. He held his breath until she finally looked at him.

'Well?' he said again. 'What's going on?'

'They … she wanted me to go out again tonight. To a party. She's been asking me for the last few days and I've been telling her I can't.'

'Is that all?' Josh felt relief flood through him.

'Yes. Well, you can guess what these parties are like. There'll be plenty of alcohol and smoke and I knew you wouldn't want me to be around all that.'

'Steph, I don't mind you going out enjoying yourself. I just don't want you partying too hard.'

'I know. And that's why I've been saying no to Coco. I'm not sure that crowd are good for me. They party way too hard and it's difficult to resist temptation when I'm with them.'

'Well, I don't want you giving up your friends on my account, but if I'm honest, I'm glad you're not going to the party.'

'Good,' she said, standing up. 'Now, let's go and watch the end of that movie.'

They went back into the sitting room and resumed their previous positions. But Josh couldn't concentrate on the movie. He was thinking about Holly. He was going to meet her as planned the next day but he now knew what he had to do. Stephanie was making great efforts to get their relationship back on track so he needed to do the same. He needed to stop dreaming of what could have been. But first he had to exorcise the demons of his past.

Chapter 31

20 August 2002

Something wasn't right. Josh had cancelled their date for the second day running and it just wasn't like him. Holly sat on her bed looking out the window, fear coursing through her. He'd rung her yesterday to say he wouldn't make it to the cinema and this evening it was just a text to say he couldn't see her. She'd tried ringing him back but it had just gone straight to voicemail. His parents had moved to Dublin a few weeks earlier but he'd stayed in Kildare, sleeping in the spare room of his friend's mother's house. Holly knew the set-up wasn't ideal and he hated feeling like a guest but he'd insisted he was happy once he was close to her. But in all the time she'd known him, he'd never been cold towards her. If he ever had to cancel something, he'd do it apologetically, promising to make it up to her another time. Holly was blessed with a sixth sense. Her mother always said it. She just knew when things were going to happen. And something was telling her that her life was going to change dramatically. But not in a good way.

The sound of the doorbell made her jump. Her mam and dad had gone out so she dashed down the stairs, praying it would be Josh. And it was. But when she saw the look on his face, she crumbled.

'Josh, what is it? What's wrong?'

'Can we go in and sit down?' he said, his hair dishevelled, his eyes red and sad. 'We need to talk.'

Holly sang to herself as she stepped out of the shower. She was going to meet Milly for lunch and she was really looking forward to hearing all the gossip from the surgery. She missed working there. She missed the staff and the customers, and especially the animals that she'd grown to love. But she was excited about her possible new venture and couldn't wait to tell Milly all about it.

She dried herself quickly and pulled on a pair of blue jeans. She was pleasantly surprised that they slipped easily up her legs when, just a few weeks before, she'd struggled to put them on. She teamed them with a long-sleeved grey T-shirt and took the bobbin out of her hair to let it fall down over her shoulders. She didn't bother with make-up, except for a smack of pink lip gloss, then she headed downstairs to where she'd left her boots.

She just needed to let Simon out before heading off so she locked up and went down to number forty-four. He was sleeping on his bed when she let herself in. As good as gold and not a sign of a mess. He must have been protesting about being taken out of his house when he ran riot in hers on Saturday, because at home he was practically an angel. His tail wagged furiously when he saw her and he ran to give her a good lick. It reminded her of how loyal animals were. How caring and loving. And it made her sad to think that David would never let her have a dog of her own. She let Simon out the back, where he obligingly tended to his business, before giving him a treat and sending him back to bed.

She was meeting Milly in O'Malley's and was looking forward to a nice carvery lunch. The food there was gorgeous since they'd changed chefs earlier in the year and it was always busy at lunchtime. As she walked out of the estate and down the main road, she thought about what the day might bring. She'd be making two visits to O'Malley's today because she was due to meet Josh there later also.

Milly was already in the queue for food when Holly walked in so she went over to join her.

'Great timing,' she said, hugging Holly and pointing to the line behind them. 'If you were any later, I'd have had to get my own and you'd be queueing for ages.'

'It's good to see you, Milly. I'm dying to hear all the gossip.'

'Well, from what you've been telling me, I think *you're* the one with all the gossip. Now let's get this food and get back to a table so you can tell me all.'

Ten minutes later, they were sitting on barstools at a high table at the back of the pub, tucking into lasagne and chips and laughing at Milly's stories.

'Oh God, I can't tell you how much I've missed this,' said Holly, wiping tears from her eyes. Milly had just told her about how Mrs Duggan's cat, Fifi, had scared the life out of Gerry O'Brien's Great Dane. Fifi was barely the size of the dog's head and yet she'd hissed and spat so much that the poor dog had cowered behind his owner's chair for twenty minutes.

'Right,' said Milly, shoving her plate away and gulping down some water. 'I have forty minutes left before I have to be back to work, so I want to hear everything!'

Holly sighed. 'Where do I even begin? There's so much to tell you.'

'Well, first tell me about this business idea. Then you can get onto the juicy stuff!'

Holly laughed at that before telling her about Mr Fogarty and what he'd done for her. She told her about his idea that she could start small by walking dogs and dog-sitting while owners were out. And then maybe she could expand the business to something bigger, like grooming or even opening a kennels. Milly was delighted.

'You were born to work with animals,' she said. 'And since your business would be local, we could refer people from the surgery to you. Honestly, Holly, I think it's a great idea. What did David have to say about it all?'

'He thinks it's a great idea too.' That wasn't strictly true. He'd said it was a nice idea. For a *hobby*! She'd argued that it could be a great money-earner and she could turn it into a big business but he'd waved a dismissive hand. 'Too much work for too little money,' he'd said. 'It just wouldn't make financial sense.' What he really meant was it wasn't a safe, pensionable job so it wasn't worth looking into. She hadn't spoken to him any more about it but she certainly wasn't giving up. She'd sacrificed too many of her dreams already.

'So come on then,' said Milly, breaking into her thoughts. 'Tell me about the gorgeous Josh.'

'Milly!'

'Well, he is, isn't he? That's what you said.'

'I'm meeting him later.'

'Ooh, now this is the gossip I've been waiting for. Where? How? What for?'

'Don't get too excited, Milly. We're just going to talk. I met him the other day and he said he wanted to speak to me. About the past and what happened. About us.'

Milly nodded sagely. 'He wants to get back with you, Holly. I bet he does.'

'No, he doesn't,' said Holly, shaking her head. 'He has Stephanie so he's not going to abandon her for *me*.'

'And if he *did* want to?'

'But he doesn't.'

Milly persisted. 'But let's say he did. Let's say he's going to declare his love for you tonight. Let's say he's realised he doesn't want to be with Stephanie and he wants to be with you.'

Holly sighed. 'I'd certainly give it some thought.'

'Would you really? And what about David?'

'David is fabulous. And I love him. I really do.'

'But?'

'But ever since Josh came back into my life, I'm comparing the two of them. I don't think I'll ever be able to replace the love I had for Josh. It was special. Really special.'

'You still never told me what happened in the end between you two,' said Milly, sitting forward and leaning her elbows on the table. 'I mean, I know you said he broke your heart, but was it sudden? Unexpected?'

'It's a long story.'

'Tell me. Please. I really want to know. I want to understand this bond you seem to have with him. It's been such a long time, but you're obviously still in love with him.'

Holly nodded. 'I suppose I am. Well, you know that we were friends since preschool. We lived around the corner from each other and we just clicked from day one. We were so close that nobody else really got a look in. We had other friends, of course, but we just loved each other's company so most of the time it was just the two of us. We had our first kiss when we were thirteen. And it grew from there. That's when we stopped being just friends who loved each other – we became two people in love.'

'That's so sweet,' said Milly, tears in her eyes. 'Such young love.'

'Anyway,' continued Holly, 'the years went by and we grew closer. We just took for granted we'd always be together. We'd even planned the wedding we'd have some day.'

'The one where you'd get married in the snow in a castle on a hill?'

'That's the one.' Holly had confided her dream wedding to Milly one day in work and had confessed that her planned summer wedding to David wasn't filling her full of joy. 'We left school in 2000, but by the following January, everything had changed.'

'Changed how?'

'I got pregnant.'

Milly's mouth gaped. 'What? Wow! What happened?'

'It was a shock at first, but then we accepted it. It was just another part of our journey. It wasn't going to be easy, but we had a lot of support from our families, so I was going to have the baby. We were going to be parents.'

Milly's eyes were wide. 'Go on.'

'But in May that year, when I was around twenty weeks pregnant, I went into early labour. There was nothing they could do.' Her voice caught in her throat but she continued. 'It was a girl. Lara. She was stillborn.'

'Oh, Holly.' Milly reached across the table and gripped Holly's hand. 'That's so sad. I can't believe you went through all that. You and Josh. So is that what caused you to split up in the end? They say that tragedies can either bring a couple closer together or tear them apart.'

Holly shook her head. 'No, we were okay after that. It took me ages to lift myself out of the depression and start to live again, but with Josh's help, I got better. And we were stronger than ever. You don't go through something like that and not develop a bond. We were united in our grief and we felt nobody could understand how we felt except each other.'

Neither Holly nor Milly spoke for a few moments, both lost in thought. It was painful for Holly to talk about her daughter. But it was also good. It was good to share what had happened. To be able to talk about it to somebody. Her family never spoke about it, hoping she would have forgotten in time and not wanting to remind her. But of course Holly had never forgotten, nor would she ever want to. Lara was her daughter and although she'd never taken a breath in this world, Holly had loved her and always would.

'So do you want to go on?' Milly's voice was barely a whisper as she blew her nose and wiped her eyes. 'Do you want to tell me what split you two up in the end?'

Holly nodded. 'It was more than a year later. August of 2002. Josh had been acting strange for a couple of days. Cancelling our dates and not answering my calls. It was so unlike him that I began to worry. And as it turned out, I was right. He arrived at my house one night, all teary-eyed and upset. And that was it. He said it was over.'

'No way! Why? What did he say?'

'He just said that he'd been thinking about it and, although he still loved me, he thought that maybe we should have some time apart. I asked him how long, thinking at first he meant a couple of weeks or something, and that's when he said he thought we should split up. He said that we'd spent our whole lives together and we both needed to go out into the world and experience other things, other people.'

'God, I can't even imagine how you must have felt. What did you say to that?'

'I pleaded with him of course,' said Holly, remembering the scene. 'I asked him what had made him think that way. What I'd done. But he said that he'd been thinking about it for a while and he just hadn't known how to speak to me about it. He said he knew I wanted to travel and that he was holding me back because he still had a few years of teaching college to do. I said I'd wait for him – I didn't want to travel unless he was with me – but he told me to go. He said I should broaden my horizons, travel the world, be the person I'd always wanted to be.'

'So there was just no changing his mind?'

'There was nothing I could have said. I tried everything, but his mind was made up. He said we shouldn't stay in touch because it would be too painful. He said maybe in years to come we could get in touch again, but right at that time, it wasn't a good idea.'

'You must have been devastated. So what happened after that?'

'That was it. He went, and I never saw him again. Until he moved into the house across the street a few weeks ago.'

'And did you go travelling in the end?'

'Yes. A while later. I waited for him, convinced he'd knock at my door and tell me he'd made a huge mistake. But he didn't, and I decided to get out of the country and try to kick-start my life again. I went to Australia with a friend and spent a year travelling around. And when I came back, I was determined to meet my Mr Right and put Josh firmly out of my head. So I kissed a lot of frogs, until David came along, and the rest is history.'

Milly sat back in her chair and shook her head. 'That's unbelievable. So what happens now? What are you going to say to Josh?'

Holly thought for a moment. 'I'm going to tell him how hurt I was and to find out once and for all what happened. I want to know why he had a sudden change of heart about me. I've always wondered if he'd found someone else and didn't know how to tell me or if he'd just gone off me.'

'And after that?'

Holly shrugged. 'After that, we'll see. I love him, Milly. I've never stopped loving him. And if I'm being really honest, if I thought there was a chance of us being together I might just take that chance.'

'Even with David and Stephanie in the picture?'

'I don't want to hurt anyone, Milly. And I know I'd be throwing away the possibility of a lovely life with David. But seeing Josh again has made me realise that maybe lovely isn't enough. I want my heart to beat out of my chest when I look at my partner. I want my knees to turn to jelly in anticipation of his touch. I can't help how I feel. And if I'm reading things correctly, I think maybe Josh feels the same way too.'

Chapter 32

'Bye, love,' said Josh, kissing Stephanie on the lips. 'I won't be long – two hours maximum – and I'll pick us up something for dinner on the way home.'

He slung his gym bag over his shoulder and headed out to the car. He felt awful lying to her – he was the very one who condemned lies in a relationship – but he just didn't want to hurt her. Things were beginning to look up for them. Josh had received a cheque from the tax office the previous day and it was enough to keep them going for another while. He'd think again about a second job once Christmas was over. He was feeling good about his relationship with Stephanie now too. They seemed to have turned a corner and he was committed to her and the baby. They'd promised each other honesty and openness in their relationship and, after today, he wasn't going to keep anything from her.

A few minutes later, he'd parked on the main street just a bit down from O'Malley's and was heading inside to meet Holly. It was pretty quiet so he spotted her immediately. She was sitting at a corner table down the back, a pint of cider in front of her and a pint of Guinness ready for him. He went over to join her and, although he was driving, he couldn't resist taking a slug of the drink before speaking.

'Thanks for this,' he said, taking off his jacket and sliding into the seat beside her. He could smell her perfume. The Body Shop White Musk. It was the one she'd always worn when they'd been together and he closed his eyes for a moment as it brought him back to the past.

'Are you okay, Josh?'

He opened his eyes quickly. 'Yes, sorry. It was just the … never mind. So how are you?'

'I'm okay,' she said, sipping her pint. 'You said you wanted to talk?'

He nodded. 'Yes, I think we need to clear the air, don't you?'

'Yes.'

She held his gaze until he was forced to look away. He knew she'd be able to read his eyes. Read what was in his heart. And he didn't want that. He was going to do the right thing. They sat in silence until she spoke again.

'Is everything okay with you and Stephanie?'

That took him by surprise. 'Yes. Why do you ask?'

She shrugged. 'I just get the feeling that … that maybe things aren't too good between you two.'

'Everything is fine. We have a few issues, but who hasn't?'

'Josh,' she said, putting a hand over his, 'you can talk to me, you know. As you said yourself, I'm a good listener.'

Her touch was like a bolt of electricity shooting through him and he could barely get the words out. 'You're right, Holly. Things have been a bit strained between Steph and me lately.'

'Any particular reason?' She was watching him carefully.

He knew what she was thinking and he needed her to stop. 'It's not because of us.'

'Oh, I wasn't … I mean …' She flushed bright red and Josh was quick to reassure her.

* * *

'What I should have said was that there's been a strain on our relationship since well before we moved onto the street. Some of her friends, and I use the term *friends* lightly, have been putting ideas into her head and it's causing tension between us.'

'Do you want to talk about it?'

Her hand was still on his and he couldn't think straight. He wanted to tell her all of it. To tell her about Stephanie's wild nights. About her smoking joints. About the wrong dates on the scan. He wanted to spill it all out and have Holly put her arms around him and tell him it would be all right. He'd had this crazy notion that maybe something might happen between him and Holly. But now he knew where he needed to place his loyalties.

'Josh?'

'I actually had a good chat with Stephanie about things last night. It was great to clear the air and we've agreed now that we're going to make a fresh start. Onwards and upwards.'

Holly subtly moved her hand away from his. 'That's good. I'm very happy for you both. So there's no drama then?'

'No, thankfully. But I don't want to talk about me and Stephanie any more, Holly. I want to talk about *us*.'

'Us?' Her eyes glistened as she looked at him.

'Yes, us. I want to talk about what happened back then.'

She opened her mouth to say something but no words came out.

'Just say it, Holly. Say what's on your mind. That's why we're here.'

'Do you ever think of her?'

She didn't have to tell him who she was talking about. He felt a lump in his throat as he nodded. 'All the time.'

'Really?' She sounded surprised.

'Of course. Lara was my daughter too.'

They sat in silence for a few moments. 'But you never go to the grave,' said Holly, looking at him, her big brown eyes glistening with tears. 'At least, I've never seen you there.'

'Maybe *you* find peace at the graveside, Holly, but it's not for me. Lara is in here.' He pointed to his head. 'She's with me all the time no matter where I am.'

'I ... I didn't realise.'

'What? You thought I'd forgotten about her?' He shook his head. 'I thought you knew me better than that.'

'I should have known,' she said, looking at him with sad eyes. 'Do you ever wonder what would have happened if ... you know ...?'

'If she'd been okay? If she'd lived?'

Holly nodded.

'I used to wonder that all the time. But who knows? A lot of time has passed now and a lot of things have happened. I guess we'll never know what might have been.'

They sat in silence for a while, each lost in thought, until Holly eventually spoke. 'I can't remember the last time we kissed, Josh.'

It took him by surprise and he looked at her, half-expecting her to be joking, but her eyes told him she was deadly serious. 'What do you mean?'

'Our last kiss. I can't remember it. We were so in love, Josh. Every moment together was so special to me and yet, when I try to remember, I just can't picture it.'

He didn't know what to say to that. He couldn't read her. Did she want to be reminded or was it better to have it blocked out of her mind. 'Maybe it's for the best,' he said.

'Can you remember it?'

He shook his head. 'Look, Holly. What's the point in dredging up stuff like that? It's all irrelevant now.'

'I suppose,' she said, looking away from him. 'What does it matter now anyway?'

'What happened to us?' Josh said suddenly. 'How did it all go so wrong?'

Holly looked at him and her previously sad eyes shone with anger. 'I'll tell you how it all went wrong, Josh. You left me. You broke my heart into a million pieces. That's how it all went wrong!'

He tried to take her hand but she pulled it away as she continued to rant, the tenderness of the previous conversation long forgotten. 'How could you have done it, Josh? How could you have dumped me like that? Like I didn't matter to you? Did you have somebody else? Was that it? Was I not enough for you?'

'Of course I didn't have anybody else. You were the only one for me.'

'Well, that's obviously a lie.' Her brown eyes looked almost black as she looked at him in anger. 'You moved on, didn't you? You found someone else. Was *she* there in the background all the time? Waiting for you to dump me?'

'Holly, stop this. I didn't know Stephanie back then. And you've moved on too. It's not just me.'

She nodded and he was shocked to see tears roll down her face. 'Yes, and I've moved on with a fabulous man. A decent, kind, reliable man. A man who adores me and would never break my heart. A man who wants to marry me and spend the rest of his life with me. So things didn't turn out too badly after all.'

'Holly, please. Let's talk about things without getting too emotional. We need to sort it out.'

'Without getting too emotional?' She raised her voice and people started to look around at them. 'Do you know how you made me feel back then? Do you? Do you know that I felt like my life was ended because you didn't love me any more?'

'But, Holly, I told you. I *did* love you.'

'Don't be ridiculous, Josh. Stop lying to me and stop lying to yourself. If you'd loved me, you wouldn't have left me.'

He shook his head. 'It was *because* I loved you that I left you.'

She stopped crying for a moment and looked at him. 'That makes no sense whatsoever.'

'If you'd just let me explain,' he said, close to tears himself. 'When Carina came to see me, she told me that …'

'Hold on. What's Carina got to do with this?'

'You mean you don't know?'

Her brow furrowed and she looked scared. 'Know what?'

'Holly, Carina was the one who came to me and told me I had to let you go.'

19 August 2002

Josh was surprised to see Carina at the door. The owners of the house were out so he gestured for her to come in.

'What's up?' he said, leading the way into the sitting room. 'Is Holly okay?'

She sat down on the sofa. 'She's fine, Josh. But that's why I'm here.'

'Go on.'

'I know this is going to be difficult for you, but you have to let her go.'

'Excuse me? Let her go? Where?'

'Josh, you need to split up with her. She's had a tough couple of years and what she really needs now is to get out there and live her life.'

Josh laughed. 'Is this a joke? Holly and I aren't going to split up. We love each other. You know that.'

Her face was serious. 'I know you love each other, but believe me, that's just not enough. You've been together all your lives and it's not good for either of you.'

'I think we can be the judge of that.' Josh was beginning to regret having let her in.

'She wants to travel, Josh. She's desperate to leave this country behind and spread her wings. The only thing that's stopping her is you.'

'But we've discussed this. She said she was happy to wait until I'm finished college.'

'What else is she going to say? If you really loved her, you'd let her go.'

Josh was beginning to feel sick. 'Carina, I know you only want the best for Holly but, no disrespect, I need to hear this from her.'

'That's just the point, Josh. You'll never hear it from her. She'll never break up with you. But she's stuck in a rut. She's depressed. She still hasn't gotten over the baby. It's different for a woman. She'll have the scars, physical and mental, for a long, long time. The only thing that will make her whole again is to do as she's always wanted to do and travel the world. It will help her forget. It will help her start living again.'

'I … I know she's been depressed. But I've been helping her through it. She was beginning to feel happy again. She said so.'

'She's trying, Josh. But she needs to find where she fits in the world. She needs to explore other avenues, try other things.'

Josh didn't know what to say. He sat forward and put his head in his hands. Of course he'd known how desperately sad she'd been the previous year after the baby. Because he'd been desperately sad too. But he'd thought they'd begun to move forward and put that horrible year behind them. He sat back up and looked at Carina.

'Do you really think she'd be better off without me?'

Carina reached out and took his hand. 'I do. And I don't mean that to sound cruel. You're a great guy and you've made her very happy, but I think it's time to let go.'

'I love her so much, Carina. I can't imagine my life without her. She's everything to me.'

Carina looked at him, tears in her own eyes. 'Well then, if that's true, Josh, it's time to give her wings and set her free.'

Chapter 33

'I … I can't believe it,' said Holly, after she'd listened to the whole story. 'I can't believe Carina did that and I never knew.'

Josh took her hand. 'I always thought she'd have told you at some stage. So you honestly thought I just left you? That I just broke your heart for no reason?'

Holly nodded and a sob escaped her lips. 'I thought you didn't love me any more. I know you said you did, but that's what everyone says, isn't it? I always wondered if maybe you'd met somebody else but didn't want to tell me. Or if you were just fed up with me.'

'Well, now you know. And maybe I handled it all wrong. Maybe I should have spoken to you about it. But Carina convinced me that if I spoke to you you'd just say everything was fine. She said you were depressed. That the only way to make you better again would be to set you free. I was worried when I heard about the depression. You hear about things – about people doing stupid things. I got scared, I suppose. I loved you so much and I just wanted you to be better. To be happy. She said I should just tell you that we needed to go our separate ways, so that's what I did.'

'Just like that. And you never looked back.' Holly was still in shock.

'That's not true at all. After some time had passed, I began thinking that I shouldn't have taken Carina's word. I felt desperately lonely without you so I was planning on going to talk to you.'

'But you didn't.'

'I made some enquiries and found out that you were gone. To Australia. So I realised then that Carina had probably been right and you needed to spread your wings.'

'God, Josh. I only went because I was so broken-hearted and couldn't stand to stay there without you. I can't get my head around the fact that Carina did this. She knew how much I loved you. How much we loved each other. Why did she do it? I just can't figure it out.'

Josh shrugged. 'Who knows? But maybe it was the right thing to do, even if it didn't seem like it at the time.'

'Do *you* think it was the right thing?'

'Well, if we'd stayed together, you never would have met David and I wouldn't be with Stephanie. You're happy, aren't you?'

She desperately wanted to tell him she wasn't. She desperately wanted to say she was still in love with him and would leave David in a heartbeat to be with him. She wanted to throw her arms around him and hold him close. But she did none of that. 'Yes,' she said, her voice barely a whisper. 'And you're happy with Stephanie.'

'I am. So it's all ended well.'

'I have to go,' she said, suddenly standing up. 'I'm sorry, I just can't do this.'

'Holly, wait.' He got up and started to walk after her.

'No!' She spun around to look at him. 'You stay here. Let me go. Just like you did thirteen years ago. Just let me go.'

She ran out of the pub and down the street until she could barely breathe. Leaning against a wall, she began to cry. Big fat sobs, as tears streamed down her face. All those wasted years. All the years of wondering why Josh didn't love her any more. All the years of wondering what had happened to make him fall out of love with her. To make him leave her. And it was all down to Carina. Her lovely, reliable big sister. The one person in the world she'd thought she could trust. Well, she was going to confront her. To make her admit what she'd done. And then she was going to walk away and forget she'd ever had a sister.

Tears poured down Holly's face as she drove through Kildare town on her way to see Carina. She'd rushed home from the pub earlier to find David had just arrived, so she told him she needed the car. She'd made something up about Carina having a marriage crisis and needing Holly's advice. David had looked dubious but had handed over the keys without question. If he'd noticed her tear-stained face, he hadn't said, but at that point, Holly couldn't have cared less.

She pulled the car up outside the house and saw that Jason's car wasn't there so at least she'd be able to confront Carina without an audience. She hoped the girls weren't there either, because the way she felt, she wasn't sure she'd be able to do the nice-auntie thing with them. She didn't bother with the doorbell but banged on the glass pane of the door with her fists. She'd always wondered why they did that in movies but she realised now that it felt more urgent, more serious, than a mere ding-dong of a bell.

'Holly!' said Carina, swinging the door open. 'I wasn't expecting you. What's the panic?'

Holly stepped inside and brushed past her. 'Are the girls here or are you alone?'

'Holly, what's wrong? Has something happened?'

'Carina, just tell me. Who's here?'

'It's just me.' Carina looked worried and Holly was glad. 'Jason took the girls to football practice and I was just making dinner.'

'How could you do it, Carina? How could you ruin my life?'

They stood there in the hall, staring at each other, like two cowboys during a standoff. 'What on earth are you talking about, Holly? Is this a joke?'

'It's no joke,' spat Holly. 'I've just had a conversation with Josh.'

Realisation slowly swept across Carina's face and her voice came out as a whisper. 'Let's go into the sitting room and we can talk about it.'

Holly shook her head. 'This isn't going to be one of those conversations where you make tea and talk me down. What were you thinking, Carina? Why did you do it?'

Carina sighed and walked into the sitting room and Holly was forced to follow. 'Sit down, Holly. It's not what you think.'

'Oh and you know what I think, do you? If you really knew what I thought right now, what I thought about *you*, you'd be pretty shocked.' She sat down on the armchair furthest away from Carina and perched on the edge. She took a few deep breaths to calm herself because, despite the fact that she hated Carina right at that moment, she wanted to know why she'd betrayed her so badly. 'Right, I'm listening.'

'Holly, please understand that anything I said or did in the past was for your own good. Well, at least I did it with good intentions.'

'Are you actually serious? How can you say that splitting me and Josh up was for my own good? Didn't you see what I went through? The heartbreak? The depression? How can you sit there, having witnessed the lowest moments of my life, and tell me it was for the best?'

Carina began to cry but Holly cut her off straight away. 'You don't get to be upset, Carina. *You* don't get to play the victim. Now, just tell me everything.'

'Okay, okay.' Carina took a tissue from her pocket and wiped her running nose, then cleared her throat and began to speak. 'Look, before I explain, I just want to say I'm sorry. You have no idea how sorry I am for everything. And whether you believe it or not, I really did have good intentions back then. It just all went wrong and I didn't know how to fix it.'

'Go on,' said Holly, sitting back in the chair.

'After you lost … after the baby died –'

'Lara. Her name was Lara.'

'I'm sorry. After Lara died, I just saw something inside you die too. You were depressed and nothing seemed to make you happy.'

Holly bristled. 'Of course I was bloody depressed. It takes a long time to get over something like that. Actually, you *never* get over it.'

'I know,' said Carina. 'But I wanted to make things better for you. You were always talking about travelling the world and moaning because you had to wait for a few years until Josh had finished college. You two had been together most of your lives and I really felt it had become habit. You were great together, I know, but I felt there was so much out there for you to explore, for you to discover, and you'd never have had the opportunity if you'd stayed with Josh.'

'But, Carina, that wasn't your call to make. You don't get to play God and decide what I should do. Yes, I wanted to travel and, yes, I hated that I couldn't just get up and go at that stage, but given the choice, I would have chosen Josh above travel every time.'

'I know that now, but I just got it into my head that I had to do something to give you opportunities. I felt you were festering away, doing menial jobs around the town and just living your life waiting for Josh.'

'It wasn't like that and you know it. Josh was committed to me, and if I had forced his hand, he would have given up college just to go travelling with me. But I'd never have done that to him. I'd never have made him choose.'

'You see,' said Carina. 'That's exactly what I thought. You never would have done it yourself. I honestly thought that I was doing a good thing. Giving you the opportunity that you wouldn't take for yourself. I told him you needed to be set free to live your life and he understood.'

'Are you saying he agreed, then? Are you saying that he thought it was a good idea too?'

Carina shook her head. 'He was upset. He didn't want to do it but I convinced him that you needed to be released to be truly happy.' Holly went to interrupt but Carina stopped her. 'I'd been in a relationship with Jason since I was very young too. I'd settled down at an early age and had already started a family at that stage. I was happy, but I also felt I'd missed out on a lot. I'd have loved to travel, see the world, have a few adventures before motherhood took hold of me and kept me captive.'

'Wait, so you're saying that you wanted to live your life through me? You stayed in your nice, safe relationship and split mine up so that you could see what it would have been like?'

'It wasn't like that, Holly. You know I'm not that sort of person.'

'I'm beginning to wonder.' Holly felt tears prick the back of her eyes.

'Anyway,' Carina continued, 'after you two split, I began to regret what I'd done. I honestly thought you'd be sad for a bit but then get excited about the future. I thought you'd feel happy to be free to be your own person and do what you wanted with your life.'

'But why didn't you say something then? You could have fixed it. It wouldn't have been too late.'

'I did try to fix things,' she said, her eyes looking pleadingly at Holly. 'I went to Dublin, to his college, to find him. To talk to him.'

Holly's eyes widened. 'And did you? He didn't tell me that. Did you talk to him?'

Carina shook her head. 'I made some enquiries and was directed to a local pub. I went in and saw him. He was with ...' Her voice trailed off and she looked at Holly.

'Go on,' said Holly.

'He was with another woman. They looked cosy, loved up. He looked happy. I didn't know what to do. I'd already done enough damage so I thought I'd go home and have a think about it. I wanted to make things right but I just didn't know how.'

'So that was it? One pathetic attempt to fix things and then you gave up?'

'It was more complicated than that. After I'd seen Josh, I thought about things for a few days. And then you announced you were going to go to Australia with Sarah. You said you were going to travel, to get out of "this hell-hole" and see the world.'

'But that was only because of what had happened. Can't you see that? It was only because Josh had left me and I couldn't bear to stay here any more with the memories.' She couldn't hold the tears back any longer. One escaped from the corner of her right eye and it seemed to unlock a lifetime of hurt and sadness. She began to sob, big loud sobs that quickly turned to wails, and Carina was quick to run to her and tightly wrap her arms around her.

'Holly, I'm so, so sorry. I don't know what else to say. I know I was wrong. But my only defence is that I didn't do it out of any malice or badness. I love you so much and I just wanted to help.'

Holly couldn't respond, as her body heaved and shook, and she felt like she was going to be sick. They stayed like that for a while and, despite how Holly felt about Carina, she was glad to have her comforting arms around her. Eventually the sobs subsided and gave way to hiccups. She pulled away from Carina then and looked at her.

'I understand that you weren't being malicious, Carina. But I'm not sure I can forgive you.'

Carina nodded and went back to sit on the sofa. 'I can't say I blame you. I probably wouldn't forgive me either. And what does Josh have to say about it all?'

Holly wiped her eyes. 'He just said he did what he thought was best for me at the time. He's moved on now and he's in love with Stephanie.'

'And you and David?'

Holly shrugged. 'We're in love too. And we're planning a wedding, so I've just got to put the past behind me and move on.'

'It's probably for the best,' said Carina. 'You have a good man who loves you. You need to think about the future now.'

'With all due respect,' said Holly, standing up, 'I don't think you're in any position to tell me what's best for me. Look where that got me last time.' She walked out towards the hall door.

'You're right to be angry with me, Holly. But maybe in time you can forgive me.' Carina went to hug her as she opened the front door but Holly pulled away.

'Maybe,' said Holly, looking at her sister with sad eyes. 'But it could take a long time.' She strode out to the car without a backward glance. She'd loved Carina so much. And now she felt like she'd lost her. Just like she'd lost Josh thirteen years ago and again today when he'd declared his love for Stephanie. She'd never felt more alone as she drove off, back to the life she'd once thought had made her happy.

Chapter 34

'See you tomorrow, Mr O'Toole,' said Jane O'Driscoll, waving as he passed her on the corridor. Jane was a fourth-class teacher close to retirement and had a soft spot for Josh. Except she insisted on calling him by his formal title, despite the fact he'd told her a hundred times to call him Josh. But she was old school and had very definite ideas about how to behave so she wasn't going to change her ways.

'I won't be here tomorrow, Miss O'Driscoll,' he said, giving her a wink and making her blush. 'But I'll see you on Thursday.'

'Oh, yes. Okay then. I'll see you Thursday.' She rushed off down the corridor and Josh smiled to himself at how she'd gotten herself all flustered when he'd winked.

It suddenly dawned on him that this was the place where he was happiest at the moment. Being in school, with the students and the teachers, made him feel content. There were no dramas other than boys misbehaving, and life seemed relaxed and simple. Because outside of here, everything was a mess. In theory, he should have felt happy. He had a partner who loved him and a baby on the way. But it was way more complicated than that, and he'd made it even more complicated by his actions the previous night.

When he'd come home after meeting Holly the previous evening, he'd been glad to find that Stephanie had gone out. His head had been all over the place and he'd needed time to think. Delving into the past had unsettled him and he'd found himself asking the dreaded question 'what if?' What if he'd ignored Carina's advice back then? What if he'd spoken to Holly about it instead of acting on Carina's words alone? What if, what if, what if? But he'd realised that no amount of soul-searching was going to change things so he'd found a bottle of red wine in the cupboard and opened it while waiting for Stephanie to come home. He'd needed something to take the edge off how he was feeling. By the time Stephanie had arrived, he'd polished off the whole bottle and thought he had his life sorted. He'd sat Stephanie down and told her he loved her. That she was the only one for him and he couldn't wait to have a future with her. And then, to her surprise, he'd gotten down on one knee and asked her to marry him. She'd said yes, of course, and he'd felt like the happiest man in the world.

Then he'd woken up this morning, his head like a lead balloon and his stomach in knots, and bit by bit the conversation had started to come back to him. He'd glanced to his left to see Stephanie snoring contentedly and wondered what the hell he was going to do. Should he tell her he'd been so drunk that he hadn't known what he was saying? Or should he just go with it and get on with his life, just like Holly was doing with hers?

He was lost in thought as he headed out to the school car park and was suddenly jolted back to the present when his phone beeped. He opened the message as he hopped into the car. It was Stephanie.

'I'm making dinner. Can't wait to see you and talk about our plans. Your fiancée, Steph. x'

He winced at her words and threw the phone down on the passenger seat. She'd hinted for years that she wanted them to get married and he'd always resisted it. It had never felt right. And now, all because of a drunken moment, he'd asked her to marry him and it still felt wrong. It was like he wasn't in control of his own life any more. He was just a spectator, watching his life unfold, and there was nothing he could do about it.

His head was beginning to throb again, despite the painkillers he'd loaded up with, and the pain in his stomach had come back. He was due at the hospital the next day for more tests so at least he might have some answers after that. As he drove down the Navan Road, he pictured Stephanie at home, singing to herself as she made dinner. He'd made her so happy with his proposal – there was no way he could take it back now.

'Hi, love,' she said, opening the door for him before he was even out of the car. 'I hope you're hungry. I've made loads.'

He kissed her on the cheek. 'I'm starving. I've barely eaten anything all day.'

'Well, your timing is perfect because it's all ready.'

He followed her into the kitchen where she had the table set for the two of them. His stomach lurched when he saw the pasta in cream sauce, her speciality and one of the few things she could cook. But still, she'd made the effort, so he couldn't complain. Maybe he'd go to the chipper later for a big juicy burger if he was still hungry.

'So, did you tell them?'

He looked at her as he dished up some pasta onto his plate. 'Tell who what?'

'People at work. Did you tell them we're engaged?'

'Oh.' It hadn't even occurred to him to tell anybody. It still didn't seem real and the memory of it was fuzzy in his brain. 'I didn't get a chance.'

'What does that mean?' She looked at him suspiciously. 'Don't you get a lunchbreak? Were you not dying to tell everybody?'

He stuffed some pasta into his mouth to buy him some time as he nodded. 'Of course,' he said, through a mouthful of food. 'And I'll tell them on Thursday when I'm back in. I just wanted to savour the news for ourselves at first.'

'That's the stupidest thing I've ever heard.' She picked at her salad as she talked. 'I've been on the phone to everyone. And they're all asking about the ring.'

'The ring?'

'Yes. My engagement ring. You know, the thing that the man usually puts on the woman's finger when they get engaged?'

It hadn't even crossed his mind. 'Oh, yes. Well, of course we'll have to go shopping. I reckoned you'd want to choose something yourself.'

'Well, it would have been nice, in a way, if the proposal had come with a ring, but I suppose you're right. I'd be fussy about the type of ring I want so I'm probably better off choosing it myself. So when are we going to go? The shops are open late tomorrow night.'

Josh thought about their finances and knew they couldn't afford such an extravagance. 'I have the hospital tomorrow, remember? I don't think I'll feel like going out shopping afterwards.'

'Oh, of course. I'd forgotten. Thursday after work then?'

'I might have a lot of work to catch up on because I'll be out tomorrow. Let's wait until Thursday to decide.'

'It's so exciting, isn't it?' she said, her eyes dancing. 'When do you think we'll set the date for? Could we fit it in before the baby, do you think?'

'Whoa! Hold on there. That's not giving us much time.'

'But wouldn't it be lovely to be married when the baby arrives? Wouldn't it be a better start for him or her?'

'I don't think he or she would notice, to be honest. Let's just relax about it, Steph. There's enough to think about with the baby coming along. When things settle down, we can start to plan the wedding.' He was saying the words but he didn't fully believe them. He still couldn't picture himself marrying Stephanie, despite the fact that he loved her.

He began to relax as the conversation moved on to other things and he realised, well after they'd finished their meal, that he'd really enjoyed her company. That's how it used to be between them. Relaxed and easy. Until all the complications of the last year had made things tense and difficult. They worked together to clean the kitchen afterwards and, as Josh looked at her, he began to think that maybe getting married wouldn't be such a bad idea after all. What was stopping him? He'd be thirty-three on his next birthday and he had a baby on the way. Seeing Holly again had made him doubt himself and his relationship, but he was going to do his best to keep things with him and Stephanie on track.

'I'm just popping upstairs for a shower,' Stephanie said, putting the last few things in the dishwasher. 'Why don't you see what's on the telly and we can watch something when I get down?'

When she'd gone, he rooted around in the medicine cupboard in the kitchen for some more painkillers. The pain was building in his stomach and he wanted to keep it at bay. He had to fast from this evening and drink some awful stuff in preparation for one of the tests he'd be having tomorrow, so he didn't need pain to add to his list of woes. He found what he was looking for and swallowed two down with a glass of water.

Back in the sitting room, he scanned through the TV guide on the telly, but his mind wasn't on it. He wondered how Holly was. She'd been really upset when she'd rushed off the previous day but he hadn't wanted to upset her more by following her. She'd made it very clear that she hadn't wanted to talk any more so he'd had to respect that. It was weird knowing she was just across the road yet he couldn't call to check how she was. He wondered if she'd told David any of it, if things would now be awkward between the two men if they met on the street. He hoped not.

Standing up, he headed over to the window to look across the road. David's car was there so he must have come home from work early. He tried to imagine the scene inside. Was she crying on his shoulder, telling him about how Josh had hurt her? Or had yesterday's conversation helped her to move on? Suddenly, the front door opened and David walked out. He looked smart, as he always did, in a suit and tie. And behind him came Holly. Josh's breath caught in his throat when he saw her. She looked beautiful. She wasn't particularly dressed up but her hair shone in the December sun as it fell loosely over her shoulders. Her smile lit up her face as she laughed at something David had said, and Josh felt a little stab to his heart. He couldn't peel his eyes away from them. David opened the car door for her, but before she stepped in she placed her hand on the back of his head and pulled him towards her. Their lips met and, for Josh, time seemed to stand still. David cupped his hands around her face and she put her hands over his, reassuringly. Holly loved David. Josh could see that. They were happy. She'd moved on. It was time for him to do the same.

He watched them drive off and sighed. He was going to put Holly Russo right out of his mind from now on and concentrate on Stephanie – his fiancée. She was his life. His future. He began to root through their DVD collection until he found what he was looking for. *Miss Congeniality* – Stephanie's favourite. It was about time he started paying his gorgeous girlfriend some attention and stop hankering after something he'd never have. They'd watch the movie and then he'd suggest an early night. He'd make slow, gentle love to her and tell her that he couldn't wait to be her husband. He suddenly felt very lucky. Lots of men would kill to be in his shoes. He had everything he'd ever wanted and he was going to make sure he didn't mess it all up. He wouldn't make the same mistake he'd made thirteen years ago.

Chapter 35

Holly felt numb as she sat in the car beside David, on their way over to his mother's for tea. She was trying her very best to act the part of the dedicated wife-to-be, but her heart wasn't in it. After everything that had happened the previous day, she was exhausted. She wished she could head off to a desert island. Somewhere she could just be alone to think. To sort out the mess in her head.

She glanced at David, who was concentrating on the road, and she felt a rush of affection for him. She knew she could have a good life with him. He treated her well and she knew she'd be well looked after. The problem was that affection wasn't love – at least, not love the way she'd known it with Josh. But she also knew that her love for David could grow, given time. If she could just put Josh out of her head and accept the fact that he'd moved on then she could put all her energy into being happy with David.

The tea with his mother had been her idea. When she'd come home the previous evening after seeing Carina, David had noticed that she looked upset. He'd made her a cup of tea and gently asked if he could help. She'd spun him a story that she and Carina had argued about something stupid. She'd said it was a sister thing and it had just upset her. He hadn't pushed her to tell him more but he'd been attentive and loving towards her for the rest of the evening. It had made her want to try harder with him. To try and be grateful for what she had. To love him better. So in a moment of madness, she'd offered to have his mother over for tea. He'd been delighted with the offer and had rung his mother immediately. Mammy Wood, of course, couldn't just accept an offer graciously. She had to turn it around and tell them to go to *her*. Holly had been somewhat relieved because it meant that she wouldn't have to cook or to worry about cleaning the place from top to bottom.

They pulled up outside the house and David hopped out to open the door for Holly. Doreen had the front door open before they could ring the bell and, after much air-kissing and pleasantries, they were ushered into the grand dining room. The house was an old Georgian one, with beautifully laid out rooms with exquisite furniture. Doreen's husband had been a wealthy man and they'd bought the house for cash when they'd first got married. He'd signed it over to her when he'd left and she'd managed to maintain it beautifully over the years. The mahogany table was set for three, with her best cutlery and china, and Holly drooled at the sight of the food. There were bowls of chicken wings, mini-quiches, sausage rolls and vol-au-vents. There was smoked salmon on brown bread, platters of mozzarella and tomatoes and plates of various cold meats.

'Come on,' Doreen said, pushing them forward. 'Sit yourselves down and tuck in. I thought you'd both be glad of a decent meal.'

Holly bristled but kept her mouth shut. She smiled sweetly at her soon-to-be mother-in-law and sat down where Doreen indicated. David's eyes were almost popping out of his head as he piled up his plate and Holly sighed as she realised that she'd never be able to live up to the cooking abilities of the great Mammy Wood.

Doreen delicately placed a few things on her own plate and proceeded to pick at them. 'So, how are the wedding plans coming along?'

'Fine,' said David, through his mouthful of quiche. 'With the church and hotel booked, we can relax a bit about the other stuff. It's still early days.'

'Early days?' Doreen looked as though he'd said something obscene. 'It's never too early, David, love. There's so much to organise. Now, Holly.' She turned her attention to Holly, who would have been happier to be an observer. 'We need to talk dresses. I have a few magazines here and I've marked a few out that you might want to have a look at.'

'That would be lovely,' said Holly. She could think of nothing worse than looking at dresses with Mammy Wood. 'I have a few ideas myself but I'll have a look anyway.'

'Good, good. And flowers. I know carnations are popular as buttonholes but they're a bit common, don't you think?'

'Buttonholes?' said Holly, looking confused. 'What's that?'

Doreen laughed and shook her head. 'Don't you know anything about weddings, dear? Everyone has to wear a flower in their buttonhole or pinned to their jacket. It's traditional.'

'Maybe roses then?' David offered. 'You can't really beat a nice red rose.'

Doreen nodded. 'That's what I was thinking. But they'd have to be jazzed up a bit. Maybe a bit of fern or I saw in some magazine where they had a rose with small green feathers that looked like leaves. I want people to remember this wedding. To see that we went all out to make it special.'

Again, Holly was a spectator in her own life. David and his mother were talking about the wedding as though she wasn't there. As though she didn't matter. She couldn't care less about buttonholes or things like that. She didn't want to have to do something because it was traditional or expected. Their voices became a dull murmur to her as she thought about the wedding she'd once dreamed of. The one she'd never have.

'So what do you think, Holly?'

David was looking at her and she didn't have a clue what he was talking about.

'Sorry, I was miles away. What were you saying?'

'Mum was suggesting that we arrange a night with her and your parents so she and your mum can discuss what they're going to wear. She doesn't want to end up with the same dress or the same colour as her.'

'Um, yes. That's a good idea.' Her mother wasn't really into fashion and she certainly wouldn't be deciding on a dress a year and a half before the wedding. 'When were you thinking?'

'I was thinking some time over Christmas,' said Doreen. 'I'll need to pick out material soon and discuss styles with my dressmaker.'

'And we'll have to decide about bridesmaids, best man and groomsmen,' said David. 'Obviously you'll have Carina and Milly so I'll have to think who I'm going to ask. And if you want more than two, I'll have to have the same, obviously.'

Doreen joined in. 'You'll have to think carefully about who you ask, Holly. From what I can remember, Carina is very tall and Milly is tiny. You don't want your wedding party looking like a circus. Oh and that reminds me about a photographer. They get booked up really quickly.'

'James from work has a brother who's a photographer. I'll ask him about it tomorrow. And do we want a video?'

'I'm not sure about that,' said Doreen, scratching her head. 'Is it a bit tacky?'

Holly felt like she was watching a game of tennis, her head swinging from one to the other as they came up with suggestions and ideas, none of which she was particularly interested in. Then all of a sudden, her head began to spin and everything became fuzzy. It was like an out-of-body experience and she felt as though she was looking down at the scene.

'Holly, Holly, are you okay?' She tried to focus and saw David kneeling in front of her. 'Holly, love. What's wrong? Are you sick?'

'I … I …' She couldn't speak and feared she was having a stroke. David's and his mother's voices were blurring together as she tried to understand what was happening.

'Let's get her into the sitting room.'

'Should we call an ambulance? A doctor?'

'Maybe we should lie her down.'

'Holly, Holly, can you hear us?'

Next thing she knew, she was being led into the sitting room and pushed gently down onto the sofa. It felt good, like sitting on marshmallows, and she gratefully lay back and closed her eyes. She wasn't sure how long it took, maybe only minutes, but eventually her breathing became even again and she was able to open her eyes. David was kneeling down beside her, a glass of water in his hand.

'Here, take a sip of this,' he said. 'Are you feeling better now?'

She pulled herself up into a sitting position. 'What happened?'

He held the glass to her lips while she took a grateful sip. 'You got dizzy and fainted. You gave us a right fright there.'

'Sorry,' she said, feeling stupid. 'Where's your mother?'

'She went to see if Mr Gleeson next door is home. He's a doctor.'

Holly panicked. 'Oh God, stop her. I don't need a doctor. I'm fine.'

'He's not there,' said Doreen, bursting into the room. 'Oh, Holly, you're back with us. Thank God. Are you okay?'

'I'm fine,' she said, unaccustomed to Doreen's softer tone. 'I just felt a bit weak.'

'Well, I'm glad to see some colour come back into your cheeks. You were pale as a ghost – wasn't she, David?'

David nodded and Holly noticed that he looked pale himself.

'Now,' Doreen said, looking at David. 'You take Holly home and make sure you look after her. She'll need plenty of rest and you'll need to make sure she's eating okay.'

'I'm fine, honestly, Doreen.'

'Nonsense. You need to take it easy after an episode like that. I'll put some of the food in containers so you can take it home. It will save you cooking for tomorrow at least.'

Holly nodded and thanked her. And then it dawned on her. Doreen may have been a pain in the ass, an over-bearing meddler who always wanted things done her way, but she was obviously lonely. She wanted to feel needed. To feel useful. Holly had never thought of her like that before and it was a real eye-opener. All of a sudden she stopped hating the woman and felt a rush of affection for her. Affection. Just like she felt for David. And that's when she knew that it wasn't enough.

Holly stood at the sitting-room window looking across at number three. She now believed that fate *had* brought Josh back into her life. But not for the reason she'd initially thought. She'd thought in the beginning that maybe fate was trying to bring them back together, but that wasn't it at all. Fate was trying to tell her that she and David weren't suited. And she never would have realised that without see-ing Josh again. She loved David. She really did. But she wasn't *in* love with him. And it wouldn't be fair to marry him. Now she just had to think of a way to tell him.

'Here you go, love,' said David, coming into the room with a mug of tea for her.

'Thanks, David. You're very good to me.'

He walked over to the window and handed it to her. 'It's only what you deserve.'

She cupped her hands around the mug but didn't move from the window. She needed to think about what she was going to say. Because it wouldn't be fair to let things linger. Not now that she knew. She was aware of him standing behind her, but she continued to stare out the window, lost in thought.

'You're in love with him, aren't you?'

She swung around. 'Wh– what?'

'With Josh. You're in love with him.'

She laughed nervously. 'What are you talking about? Of course not.'

He sighed and sat down on the sofa. 'Holly, I'm no fool so don't treat me like one. I've probably known from that first day when you and Josh clapped eyes on each other at our front door.'

She was about to object again but instead sighed and went to sit beside him. Neither of them spoke for a few minutes and Holly desperately tried to decide what to say. Should she lie to save David's feelings? But what would that achieve? Especially when she knew she wasn't going to marry him anyway. She took a deep breath, before her words came out as a mere whisper.

'How did you know?'

His eyes filled with tears. 'So I'm right? You're in love with him?'

She nodded. 'Yes, David. I probably have been all my life.'

'It was the look.'

'Sorry?'

'It was the look,' he repeated. 'How you looked at him. I'd never seen you look at me that way. So intense. It was as though you were looking right into his soul.'

Holly couldn't believe he'd been so perceptive. 'I'm sorry, David. I really am. What Josh and I had – it was special. And very rare. After we split, it took me a long time to get over him. But I did. Until he arrived onto our street and all the memories came flooding back.'

He held up a hand to stop her. 'I don't really want to hear the details, Holly. Just tell me, are you two getting back together?'

She shook her head adamantly. 'Of course not. He's happy with Stephanie and they're going to have a baby. I can't help how I feel but he doesn't feel the same way.'

She watched as the information sank in with David. His eyes were brimming with tears and Holly wanted to comfort him, but she didn't dare. She'd given up the right to do that the moment she'd told him she was in love with another man. So she waited patiently until he spoke.

'We can work it out, Holly,' he said, reaching out to take her hands in his. 'We have something special too. If nothing is going to happen with you and Josh, we can work on things. On us.'

She didn't know what to think. Maybe he was right and they *could* work it out. They'd been happy before Josh had arrived back on the scene. They'd been planning to get married. Surely they could get back to that couple. And maybe in time she could forget about Josh and she could grow to love David even more.

'So what do you think, Holly?' His eyes were dancing on a bed of tears. Almost manic-looking. Pleading. 'We could move. We could sell up here and move far away from all your memories. It would be a fresh start for us. I love you, Holly. I have enough love for the both of us and I can make you love me in time.'

'David, I –' She couldn't finish as a sob escaped her lips and all of a sudden she was crying.

'Come here, love,' he said, folding her into his arms. 'It's going to be okay. Everything is going to be okay.'

She couldn't do it to him. She allowed herself a few moments to lean her head on his shoulder, knowing that it would be the last time, and then pulled away. She spread her left hand out in front of her and wriggled the engagement ring off her finger.

'No, Holly. Please –'

'David, I'm so sorry. But we can't do this.'

'Of course we can,' he said, taking a cloth hanky out of his pocket to wipe the corner of his eyes. 'You and Josh were children. You said so yourself. And we always look at the past with rose-coloured glasses. Your mind is clouded by the memories of the past but we can make memories too. Wonderful memories. And in time, those memories will replace the ones you have of him.'

She shook her head and gripped his hand tightly. 'I love you, David. I really do. But it's not enough. I don't feel the way I should feel about somebody I'm about to marry. I know that now. And I can't marry you in the hope that those feelings will grow. It wouldn't be fair.'

'Well, we don't have to get married.' His voice was going up a notch and he was beginning to sound desperate. 'We can just take things back to how they were before the engagement. Forget all the wedding stuff. It was putting you under too much pressure. And I can tell Mum to back off from –'

'David, no!' She had to be firm with him. To make him understand. 'I'm not going to change my mind. I'll pack up a few things tonight and come back for the rest over the next few days.'

He opened his mouth to speak again but she stared him down and he seemed to get the message. His head dropped and she watched as tears spilled down his face. She could hardly breathe as she watched him, and she was reminded of a nineteen-year-old girl who'd just lost the love of her life. She felt her own face wet with tears as she thought about her childhood and how simple and wonderful everything had been.

'Promise me we'll be best friends forever,' said Holly, swinging her legs as she balanced on the silver-coloured railings outside her house. 'Say it.' She looked pleadingly at the seven-year-old boy who'd been her friend since preschool. 'You have to say "best friends forever" and we link our little fingers and then it will come true.'

Chapter 36

Josh didn't have cancer. He sat in his car outside the school, relief coursing through his body. The bell had rung just fifteen minutes before, signalling the end of the school day. He'd switched on his phone as the boys lined up impatiently to leave, and his heart had leapt with fright. Two missed calls from his doctor. He'd gotten the boys out as quickly as possible and dashed out to the car to return the call. He hadn't been able to breathe as he'd waited for Dr Kim to come to the phone.

The preliminary results were in and they were all clear. She hadn't wanted to keep him waiting, in light of how worried he'd been. He'd been reassured to a certain extent with the blood tests, but when they'd prepped him to have that camera inserted, all his fears had come rushing back. He'd been convinced he was going to get bad news and had barely slept for the last couple of days as a result. He couldn't actually believe that he was okay. She'd suggested that he probably had irritable bowel syndrome – or IBS, as she'd referred to it. His flare-ups seemed to be connected with stress so, given the tests were clear, IBS seemed to be the most likely diagnosis. She was going to prescribe him tablets for it and monitor how he felt for the next while.

He couldn't wait to get home to tell Stephanie. Things had been good between them this week. She'd said she felt more energised and was in much better form. And he'd managed to put thoughts of Holly aside and was making a better effort with Stephanie. He headed out of the school gates in the direction of home. And it really *did* feel like home now.

'Come on, Steph,' he said, bursting in the door twenty minutes later. 'We're going out.'

'Are we?' She appeared at the kitchen door. 'Where are we going? I was just about to make us some lunch.'

'We're celebrating so I'm taking you to that new Italian restaurant in the village.'

Her eyes lit up. 'That's supposed to be gorgeous. And what are we celebrating?'

'Loads of things,' he said, walking towards her and wrapping his arms around her.

'Such as?'

'Oh, I don't know … the baby, our relationship, the fact I love you so much …'

She pulled away to look at him. 'You're acting really weird, Josh. Did something happen?'

'Just a little phone call to tell me I have the all-clear and I'm not going to die after all!'

'Oh, Josh, that's fantastic,' she said, hugging him tightly. 'I'm so happy for you. For us. And for this little one, of course.' She patted her stomach and Josh's heart soared.

Suddenly her phone began to ring in her pocket, breaking the spell of the moment. But she pulled it out and ended the call, without even looking to see who it was.

'You didn't have to do that,' said Josh. 'You could have taken it.'

'I did have to do it, Josh. The rest of the day is about you and me. Nobody else.'

The phone rang again and this time she switched it off altogether. 'There,' she said. 'No phone for the rest of the day.'

'But what if it was an emergency? What if it was your mother?' It wasn't like Stephanie to ignore a call.

'Well then she'd ring *your* phone if she really needed to get me. Anyone who matters to me has your number so it's not as though I'm not contactable.'

Josh was happy to have Stephanie's full attention. She was so attached to her phone that it was sometimes difficult to have a proper conversation with her. If she wasn't answering phone calls, she was checking her Facebook or Twitter. 'Shall we go, then? It's past lunchtime so it shouldn't be too busy.'

'But I haven't showered yet and I'll need to change.' She indicated her jeans and T-shirt but Josh thought she'd never looked so beautiful.

'You're perfect as you are, Steph. Maybe we can shower together later.'

She giggled at that and they headed outside to the car. But just as they were reversing out of the driveway, Josh spotted his mother pulling up outside. She never visited unannounced and liked to wait for an official invitation before she'd call to see them. Josh parked the car, hoping nothing was wrong.

'Mum, what are you doing here?' he said, hopping out of the car and walking across the road to her. 'Stephanie and I were just heading out.'

'Well, that's a lovely way to greet your mother.' She took a Tesco bag out of the car, and Josh noticed she had a twinkle in her eye. 'I thought you'd be delighted to see me.'

'I … yes, of course. You know I always love to see you. I'm just surprised, that's all. To what do I owe the pleasure? Actually, hang on. I'll just let Stephanie know we're not going out.'

'Hold your horses, Josh. You two can head on out. I'm not here to see *you*.'

'You're not here to see me?' He looked around him, confused. 'What do you mean?'

'I have a date.'

'You have a date?'

'Josh, stop repeating everything I say. Yes, I have a date. Is that so unbelievable?'

'Of course not.' He wasn't sure whether she was joking or not. 'Anyone I know?'

'Well, yes, as it happens. It's John. And it's not really a date. I was just teasing you.'

'John?'

'What did I say about repeating everything I said?' She smoothed down her grey coat and Josh recognised it as her Sunday best. 'John Fogarty from number forty-four. And Simon, of course.'

Josh was gobsmacked. 'But how … when …?'

'John and I have chatted a bit on the phone since we met here last month. And did you know he's been in hospital?'

'I did, yes. To have his hip done.'

'And did you also know he doesn't have a single family member around? His wife is dead and his only daughter is in Australia. There's nobody to visit him or to see if he's okay.'

'I didn't, actually. He always seems so upbeat. So happy. I suppose I never asked.'

'Loneliness isn't a badge, Josh, love. It doesn't scream out to announce its presence to the world. John is lonely. Much like myself. I went to visit him in hospital. He's a good man.'

Josh suddenly realised his mother looked relaxed and happy. She looked younger somehow and her eyes were full of life. 'That's great, Mum. So are you two, you know …'

'Josh O'Toole! Get your mind out of the gutter. We're friends, that's all. Two lonely old souls keeping each other company.' She indicated the bag in her hand. 'I picked him up a few bits in Tesco since he won't be able to get out for a few days, and I'm going to make him some dinner.'

'Well, I'm delighted for you. For you both.' He reached over and kissed her on the cheek. 'Tell him I said hello and I'll pop in tomorrow to see if he needs anything.'

He hopped back into the car where Stephanie was listening to the radio, oblivious to what had just transpired. 'Wait until I tell you about Mum,' said Josh, starting the engine again.

'So we're still going? Thank God for that. I didn't want to get out of the car in case we wouldn't be able to get rid of her.'

Josh didn't bother telling Stephanie about his mother. She wasn't interested. She'd *never* been interested in his family. It didn't usually bother him but this time he felt angry. Upset. Something his mother had said struck a chord with him. Loneliness. It doesn't scream out to announce its presence. It was a shock for him to realise it but, just like his mother, he was lonely too.

After just an hour at the restaurant, where they'd talked mostly about what type of engagement ring Stephanie wanted, they were back home. It was only just gone five but Stephanie had changed immediately into her pyjamas, stating that she was fit for nothing except lying on the sofa for the rest of the evening.

'Why don't you head up for a bit of a sleep, Steph? You look exhausted.'

'Maybe. But only if you come with me.' She fluttered her eyelids and Josh smiled.

'I'll join you later but I fancy going to the gym for an hour first.'

'To the gym?' she said, looking at him strangely. 'After all that food?'

'I'll just do some weight training. All upper body, so it'll be fine.'

She flicked the telly on and Josh was glad she'd lost interest in the conversation. He ran upstairs to throw some things into a bag and was back down in minutes. 'See you later,' he said, kissing her on the top of her head. 'I won't be long and I have a key if you decide to go to bed.'

He sped off down the road, his head awhirl with thoughts. If he was really quick, he might just about make it on time. He hated lying to Stephanie. But he had no choice. There was something he needed to do and he couldn't tell her about it. Somebody he needed to see. He drove through the village and was pleased to see the little flower shop on the main street was still open. He parked right outside, hoping there weren't any traffic wardens about, and rushed in just as they were putting the Closed sign up.

'Sorry, sir,' said an elderly lady. 'We're closed.'

'Please,' he said. 'It's important.' He glanced quickly around the shop and pointed to a small arrangement of lemon and white roses. 'Those. I'll take those. Look, I have the exact cash.'

She nodded and handed him the flowers, taking his twenty euros from him. He breathed a sigh of relief as he got back in the car and went on his way. Thankfully most of the traffic was going in the opposite direction so he made it to his destination in twenty minutes. He got parking easily enough and rushed across the road, carefully carrying the flowers at arm's length so they wouldn't get damaged. His heart began to beat quickly as he approached the gates and he had to stop for a moment to catch his breath. He'd spent so many years being afraid of this. Afraid of the power of his emotions. But he was determined. The air seemed to turn icy so he zipped his jacket right up before striding purposefully through the gates of the cemetery.

Chapter 37

'My head is spinning,' said Milly, staring at Holly. 'I can't believe so much has happened in less than a week. It was only Monday when I saw you last.'

Holly sat forward and poured some more tea into her cup. '*Your* head is spinning? Imagine how I feel. I still can't get my head around everything. My life is a mess and I honestly don't know what to do about it.'

It was Saturday morning and Holly was having breakfast with Milly in Avoca in Rathcoole. Since Holly had moved back home with her parents in Kildare, Avoca was a handy midway point to meet. They'd ordered cheese and tomato scones, which were almost the size of their heads and were served with cream cheese and tomato relish. Usually Holly would get stuck into a treat like that, but she wasn't very hungry. In fact, she'd barely eaten since she'd left David on Wednesday.

'So go on,' said Milly, cutting little pieces from her scone and popping them into her mouth. 'Did you leave straight after the conversation? Was it awful, packing up to go?'

Holly shook her head. 'I stayed on Tuesday night. I slept in the spare room and told him I'd be gone when he got back from work the following day.'

'Oh God. And were you? Did you not see him again?'

'He didn't go to work, Milly. It was awful. I didn't sleep most of the night and fell asleep in the early hours. When I eventually got up around ten, I came downstairs to find him waiting in the kitchen, a cooked breakfast keeping warm in the oven. He said he couldn't let me go without fighting for me. He said he loved me – would always love me – and that he'd hoped that I'd changed my mind after a night's sleep.'

Milly's eyes were wide listening to the story unfold. 'And were you tempted? To change your mind, I mean.'

'No, not at all. I felt sure at that stage. It was desperately sad. David did nothing wrong. And I really didn't want to hurt him. But I was sure.'

Milly nodded. 'So you went back home to your parents. What did they say?'

'Mum and Dad are great.' Holly smiled. 'They really liked David and wanted us to work out but, at the end of the day, all they want is for me to be happy.'

'So what are you going to do now?' said Milly. 'Are you going to try and rebuild your life back in Kildare?'

Holly shrugged. 'I honestly don't know what's next for me, Milly. I'm really going to have to think about where I'm going to live. Mum and Dad are great and it's comforting to be back home at the moment, but I'm thirty-two years old. I really don't want to be back where I was a few years ago, a lonely spinster living with my parents.'

'And what about the new business idea? I know you're probably not in the right frame of mind to think about it now, but I'd hate to see you let an opportunity like that pass.'

'I won't,' said Holly. 'I'm just going to take some time over Christmas to get my head together and then I'll contact potential clients. I'll figure something out.'

'And Josh?'

'What about him?'

'Is there any hope there? Are you going to tell him about you and David?'

'Definitely not,' Holly said, probably a little too sharply. 'I'm sure he'll find out in time. He'll bump into David no doubt at some stage, but why would I go to him and tell him?'

Milly looked at her warily. 'Maybe because you're still in love with him?'

'But that's not enough.' There was no point in denying the fact that she loved him. Because she did. She was so much in love with Josh that it hurt to even talk about him. 'He made it clear on Monday night that he and Stephanie have a future together. They're having a child, Milly. Josh is going to be the father of another woman's child.' The words caught in her throat and she could feel tears form at the corners of her eyes.

'Oh, Holly, I'm sorry. I really am. Please don't cry.'

'I'm okay,' Holly said, wiping her eyes with a serviette. 'It's just all so raw. Everything seems to be happening so quickly that I feel like I have no control of my life.'

Milly indicated to a waiter to bring them some fresh tea, as the other pots had gone cold. 'Just take it one step at a time. There's no rush to make any decisions so maybe you should just relax for a few weeks with your parents over Christmas and then decide in the new year what you're going to do.'

Holly began to cry again. 'Six days to Christmas, Milly. Just six days. And it's my favourite time of the year. Or should I say, *used to be!*'

'Look, Holly. There'll be plenty more Christmases. You just need to concentrate on yourself and getting through each day.'

Holly knew Milly was right. But everywhere she looked there were Christmas trees and decorations, carollers singing on the streets and Christmas music on almost every radio station. These were the things that usually made her happy, but not this year. All the Christmas cheer just made her think about what she'd lost and added to her sadness.

'I have to go,' she said suddenly. 'There's somewhere I need to be.'

Milly looked alarmed. 'Don't go yet, Holly. You haven't even eaten your scone and I've ordered more tea. Stay for a while. We can talk some more about things.'

Holly took her coat off the back of her chair and grabbed her handbag from under the table. 'I'm all talked out, actually. I just need to be somewhere quiet now. Somewhere peaceful.'

'Holly, no. Don't go, please. I'm worried about you. What do you mean? What are you going to do?'

She smiled at her friend's concern. 'I'm okay, Milly. Honestly. At least I will be. Thanks for being such a good friend and I promise I'll ring you tomorrow.'

She didn't wait for Milly to object again but dashed out of the restaurant and down the stairs to the exit. She knew where she needed to be. Somewhere away from all the happy Christmas songs and bright, twinkly decorations. She needed to be alone with her thoughts so that she could try and figure some things out. She hopped into her dad's car and headed towards Dublin.

Holly's mood was reflected in the black clouds as she stepped inside the gates of the cemetery. There was a distant rumbling of thunder and it looked as though the sky was going to open and spill its contents. She stepped back as a funeral passed by and it struck her how sad it must be to lose somebody so close to Christmas. Of course, no time was a good time to lose a loved one but it just seemed particularly unfair to have such sadness when the world was celebrating.

She made her way down the well-familiar pathway, zig-zagging around the graves, until she got to where her daughter lay.

As she approached the grave, she noticed a beautiful fresh arrangement of yellow and white roses. It startled her a little because, other than her mum and dad, she was the only one who visited on a regular basis, and she was sure they would have mentioned to her if they'd been. And then it dawned on her. Carina. Holly hadn't spoken to her since their argument on Monday and she had no doubt that her sister was feeling guilty about what she'd done. Carina didn't visit the grave often, but when she did, she always said she felt peaceful there. Holly was beginning to feel bad about how she'd spoken to her. Carina may have messed up, but she hadn't done it with any ill intent. And hadn't they all made mistakes they wished they could erase?

She sidled her way through the surrounding graves until she was right in front of Lara's. Her breath caught in her throat, as it always did, when she read the words on the gravestone.

Sweet dreams, Lara, our precious angel. Love always. Mum &
Dad. 3 May 2001.

She closed her eyes and said a silent prayer. Although she wasn't religious, it gave her great comfort to imagine Lara in some heavenly place and to believe that, wherever she was, she knew that her mummy loved her and would never forget her. After a few minutes, a great sense of peace enveloped her and she began to feel calm. She'd been questioning herself all week. Wondering if she'd done the right thing and worrying that she'd end up alone for the rest of her life. But she knew now, without a shadow of a doubt, that she'd been right to leave David. She just didn't love him enough, and fear of being alone wasn't a good enough reason to stay with somebody.

Flowers from previous visits lay wilted and dead on the grave so Holly bent down on her hunkers to gather them up. She'd been so anxious to get into the graveyard that she hadn't stopped for flowers herself, so she was glad of Carina's brightly coloured arrangement. Just then, she noticed a little card buried in between the heads of the flowers. Placing the dead flowers carefully beside the grave to take to the bin after, she reached forward and pulled the card out. The writing wasn't Carina's, yet it was weirdly familiar. And then it dawned on her. Before she even read it. She'd always admired his artistic writing style and her heart began to beat quickly as she read the words.

To my precious Lara. Always on my mind. Love, Daddy. xxx

She stood holding the card for a very long time, allowing tears to spill down her face. Josh was the only person in the world who truly knew how she felt and it gave her great comfort to know that he felt the same way too. Lara would connect them to each other for the rest of their lives, no matter what the future held.

She was suddenly aware of movement beside her and realised somebody had come to visit a nearby grave. She glanced over and saw it was an old lady, her head bent in prayer, a tissue dabbing the corners of her eyes. It was time for Holly to leave and let the woman have her time alone. Holly kissed her hand and placed it on Lara's name on the gravestone before turning to walk away. Her thoughts turned to Josh and she wondered if he'd ever tell Stephanie about Lara. It didn't seem right that Stephanie was having what she thought was his first child, when really it was his second. But Holly had enough going on in her own life and didn't need to be worried about his. He was no longer her problem. No longer her worry. He was no longer hers. Tears began to fall again as she drove off, heading back to a life that she'd once thought she'd left far behind.

Chapter 38

Josh paced up and down the living room. He was worried sick. It was early on Sunday morning, and after having such a lovely evening on Friday with Stephanie, the rest of the weekend had fallen apart. Stephanie had been really moody all day Saturday and hadn't wanted to do anything. He'd suggested they go to town to do some Christmas shopping, but she'd shaken her head and said she couldn't face the crowds. He'd then tried to talk to her about Christmas Day but she hadn't wanted to discuss it. He'd already given in to her wishes to have Christmas dinner together at home, but he'd wanted to talk about the evening time and whether they'd have some people over or maybe go visiting. It was only five days to Christmas Day and Josh had never felt so unprepared in his life.

He checked his phone again but there were no missed calls or messages, so he went into the kitchen to make himself a cup of tea. As he waited for the kettle to boil, he thought back to the previous day and wondered if he could have handled things better. But he honestly wasn't sure what he could have done differently. After a day of trying to cajole Stephanie out of her mood, he'd eventually given up around tea time. And that's when she'd turned on him. She'd told him she felt like he was her jailer. That he was keeping her at home, trying to make her into some sort of 1960s home-maker, and that just wasn't her. He'd been shocked at that because he'd never meant her to feel that way. But once she'd started, there was no stopping her. The words had spilled out. It was as though she had months' worth of pent-up anger and she was letting it all out at once. Josh was too controlling. He wasn't supportive. He didn't understand how she felt. She wasn't loved enough, appreciated enough, supported enough. It was like a slap in the face to Josh and he'd been really upset at her vicious words. He'd argued back a little but hadn't wanted to upset her further. So he'd ended up apologising and asking her what she wanted him to do to make things better. But her response to that had been to go upstairs, get herself dolled up and announce that she was going out for the night. He hadn't wanted her to go out angry and he'd tried to make up with her before she'd left, but she'd stormed out, telling him not to wait up.

But he *had* waited up. And waited, and waited. He'd sent her a few texts, which she hadn't answered, and had tried to ring her a couple of times but the calls had been cut off. It had been two o'clock in the morning when she'd eventually responded to one of his texts and told him that they were all going back to Coco's apartment for a while and she'd get a taxi home later. But it was now almost 8 a.m. and he hadn't heard from her since. He took his tea into the living room and sat back on the sofa, cupping his hands around the steaming drink. Flicking around the television channels, he eventually settled on the early-morning news but muted the sound to allow himself to think.

He'd been trying so hard to make things work between himself and Stephanie that he hadn't really considered the fact that maybe they just weren't compatible. He loved her – there was no doubt about that – but it was becoming more and more difficult to be with her. Being with somebody you love shouldn't be such hard work. And that's what Stephanie was a lot of the time – hard work. Her moods dictated everything but he'd overlooked that because she was pregnant and had, as she said herself, raging hormones. But as he sat sipping his tea, he asked himself the question that he'd been trying to avoid. Was he really happy?

Just then he heard a rattle of keys and the front door opening. At last. She obviously thought he was in bed because the next thing he heard was the sound of her footsteps on the stairs. He jumped up, leaving his tea on the little coffee table, and went out to the hall to see her.

'Steph, I'm down here.'

She turned around and he was shocked at how dishevelled she looked. 'Oh, hi, Josh. I thought you would have been fast asleep.'

'Are you kidding me? I've been worried sick about you. You've been out all night.'

She giggled. '*No!* Have I? I hadn't realised.'

He noticed how she was slurring her words and fear coursed through him. 'Steph, have you been drinking? Please tell me you're not drunk.'

She sat down on the stairs. 'Okay. I'm not drunk.'

'Come into the kitchen and let's talk,' he said, panicking. 'I'll make you a cup of tea.'

'I don't want tea. I just want to go to bed.' She stood up and swayed, and he rushed up to steady her before she fell down the stairs.

'Thanks, love,' she said, slobbering a kiss on his cheek. 'I just need some sleep. That's all.'

'Right, let's get you upstairs.' He knew she was either drunk or high but he wanted to get her into bed, out of harm's way. When she plonked down on the bed and began to strip off her clothes, he tried again. 'Steph, just tell me. Have you been taking that stuff again?'

'Stuff, schmuff!' She seemed to find that hilarious and threw her head back, laughing. 'You're my fiancé, Josh. Not my father. Lighten up, would you?'

He began to feel angry. 'Steph, if you weren't pregnant, I wouldn't care so much about what you drank or what you took. And we've been through all this before.'

'Yes, we have,' she said, looking suddenly sober. 'And I don't want to keep going through it again and again.'

He sat down beside her and took her hands. 'But we will keep going through it if you keep acting like this. You said I'm not your father but you've got to stop acting like a child.'

'I'm just enjoying the last of my freedom until this thing,' she prodded an index finger into her stomach, 'comes out.'

Josh felt his blood boiling. 'You don't mean that, Steph. You're not thinking straight and you're saying things you'll regret. Just get some sleep and we'll talk about this more later.'

She'd laid her head on the pillow and looked as though she was ready to drop off, but as soon as he told her to sleep, she became alert and sat up. 'No, Josh. We won't talk about this more later. I'm sick of talking. Talk, talk, talk. That's all you ever want to do. *Let's discuss Christmas, Steph. Let's talk about you getting a job, Steph. Can we talk about the baby? The house. The future!* Talk, talk, talk. Well, I'm bloody well sick of talking.'

He knew that there was no point in continuing. Even when she was sober, it was difficult to make her see his point of view, so in her current state, it would be impossible. She was staring at him, willing him to argue back with her, but he wasn't going to do it. Not now. He walked towards the door.

'Look, Steph,' he said, rubbing his hand on his forehead. 'You've been up all night. Just sleep for now. We'll work it all out later. I don't want to fight with you.'

'Well, maybe *I* want to fight,' she said, standing up and walking towards him. She brushed past him and headed for the stairs. 'Okay, so you wanted to talk. Let's talk.'

He sighed as she stormed down the stairs and he had no choice but to follow her. It was all getting out of hand. He was coming across like a strict parent and she was acting like a petulant child. He didn't want it to be like that with them. They were equals. Partners. And they should have been pulling together and not ripping each other apart. She was already sitting at the kitchen table, tapping her fingernails on it, when he came into the room.

'So, go on, Josh. What did you want to talk about? Give me your words of wisdom.'

He shook his head. 'Come on, Steph. Don't be like this. You know that I only want, I've only ever wanted, the best for you and the baby.'

'You're so bloody obsessed with this baby,' she said, spitting out the words. 'It's only a baby, not the second coming.'

'But it's *our* baby. Our first child together. Of course I'm obsessed with it.'

'Hmph!'

'What does that mean?'

'Work it out, Josh.'

Josh felt a chill running down his spine. 'Work what out? What are you talking about?'

She shifted uncomfortably on her chair. 'Nothing. Forget I said anything.'

'Oh, for God's sake, Steph. Just spit it out. What are you trying to say?'

She pulled a tissue out of the box on the table and began ripping it into tiny pieces and Josh suddenly felt angry. Everything he did was for her and the baby. All his thoughts, all his energy went into making sure the future was secure for all three of them. He'd only ever wanted to make Stephanie happy and he was fed up with how she treated him. Well, he wouldn't let her away with it any more.

'I don't know how you can take the high moral ground,' he said, tears of anger forming in his eyes. 'I've been nothing but good to you and this is how you treat me. You know how important this baby is to me. And I foolishly thought it was important to both of us. But you go out boozing and taking stuff, with not a thought for how it's affecting the baby. Do you not care if you're damaging him or her? Does it not matter to you?'

'It shouldn't matter to you either, Josh.' She spat the words at him and he was momentarily confused.

'Why shouldn't it? Of course it matters.'

'Well, it shouldn't.' She stood up and went to the sink and poured herself a glass of water from the tap.

The next exchange happened in slow motion for Josh as he suddenly knew what she was going to say before she even said it. The word came out as barely a whisper. 'Stephanie?'

She turned around and looked him right in the eye. 'Because, Josh, the baby isn't yours. It's not yours, okay? You're a school teacher, for God's sake. Could you not have figured it out?'

His eyes went to her stomach and the room began to spin. His baby. *Not* his baby. He couldn't believe it. All this time and she'd been pregnant with someone else's baby. He couldn't get his head around it. He wasn't going to be a daddy. He wasn't going to have his little bundle of joy. Tears began to spill down his face and he had to reach out to the kitchen counter to balance himself.

'Say something, Josh,' said Stephanie, her voice beginning to sound worried. 'I … I wanted to tell you. But you were so happy. So excited. I *wanted* it to be yours. I really did. And it still can be.'

'Who?' That was all he could manage.

'That doesn't matter,' she said, standing up and walking towards him. 'I don't want to be with him. It's you I want. It's always been you.'

'*Who is he?*' The words came out as a roar, surprising even himself, and Stephanie backed away.

'You don't know him,' she said. 'Leo. He's a film director I met at a party last summer. It was a mistake, Josh. I promise. It was only that once and it will never happen again.'

Josh felt as though he was in a nightmare and closed his eyes, willing himself to wake up. But when he opened them again, Stephanie was still staring at him and the reality of the situation threatened to choke him. He walked in a daze over to a chair and sat down heavily.

'When?'

Stephanie looked scared. 'When what?'

'When were you with him? How do you know the baby isn't mine?'

She had the grace at least to look guilty. 'While you were away. Last summer. As I said, it was only the once but –'

'The scan!'

'What?' said Stephanie, looking at him uncertainly.

'The dates on the scan. They were right after all. How could I have been so stupid?' He leaned forward on his elbows and put his head into his hands.

'I was just waiting for the right time to tell you, Josh. I shouldn't have told you like this, but Leo said if I didn't tell you, *he* would. It's been so difficult for me these last few months.'

He glared at her then. 'For *you*? Difficult for *you*? It's always about you, isn't it, Stephanie. Poor little girl. Well, you've rightly made a mug of me, haven't you? You weren't a poor little girl when you jumped into bed with that guy the moment my back was turned. Where did it happen? Was it in our house? Our bed? Oh God, I feel sick at the thought.'

'Stop, Josh,' she said, beginning to cry. 'Don't do this.'

'Don't you *dare* play the victim this time, Stephanie. Don't you *dare!*' He was more angry and upset than he'd ever been in his life. His whole world had come crashing down around him and he wasn't sure what to do. All the happiness he'd thought was in his future had just been wiped out and he'd never felt more alone. He looked across the table at her and took a few deep breaths before he spoke again. He needed to know for sure.

'Are you absolutely sure? I mean about the dates? Is it definitely not mine?'

She nodded slowly. 'I'm sure. The dates match up. It's not your baby. But it could be, Josh. Nobody else would have to know.'

He couldn't believe the words coming out of her mouth. 'I'm going to pack a few things and go to my mother's. You can stay here if you like but I won't be paying the rent any longer.'

'What? Josh, no. I don't want you to go.' She followed him up the stairs. 'I want us to work this out. Stay and we can talk. You said you wanted to talk.'

He pulled out a rucksack from under the bed and began to throw random clothes into it. 'It's too late for talking, Stephanie. Way too late. You can go and talk to *him*. See if he'll take you because I sure as hell won't.'

She tried to stop him from packing but he shrugged her away. 'Please listen to me, Josh. I wish I hadn't told Leo about the baby but it was a spur-of-the-moment thing. I was panicking and I thought he'd help me to get rid of it before you even knew. But it turns out he wants a baby and he's been trying to get me to move in with him. He's really wealthy and said he could give me and the baby every-thing we needed.'

'Well, there you go.' Josh couldn't even look at her.

'But you don't understand. I keep telling him it's *you* I want. It's *you* I love. Don't you see, Josh? I chose you.'

'Well, Stephanie.' He zipped up his bag and glared at her. 'I don't choose you.'

'Josh, please. I love you. And I know you love me. Please don't go.'

He didn't want to hear it. He took his car keys from the hall table and his jacket from the bannisters. 'Goodbye, Stephanie. I hope you'll be happy.'

He could hear her sobs as he got into the car but he wasn't going to look back. She'd hurt him beyond belief and it was going to take him a long time to recover. When he turned out of the estate, he finally let the tears fall. They spilled down his face, soaking his top and blurring his vision. He turned onto the main road and all of a sudden there was the loud blare of a car horn. Lights blinded him and he began spinning out of control. Everything seemed surreal as he felt the seatbelt eat into his shoulder and pain seared through his neck. A loud bang like a shotgun was the final noise he heard before there was nothing but blackness.

Chapter 39

Holly felt as though her life had been rewound. She was back living at home, eating her meals with her parents and fighting for control of the telly in the evening. Except she was older and wiser than when she'd lived there before. The scars of her heartache had surfaced again but now they were even deeper. Not only had she lost Josh for a second time, but she'd lost David, a loving, caring, wonderful man who had done nothing wrong except love her. Her life was a mess.

It was Sunday afternoon and she was alone at home, half-heartedly hanging silver and gold chain decorations on the living-room ceiling. Her love of Christmas came from her parents, who always threw themselves into the festive season with gusto. They'd gone out to buy some more fairy lights and had asked her to do the ceiling decorations, on account of her mam's bad leg and her dad's lack of balance. She came down from the stepladder to survey her work and couldn't help smiling. They'd had those chains for as long as she could remember. They were old-fashioned and worn yet she couldn't imagine the house without them. She felt suddenly glad for the warmth and protection of her childhood home and made a mental note to thank her parents for being there for her.

She'd spoken to David a couple of times since she'd left and, although he said he missed her, he seemed to have accepted their fate. And although it was she who'd ended it, she missed him too. How could she not? They'd had some special times together and she'd always remember him fondly, but the fact remained that he just wasn't the one. She fixed the final decoration into place and stepped down again from the ladder. Her parents had said they'd be home around three, so if she was quick, she could rustle up some lunch and have a nice quiet hour in front of the telly. It was lovely to spend some time with them, but they were a little over-bearing in their efforts to make sure she was okay.

Ten minutes later, she was settling down on the sofa with a toasted ham and cheese sandwich and a packet of crisps when the doorbell rang. Damn! There was no way she was going to entertain some canvasser or salesman at the door when she had precious little time to enjoy alone. So she stayed very still and hoped they'd go away. But no, the bell rang again, and again, and it became clear that whoever it was, wasn't going to give up. Sighing, she put her sandwich down and went to answer the door. She'd tell them that she was just the lodger in the hopes they'd go away. She swung open the door and was about to launch into her speech when she saw who was there.

'Hi, Holly,' said Carina, pushing past her into the hall. 'You wouldn't answer my calls and when Mum told me what had happened between you and David, I just had to come to see you.'

'Well, I don't want to see *you*, Carina. Not yet. I have enough things to worry about.'

'Please, Holly. Let me be your big sister. I think you need me. You must be devastated. I really thought you'd found somebody who'd make you happy.'

Holly sighed. 'So did I.'

It was awkward, both of them standing in the hall looking at each other like strangers who'd just met. Holly hated that things had come to that but she wasn't ready to forgive Carina for what she'd done. It may have been a long time ago, but for Holly it was new and raw.

'Right,' said Carina, heading into the kitchen. 'Let's have some tea and we can chat.'

Holly followed her in. 'No – I told you, I don't want to talk. I have nothing to say to you.'

Carina filled the kettle regardless and turned to face Holly. 'I know you hate me for what I've done but –'

'I don't hate you, Carina. Am I hurt? Yes. Am I ready to forgive you? No. But I could never hate you. And I know you did what you did out of misguided loyalty, but it still resulted in my life being shattered into a million pieces.'

Carina went to her and tried to put her arm around her but Holly bristled. 'Please, Holly. Don't turn your back on me. I'm your big sister. I care about you. About what's happened to you. Don't shut me out.'

Holly was torn. Part of her wanted to feel her sister's reassuring embrace but she wasn't ready for that yet. She was still too hurt, too devastated by what she'd found out.

'Look,' Carina continued, pouring two cups of tea. 'I know it's going to take a long time for me to earn your trust again. I know you don't want to talk about what happened back then and, to be honest, I've probably told you everything anyway. I've explained myself as best I can and I'm not sure what more I can say except how sorry I am.'

'We've been through –'

'Just listen, Holly.' Carina put a hand up to stop her talking. 'What I'm trying to say is that I think you need me at the moment. I want to help. And I don't mean interfere. I just want to be here for you, like I always am. We don't have to go over the past and what's happened. Just talk to me about what's happening now. Why you and David split up and whether or not you'll go back to him. Tell me how you're feeling. What you're thinking. Just talk to me, Holly, and I'll listen.'

Holly was about to object but instead began to cry. She sat down heavily on a kitchen chair and put her head in her hands.

'Oh God, is there more to this than I thought? Did David do something to hurt you?'

'No! Nothing like that.'

'Well, then what is it? Why did you leave him?'

'Because,' said Holly, her voice a mere whisper, 'he's not Josh.'

Carina nodded and looked unsure what to say next. When she eventually spoke, she had tears in her own eyes. 'So you really are still in love with Josh.' It was a statement rather than a question.

Holly nodded. 'I always have been. I suppose I blocked him out over the last number of years. It was the only way I could get on with my life. And then he arrived back and nothing has been the same since. I love him so much, Carina.' She patted her chest over her heart. 'So much that it actually hurts physically. He's all I think about and I don't know if I'll ever get him out of my head.'

'Have you told him this?'

'Of course not. How could I? He doesn't feel the same so there's no point.'

'How do you know?'

Holly looked at her sister. 'How do I know what?'

'That he doesn't feel the same. How do you know?'

'Because he's with Stephanie.'

'But you were with David until a few days ago. Nobody knows what goes on behind closed doors and you're proof of that. Josh could be thinking that you and David are happily in love. Maybe if he knew that –'

'Carina, *no!*' Holly's voice came out sharper than she'd intended but she didn't want her sister sticking her nose in again. 'I'm sure Josh will find out in time that I've moved on but I'm not going to tell him. And neither are you, do you hear me?'

Carina nodded. 'But wouldn't you like to know what he's thinking? How he feels?'

'I don't need him to tell me. And anyway, he has a baby on the way – even if he did feel something for me, he's not going to walk away from his family. From his child. From something he's always wanted.' She began to cry again and this time Carina came to her and, squatting down on her hunkers, enveloped her in a hug.

'I just wish I could do something to make it better for you, Holly. I feel so helpless. Only for my meddling, you two would still be together. I'm so, so sorry.'

Holly wiped her eyes and looked at her sister. 'It wasn't just *your* fault, Carina. Nothing is as straightforward as that. We can all take some of the blame. Josh shouldn't have taken your word. He shouldn't have just done what you said without talking to me about it. And I should have pushed him further when he said he wanted us to split up. We all could have done more. But we were young, and impulsive, and hadn't learned that happiness has to be worked for. It doesn't just get handed to you.'

Carina sat back down on her chair. 'So what are you going to do now?'

Just then the front door opened and there was the sound of animated chatter in the hall. 'We're home. And we got so many more Christmas decorations. Wait until you see them!'

Holly smiled. 'I guess I'm going to put up some more decorations.'

'Holly. Really. What's next?'

'Who knows?' she said, her eyes becoming moist again. 'Right now, all I know is that I need to get through Christmas. And at least I have you and Mum and Dad to help me.'

But despite being surrounded by so much love, Holly had never felt so lonely in all her life.

Chapter 40

Josh plastered a smile on his face as he waved goodbye to his mum. He wanted to assure her he was okay because, the way she'd been talking, he'd thought she was going to move in to look after him. He closed the door when she disappeared around the corner and his hand went automatically to his bruised face. He winced when he touched it and headed into the kitchen to get some of the pre-scribed cream to apply to it. He'd been lucky to walk away from the crash with just bruising, but his injuries went way deeper than that. He couldn't really care less about the physical stuff: it was the mental torture he had to endure that was causing him the most pain.

He applied the cream, popped a couple of painkillers and headed into the living room. A lot of the past twenty-four hours were a blur, which was just as well because they were among the worst hours of his life. According to eye-witnesses, he'd come around the corner veering onto the wrong side of the road. A couple of cars had swerved to avoid him but he'd spun out of control, crashing into a post-box on the pavement. Thankfully there'd been no pedestrians around and nobody else had been injured. Another driver had called an ambulance and stayed with him until it arrived. The seatbelt and airbag had saved him, they'd said. Otherwise things could have been a hell of a lot worse. He had whiplash, bruising and a cut over his left eye and they'd kept him overnight because he'd had a headache.

When they'd asked him in the hospital who they should ring for him, his mind had briefly flicked to Stephanie, before he'd remembered the events of the morning. He'd given them his mum's phone number instead and she'd arrived soon after. He'd been feeling vulnerable and had told her about Stephanie and the baby, and she'd sat with him while he cried. It was funny, for years he'd protected his mother. He hadn't told her things that he thought might upset her and he hadn't shared a lot of his worries with her for fear that it would make her anxious. But lying in that hospital bed the previous day and having her there to comfort him, he'd realised that she was a strong woman – way stronger than he'd ever be. Despite his protests, she'd insisted on ringing Stephanie to tell her what had happened. According to his mother, she'd listened to the information, wished him a speedy recovery and said she'd text him.

When the text had eventually arrived at nine o'clock that night, it had shocked Josh to the core. He couldn't believe the speed at which everything was happening. His life felt like a freight train and he was running along the track trying to keep up with it. The text had simply read:

Josh. I'm sorry for everything. You can come home because I'll be gone. I'm going to stay at Leo's. He wants to look after me and I think it's the right thing to do. I hope you recover soon. Stephanie x

He'd stared at the phone for a long time, aghast at the fact that she could be so cold, so calculated. Less than a day before, he'd thought he was going to be a father bringing up a baby in a loving relationship. Now, not only had she crushed him by admitting she'd had an affair and the baby wasn't his, but she'd insulted him further by going to live with the guy while their bed was still warm from where they'd lain together.

He lay down on the sofa and positioned a cushion underneath his head. He remembered feeling a stabbing pain in his neck before he'd blacked out and when he'd come to he'd feared he'd broken it. But thankfully it was only whiplash, and in time it would go away. If only it was the same for his broken heart. The funny thing was that he wasn't broken-hearted about Stephanie. Not really. His heart was breaking for the baby that he'd lost. Not that he'd ever had him or her. But all the same, it was a loss. A loss of a future he'd thought he had. A loss of the happiness he'd looked forward to. But if he was really honest with himself, he hadn't loved Stephanie the way he should have. He'd been used to her. They'd been together a long time and had gotten comfortable with each other.

He was just about to drift off into a drug-induced sleep when the sound of the doorbell startled him. Oh God. He hoped his mother wasn't back. She'd brought him home, gone out shopping to stock the fridge, cooked up a storm and then left. Surely she wasn't back to cluck over him again. If he just stayed still, whoever it was would probably leave, thinking there was no one at home. Or if it was his mother, she might realise he was asleep. But no such luck. The doorbell rang again and there was a knocking on the door for good measure. He hauled himself up off the sofa and went to answer it.

She was the last person in the world he would have expected to see at his door again. The last time he'd seen her, she'd shattered his dreams, and seeing her again brought a myriad memories flooding into his head. He opened his mouth to say something but no words came out.

'Hi, Josh. My God, what happened to you?'

'What are you doing here, Carina?'

'I wanted to talk to you. I know from Holly that you work in a school so I guessed you'd be home by now.' She looked past him into the hall. 'Are you alone?'

He nodded, confused by her presence. 'There's nobody else here but I'm really not in the humour for chit-chat. What is it you want?'

'Please, can I come in? There are just a few things I need to say.'

Josh sighed but opened the door further. 'Okay. But not for long. As you can see, I've been in a bit of an accident and I really just need to sleep.'

She followed him into the kitchen where he indicated for her to take a seat. 'What happened? You look pretty beaten up.'

'A car crash. It looks worse than it is.'

'Your girlfriend and the baby – are they okay?'

He opened his mouth but no words came out.

'Oh God. Are they hurt?' She looked genuinely worried.

He shook his head. 'No, Carina. They're both fine. But I'm sure you're not here to talk about them.'

'I … I just came to say I'm sorry, Josh. You can't imagine how sorry I am for everything that happened back then. I promise you, I never meant to hurt anyone and I only did what I thought was best for Holly at the time. She was hurting. And I thought she needed to be her own person for a while.'

He nodded but the mention of Holly's name was like a stab to the heart. 'It's okay, Carina. Let's just leave the past where it belongs.'

'But *is* it the past?'

Josh looked at her quizzically. 'What do you mean?'

'You and Holly. Is it really the past? Don't you feel anything for her any more?'

He thought of Holly's silky hair and how it smelled of lavender. Her translucent skin. The dimples on her cheeks. The smile that lit up her face. He remembered how they'd laughed together, cried together, vowed they'd always be together.

'Well?' said Carina, staring at him. 'Do you still love her?'

It was all too much of a mess. 'No, Carina. I don't.'

She looked as though he'd punched her in the face. 'I don't believe you.'

'I don't really care.'

'She loves you.'

'Come on, I think it's time you went home.' He stood up and ushered her from her seat. 'Holly is with David now. Engaged to be married to David. I don't think she'd appreciate you coming around here and sticking your nose in again. Did you learn nothing from the last time?'

She walked towards the front door. 'Don't you see, Josh? I'm trying to fix the damage I did the last time. I'm trying to make up for all the hurt I caused. Any fool can see that you two are meant to be together – were always meant to be together. I know you have a baby on the way and things aren't as straightforward as they could have been, but look into your heart, Josh. Think about what you really want before it's too late.'

'Even if I did feel something for Holly,' he said, opening the front door, 'I would never tell her. I'd never wade in and ruin what she has with David.'

'Oh God. I promised her I wouldn't tell you.'

'Tell me what?'

'I … I can't.'

'Oh, for God's sake, Carina. Just tell me and then go.'

'Holly has left David. She's back living with Mum and Dad. And she's going to kill me. Again.'

Josh's thoughts whirled and he didn't know how to respond. Holly wasn't with David any more. He wasn't with Stephanie. He wasn't sure what to do with that information and his head was beginning to throb from the pressure.

'Josh?'

'Stephanie's gone too.'

'What? Do you mean gone as in left?' Steam rose in the air from her warm breath. 'What about the baby?'

'Not mine.' He felt the sting of tears at the backs of his eyes as he said the words.

'Oh, Josh. That's awful. I really am very sorry.'

'Well, now you know. And tell Holly I'm very sorry too. For what it's worth, I thought she and David made a lovely couple.' That was a lie.

'Wait,' said Carina, as Josh was about to close the door. 'Doesn't that change things?'

'What? Just because we're both single now? How does that change anything?'

'There's nothing in your way now. You can at least get together and talk about things.'

'No.'

'Josh, come on. I know you still love her.'

'Holly and I won't be getting back together, Carina. I know you mean well, but you can stop with your matchmaking. Too much has happened. There's been too much hurt and we're not the people we used to be. It's thirteen years too late for Holly and me.'

He closed the door and walked back into the living room in a daze. His head was throbbing and he was finding it difficult to compose his thoughts. So much had happened in such a short space of time and it was all too much to take in. There'd been so much heartbreak. Josh was going to have to figure out a way to move on with his life and face the future. Without Holly. Because there was just no way they could ever get back together. Was there?

Chapter 41

'You what?' said Holly, glaring at Carina. 'Please tell me you didn't.'

Carina nodded. 'I did. But I had to. And as it happens –'

'No, you bloody well *didn't* have to. I told you to keep out of it. I honestly can't believe that you went high-tailing it over to his house to tell him after I specifically told you not to.'

'I'm sorry, Holly. I just thought –'

'That's your trouble, Carina. You *don't* think. If you'd thought about it, you wouldn't have waded in again. God, Josh must think I'm a helpless, pathetic woman, getting you to go over to him to announce I've split with my fiancé.'

She stood up and began pacing up and down the kitchen. It was late on Monday night and Carina had arrived unannounced just ten minutes before. As soon as Holly had seen her face, she'd known something was up. And then Carina had blurted out the whole story. How she'd gone to Josh's to apologise for her past interference. How he'd been all beaten up from a car crash. And how she'd accidentally told him about Holly's newfound single status.

'Four days to Christmas,' said Holly, continuing with her rant. 'Just four days to what's usually the highlight of my year. And you couldn't leave things alone. It's enough that I'm worried about David and worried about my own future, but now I have to stress about what Josh must think of me. I mean, did he think I was sending you over to try and break up his relationship? I know what that baby means to him and I'd never do anything to upset things between him and Stephanie.'

'Holly, if you'd just listen to the rest of the story. Come and sit down.'

'The rest of the story? Oh God, there's more? I don't know if I want to hear it.'

'Trust me,' said Carina. 'You do.'

Carina's voice was soft. Calming. And Holly felt herself beginning to relax a little. Much as she hated the idea that Carina had gone over there to talk to Josh, she was also a little bit curious. Had he been shocked at Carina's revelation? Had he been upset for her? Or was a teeny bit of him happy that she was now single?

'Okay,' said Holly, sitting back down. 'Tell me the rest.'

Carina leaned forward on her elbows. 'Well, as it turns out, you're not the only one who's now single.'

It took Holly a moment before realisation dawned. 'What? Josh and Stephanie? Split up? You must have got that wrong.'

'It's the truth all right. Josh told me himself. I don't know the details, but he said she was gone.'

Holly shook her head in disbelief. 'I can't believe it. But what about the baby? I hope she's going to be fair to him and he doesn't end up in a terrible custody battle. You hear about things like that. You know Rory Kilduff from the Avenue? His girlfriend wouldn't let him –'

'It's not his.'

Holly glared at Carina, trying to make sense of what she'd said.

'It's not his, Holly. The baby isn't his. That's what he told me.'

'Oh my God.' Holly's hand shot up to her mouth. 'Poor Josh. And he didn't know? Well, of course he didn't. He was making plans and he was so excited. That's awful. Really awful.'

'I know. I felt so sorry for him. He was all battered and bruised and he looked so miserable. And all alone.' Carina raised her eyebrows at Holly.

'Stop it, Carina. I am *not* going to see him.' But she couldn't help smiling at Carina's persistence. 'Right, I'm putting the kettle on. I assume you'll have tea? Mum bought a tin of Chocolate Kimberly earlier. They're supposed to be for Christmas but I think even she'd agree that this is an emergency, requiring only the best confectionery.'

'Does this mean I'm forgiven?' Carina batted her long black eyelashes at Holly.

'I can forgive you this time, Carina,' Holly said, leaning against the kitchen counter, 'because it's not as though my split with David would have remained a secret. He was bound to find out. But please, please, please, can you just stop it now? Stop interfering in my life, whether you think I need it or not. I'm old enough to look after myself, and if there are mistakes to be made, I need to make them myself.'

'Deal,' said Carina, looking relieved. 'But don't bite my head off when I ask what you're going to do about Josh.'

Holly thought for a moment. 'I'm not going to do anything. It's too late for us, Carina.'

'That's funny. That's exactly what Josh said.'

'Is it?' Holly felt a little stung. She'd said the words but hadn't really meant them. Hearing that he was no longer with Stephanie had ignited some hope in her and, although she hadn't wanted to admit it to Carina, she'd wondered if maybe there was a chance for her and Josh. But obviously not. 'What exactly did he say, Carina?'

Carina shifted awkwardly in her chair.

'Just tell me!'

'He said that you're not the same people you used to be. He said that a lot has happened and that it's …'

'Go on.'

'It's thirteen years too late for both of you.'

It was like a knife to Holly's heart. She swallowed back the tears enough to reply. 'Well, there you go. That's your answer. Josh and I need to move forward with our lives and it would be wrong to get too caught up in the past. Onwards and upwards.'

'But, Holly –'

'No, Carina. I don't want to hear any more about it. There are only a few days left until Christmas so I'm going to stick on my happy face and join in with the festivities. And when it's all over, I'm going to have a think about where I go from here. I have a business plan to work on, which will keep me busy, and I'll need to move out and stand on my own two feet again. But one thing is for sure, I don't want to hear the name Josh O'Toole mentioned again. Are we clear?'

Carina looked as though she was about to object but Holly shot her a warning look and she just nodded instead. What a week it had been. Holly felt exhausted. She turned to make the tea and closed her eyes tight. She felt as though she was closing a door on something huge. It felt so final. Josh had said it was too late. Thirteen years too late. She gripped the kitchen counter but suddenly she had no strength in her body. She began to slide to the floor before everything went black.

Chapter 42

Josh hadn't enjoyed Christmas Day one bit. He'd spent it with his mother – just the two of them at her house. She'd cooked and the food had been spectacular, but he hadn't been all that hungry. He was usually a massive fan of Christmas, but this year he just wanted to get it over with. He wanted to forget the pain that the last year had brought him and try to look ahead to a brand new year. But at least the day was almost over and he was heading home. His mother was going to spend the evening with John and despite Josh offering to bring her, she was insisting on driving herself.

'Right,' she said, joining him in the kitchen and wrapping a warm scarf around her neck. 'Let's head off. John is expecting me at seven so I don't want to be late.'

'Okay, Mum.' He bent to kiss her on the cheek. 'Safe driving and I'll see you soon. Thanks so much for dinner. It was delicious.'

She clicked her tongue disapprovingly. 'You barely ate a thing, love. I know you're hurting but you've got to look after yourself. Now, I've put together a few bits and pieces to keep you going for a few days.' She took a heap of containers out of the fridge and handed them to Josh.

'That would feed an army,' he said, eyeing up the food. 'You don't have to give me all this.'

'It's just turkey and ham. And a few nice bits. And you can freeze anything you're not ready to use.'

'Thanks, Mum. And are you sure you don't want a lift to John's? You could get a taxi home later.'

'Not at all, love. I like having my car with me.' She winked at him as they walked towards the front door. 'That way I can be ready to escape if I don't like how things are going.'

Josh laughed at that and turned suddenly to hug her. 'I'm glad you're happy, Mum. You deserve it. And John is lovely. A really, really lovely man.'

'He is, love. And great company. Sure we're just two golden oldies trying not to be lonely.'

Josh nodded, a lump in his throat, and kissed his mother again before heading out to his replacement car. The garage had given it to him while he was waiting for the Micra to be fixed. It wouldn't be ready until after Christmas, they'd said, but he was quite happy driving around in an almost new Volkswagen Golf in the meantime. It made him think about trading up to something nicer, more modern, now that he'd have more money. He'd spent the last few years supporting Stephanie financially while she swanned around the place trying to be an actress, and in the last few months, he'd been saving for the baby. Tears sprang to his eyes when he thought of the baby. The baby he'd thought was his. It would take him a long time to get over that.

He parked in his driveway and looked across, as he'd done so often these last few weeks, at number forty. He stood for a moment, thinking about the day he'd realised Holly was living there. The day he'd realised he'd never stopped loving her. Just then the door opened and David walked outside, zapping the lock on his car and opening it to take something out. He locked it again and glanced across the road to where Josh was still staring. They looked at each other for a moment until David raised his hand and waved. 'Merry Christmas,' he said, before turning and going back inside.

Inside the house, Josh filled his fridge with the cartons of food then took out a beer. It was strange to be alone on Christmas night. It certainly wasn't the way he'd imagined spending it. In the living room, the Christmas tree looked tired and sad. Josh hadn't bothered putting on the lights, nor had he put the lights on outside the house. There didn't seem to be any point. He wasn't happy, so why should he put on a happy front?

He flicked on the telly but he wasn't in form for the Christmas cheer that seemed to be on every channel. So he stuck on Sky News, which was more reflective of his mood. A picture of Holly filled his mind as he lay there on the sofa, and before he knew it, tears were falling down his face. Holly Russo. The great love of his life. She'd always been the one. Just then the doorbell rang, jolting him out of his reverie. He wiped away his tears with the sleeve of his shirt and went to answer the door.

'Josh, love,' said his mother, stepping into the hall, 'I have your phone here. I think you must have taken – What's wrong? Are you crying?'

'Of course not. I ... I was just sneezing. Do you want to stay for a cup of tea before you head over to John's?' He prayed she'd refuse because he just wanted to be on his own.

'I won't stay, love. I don't want to be late for John. But I don't want to leave you until I know you're okay.'

'I'm fine, Mum. Honestly.' He led the way into the kitchen where he'd left the phone. He hadn't even noticed he'd taken the wrong one.

'Well, Josh O'Toole,' said his mother in a stern tone, 'you're not fooling me. Listen, I didn't bring up the subject today because I reckoned you'd talk about it if you wanted to, but what are you going to do about Holly?'

The question took him by surprise. 'What do you mean?'

'Do you still love her?'

'Mum!'

'Well, do you?' She fixed him with a steady gaze and he had to look away.

'Josh?'

'Yes. Yes, I do.'

'Well, then, what's keeping you away? You're both free now and didn't Carina tell you she loves you too? It seems to me that you're both as stubborn as each other.'

'But it's more complicated than that, Mum.'

She sighed. 'It doesn't have to be. Stop putting obstacles in the way. If you truly love the girl, go and get her. Life is too short for indecision.'

'I'll think about it.'

'You do that,' she said, turning back towards the front door. 'But don't let happiness pass you by. If you have a chance to get it, grab it with both hands and hold on for dear life.'

They said goodbye again and he resumed his position on the sofa, mulling over his mother's words. And then he noticed the weather forecast on the telly. There was going to be snow. The reporter was wrapped up in his winter woollies. Behind him was a castle, regally reaching up towards the filled clouds. And just as he was talking, snow began to fall lightly, covering his hair with a delicate dusting of white fluff. That's when Josh knew. It was a sign.

He jumped up from the sofa, wincing at the pain in his neck as he rushed upstairs. He brushed his teeth quickly and ran a comb through his unruly hair. Back downstairs, he put on his navy parka and wrapped a colourful scarf around his neck. This felt right. For the first time in a long time, he felt certain. Certain of the future that he knew he deserved and certain that, if all went to plan, he might just get his happy ever after.

Chapter 43

It was the worst Christmas Day ever. Holly had managed to plaster a smile on her face all day while she sat around the table with her family. Carina and Jason had been all loved up and the only thing she'd had a cuddle from were her mother's two cats. It had filled her with the fear she'd always had of becoming an old matronly cat-woman, sinking lower and lower into a spinsterly depression. She'd been saved once from that fate but now she feared she'd never be saved again.

She finished drying the last of the dishes and, for about the millionth time that week, cursed the fact that her parents shunned modern appliances like dishwashers, preferring the old reliable Fairy Liquid and a pair of rubber gloves. She'd sent them all off to Carina's half an hour before, promising to follow as soon as she'd finished in the kitchen. Going to Carina's house on Christmas night was traditional. They'd start the evening with karaoke on the PlayStation, moving on to a more sedate game of poker later for the die-hards. The funny thing about it was that, cheesy and all as it was, she usually enjoyed it. And David had enjoyed it too when he'd been there for the last couple of years. But this year, she wasn't in form for it.

She wiped down the counter when she'd put the last of the plates away and threw the soaking tea-towel into the washing machine. Her mother was always giving out about the washing machine, claiming that it was like a plane taking off when it was in full spin. She kept an ancient wash tub with a clothes wringer on top out in the shed and Holly feared that she'd one day replace the modern machine with it. She glanced around the kitchen. It was sparkling clean so there was no reason to delay any longer. She'd have to join them at Carina's house or they'd be sending a search party over to get her.

She'd suggested earlier that she might just stay home, but she'd been met with objections from everyone. 'You can't be on your own right now,' her mother had said. 'You need to have people around you.' And 'Of course you should come with us,' her dad had added. Carina's offering wasn't as obvious but had the same intent. 'We'd miss you if you weren't there, Holly. It wouldn't be the same.' In truth, ever since Holly had fainted in the kitchen a few days before, they'd all been afraid to let her out of their sight lest she'd collapse and do herself damage.

She was just about to head upstairs to get herself ready to go when there was a knock on the door, which almost made her jump out of her skin. She couldn't imagine who'd be calling on Christmas evening and, for a brief moment, she thought it could be David. She hoped he wasn't there to beg her to go back to him. Because one thing was for sure, she and David just weren't meant to be. She crossed her fingers behind her back as she opened the door, but her legs almost collapsed beneath her when she saw who was there.

'Josh! Wh– what are you doing here?'

His face was flushed from the cold but he was smiling as his words tumbled out. 'It was at the bus stop in Dublin city centre. Four o'clock on a Friday afternoon.'

'What was?' Holly's voice was barely a whisper as she stood looking at the man she adored.

'You were wearing a pair of white jeans and a yellow T-shirt. It was hot. Really hot. And you were worried you'd feel sick on the bus.'

'Josh, I don't follow.'

He put up a hand to shush her. 'You hated travelling alone but I was going to stay with a friend in Dublin because I had an interview for a part-time job the next morning.'

Realisation began to dawn on her but she stayed quiet, holding her breath as he spoke.

'The bus was rattling towards the stop and you were hyperventilating. So I kissed you. Long and soft. And you calmed down instantly. You got on the bus and I waved you goodbye. That was our last kiss, Holly. I never forgot it. I never forgot anything about you.'

Holly couldn't find any words as tears began to pour down her face. It was the thing that had haunted her. Their last kiss. She'd blocked it out of her mind but he'd kept the memory. He'd remembered every little detail, even after all this time.

'Come with me,' said Josh, holding out his hand. 'Please. I want to take you somewhere.'

'I can't. Everyone is at Carina's and they're waiting for me. It's a tradition.'

'Do you *want* to come, Holly?'

All she could do was nod.

'Right then, let's go. We'll be no longer than an hour and I promise I'll drop you to Carina's on the way back. How does that sound?'

'Okay.' Her head was spinning trying to keep up with what was going on as Josh took her hand and led her out to his car. She got in without question and actually pinched her own arm hard, just to make sure she wasn't in the middle of a dream.

'Where are we going?' she said, looking at his face and noting the cuts and bruises. She instinctively wanted to kiss each and every one of them but she didn't dare. Not until she knew what was happening. A bolt of excitement shot through her and, although she'd just been whisked away from her house on Christmas night by a man she'd broken up with thirteen years before, there was nowhere else she'd rather be.

'Just wait and see,' said Josh, keeping his eyes on the road. 'Sit back and relax, Holly. Trust me, I have a lot to say but I want to wait until we get there.'

They sat in silence for the next twenty minutes, during which time Holly went through every possible scenario in her head. She hadn't a clue what he was up to, but it wasn't long before they were in a quiet part of the countryside and he was parking the car in what seemed like the middle of nowhere.

'Put this on,' he said, handing her his jacket. 'It's going to be freezing.'

Holly did as she was told and they got out of the car. It was almost pitch dark but she took his hand and allowed him to lead her. It occurred to her that she trusted him implicitly. And she would have followed him anywhere he'd asked. Josh had been right about the cold and she could feel the tip of her nose go numb as they headed into the darkness. They were going uphill and Holly was beginning to get out of breath.

'Almost there,' he said, putting a supportive arm around her.

And then she saw it. It was like the one she'd always imagined. A castle on top of a hill. It was in ruins but it was beautiful to her. He'd brought her to the place of her dreams and she gasped at the sheer beauty of it as it rose into the darkness. Tears sprang to her eyes as she looked up, and she let them fall. And then Josh took her two hands, turning her to face him.

'Holly, I know we're both a little broken at the moment. I know we have scars which will take a long time to heal. But I'm hoping you'll allow us to heal together.'

'You remembered, Josh,' she said. 'You remembered about the castle on a hill.'

'Of course I remembered. I told you, I never forgot a single thing about you. And I know it's not exactly as it was in your dream, because in your dream you were getting married. But I thought the next best thing was to bring you here so that I could ask you.'

Holly's heart began to beat almost out of her chest. 'To ask me what?'

He gazed into her eyes and, despite his beaten-up face, she thought he'd never looked so beautiful. His piercing blue eyes shone in the dark and the dimple bounced in and out on his left cheek. And suddenly he was down on one knee, putting one of her hands to his mouth and kissing it gently.

'Marry me, Holly Russo. Please say you'll marry me. I let you get away once before and I'll do anything to keep you from getting away again. I love you. I love you so much that it hurts. Please say you'll marry me and we can make your dream come true right here, at your castle on a hill.'

Tears poured down Holly's cheeks but she didn't care. 'I love you too, Josh. I've always loved you.'

'Is that a yes?' he said. 'Because if I don't get up from this position soon, I'm likely to add a dodgy back to my list of injuries.'

'Yes, yes. Of course it's a yes.'

He stood up and wrapped his arms around her. And then suddenly the sky seemed to brighten and they looked up to realise it was snowing. Big fluffy snowflakes falling all around them. Just like in her dream. But this was reality. And Holly had never felt so happy in all her life.

One day they'd get married in a big castle on a hill. It would be Christmas time and it would be snowing. Her dress would be white and she'd have red roses for her bouquet. It would be like a fairy tale and they'd live happily ever after. One day.

Acknowledgments

For me, writing is the most wonderful job in the world. I feel lucky and privileged to do something I love every day and call it work. I adore the process of thinking up new characters and giving them life. I love forming their personalities, deciding what they'll do for a living and being in charge of their destinies. If I like a character, I can reward him or her with a nice new job, a fancy car or even a lottery win. If I don't like them, I can give them a nasty toothache, fire them from their job or push them under a bus. I love, love, love losing myself in another world – a world of my own making – a world where I literally rule! But like all jobs, sometimes things don't go to plan. Sometimes I sit in front of a blank screen and can't write a single word. Or worse still, I read back what I've written and realise it's nothing but a load of rubbish. They're the times that I want to hurl my laptop out the window and wish for a nice, steady nine-to-five job where I can clock off at the end of the day and go and watch Coronation Street. There have been a lot of those times over this last year. I've had moments of real doubt, wondering if I'd ever get this book written. Wondering if my writing days were numbered. Wondering how the hell I'd managed to have five books published when number six was refusing to cooperate! There've been tears, tantrums and a lot of over-eating (it's important to feed the brain – mainly doughnuts and Belgian chocolate). I suppose what I'm saying, in a very roundabout way, is yay for me! I've managed to work through the storm and produce a book that I'm very proud of at the end of it all. But the truth is, I would have given up on many occasions if it wasn't for the wonderful people in my life who cheer me on, encourage me, support me and love me through it all.

I've said it so many times before but my husband, Paddy, is not only the love of my life but he's my very best friend. He's such a support to me, both practically and emotionally, and I really couldn't do any of this without him. Our four wonderful children – Eoin, Roisin, Enya and Conor – are such a blessing and again, I couldn't do this job without their input. I often discuss storylines with them and they'll go away and think about what we've discussed and come back to me with their ideas. They read my books and let me know (sometimes with brutal honesty) what they think. Having four children and a crazy dog makes our house pretty chaotic, but I wouldn't change it for the world. So thank you Paddy, Eoin, Roisin, Enya and Conor (and a special mention to Bella!) for all your love and support and for bringing so much joy into my life.

Thanks to my wonderful parents, Aileen and Paddy Chaney, who I love very much. They've always encouraged me to follow my dreams and I wouldn't be where I am today without their endless support. Thanks to my brother and friend, Gerry Chaney, for all his help with photographs, technical stuff and especially for all the good advice. Thanks also to his wife, Denyse, who I consider to be the sister I never had. Denyse reads all my first drafts and her honest and straight-forward input is invaluable to me. Thanks to my extended family – brothers-in-law, sisters-in-law and especially my very lovely mother-in-law, Mary Duffy. Family is very important to me and I feel lucky and blessed with the one I have.

I have so many friends who've been my cheerleaders over the last year and I know, without a shadow of a doubt, I couldn't do this without them. To my very best, long-time friends, Lorraine Hamm, Angie Pierce, Dermot and Bernie Winston, Rachel Murphy and Sinead Webb – thank you for always being there. For putting up with me not returning your calls for ages and for forgetting special occasions (I'm not coming out of this well, am I?). It's a sign of true friendship when we don't speak for weeks or even months and then take up where we left off with no sign of awkwardness. Some of my writing friends I've only met in recent years but consider them now amongst my best friends. Michelle Jackson, Niamh Greene and Denise Deegan – thank you for the weekends away, the laughs and the drunken book ideas which will never see the light of day! Your friendship means a lot to me. Thank you Niamh O'Connor for always giving good advice and reassurance and for always being there. Thanks to the Avoca gang (you know who you are!) for all the chats, laughs and potential storylines. Our coffee mornings always fill me with inspiration and more importantly send me on my way with a smile on my face. I'm very lucky to be part of a wonderful writing community both in this country and in the UK. Writers are such a support to each other and without them, I wouldn't have the confidence to do what I do. There are way too many to mention but I want to thank all of you writers who've helped and encouraged me since I began to write. You've come to my launches, listened to my moans, advised, encouraged and made me believe in myself. I'm very thankful for each and every one of you. I want to give a special mention to one person without whom, my writing would probably still be in a drawer at home. Vanessa O'Loughlin from Writing.ie and Inkwell Writers is a wonderful source of knowledge and help to aspiring writers in this country. She's always on hand with advice and encouragement and I'm lucky to call her a friend.

I seem to be using the word 'lucky' a lot but it's exactly how I feel. Writing the book is just one part of the process and I feel extremely lucky to have such a wonderful team of professional people around me who work so hard to get the book onto the shelves. To my agent, the very fabulous Madeleine Milburn from the Madeleine Milburn Literary, TV and Film Agency. Thank you, Maddy, for all your help and support and for believing in me. I love being a part of the agency and look forward to many years ahead of working together. Thank you to the wonderful team at Hachette Ireland, especially my editor, Ciara Doorley, whose magic touch always makes my books better. Sometimes I think Ciara is crazy when she asks me to drastically change a scene or a character, but annoyingly, she's always right! Thanks to Joanna Smyth for all her patience and help, and for always knowing the answer. Ruth Shern deserves a special thanks for putting up with me on our annual day out, when we visit book-stores. I'm sure she goes home with her ears ringing and her head pounding from listening to me chatter all day. Thank you to the rest of the team at Hachette – Breda, Jim, Bernard and Siobhan. It's a pleasure to work with you all. Lastly, thanks to Emma Dunne for her editing on this book also. Her keen eye spotted a lot of things that I was just too goggle-eyed to see myself.

Book bloggers are a very important part of the writing process for authors as we wait with trepidation for that first review. Most of these bloggers don't get paid for what they do and yet we'd be lost without them. So I want to say a huge thanks to all the wonderful bloggers who read and review my books. Again, there are too many to mention but I want to say a special thank you to one in particular. Margaret Madden from Bleach House Library is a wonderful lady who offers endless support to authors. She's completely selfless with her time and even sends out 'Happy Mail' if somebody needs cheer-ing up! So thank you, Margaret, for everything. Thank you also to the book-sellers who do such a wonderful job in promoting my books. I still get teary-eyed when I walk into a shop and see a dis-play of my books or spot some in a window. I don't think I'll ever get used to it.

So last but not least, to my readers. I still can't believe that people go into actual book shops and pay actual money to buy my books! It's a real honour and it fills me full of pride. Your generosity allows me to wake up every morning and do what I love and call it a job. And hearing from my readers is my favourite part of the whole process. I love getting emails, tweets or facebook messages so please keep them coming. You can contact me through my website at www.mariaduffy.ie or on twitter at @mduffywriter. You'll also find me on Facebook. So thank you from the bottom of my heart, my lovely readers, for your continued support. I hope to entertain you with my words for many years to come.

Lots of love,
Maria x